JL ESQUIRE

Enchanter's Quest: Curse of the Necromancer

PRIVATE DRAGON
Publishing

First edition

ISBN: 978-1-951405-29-8

Editing by Samantha Knight
Cover art by Samantha Knight

This book was professionally typeset on Reedsy.
Find out more at reedsy.com

To Grandpa Don
For always letting me be your sidekick

Contents

Map of Cray

Prologue

Kernil Ravenhigh was coming home.

He had spent the past few weeks alone on a hunting expedition in the forests south of his home of Vain. Ioc, Kernil's horse ambled on the path northward, its breathing growing heavier with every step. Kernil patted the horse on the neck as they rode together.

"We're almost there," he said, seeing Vain on the horizon.

The horse was rightfully wary, as was he. Kernil went too far hunting a beautiful stag. Their return was now more difficult, and the horse Ioc had endured the worst of it. What made it worse was Kernil had failed to catch the stag. He had a clean shot, and the unsuspecting deer was only a few yards away. Yet, just as he was about to release the arrow, a sudden earthquake caused him to miss and the stag to flee.

"What an embarrassment," Kernil said as he recalled the event. "What will my father say about this?"

Lord Kreed Ravenhigh, Kernil's father, was an excellent hunter and had spent several seasons in Kernil's youth teaching his son everything he knew. Lord Kreed was a loving but judgmental man. When his only son succeeded, there was no one more proud than he. Yet, when Kernil failed, he was more critical or scrupulous. This had been Kernil's first expedition alone, and he had set out to prove himself.

Kernil's hand fingered the hilt of the sword strapped to his back. The Sword of Vain. It was a family heirloom passed down through nine generations. The stewardship of Vain passed with the sword. Kernil had received the blade from his father upon his departure for this trip.

"This is yours now," Lord Kreed had said to him. "Keep it with you always until your child is ready. The strength of your ancestors will be with you each time you wield it. When you return, I shall make you governor of Vain. King Chamish already approved it."

"Will he still think I'm ready?" he asked himself.

Kernil cued Ioc to a stop and dismounted to stretch his cramped muscles. The summer sun had just set, and a slight breeze of early evening air was cool against his dark skin.

Kernil was a tall, muscular, young man, over six feet in height. He had hazel eyes and his dark hair was cut very short. He had a face that made him appear younger than he really was. This caused many people to trust him and put them at ease with him quickly. Kernil had gotten that trait from his mother.

As he stared at the city in the distance, Kernil noticed a figure coming toward him and it was moving fast. The Son of Vain readied his stance and drew his sword, the golden hilt and polished blade gleaming in the moonlight.

As the figure neared, Kernil could hear the clomping of horse hooves and a voice calling out, "Kernil! Kernil, it's me! You have to turn back!"

He recognized the voice as Rivith Farn, the cook in his father's house. Kernil relaxed his stance and put the Sword of Vain back in its scabbard, as he waited for the gnome to arrive.

"Kernil," Rivith huffed as his horse come to a sudden halt next to Kernil. "I'm so glad I got to you first. You have to leave, now!"

"What are you talking about?" Kernil replied. "I haven't been home in weeks. I'm tired and hungry, and I just want to sleep in my bed tonight."

The overweight gnome wheezed as he tried to catch his breath. "But you can't. Kernil, while you've been away, something terrible has happened."

"Is my father okay?" Kernil asked urgently.

Rivith shook his head and the Kernil's heart sank.

"No," Rivith answered solemnly. "There was a coup. Not just in Vain, but in all the southern providences. Your father, along with all those loyal to him and King Chamish, were killed."

"What?" he gasped in disbelief. "No, that can't be true. It can't be..."

The gnome lowered his head, the pain visible in his eyes. "It is true. I'm sorry, Kernil. It was my job to save you from the same fate. You and I are all that's left."

Kernil faltered and fell to his knees. His head was spinning, and his heart felt like someone had ripped it in two. His fist hit the grounds with a soft thud. He closed his eyes, wishing the entire world away. His whole body shook as tears poured from his eyes.

"When did it happen?" Kernil asked, trying to hold back his sobs.

"A day or two after you left," replied the gnome, not wanting to make eye contact. "But it's not your fault. There's no way you could have known."

"A day?" cried Kernil in despair. "I should have been there. I could have stopped it."

"No," Rivith shook his head. "Kernil, you would have been killed too. As it is, Nemul will have you dead as soon as you enter the ci-"

"Wait, Nemul?" Kernil interrupted. "Father's cousin led the coup? He killed him?"

The gnome nodded.

Then, Rivith saw something change in the Son of Vain's eyes. The sorrow had turned to anger and hate.

"I'll kill him!" vowed Kernil as he got back to his feet and began to mount Ioc.

"No, you can't," called Rivith as he grabbed hold of Kernil's tunic, keeping him from getting on his horse.

Kernil tried to push the gnome off of him, but Rivith held him tight and pulled him even closer.

"Let me go!" he yelled in frustration. "Nemul must die for what's he did to my father!"

"I know," Rivith replied, trying to keep calm. "But he's waiting for you. Don't you understand? If you go now, you'll be walking into a trap."

The Son of Vain shook his head and again tried to pull away. "No, he will die. Nemul will die today!"

Rivith could see that the boy wasn't listening to him and would leave the minute he broke from the gnome's grasp. Rivith knew this would happen, and that's why he hadn't wanted this job. Nobody listened to him. He wasn't an aggressive or persuasive person by any means.

"I'm not the right man for this job," he thought. "Someone more assertive and stubborn was better suited for this. Some-one like Dahrik."

"Dahrik," he whispered to himself as Rivith remembered his closest friend.

"What?" snapped Kernil.

"What would Dahrik do?" he thought to himself, keeping his grip on the Son of Vain.

The gnome knew instantly what the irritable dwarf would do, and he acted before talking himself out of it. With a deep breath, Rivith brought up his right hand and slapped Kernil across the face as hard as he could.

WHAP!

"Ow!" the young man yelped, rubbing the right side of his face.

Rivith pulled Kernil closer, getting inches from his face, and glared at him fiercely.

"Now, you listen to me," Rivith barked. "If you go back there, your father and hundreds of others will have died for nothing. By a miracle, you haven't been killed yet. Do not just throw that away for some foolhardy and idiotic attempt at revenge. Nemul has an army around him now. The best thing that you could do is wait for this civil war to be over. Better yet, join King Chamish in his efforts. He wants Nemul dead almost as much as you do."

"But..." he began, but the words got lost in his quivering lip.

"I know it feels wrong," Rivith added, now in a much softer tone. "I know it's sudden and unfair, and all you can think about right now is the pain that you're feeling and who caused it. I've felt that very pain. I watched all of my friends fight back and die by Nemul's hand, just days ago. You can't let it control you."

Kernil stared back at Rivith, tears reforming in his eyes. The gnome's words made sense and his compassion was tangible. Yet, in his soul, grew a ferocious fire. It burned with the hate and agony of his father's death.

The gnome continued, "If you want your revenge, if you want your city back, then you need to act wisely. Charging in alone, with no plan, won't solve anything."

"You're right," Kernil admitted softly. "I'm not thinking straight. Going to Chamish is the right move. He'll help me avenge my father and my city."

Rivith nodded. "Good. I'm glad you understand that. Now, you should leave. Make for Tyran City at once."

"Thank you, Rivith Farn. I owe you a great debt," said Kernil as he offered a hand to the gnome.

Return the gesture with a smile, Rivith replied, "Just don't forget me when you're the governor of Vain."

"I won't," Kernil said as he calmly mounted Ioc. "Now, let's just hope that is the outcome because I don't know what I'll do if it's not."

The Son of Vain took three deep breaths. He stared at the outline of the city ahead, wiping a single tear from his eye. With a wave goodbye to Rivith, he steered Ioc west.

Kernil Ravenhigh was not coming home.

When Magic Fails

I left my bedroom as soon as Rebeca and our two sons fell asleep. The door creaked as I shut it, but otherwise, my departure was noiseless. Five years of marriage and just as long of sneaking out the squeaky door, and each time I cursed myself for forgetting to fix it. I could have just enchanted the door to stop squeaking, but my pride stopped me. Years ago, my wife had accused me of not being able to fix anything without the use of magic. She was mostly right, of course, but I denied it.

I traced the door frame with one end of my scepter, setting a ward upon my family's room within the Tyranian castle. Wards are invisible barriers meant to protect a certain place or person from magical threats. Just as any armor or barrier, however, it does not guarantee protection. Over time, the ward fades and must be recast. For this reason, I put a ward on the room each time I left home. The house of Regalock had been victim to a magical attack once already, and if it ever happened again, I needed for there to be a safe place in case I wasn't around.

I looked up and down the torch-lit hallway. I was alone.

"Where is he?" I asked myself out loud. "Joel's never this late."

I decided not to wait and began walking to the servant lodging. The stone castle was enormous, and it took several minutes to get from one end to the other. I passed several guards who groggily stood watch, each one nodding as they acknowledged my presence.

Even after five years, I hadn't adjusted to living in the castle. So much of my life had changed since that time, and on occasion, it was all overwhelming. Just as I had gotten used to being an enchanter, five years ago, I had gone on a quest and destroyed an evil demon called the Vios Almna. On that quest, it was revealed that my destiny wasn't merely to be an ordinary enchanter, but the god Jard's chosen Prodigy. Rebecca had gone on that quest with me. We fell in love and married in less than a month of our return. She is the princess of the human kingdom of Tyran, King Chamish's only daughter.

Once married, I started living in the castle. Soon after, I became a father. First, to our elder son, Elias, and about two years later to our younger son, Samuel. So much had changed in just a short time, and I had grown accustomed to most of it. Oddly enough, living in a castle was not one of those things.

As I walked through the dark castle, the green gems at each end of my scepter glowed faintly in the dim light. The air was cool and smelled of autumn.

The servant houses were outside the castle on the northeast side but within the inner wall. After several minutes, I arrived. All the rooms were dark except one. As I approached, I could hear the frantic voice of Alexandria and the excited shouts of her son Joel.

Joel saw me through the window and ran to open the door. The boy was a half-elf, his father a human, and his mother an elf. Joel had the pointed ears signature to an elf, although they were not as pointed as a full elf. His eyes were a sea green that seemed to pulse with energy. His shaggy brown hair was grown out long to hide his ears from view.

"He's here! He's here!" the boy called to his mother as I enter the small home.

"Hey Joel, you ready to go?" I asked.

The half-elf boy nodded.

"I'm certainly not ready," said Alexandria as she handed her son an overnight bag.

Alexandria's deep green eyes glimmered in the candlelight. Her elven face looked stressed and sad as she looked upon her son, who was jumping with enthusiasm. I understood her concern. Joel was her entire world, and I was here to take him to the Sorcerer's Keep. A few days earlier, I sensed magic developing within Joel and was here now to take him to Ginn. Ginn was the grandmaster of the Sorcerer's Keep and the person who would determine if and when he should be allowed to join our order.

Although she didn't want to be separated from her son, Alexandria wanted what was best for Joel. That had been clear from the moment I met her five years ago. She was trapped in a city in the Beyondus desert for many years, and when I had been trapped there also, she helped me escape. The price of her help was to come back for Joel. After I had destroyed the Vios Almna, I fulfilled my promise and went back to the desert city and freed everyone. With my recommendation, Alexandria took a job here in the castle as Rebecca's maidservant.

"We won't be gone for long," I said, putting a hand on her shoulder. "A few days at most, then he's coming right back."

She sighed. "I know. I'm just nervous. He's never been away from me for this long."

"This time around won't be long at all, I promise," I said, "but once they assign him a master and his training officially begins, then he'll have to be gone for longer periods. I'll make sure it's not too long, but there's only so much I can do."

"Will you train him?" she asked hopefully. "Then he could come home whenever you do."

I immediately felt sad for her. As much as I wanted to tell her yes, I knew it wasn't likely to happen. The Grand Council of the Keep had given me special permission to split my time in between home here in Tyran City and the Keep. Every two weeks I went back and forth. I received this permission due to my status as the Prodigy. Joel wasn't likely to get the same deal.

"I want to, but I can't," I admitted, removing my hand. "Since I'm the Prodigy, it's not likely that I'll ever train an apprentice, but I'll make sure he gets assigned to a skilled master."

Joel grabbed the overnight bag and put it over his shoulder. "I'm ready, let's go!"

Alexandria frowned. "Now hold on, before you go, I want..."

"Time to make me an enchanter," he cried with excitement, not noticing his mother's hesitation.

"Well, we are not going anywhere until you say goodbye to your mother," I stated with authority.

The half-elf boy's eyes went wide with surprise.

"You might not see her for a long time," I said more calmly.

He then nodded sheepishly, then turned to his mother, the excitement in his face replaced with sadness. He slowly walked over to Alexandria and gave her a big hug.

"I'll miss you," he said, sniffling his nose.

A tear ran down her face. She nodded. "I will miss you too, my boy. I will be right here waiting for you."

Alexandria squeezed him tightly, then looking him in the eyes, said, "Listen to Jes and the other sorcerers. Be careful and don't try anything you're not ready for, you have a habit of doing that."

Joel nodded. "Goodbye, Momma."

I put a hand on the boy's shoulder. "Very good. Now we may go."

I turned to Alexandria and faintly smiled. "He'll be back soon, I promise."

She wiped her eyes and nodded. "I know."

I tapped my scepter on the ground twice, calling forth a rift that would take us to the Sorcerer's Keep. Light surrounded Joel and me, blinding us. For several seconds, it felt as though we were caught in a tornado, spinning out of control until suddenly it was over. The overpowering light was gone and when I opened my eyes, we were standing just yards away from the Keep.

"Whoa," Joel gasped. "Where are we? How did you do that?"

I laughed, remembering my first time portaling to the Keep.

"That was a rift," I explained. "A magic portal that can take us to the Keep."

I gestured to the massive stone building. It was a white

rectangular building as tall as the Tyranian castle. It had no visible doors or windows, making the structure look like it was a solid piece of white stone.

"That... that's the Keep?" Joel asked in awe. "It's huge!"

I laughed again. "It's even more impressive on the inside. Come on."

Joel and I walked toward the center of the northern face of the Keep. I explained to him everything that I wish Dahrik, my master, had explained to me when I was entering the Keep for the first time. Dahrik was a sour old dwarf who wasn't much for conversation. When he had brought me to the Keep, over ten years ago, he hadn't told me anything. He just expected me to follow behind him and not ask questions. I decided to take a different approach with Joel.

"Now," I began, "once we are inside, I will take you to Ginn. She is what's called the grandmaster, the leader of the Keep. She is an elf, as most enchanters tend to be. She will ask you some questions, and then she will decide when you're training will begin and with whom."

The half-elf child nodded attentively, absorbing every word.

"Most important of all, relax. There are no wrong answers." I said, tapping my scepter to the outer keep wall, causing the door to suddenly appear.

"What the... but there wasn't... how?" Joel stammered with

surprise at the door's instant appearance.

I chuckled, stepping through the doorway, motioning for him to follow. "You'll get used to it. Come on in."

* * *

In the city of Culten, Kernil Ravenhigh sat alone on the bell tower as he looked across the night sky. It was nearly morning, the new day bringing with it the autumn equinox. The air was chill, and the sky was cloudy, as though it might rain, but Kernil suspected it would not. It was here in the bell tower near the western edge of the city that Kernil came often to think and be alone.

His friends were in the Noble Griffin, a nearby tavern, celebrating a job completed and a large payment received. Kernil joined them at the beginning of the celebration but snuck away to be alone. He didn't feel like drinking, singing, or telling exaggerated tales of adventure. Not tonight, at least, not on his father's birthday.

For the past four years, he had done everything he could to take his mind off the shame and the pain that boiled inside him. He had distracted himself, with moderate success, by working jobs with his crew and drinking lots of ale. Yet in recent days, that wasn't enough. The pain and shame of his failure weighed on him even more as time went on.

"How did it all go so wrong?" he whispered to himself as he gazed at the city below him.

He knew the answer, of course. Nemul Lamm had killed his father and assumed himself ruler of Vain and of the new kingdom he called Aris. What hurt Kernil the most, was that he had not been there to stop Nemul and save his family. He had only survived because of an extended hunting trip meant to prove his worth.

"If only I had been there," he spat bitterly to himself, punching the large copper bell that hung in the tower.

A nearly inaudible *ding* of the bell echoed the act.

Yet, he knew that if he had been there, they would have killed him, just as his entire family had been.

"If nothing else," he mumbled, "I should have gone and ended Nemul once and for all."

But Kernil had taken Rivith's advice and done the sensible thing. He had gone to Chamish Regalock, King of Tyran. Chamish knew him and his father. Kreed Ravenhigh had been the King's loyal governor over Vain.

"Your father was a good man," the king had said. "His death and this rebellion by his usurper is tragic and outrageous."

For a year, Kernil served Chamish as a captain in the Tyranian army as they tried to reclaim the new Kingdom of Aris. Yet despite their best efforts, Nemul and the armies of Aris defeated Tyran and solidified their sovereignty. It was an embarrassing defeat for Chamish and Tyran. Kernil also felt ashamed by the loss. He had been given a chance to take vengeance on Nemul and reclaim his city yet again and had failed.

Because Aris could not be retaken, Kernil was denied his birthright. King Chamish had insisted that he arrange a marriage for Kernil with eldest the daughter of Lord Delweye, the governor of Zenan. This would have kept the Son of Vain in the elites of Tyran, as well as make him the type of leader he was born to be. However, he had respectfully declined this offer. His heart wasn't in it. Vain was his home and being lord over a land that was not his own felt wrong.

Since then, Kernil had been living and working in Culten. He formed a crew where they worked as hired security, usually for visiting nobles or wealthy business owners. It wasn't what the Son of Vain had to expect from his life, but it kept him busy enough. That is, until lately. Kernil had put everything into his work, his crew, and anything else that might keep him from having to think about the past, about his failures. Normally, his attempts were successful, but as of late, thoughts of Vain kept infesting his mind.

Images of the city center market, the governor's manor that was his home, and of Adaline, his lifelong sweetheart. A sharp pain swelled in Kernil's chest as his mind lingered on the images and how he would likely never see them again.

A tear ran down his cheek. His right hand fondled the gold hilt of the Sword of Vain. The sword was meant to mark him as the heir apparent to the governorship, but now all it did was remind him of the life that was no longer his. Kernil couldn't part from it however, it was his last remaining connection to Vain and his father.

Kernil gazed over the northwestern fields. From this vantage point, he could see all the way to the Lake of Ears. The autumn breeze felt nice against his skin. The sun was just rising in the east, illuminating the west with a fiery light. Then, off on the horizon, Kernil saw something move. The ground shifted as though a massive colony of bees had created a hive on the southeast shore of the Neos River.

"What is that?" he asked himself out loud, squinting his eyes to get a better look at the wave of movement.

The odd cluster was moving toward Culten at a fast pace. Kernil studied it for several minutes, still unsure of what exactly was coming his way at an unprecedented speed. Then he heard the hissing. It started out dim and unrecognizable, but as the swarm grew closer, the sound became more intense, as though thousands of snakes were hissing at once. A shiver ran up Kernil's back as he was just able to make out the individual figures. They had vaguely humanoid bodies but moved on the ground like lizards. Each one ran synchronized with the other, as though they were all part of one organism.

An internal alarm started screaming at Kernil. Whatever these things were, they were dangerous, and the Culten was in their path. Without taking his eyes off the hissing mass of figures approaching the city, he shoved the large, copper bell next to him with all his might.

Dong! Dong!

The bell clamored thunderously, the noise nearly deafening the Son of Vain. Kernil withdrew the Sword of Vain, its polished blade gleamed in the early morning sunlight.

"The city is under attack!" he yelled, his ears still ringing from the bell. "To arms, everyone. Enemies on the northwest!"

* * *

Joel only spoke with Ginn for a few minutes.

"Jes is right, you have magic growing inside you," Ginn said in a warm voice.

The boy's face lit up with joy, and his feet tapped with excitement.

"However, the magic is still very new and not fully developed yet. You shall be trained but I think it best to wait a few more years," the grandmaster concluded.

Joel's face sagged, along with his entire body. The happiness and energy that had been all too apparent only seconds ago had vanished.

"I know it's not quite what you were hoping for, Joel, but this is for the best," I consoled as I walked him out of the grand council chamber.

He sighed with disappointment. "I just wanted to be an enchanter, like you."

We said goodbye to Ginn and walked together through the elegant halls of the Keep. Joel paid no attention to his surroundings, he just stared at the floor, his eyes distant, as I guided him to his room.

"And you will be," I said, nudging his side. "This is not a rejection."

"But why can't I learn magic now?" he whined. "I don't want to wait two more years."

"Magic develops and usually manifests during adolescence," I explained. "You're only eleven years old, very young. I didn't start my training until I was fourteen, so even in a few years, you'll be the same age I was."

A slight smile flashed across his face.

"Really?" he asked, looking up at me. "But you're the best enchanter ever."

I laughed. "Oh no, I'm not. I might be the Prodigy, but I'm far from the best."

Joel stopped walking. "Yes, you are," he protested. "You are the best, that's what being the Prodigy means."

"Well, yes, but that..."

13

Joel cut me off as he pointed to a large, framed painting on the wall to his left. "Your picture is even on the wall!"

I turned to see that he was right. The large painting hanging on the wall depicted me fighting the Vios Almna. Ginn had commissioned it shortly after I had returned from the quest. A friend of mine, an elf named Zorrel, painted it. He did an amazing job on the artwork. It seemed so realistic and accurate, as though he had been there painting it while the fight was taking place. Most impressively, Zorrel captured the powerful and intimidating presence of the Vios Almna. The only anachronism was that he made me look so courageous as I faced the void of souls, my face showing no fear as I aimed the silver gauntlet at its life source.

In truth, I had forgotten that it was here.

"I doubt they make those of everyone," Joel added.

I rubbed my eyes, suddenly exhausted and wanting to be alone and sleep.

"Not the point," I said with a sigh. "Even being the Prodigy, my powers showed up at fourteen years old. Had I began before my powers developed enough, I would have had an even more difficult time. I probably would have quit before ever being able to cast a spell. That's why you need to wait. If you start now, it will just discourage you."

Joel looked at the painting of me, studying it as though it held the solution to beginning his training early. A tear swelled in his eye. I put a hand on his shoulder.

I was about to speak when the painting started to rattle. Then, I felt a pulsing vibration from the floor. A loud *THUD* echoed through the halls, followed by the sound of cracking stone. The painting fell to the ground.

"Was that an earthquake?" asked Joel, his eyes wide with fear.

I shook my head, inspecting my surroundings.

"No. The Keep is impervious to earthquakes. This was something different..." I trailed off.

Then, Ginn's voice rung in the air, speaking to the whole Keep at once.

"Everyone, the Keep is under attack," she said, trying to sound calm, but fear was obviously present in her voice. "A horde of creatures unknown have nearly breached the northern face. Converge and protect the Keep at all costs."

With the message delivered, Ginn's voice was gone. Throughout the Keep, every sorcerer started moving toward the northern end, their scepters in hand and ready for battle.

"What's attacking us?" Joel asked, yelling over the roar of people now running through the halls.

"I don't know," I replied. "Follow me."

I grabbed him by the arm and began leading him south. The crowd moved against us, but I pushed my way through, keeping a tight grip on Joel.

"I have to get him to safety," I said to myself, my thoughts nearly drowned out by the noise of my own heartbeat as well as those moving through the hallway.

There was another tremor, pushing everyone to the east wall. I was the first one back on my feet and pulled Joel up to his and then resumed walking, now faster than before.

"What's happening? Where are we going?" he called as I pulled him along.

I didn't answer. Instead, I walked even faster.

"I need to get him to safety. I need to get him to safety," the thought repeated in my head. "First safety, then defend. I need to get him to safety."

After what felt like an eternity, we reached my quarters. It was a small room with only a bed, desk, and graphic rug as furniture. It was near the southeast corner of the Keep, at the opposite end from that of the attackers.

I opened the door and pushed the boy inside.

"You are to stay in here until I come to get you," I said, pointing at him to hold his attention.

"What? No!" he shouted in protest. "I want to come with you."

The gems on my scepter glowed bright green. My voice boomed through the room like thunder, "You are to stay here until I come to get you!"

Joel shrunk against the wall, nodding in compliance.

The light from my scepter flickered off. I spoke softly, realizing my overcorrection, "I promised your mother that you would be safe. Here is the safest place to be right now. I have to go and defend the Keep. Stay here."

I turned to my desk and picked up the metal gauntlet placed on top. I saw my reflection in the polished silver and in the large green gem embedded in the forearm. I smiled with satisfaction as I inserted my left arm into the gauntlet. I immediately felt the power of the weapon coursing through me.

"Wait, is that *the* gauntlet? The one you used to kill the Vios Almna?" asked Joel, pointing at the gauntlet.

"Yes, it is," I replied, walking out of the room. "Stay here."

I shut the door and sprinted through the Keep. There was no longer any traffic in the halls, as by now all had probably made it to where the attackers were trying to breach. As I neared, an overwhelming hissing sound filled the air. It grew so loud that I could barely hear myself think. The hissing sound seemed like it was coming from the combat training room, which was one of the northern-most rooms.

I came around a corner and the next thing I knew, I was on my back. Crouched on top of me was a horrifying creature I had never seen before. It had scaly skin, like that of a snake or a lizard. The scales were checkered yellow and black. The creature was humanoid, standing about five and a half feet tall. It had big, round, red eyes with diamond-shaped black pupils. It had short and stubby fingers with black serrated claws about the length of my forearm that were hooked at the end.

The creature hissed in my face, exposing hundreds of its needle-like teeth. It raised its clawed hand to strike. I desperately tried to yank my arms free, but the creature had them pinned down. Time seemed to slow for an instant. First, its arm flinched, then began moving toward my exposed throat. Just as it did, a black iron rod came crashing down on the creature's head. Before I or the creature could react, a large, black hand grabbed it by the neck and threw it across the hall.

I turned to face my rescuer and saw the dwarf Dahrik, my friend and former master.

Stabbing at the wall with his scepter, Dahrik called out to the creature, "Get out of my house, you reptilian scum!"

Then, the dwarf used both hands to rip his scepter from the wall, taking a chunk of the stone wall with it connected to the end of the staff. With an audible grunt, he flicked his scepter like a catapult, throwing the chunk of wall down the hallway. The large piece crashed in the lizard creature's head. The stone broke into several smaller pieces and the reptile fell limp to the ground.

Dahrik spun around, grabbed me by the tunic, and pulled me to my feet.

"Where have you been?" he yelled. "The Keep is under attack and you take your time? What's wrong with you?"

I used my scepter to hoist myself to my feet. "I had Joel with me. The boy has undeveloped magic in him, so I brought him in tonight to speak with grandmaster Ginn. Had to make sure he was safe first before joining the fun."

"Ah, right," Dahrik said, remembering that I had mentioned Joel the last time we had seen each other.

"What are these things," I asked, looking at the dead creature.

The dwarf shook his head. "No idea. I've never seen these things before. Doesn't seem like anyone else around here has either. They're dangerous though, resilient too."

I nodded. I looked down the long hall that led to the combat training room where the lizard creatures were trying to enter. I could hear the shouts and sounds of battle. Just out of sight stood every sorcerer defending our home.

I took a step forward, ready to join the rest of the Keep, when Dahrik grabbed my arm, stopping me.

"Ginn is leading the defense to stop them from entering the breach," he said. "She assigned me to make sure that if any of these things get past everyone, they don't get far. I could use your help."

I could see in his eyes that he was nervous. Nervous about what, I couldn't exactly tell. Maybe he was nervous about protecting the Keep, or perhaps my safety. Maybe he feared for his own life and did not want to die alone.

Just then, the hissing returned. Ahead, three more of the creatures raced towards us, their claws readied. Dahrik and I nodded to each other and faced the creatures.

I called forth the power of my gauntlet, immediately I could feel the power surge through my body and focus on my left hand. In my palm formed a ball of swirling green energy that grew in size and power with every second. They had closed half the distance between us when I fired the energy into the trio of lizard creatures. With a twitch of my thumb, the energy burst from my palm. A flash of green light filled the hall. The gauntlet energy zipped down the hall, intent on striking the creature in the middle of the trio.

The three creatures came to stop just before the energy struck, hissing and gnashing their teeth. The creature in the middle slashed at the oncoming blast, its claws catching and stopping the green energy.

I gasped. How did it avoid harm for the magical blast? How was it handling the raw power like it was harmless? This had never happened before. The energy was always destructive and effective. How could this happen?

The green energy swirled around the creature's long claws. The creature's eyes glowed green, and the energy captured in its hands diminishing into nothing. The three creatures hisses then began running towards us again.

I stepped back in shock at what had just happened.

"Watch out!" Dahrik yelled, his scepter at the ready. "I don't think these things are affected by magic. I've just been bashing their heads in and that seems to work."

The dwarf sprinted down the hall, his scepter raised high with both hands. Just before he was upon the creatures, he used his scepter to pole vault into a flying two-legged kick. His feet smashed into the middle lizard's face and Dahrik momentum and body weight pushed it to the ground with a loud crash. Before the other two creatures knew what had happened, Dahrik whacked both of them in the head with the edges of his iron scepter.

Before the creatures could recover, I rushed in with an upper-cut punch to the creature on the right with my gauntlet. A stream of blue-colored blood dripped from its small nose. It hissed, then attacked in a flurry of claws. The long steel-like claws scraped my gauntlet, which I used to shield myself.

Dahrik stomped the neck of the lizard on the ground, and it didn't move again. The creature on the left hissed and swiped at the dwarf and caught him in his undefended shoulder. Dahrik yelped in pain, blood now gushing from his arm. The creature's claws shined brightly with white light. Dahrik shouted in anger and swung his long, iron scepter into the lizard's side. It doubled over and the dwarf kicked it in the head, knocking it on its back.

The creature in front of me swiped at me furiously, but I blocked the attacks with my gauntlet, which thankfully covered down my elbow. I waited for an opening. Once I saw it, I channeled magic through my muscles, allowing me to move faster as I struck with my scepter, stabbing it in the throat. The creature made a choking sound and clutched its neck. I took advantage and grabbed hold of its head with my gauntleted hand and bashed its head against the wall. The creature fell to the ground and didn't get back up.

After having applied the Vodro Heal to the wound on his arm, Dahrik bombarded the last creature with a flurry of magical attacks, swinging his hands and scepter around like a whirlwind. The creature effortlessly stopped all the mystical fire and electricity that Dahrik threw at it. Each time, its claws glowed as it absorbed the spell.

It jumped forward, nearly reaching the ceiling as it came at the dwarf with all of its claws. Dahrik held up his scepter in defense, its serrated claws and the iron staff colliding with an awful scraping noise.

Still using the magic to enhance my muscle and motor skills, I moved in on the creature from behind and bashed my scepter into the back of its leg. Its footing faltered and Dahrik took advantage, landing a kick into the beast's chest. The reptile fell on its back, right in front of me. Without a second's hesitation, I jammed the end of my staff in between its eyes, unleashing a surge of electricity. Its limbs flailed and twitched for the duration of the lightning, then stopped as I pulled away.

The smell of burning flesh filled the hallway. Dahrik stood next to me and patted my arm.

"Not entirely magic proof, are they? Nice work back there."

"What are these things?" I asked, looking them over. "How are they able to cut through magic like that? That shouldn't be possible."

"You can try asking them," Dahrik said, staring down the hall, his scepter held at the ready. "Heads up, more incoming."

I looked up and saw that five more of the creatures coming from the breach.

The Hissing Death

"Three Cheers for the hero of Culten!" someone in the crowd shouted.

The mass of warriors cheered thrice as Kernil was hoisted in the air by Hemm. Kernil replied by raising the Sword of Vain high above his head in triumph.

"A round of drinks at the Noble Griffin, on me," called another man. "Two for the man that warned us all in time."

The offer of drinks was followed by another roar of cheers, this one louder than any that had come before it. Before long, the Noble Griffin Tavern was filled to capacity and a roar of cheerful voices was heard throughout the nearby streets as the defenders drank abundantly. With the city successfully protected from the horde of mysterious creatures, a spirit of celebration settled over the warriors and city guardsmen who had defended it. Kernil sat among his crew, this time gladly participating in the celebration.

The Son of Vain thought back to the events of the morning. Just before the lizard monsters reached the city, Kernil led every armed warrior he could gather against them on short notice, about two hundred. The Culten Watch had comprised the majority of that force, while various mercenary teams comprised the rest.

The creatures fought like nothing Kernil had ever encountered before, but just as he did in every battle, he quickly learned their fighting patterns. They depended too much on their claws to ward off foes and didn't focus much on their footing. The Son of Vain wasn't the only one to pick up on this weakness, and soon, even the outnumbered defenders had the creatures nearing retreat. Before long, more warriors for hire like himself joined in, as did the famed Culten Militia. This added about four hundred more swords and was the turning point of the short battle.

The battle reminded Kernil of the Five-Year War against the elves. Similarly, Kernil had led a charge against an army of elves attacking his home of Vain. This time, it wasn't the elves he was fighting, in fact, many of those that fought by his side were elves. When Kernil had first moved to Culten, after Tyran failed to recapture the lands of Aris, living among elves was something that he was forced to accept. It was a difficult thing to do for a long while, after all, the elves had killed many of his close friends during the Five-Year War. Yet, Kernil eventually realized that just as he was disassociated from the humans of Tyran, so too were the elves of Culten from those that dwelt in the Bellum Forest.

Culten was a place for everyone. This includes elves, humans, trolls, dwarves, gnomes, and even some of the less sociable creatures of the land. It wasn't a nation of just one species but of any and all, the only one in Cray. Kernil liked Culten because it was different. It reminded him less of home than anywhere in what's left of Tyran did.

Those in the tavern talked and laughed among themselves, eating and drinking without restraint. Kernil's crew made a toast to him.

"To our vigilant leader," proclaimed Barris, as he raised a pint mug high in the air. "While we were off celebrating a job well done, Kernil was looking for more work."

"To Kernil," the others cheer, then drank from their mugs.

"Speaking of which, are we getting paid for this?" asked Kilt, still swallowing her drink, "I'm happy to play the hero whenever, but if I do, there better be some reward coming my way."

Hemm, who sat next to her, grunted in agreement. His massive arms that rested on the table took up most of the space. His bulky body required two stools to sit on without breaking them.

"I'm sure we'll get our fair share," Kernil offered reassuringly. "One way or another."

The crew all chuckled and took another swig of their drinks.

"Hey!" Kilt yelled to the whole of the tavern as she leaped on top of the table. "What do you say we get some music going?"

A swell of cheers and clapping followed the suggestion, and Kilt took hold of the lute that had been strapped to her back. She began to play a tune that most any resident of Culten would know. Before Kilt had finished the introduction, the whole tavern had begun to clap and stomp along with the rhythm of the song. A man at the other end of the room began accompanying Kilt with his fiddle. The entire tavern shook with the elated sounds of clapping, stomping, drinking, and singing warriors.

> *As you take in the morning air,*
> *Just enjoying yourself the view,*
> *You know that deep within your soul,*
> *This place was meant for you.*

> *It's not in Knaksis,*
> *And it ain't in Tyran.*
> *It's certainly not in the Abic of Marsh,*
> *Or even Phite or Zenan.*
> *Everyone knows the best place to be,*
> *Is right here in Culten.*

> *You've lived in towns and hamlets,*
> *And nearly every city too.*
> *But now that you have landed here,*
> *You're a Cultenier through and through.*

> *It's not in Knaksis,*
> *And it ain't in Tyran.*

It's certainly not in the Abic of Marsh,
Or even Phite or Zenan.
Everyone knows the best place to be,
Is right here in Culten.

You love the people dearly,
And the city has a fair law.
When compared to other places,
It's the best you ever saw.
So, grab yourself a plot of land,
And join the Cultenier's Hurrah!

It's not in Knaksis,
And it ain't in Tyran.
It's certainly not in the Abic of Marsh,
Or even Phite or Zenan.
Everyone knows the best place to be,
Is right here in Culten.

Everyone knows the best place to be,
Is right here in Culten!

Kernil's favorite part of the song was when everyone would shout, "Hurrah!" He liked it because at the instant of the Hurrah the song transition into somewhat of a battle cry. He had done many battle cries while in the fighting in the Five-Year War, but few since. It made him homesick again.

* * *

They left almost as quickly as they came. As if they were some sort of hive-mind, every single lizard creature simultaneously retreated and then fled toward the Neos River.

"Okay, now I'm very confused," I said to Dahrik as we watched the horde of creatures moving southeast. "They had us outnumbered and are resistant to magic. Why give up?"

Dahrik and I chased after them to see where they were headed. He and I followed them from the moment of their retreat, at first on their heels but quickly outpaced. As the distance between us and them grew, Dahrik and I used magic to push ourselves faster. We moved so fast, I didn't have time to get a good look at the battle scene near the breach. We stopped at the southeast corner of the Keep, watching the creatures in the distance.

Out of the corner of my left eye, a figure caught my attention. It was a tall, dark person, but I couldn't make out any details about them. I turned to get a better look, but when I did, the figure had disappeared.

"What are you looking at?" asked Dahrik.

I looked back at him, scratching my head in confusion. "I thought I saw someone standing over there."

He glanced over at the area I pointed to but didn't see anything but browning grass and the river's edge.

The dwarf shrugged. Before he could say anything else, Thea of Grand Council limped over to us. She was entirely covered

29

in the lizards' blue blood apart from the surrounding area of a gash on her calf.

"There you are, Jes," she said, her jaw clenched and her face red. "We needed you with us against those *things*! Ginn is furious. Where were you?"

In my ten years of knowing Grandmaster Ginn, I had never once seen her remotely upset, although Thea was Ginn's right hand on the Grand Council, so such a claim should not be dismissed lightly. Dahrik claimed that he had seen her angry once, five years ago when he had broken the Keep's code by participating in the Aris revolt against Tyran beyond his instructions.

I stuttered as I attempted to answer, but Dahrik interrupted me.

"He inside was with me, the whole time," he declared. "We stopped those that made it into the Keep from getting anywhere beyond the first hallway, just as you and Master Ginn had instructed."

The maroon-colored gems on the elf woman's pinewood scepter flickered with light. Her face flushed even darker red than before. The anger on her face was obvious. Thea would have been intimidating if she wasn't so much shorter than I. She stood at two inches under five feet, just ever so shorter than Dahrik. If it weren't for her pointed ears and slender frame, she might have been confused for a dwarf or a gnome.

"Those instructions were for you alone, Master Dahrik," Thea said, clearly trying very hard not to lose control of her temper that was currently boiling inside her.

"Yes, but-" Dahrik tried to defend himself, but Thea interrupted him.

"May I remind you, Dahrik, that Jes is no longer your apprentice. That means he is under the instruction of the Council and myself. Not to you. Catching those who made their way inside was a single-person task, not two. Especially if that second person is the living Prodigy."

I put a hand on Dahrik's shoulder. "It didn't seem to matter. Those things were immune to my magic and the power of the gauntlet all the same."

She turned to me and glared. "Not the point. Once again, Master Dahrik has ignored Keep protocols. You should have known better. Having you both inside was a waste of talent that probably cost us many lives."

The elf exhaled twice, calming herself.

"Now, if the two of you are done gazing at the horizon, there's plenty of work to be done at the breach. The wounded must be tended to, The Joining must be done for the dead and the walls of our precious Keep must be mended."

With a final huff, Thea limped away as proudly as she could, moving much faster than expected from someone her size.

31

"She's right, you know," Dahrik sighed. "I shouldn't have kept you inside."

The dwarf leaned against his six-foot-tall iron scepter, his head dinging against the metal.

"You shouldn't have kept me? What are you talking about?" I scoffed. "I saw that you needed help, so I helped you. You're good, Dahrik, but not that good. Besides, it's not like we were slacking off. We were the second line of defense, protecting all of the trainees and the acolytes inside."

He sighed again. "I suppose. Still, Thea will never let me hear the end of this one."

I felt bad for my former master. Over the past five years, his reputation had been crushed. When I was his apprentice, he was the most highly regarded sorcerer outside of the Grand Council. That changed, however, when Dahrik had broken the Sorcerer's Code by involving himself too much in a counter rebellion effort during the Aris Revolt.

It's a core belief of the Sorcerers that we don't interfere with the politics of Cray. We are to be peacekeepers and defenders against magical forces. Dahrik had been sent to Vain to stop a Warlock, an enchanter from a different Keep, from starting a civil war in Tyran. The dwarf had done so, but only after organizing and fighting in the counter rebellion alongside those still loyal to King Chamish.

This had caused the supposed incident where Ginn had grown

furious with Dahrik. He was put on probation for a long time and lost an opportunity to get on the Grand Council when Huelin's spot was opened. Instead, a human named Charlotte Rowland got the position.

After that, Dahrik seemed to be publicly over scrutinized by both Charlotte and Thea for the smallest errors, causing his high reputation to plummet. As his friend and former apprentice, it had been very hard to watch happen. This behavior shook my own view of the code as well as those who sat on the Grand Council.

I punched the dwarf in the arm.

"Quit feeling sorry for yourself. You made a choice, but so did I. We don't know who died because of what, and there's no sense in dwelling on it. All we can do now is keep moving forward, do better next time around."

Dahrik stared back at me, a thin smile creeping into his expression. "I thought I was supposed to be the one giving *you* encouragement when you mess up."

I laughed. "Don't worry, I'm sure I'll do something stupid real soon."

He smiled and patted me on the back. The two of us then walked around the Keep back towards the breach.

As we turned the northeast corner, we saw a field of red and blue carnage. Bodies, of both lizard creatures and sorcerers, covered the ground for as far as the eye could see. The usually majestic hills that surrounded the Keep were tainted by death and blood. It was so horrible, I was amazed that I missed it the first time around.

The first person alive that I saw was Merek, a member of the Grand Council and chief healer for Keep. He was instructing his team of elite healers on how they should treat the many wounded. Those that weren't treating the injured were moving the dead inside, most likely to begin The Joining ritual.

The Joining ritual is among our most sacred practices, where the souls and bodies of the dead are transfigured into magical energy, which is then fed into the Keep. That energy is then redistributed to all members of the Keep. It's a mutually beneficial process of strengthening our connection to the Keep, which is necessary for the development of magic practice.

Ginn was standing next to Thea by the breach, both studying the Keep's damage. Dahrik and I jogged toward them. As we neared, Ginn's teary eyes lit up at the sight of me.

"Jes, you're alive," she cried with glee. "When we couldn't find your body, we assumed the worst."

I glanced at Thea, who avoided eye contact with me.

"Yes, I was with Dahrik," I said with no regret in my voice. "I thought my talents were best put to use defending the Keep's interior."

She frowned. "Oh, I wouldn't worry too much about it. None of us were much use against those vile monsters, I doubt even you would have had any success against them."

Dahrik and I looked at each other, then back at Thea. However, the councilwoman was no longer behind Ginn. Thea had managed to sneak away and was now talking to Merek, some fifteen yards away.

"I trust that with the both of you, none of those things got very far," she said.

It was Dahrik who answered, "Yes, Master. None got far at all."

"Excellent," she sighed with relief. "I've sent Zorrel into the archives. Hopefully, he can find some information about them. It's odd, I've never seen anything like them but I feel like I should know what they are-"

"Master," interrupted Wulfric, also one of the seven Grand Councilmen. "The dead have been counted."

"And?" Ginn braced herself against the Keep wall.

Wulfric frowned. "Thirty-nine total fallen."

Ginn put a hand on her chest, and a new wave of tears trickled down her cheeks. My entire body tensed. Thirty-nine were killed by today's attack. Was Thea right? How many of those could I have stopped? Or was Ginn right? Would it have even mattered?

"Fifteen apprentices, sixteen members, five masters, and three councilmen," Wulfric added.

"Wait, three councilmen?" I turned and looked at Merek and Thea, then back to Ginn and Wulfric.

"Reinette, Morin, and Charlotte," Ginn confirmed. "All perished in the battle."

There was a moment of silence between us. Eventually, Ginn spoke, addressing Wulfric.

"Has the ritual begun?"

Wulfric shook his head. "No, but all have been prepared to begin. I was awaiting your verification."

Ginn nodded. "Begin. Start with the young ones, then everyone else. Alert me before you Join Charlotte, Morin, or Reinette. I think it only right for the rest of the Council to be present for that."

"Yes master," Wulfric nodded in acknowledgment to Dahrik and me, then turned and headed back into the Keep.

Ginn sighed again, then ran her hands over the cracked and damaged surface of the Keep wall near the breach.

"Thank Jard that so much death won't be for nothing," she said. "The Joining of so many should give the Keep enough power to heal this wound. Of course, it would have been better if none of this would have happened at all..."

She trailed off.

Nearly forty dead. It had been a long time since our Keep had taken so many causalities. I don't think it had ever come from a single attack. Why did they attack us? As far as I could tell, nobody had seen the likes of them before. And why did they suddenly leave? If you're going to attack an enchanter's keep and having success, why retreat before finishing the job? Most curious of all, how were impervious to magic? Never before had I heard of a creature with a resistance to magic. It was supposed to be impossible.

"Where did they go?" Ginn asked. "What direction?"

I answered, "They went southeast. Towards the river."

She nodded, mumbling something unintelligible to herself.

"And Sebastian said they came from the southwest and the northwest, converging into one group seconds before attacking," she noted, speaking more to herself than to either of us.

Dahrik and I looked at each other. We were thinking the same thing. We turned back to the pale elf.

"The Druid's Keep is southwest," Dahrik said.

"And the Mage's Keep is northwest of here," I added.

Ginn nodded, then finished our thought, "And the Warlocks are southeast of here. Now it's beginning to make sense. They have been going after all of the Keeps, not just ours. They left so suddenly because they still have the largest Keep to go, the Warlocks."

"They acted like a hive-mind," Dahrik added. "Maybe we killed enough of them that they worried their numbers wouldn't be large enough to still attack the Warlocks."

Ginn stroked her chin, then continued nodding. "Only question is, why? Why attack all the Keeps? Even if by attacking all of them you can't fully destroy them all."

"Master Ginn, what does this mean?" I asked genuinely.

The elf woman shook her head. "I don't know, but maybe someone of the other Keeps might. It's time to call a Council of the Keeps and figure this out."

* * *

Joel didn't mind the fact that he could hear the battle going on from Jes' room. He enjoyed it actually. He probably should have been scared by the orchestra of hissing and yelling, or the loud explosions of magic. He wasn't however, Joel was smart enough to know that as long as there was fighting, the attackers hadn't won and would most likely not come looking for him.

What scared him was the silence that marked the end of the battle. When the silence came over the Keep, Joel's heart began to thump against his chest. It was over now, but how did it end? Had Jes succeeded in destroying all of the attackers, or had the impossible happened and Jes failed?

The half-elf boy sat on the bed for several minutes, sitting as calmly and patiently as was possible for a boy of eleven. His leg bounced furiously as he tried not to think about the silence that encompassed him.

"Jes said he would be back as soon as the fight was over," he thought, "so where is he?"

Joel's fears started to get the best of him. He jumped up from the bed quietly crouched next to the door, pressing his ear against the wood surface to try to hear anything on the other side.

He heard nothing. It was as quiet as a graveyard.

"What if all the sorcerers are dead?" he thought, his mind panicking. "What do I do? How do I get home? What if they're looking for me? What if they're right outside the door waiting for me to walk into a trap?"

Then Joel heard a sound through the door. It was faint, but it was definitely there. It was a shuffling sound, like the sound of a single person walking or running down the hall. It was getting slightly louder; the person was coming toward Joel.

Joel panicked again. "Is it Jes? Is it someone else? Do I need to be ready for a fight?" he thought, looking around the room for a potential weapon.

The shuffling was right outside the door, but then quickly faded. The person had walked right past him. He was safe again.

The boy's curiosity spiked. If that person wasn't Jes coming for him, then who was it and where were they going?

Almost without thinking about it, Joel turned the doorknob and peeked outside. He saw an elven man speed-walking further down the hall towards a large oak door with a rounded top. The elf had a six-foot scepter in one hand, navy blue gems on each end. Was he a sorcerer, or perhaps a Warlock who had attacked the Keep?

The boy decided to not to announce himself to the enchanter. Better to keep the element of surprise. Without shutting the door behind him, Joel silently followed after him.

* * *

I stood in Ginn's private study with all of the remaining members of the Grand Council.

Ginn had just finished using the Mirror of Bonding, a powerful artifact that allowed the leaders of each of the four Keeps to send messages to one another. The mirror looked old, but rather ordinary. It wasn't very large, only about thirty-six inches in length and twenty-eight inches in width, in the shape of an oval. It hung against the study wall at eye level, at the other end of the room from Ginn's desk, the only other piece of furniture in the study. Normally, the Mirror of Bonding was covered by a brown canvas sheet, but that had been removed and placed in the corner.

The three other Keeps had an identical mirror. Thus, the four Keeps could contact one another in times of emergency. After sending the distress message requesting a Council of the Keeps, the three Keep leaders responded almost immediately. This was even rarer of an occurrence than using the mirror at all. We learned from their replies that our suspicion was correct, these unknown creatures had attacked each one of the Keeps. All had agreed to a proper meeting, either coming themselves or sending a representative of their respective council.

"The meeting is in Culten in two days," Ginn said to those of us in the room. "We always meet in the back room of the Howling Wolf Inn. Question is, which of us shall go with Jes?"

The three other council members immediately turned to me.

"Wait, why am I going?" I asked. "I'm not part of the Grand Council."

Thea scoffed. "Yes, but you're the Prodigy. Even though

you're one of us, you're supposed to be a uniting force between the Keeps. So obviously, you have to go."

"She's right," Wulfric added, "although these meetings are so rare, it's no wonder you aren't familiar with your role in them."

Thea rolled her eyes and turned towards Ginn. The grandmaster was still staring into the mirror, her gaze sad and suggesting that her thoughts were far away from the conversation at hand.

"I will go in your place, Master," Thea said to Ginn. "As Grandmaster, your place is here, and I, your right hand, should represent the Sorcerers in the Council of the Keeps."

Ginn's eyes blinking several times in rapid succession. She looked around the room, clearly confused but aware that Thea had just addressed her.

"Yes, you go," Ginn answered.

Thea smiled. "Thank you, Master, I will not fail you or this Keep."

My heart twisted in a knot. I did not want to travel all the way to Culten with Thea. I would already have to sit across from Norvic, the vile and evil leader of the Warlocks. I needed a close ally in that meeting and although we were both Sorcerers, Thea didn't feel like much of my ally most of the time. At some level, she was likely a good person, but after everything I had seen her put Dahrik through in the past five years, I didn't trust her nor did I care much to be around her. I was very certain she didn't like me either. I would have much preferred any other member of the Grand Council, alive or dead. The one who I really wanted to come with me, however, was Dahrik.

The door to Ginn's study suddenly burst open and Zorrel Highwind came in, sweating and out of breath.

"Sorry to interrupt everyone," Zorrel said as he stepped into the room. "I've discovered something that I know you will want to hear."

Thea scowled. "This better be important, Zorrel. This is a closed meeting."

"What have you found, Master Highwind?" Ginn asked, her attention fully returned to the present.

"Bring it in!" Zorrel called to a person standing just outside the door.

To my astonishment, Joel walked through the door, his arms wrapped around a large leather-bound book that looked extremely fragile and ancient.

Immediately our eyes met, and my gaze turned into a glare that said, "I told you to stay in the room. What Jard's name are you doing here?"

To which he gave a weak smile and stared back in a way that said, "You were gone for a long time. I got curious. Please don't yell at me."

Joel then avoided looking at me and placed the old book on Ginn's desk.

"I remember you," Ginn said to Joel with the first smile I had seen her make since the attack. "I spoke to you last night. I'm so glad you weren't hurt in the attack."

Joel blushed and thanked her.

"I was in the archives," Zorrel began, "searching for anything that might tell us about those strange creatures when this boy snuck up on me. He thought I was an intruder and was ready to duel me, unarmed, to the death to defend the Keep."

Merek chuckled. "Sounds like the boy's got spunk, as Huelin would have put it."

"Exactly," Zorrel replied. "He's quite the bright young lad, actually-"

"Can you please just get on with it?" Thea interrupted. "What have you found?"

Zorrel stuttered a bit, reconnecting his thoughts, then spoke again. "As I was trying to say, it was actually Joel that found it. Once I explained to him who I was and what I was doing, he helped me search. It was remarkable. The boy found it in a passage that I had overlooked. He found it in minutes."

"Did he?" I asked, nodding my head and smiling at Joel. "Sounds like he was in the right place after all."

The half-elf boy blushed and mouthed the words, "Thank you," to me.

"Indeed, he was," Zorrel confirmed. "Let me show you what we learned."

Zorrel opened the book and the spine audibly cracked, obviously very old and hadn't been used in a long time. The pages were stiff and tinted yellow. Zorrel turned the page twice, then pointed to a faded drawing. The four council members and I all leaned in to look at the image. Amazingly, it was an exact depiction of the humanoid lizard creatures that had attacked us.

"They're called 'The Hissera,'" Zorrel said as we each looked over the depiction. "Otherwise known as 'The Hissing Death.' They are a hive-mind pack species made from dark magic. Their claws can absorb magic energy of supposedly any kind. They can sense beings with magic, and they go around hunting for it, like bees to nectar. They never sleep, and they never need to eat or drink to sustain themselves. When they kill an enchanter, they can take their essence from the corpse, which is transferred to their creator."

"And who's their creator?" asked Merek.

Zorrel looked around at each one of us nervously before answering. "That's the most troubling part."

"As if magic resistant, killer lizards weren't troubling enough," Joel added.

"Precisely," Zorrel confirmed. "According to our records, the Hissera haven't been seen in Cray for about two hundred and thirty years. We have documented them in our history four times, each one resulting in large numbers of enchanter deaths."

The room went silent as we let the information sink in, but the tension was so thick, I felt like I was suffocating. I still had more questions than answers.

"You never answered the question," I noted, finally breaking the silence. "They can't just be appearing out of nowhere every few hundred years. So, who's this creator?"

Zorrel gulped. "Every single time, without fail, that the Hissera are created, it is the work of a necromancer."

The Fifth Necromancer

The Hissera moved as one towards the city of Culten. Once they crossed the Neos River, they ran for miles through the Lands of Aris. After the skirmish with the Druid, Mage, and Sorcerer Keeps, their creator had originally instructed them to head for Warlock Keep next.

"In Culten," the creator's voice spoke telepathically in their minds. "There is a single master enchanter. *His* death is crucial. Kill *him*!"

The Hissera altered their course.

When they neared the city, a large bell clanged and clamored. Just before they had entered Culten, they were met by two hundred armed warriors. Unlike the enchanters, the Hissera were not used to fighting these kinds of warriors with no magical ability. They didn't come with scepters or gauntlets, but with swords, axes, spears, clubs, and arrows.

A human with a big sword that had a gold hilt made the first cut. He cut off a hand of the one in the lead. Everyone felt the sting and cried out in pain.

"It hurts! It burns us!" the Hissera cried internally. "All shall die for the pain they cause us!"

The steel blades burned flesh when they cut into the Hissera. It was a sensation that they had never felt before. Unlike magic, the big sword was not something they could absorb or counter from far away.

"Attack, my children," came the creator's voice again. "Don't let these insects stop you from your prize. The enchanter within the city must die!"

The Hissera complied with their creator's command.

All of the warriors' weapons had the same effect. It was frustration for the Hissera to be inflicted so much pain by so few people. The worst was a troll. It swung a big wooden club, bashing and killing dozens of them at a time.

The Hissera decided to change their strategy.

"We are larger than the insects. We must surround them and kill them all."

The Hissera quickly surrounded the city defenders, then moved in all at once. The plan was working until even more warriors with weapons came from the city. The Hissera were now divided.

Many of them were dying, and all of them were in shared pain. The number of warriors kept increasing, and the Hissera were getting killed faster and faster. The advantage that the Hissera had was gone, the warriors from Culten now had them outnumbered.

"*He* is fleeing the city," the creator shouted, speaking into their minds once again. "He's going back to the Keep. After *him*! *He* must die!"

The Hissera obeyed. As one unit, they fled east. The warriors roared in triumph.

Eventually, the Hissera entered the Alley of Fire. The air didn't smell good, but it didn't bother them very much. The enchanter was close. They couldn't yet see him, but the Hissera could sense the delicious magic inside him. They nearly had him.

* * *

The five of us gasped all at once at the mention of a necromancer. The color seemed to drain from everyone's face.

"What? This can't be true! It just can't be true," reasoned Merek. "Zorrel, there has to be another explanation for these creatures."

The pain in Zorrel's expression was obvious. "I wish there was, but I'm afraid the text is very clear."

"Can someone tell me what a necromancer is? He rushed us over here without explaining anything," Joel said, pointing to Zorrel. "You have magic to protect you. Why are you all so scared?"

"Okay, remind me why this child is here again," snapped Thea.

I ignored her and answered Joel's question. "Enchanters like us are born with magic. It's a part of us. A necromancer does not have it from birth, but gained magic by stealing it from the dead. They leach off the magic of those that have it naturally, either mystical creature or enchanters."

"They use the Hissera the same way we use the Keep and The Joining ritual," Zorrel added. "But instead of using the energy of the dead the right way, to restrengthen the Keep, a necromancer corrupts the energy and uses it to make themselves more powerful. This ultimately warps the magic that they receive to become twisted and unnatural."

Joel nodded, although I wasn't sure he really understood what I was saying.

I knelt next to him and looked him in the eye, "Necromancers are a poison and a curse on the world, worse than the war-locks. They are very dangerous, even to the most powerful enchanters."

"Thank you for the refresher course," said Thea, the sarcasm in her voice nearly tangible. "But can we please get back to the matter at hand?"

I rolled my eyes in annoyance, then mouthed the words, "Good question," to Joel, and stood up.

"Yes," answered Ginn. "Assuming Zorrel is correct, then we are in danger. Our very existence is under attack. We are being exterminated."

"Even worse than that, I think the Hissera are cutting us off from the power of the Keep," said Wulfric nervously. "There's something wrong with the Keep. We have competed The Joining for all the dead, but the Keep doesn't seem to be getting any stronger. It has yet to heal itself from the attack."

I rubbed my brow as a small headache began to settle in.

"We shall work that problem later," Ginn stated. "For now, we should focus on this necromancer."

"Shouldn't we contact the other Keeps again and tell them about all of this new information?" Thea asked, pointing to the mirror.

It was Wulfric that answered. "What would be the point? They already agreed to meet in Culten in two days. Besides, they might have their own records and have learned already, just as we have."

"You have a point, Wulfric," said Ginn, walking away from the mirror and towards her desk. "But I do think that this is the time to use another relic."

She walked around the desk and sat in her chair. Ginn then opened a drawer and removed a small, rectangular object wrapped in velvet cloth. She delicately removed the cloth, revealing an ornate wooden box made of polish mahogany wood. The grandmaster opened the box and pulled out an ordinary-looking glass orb that fit in the palm of her hand.

"The Master's Eye," she said with reverence.

"What is it?" I asked.

Ginn hesitated before answering, staring into the sphere. "As you may remember, I have the gift of prophecy. Normally, when I will get visions of the future, warning me of important and dangerous events."

"But you didn't this time," Merek finished. "The necromancer must be using their power to hide from your visions."

Ginn nodded. "That is what I fear. The Master's Eye should allow me to increase my power and see what the necromancer is hiding, not only in the future but in the past as well."

"Wait, that thing will let you see into the necromancer's past?" I asked. "Why don't you use it all of the time?"

It was Thea who answered, "Using the Master's Eye is dangerous. Even a small use will leave her weakened. Using it for too long could kill her."

"Exactly," Ginn confirmed. "That is why I only use it when

there is no other option. I think now is such a time."

Ginn placed all of her fingers on the orb. Instantly, her eyes began to glow, gold beams of light flooding the entire study. Everyone turned away and shielded their eyes. Time seemed to stand still. I couldn't tell if it lasted thirty seconds or ten minutes. When the light receded, Ginn's body shuttered once, and then she stood up abruptly.

"Kaynah," she shouted. "Her name is Kaynah. She is an elf from the town of Shale."

We all looked at each other, unsure of what to make of the information.

"That's a start," Merek said. "Did you learn anything else?"

"Yes," Ginn replied, breathing heavily now. "I could not see her patron, but it began to corrupt her about ten years ago. She has been picking off enchanter's one by one, going unnoticed for many years. About a year ago, she found something buried in the earth. What exactly it is that she found, I could not see what it is. But since then, she has been able to create thousands of Hissera. She's taken up residence in the Abandoned Fortress, deep in the Abic of Marsh."

"What's a patron?" asked Joel.

I opened my mouth to answer, but Zorrel answered first.

"A patron is a magical being that shows the necromancer how

to use The Joining ritual to steal power. You can't just decide to steal magic, it must be learned by someone who knows already. If my memory for the history is correct, every patron of a necromancer thus far has been angry sprites, fairies, or spirits."

"Is there anything else you can tell us, Master?" asked Thea, ignoring Joel completely.

The Grandmaster shook her head. "I am afraid not. That is all I could see."

"Well, then, with your permission," Thea began, "Jes and I should be going. We have a deadline to be in Culten for the council."

"About that," I interjected before Ginn could reply. "I would like to request that Dahrik accompany me instead."

Thea's eyes first expanded in surprise, then turned into a scowl. "Excuse me? Master Ginn already declared that I should be the one to go. Besides, Dahrik Ironhelm can't represent the Keep, he is not a member of Grand Council."

"I am aware of that," I started, careful to word everything just right. "But now that we know what these Hissera are, and that a necromancer is creating them, we're going to need Dahrik. Despite not being a member of the Grand Council, he's better in combat than any of us, myself included. If it comes to facing down a necromancer, I'll need Dahrik by my side."

"The Prodigy has a point," Merek said, avoiding Thea's scowl.

Ginn nodded. "We have already lost three council members, perhaps sending you, Thea, is not our best move."

Thea's mouth hung open in disbelief.

The grandmaster looked at me and nodded. "Very well, Jes Nulkin, Dahrik shall go with you to the Council of the Keeps. You should leave at once."

I nodded to Ginn and walked out of the study. Seconds later, Zorrel raced up from behind and grabbed me by the shoulder.

"Wait up," he said as I turned to face him. Joel stood next to him, once again holding the ancient book.

"Ah, yes," I said, looking at the young half-elf. "Afraid I'm going to have to send you home without me."

"That's what I wanted to talk to you about," said Zorrel. "The boy is smart and even though his powers aren't ready for development, I believe he can still be of good service to the Keep. I am going to ask Ginn if I may take him on as my apprentice. He will start in the archives and library. When he is ready, then we'll move on to practicing and strengthening his magic."

I looked back at Joel and saw his face bright with joy. This was exactly what he had been wanting. Despite being too young for training, he had found another way in. It was impressive.

Joel was so determined and clever, it was admirable.

I turned back to Zorrel. He had become a full sorcerer about the time I had started my apprenticeship. Less than a month ago, they had given him the rank of master and chief librarian. Zorrel had long black hair that went past his shoulders. His eyes were a dull gray but were complemented by black, bushy eyebrows. Even for an elf, his ears were very long and sharply tipped. He had a kind and honest face which was backed up by his supreme loyalty and sense of duty. For those reasons, I had always liked him.

"I don't know what to say," I admitted. "It feels like you're asking for my permission, but it's not mine to give."

Zorrel smiled. "No, not permission. I just wanted to let you know what I was planning. You're the one who brought the boy here, after all."

"Well, then I support you, and am happy for you both," I said.

"It's a dream come true," called Joel, now shaking with excitement. "I just hope the elf lady says yes."

Zorrel and I chuckled.

"The elf lady's name is Grandmaster Ginn, and I think she will this time," I said. "Which reminds me, even if she does, I promised your mother that you would go back home before you begin any sort of training."

56

Joel's eyes filled with dread. He cried, "What? No! I want to stay here."

"If that was the promise, then we need to honor it. A sorcerer keeps his word," instructed Zorrel.

I nodded, admiring how Zorrel was already acting as a good mentor, then added, "Besides, I need someone to tell Rebecca that I'll be longer than the standard two weeks. Will you do that for me?"

Joel looked unhappily at the ground. "Yes," he muttered.

Zorrel put a hand on the boy's shoulder.

"Don't worry, Jes. I'll make sure he gets home safe," he said assuringly. "I might not be able to go the whole way but I'll drop him off as close as I dare."

I frowned. I would often forget that humans and elves hated each other. It had once been a part of my own life but now seemed so foreign to me. Enchanters were apart from any kingdoms or governments, so they were technically welcomed anywhere. Yet, there was so much prejudice against the elves in Tyran, that even elven sorcerers only entered if it couldn't be avoided. Joel and Alexandria rarely left the central part of the city, and even then, they wore either a hat, a headband, or a hood to cover the tips of their ears.

"Thank you, Zorrel," I said with a smile. "I have to get Dahrik and go, but best of luck to you both."

"And to you, Jes" replied the librarian.

"Good luck. Don't die!" called Joel.

Council of the Keeps

Dahrik and I spent the next hour with Zorrel going over the records of the previous four necromancers. After getting a rundown of their rises and falls, we hastily packed and readied the horses to leave. I mounted my loyal steed, Arrig, which I named after the ancient dwarfish word for haste. I slipped my scepter through two straps on the right side of my saddle. I looked over to Dahrik, who had just finished strapping in his own scepter. We each nodded, indicating to the other that we were ready to start our journey towards Culten.

We guided our horses out of the stable, and once we passed through the exit, we gazed out on the countless grassy slopes of the Hills of Cray. The air smelled of autumn, and the morning sun had just come over the Pryre Mountains.

With our backs to the Keep we faced north, and I assumed we would head in a northeasterly direction, just as we always did, until escaping the Hills of Cray and enter the Valley of Glorious. Once there, we would find and follow the road south until we reached Culten. A journey of several days. Even if we traveled as far and as fast as our horses would go, I doubted that we would arrive in Culten in two days.

Without speaking a word, Dahrik guided his horse east, following the face of the Keep at a speedy trot. It took me only a few seconds to realize that he had left, and I followed shortly after him. Instead of turning north, the dwarf turned southeast. I was confused but didn't vocalize my confusion. Through my ten years of knowing Dahrik, I had learned that he generally had a plan for anything he did. If on the off-chance he didn't have a plan, he would tell me so. I followed him southeast.

After a few paces, Dahrik cued his horse to move faster into a gallop. I did the same to Arrig. We traveled up and down dozens of hills, the breeze feeling nice on my face. The temperature was perfect for riding. I thought of my wife, Rebecca. Riding had become one of our favorite activities to do together. She enjoyed it more than I did, I always thought of riding as more a task rather than a hobby. I went riding with her, mostly to make her happy.

A sense of fear swelled in my gut. If my instincts were right, then this necromancer, Kaynah of Shale, was dangerous, possibly even more dangerous than the Vios Almna. How do I even fight a necromancer? Was it any different from fighting a warlock? I only hoped I was up for the task. Unlike last time, I have a family counting on my safe return.

We came up a particularly large hill and when we reached the top, we brought our horses to a halt. Looking south, I saw less than a mile ahead, the bank of the Neos river.

"Oh, I get it now," I said to the dwarf. "We're going to cross the river, then travel out from Panorl."

Dahrik snorted. "Well, of course we are. Wasn't it obvious? We can't go around the river, we would never make it in time."

I frowned. It did seem obvious as I thought about it again.

"Well, I was too busy thinking about how much you owe me for getting you on this quest," I said with a smirk.

He gritted his unnaturally white teeth. "Don't be getting an ego, boy."

I couldn't help but laugh. We made our way to the riverbank. At which point, Dahrik dismounted. He pointed to the other side of the river where there stood a single cherry tree.

"That tree is the marker," he noted. "It's the only cherry tree until you get to the Bellum Forest."

He stomped his scepter twice on the ground, the orange gem at the end clinking against a round, knotted tree root that protruded from the surface of the ground. Then there was a flash of light. I was shocked to see a bridge had appeared. It was at least a hundred feet wide and made of polished cherry wood, stretching from one end of the river to the other. I blinked several times, so to convince myself that I was not imagining the sudden appearance of the structure.

"This is perfect," I said to Dahrik with a smile. "Why don't we come this way more often?"

The dwarf mounted his horse again. He looked me in the eyes and said, "this bridge is a secret. Only you and I know about it."

"A secret? Why keep this a secret?" I asked as we began walking over the bridge. "It seems so useful."

Dahrik said nothing for several seconds. Then, finally answered with a sigh, "I made it years ago, about a year or two before I recruited you. I thought it was clever, and it is, but at the time there was a warlock patrol that had nearly found the Keep. As you know, our Keep stays hidden from those who are not members. Yet, somehow, these warlocks nearly found it."

"And the Grand Council were being strict about maintaining the Keep's secrecy," I guessed. "So, you kept the bridge hidden so you wouldn't get in trouble."

He nodded, his head lowered. "I nearly came clean to Ginn around the time of the Vios Almna, but since the whole Vain incident, I have kept it secret. I'm on thin ice as it is. You are the first person to learn of this."

We reached the opposite bank, and Dahrik snapped his fingers thrice. There was another flash of light and when I looked behind us, the bridge was gone, as though it had never been there.

We rode onward for the rest of the day and the whole night, stopping as little as possible. We were able to keep our horses from becoming exhausted by fueling them with magic. They were able to gallop at full speed the entire time. It was exhausting both Dahrik and me to do this, but it turned out to be worth it, as we arrived in Culten just before dawn. We purchased rooms at the Howling Wolf Inn and slept until after dusk.

Dahrik knocked on my door, waking me up.

"The meeting is in a few hours," he said, louder than my groggy self would have preferred. "As far as I know, the others are not here in the city yet, but we should expect them all to arrive soon."

"Well," I began, getting out of bed, "They all have a lot further of a way to go than us. Except the warlocks. They should be here by now."

"Norvic probably just wants to make a grand entrance," Dahrik said as we left my room.

The Inn was nearly empty, only one other person besides us staying the night. We were hungry, but the inn's kitchen was closed for the night, so we went out in search of some food. In our search for food, we stopped by Culten's renowned notice board to check the news. Oddly enough, there were still a handful of people around it, chatting amongst one another.

"What do you think those things wanted?" asked a woman to what looked like her brother.

"No idea," answered the brother. "It doesn't make any sense. Why charge the city only to retreat?"

"Where do you think they came from?" asked another man with them.

The woman answered, "Who knows? Crazy lizards could be from anywhere?"

"What did you just say?" I interrupted, overhearing their conversation as we approached the notice board.

The woman turned and faced me, a confused look on her face.

"You said something about lizards," I added.

"Yeah," she said, only a little less confused than before. "The lizard-things that attacked the city nearly two days ago, no one knows where they came from."

"The Hissera were here," Dahrik answered, picking a large announcement paper off of the board. "It says here that they attacked the morning after the Keep was hit."

I nodded to the trio in thanks, then joined Dahrik studying the paper. As he said, the Hissera had attacked Culten the morning following their assault on our Keep. They were first spotted by a human named "Kernil," who rung the city's giant bell in warning. He was some kind of warrior for hire, the leader of a crew called, "The Lute Brutes." The Lute Brute crew led the Culten Watch against the invading Hissera.

They were outnumbered, but suddenly the Hissera fled east, ignoring Culten completely. An investigation was underway.

"They must have come here on their way to the Warlock Keep," said Dahrik.

I frowned. "But why come to Culten at all? They're after enchanters. All they did was decrease in numbers by coming here. Going straight for the warlocks makes much more sense."

The dwarf shook his head. "No idea. One thing I will say is it the Hissera don't seem to be very effective against anything *but* magic. It says here that the soldiers who defended the city against them kill certainly a lot more than we did. Plus, very few were injured, and none died."

Something didn't make sense. If they went after magic, why bother coming to Culten at all? We pondered this in silence for a few minutes, when the hair on the back of my neck stood up, followed by a blast of cold air.

I looked at Dahrik. He felt it too. What we were both sensing was the presence of another enchanter. Then the cold feeling increased. A second enchanter was close by. Less than a minute later, the sensation grew even colder, marking the arrival of a third enchanter.

"It seems the Council of the Keeps is ready to convene," Dahrik said as we walked back to the Howling Wolf Inn.

* * *

The journey home on horseback was a lot less fun than portaling to the Keep. Joel didn't have a horse of his own and he didn't want one. He saw his first horse when he was six years old and had been rescued from Suffer. Joel had been immediately suspicious of the riding animal, mentioning to his mother that he didn't like how their heads were shaped or the sound of their hooves clip-clopping when they moved around. Everyone had assured him that horses were safe but even after five years of being around them and having to ride horses, Joel's opinion hadn't changed.

"You're tense," noted Zorrel as they rode north together on his horse. "Anything you want to talk about?"

Joel hesitated to speak. Every time he talked about his discomfort towards horses, he was met with big speeches on why he shouldn't hate them. They always made the same arguments.

"It's Amlico, isn't it?" Zorrel asked, patting the horse on the side. "You don't trust horses."

"How did you know?" the boy asked him, looking back at him, surprised.

The elf looked up at the clouds in the sky, then said, "Just a guess. My master once told me that I'm pretty good at noticing how people feel."

66

"Well, he's right," Joel replied, "I don't trust horses. They just seem too big and wild to trust."

"My master was a she, not a he," corrected Zorrel. "And what do you mean by wild? Amlico here is very tame."

Joel avoided looking at the horse. "I don't know, maybe not wild, but they just seem dangerous."

"Do you feel in danger?" the enchanter asked.

"I don't like how you can't walk behind them without them kicking you," the half-elf boy replied, getting worked up. "How am I supposed to trust an animal that will kick me if I walk behind it, no matter what of my relationship with it?"

Zorrel nodded, saying nothing immediately. Then, after a moment of silence, he asked, "Do you know what I find very interesting?"

"No, what?"

There was a hint of amusement in the elf's voice, "My former master didn't trust horses either."

Joel turned and looked at Zorrel, who had a childlike smile on his face.

"You're playing a joke on me, aren't you," asked Joel.

"No, I'm serious," answered Zorrel. "Her name was Boh

Bannon. A human from Culten. You can ask anyone in Keep that knew her and they will tell you the same thing. She hated horses, absolutely dreaded riding them."

Joel could tell by his eyes that Zorrel was telling the truth. "Whoa, I guess you're right. That's weird. What does it mean?"

"Could be just a coincidence," the librarian admitted, "but I think it's a sign that I am meant to train you."

The boy nodded, facing forward again, and another moment of silence passed between them as they continued north through the Valley of the Glorious.

"Wait a minute," Joel shouted suddenly. "You said, her name *was* Boh Bannon, and that people *knew* her. Is she dead?"

Zorrel frowned. "Five summers ago, yes. She was ambushed by warlocks in the Pryre mountains."

"Five summers ago? Pryre Mountains..." the boy muttered to himself. "Why was she in the mountains five years ago? Wasn't that the summer when Jes killed the Vios Almna?"

"The very same summer," the librarian confirmed. "Boh was part of a diversion mission through the Guarded Strait."

Joel squinted his eyes in thought. "Wait, Jes and Rebecca had a diversion the first time they tried getting to Ryone Peak. She was part of *that* diversion?"

Zorrel replied with a vacant, "Yes."

Joel frowned, staring off in the distance. He had never thought of it before, but Joel realized that being an enchanter was dangerous, even more so than horses. A wave of shame flooded his heart, making him sick to his stomach. In the past day alone, about thirty sorcerers had died in the Hissera attack, and he had been too caught up in his own fantasy to think about it for more than a passing second. Not all of them survived long enough to save the day. Not everyone was Jes Nulkin.

* * *

Dahrik and I were the last to arrive at the back room of the Howling Wolf. When I opened the door, I immediately met eyes with Norvic, grandmaster of the Warlocks who sat at the far end of the square table that took up most of the room. Two other enchanters that I did not know were also seated, on each side of the table.

"Now that we're all here," Dahrik said as he and I sat down across from Norvic. "We can get to the matter at hand."

"Please excuse my grandmaster's absence," said the woman to my right. "I have been sent in her place. I am Dalia Longroot of Knaksis, member of the Druid Council."

Across from Dalia, the enchanter from the Mage's then spoke, her voice was soft yet prideful, "I too was sent in the place of my grandmaster. Our Keep was badly damaged and the repairs are not going as smoothly as we had hoped. I am Kylora Galen, second seat on the Mage Grand Council."

Both Kylora and Dalia were elves, meaning that Dahrik and I were the only non-elves in the room. This was normal enough, the majority of enchanters tended to be elves.

Dalia had long, braided brown hair, pale skin, and deep green eyes. She had a scar on her lower lip in the shape of a fishhook. She was very short for an elf, only a few inches taller than Dahrik. Her ears were long, even for an elf, and each came to such a sharp point that they looked like they could stab an eye out. She looked young, maybe mid-thirties, but elves age half as fast, which meant that she was at least in her sixties.

Kylora had dark hair with light brown skin and hazel eyes. By the wrinkles on her face, she looked to be older than Dahrik, meaning that she had to be over ninety years old. She looked wise and experienced, yet still very beautiful.

"It appears that my Keep is the only one able to take care of itself without the grandmaster. Not a surprise," said Norvic with a smile.

Ignoring the warlock's comment, Kylora asked Dahrik and me, "Where is Master Ginn? Wasn't she the one to call this council?"

I opened my mouth to speak, but Dahrik beat me to it. "Ginn called the meeting, but I was chosen to represent our Keep. It was her decision."

"And why is the boy here?" Norvic asked, resting his feet on the table. "The rules of these meetings are very clear, one delegate each."

"Jes is the Prodigy," snapped Dahrik, "and you know that! It's his right to be here."

The warlock laughed to himself. Then we locked eyes. "Jes? Didn't you say your name was Tiddoh?"

My eyes widened with surprise. I had forgotten that when last I saw Norvic, five years ago during my quest to defeat the Vios Almna, I was in disguise and had told him my name was Tiddoh Graymark. At the time, I wasn't sure if he knew I was lying to him, and at this moment I still wasn't exactly sure. Had he known all along or did he just figured it out once I destroyed the Vios Almna?

I decided to ignore the question and addressed everyone in the room. "Does anyone else think I don't deserve to be here?"

Dalia answered, "I think your place here is more than deserved. Human or not, you saved all of Cray from the Vios Almna, just as Yep's successor was foretold to do. You rose to the defense of us all while others sought to manipulate the events for their own benefit."

All eyes were on Norvic again. This was exactly what the warlocks had done, both in the ancient times when the Vios Almna was created, as well as five years ago when it was being released from its imprisonment.

The warlock leader shrugged, no shame in his expression.

"Kylora," Dahrik asked, "what say you and the Mages?"

She didn't make eye contact with either me or Dahrik, instead staring at the table in front of her. After a few seconds' pause, she answered. "You're already here, so you may as well stay."

Satisfied, Dahrik said again, "Let's get to the matter at hand. These creatures that attacked us."

"Yes, what are these things?" replied Dalia. "Where did they come from? Our achieves had no records of them."

It was Norvic that spoke next. "That's because they haven't been around for a long time, and whenever they do show up, it's a time that we all try to forget."

"And how would you know that?" asked Kylora, almost yelling. "This another one of your plots to kill us off?"

Taken aback by her sudden outburst, Norvic took his feet off the table and leaned forward in his chair. "Hey now, my Keep was hit too. My plots require intelligence, these things are mindless monsters that feed on magic."

Kylora rolled her eyes. "Ironic, you calling *them* mindless."

The warlock's confident smile was replaced with are dark scowl.

"Say that again, Mage. I dare you," he hissed.

She looked Norvic in the eye and scoffed, "Typical. Your first reaction is to threaten."

"Alright everyone, that's enough," I said in a firm, yet calm voice. "There's no use in throwing accusations around."

"Oh please, you sorcerers are just as bad," she scoffed again.

Dahrik stood up and slammed his fist on the table.

"Excuse me, we are nothing like him," he shouted, pointing to Norvic.

"You're more alike than you than I'm sure you'd think," Dalia mummed under her breath.

"What is that supposed to mean?"

The Druid met Dahrik's scowl. "You're both just as arrogant and self-righteous."

"Okay, let's all just calm down," I said, trying to keep the peace, but nobody seemed to hear me.

"Always stirring up trouble for everyone too," Kylora added.

Dahrik's face turned red, his hands trembled with fury, "At least we make us of our magic. Both of your Keeps are practically worthless in the scheme of things!"

"That's how it should be," the Mage snapped. "All we want is to be left alone. Yet, every time without fail, we're a target, all because of you and your kind! Everything from Vios Almnas to these reptile magic eaters."

"Enough!" I cried, filling the room with a green light from the glow of the Gasper Emerald.

Everyone went quiet, their eyes fixed on me.

"We're not going to solve anything by barking at each other like a pack of rabid dogs. Everyone sit down and speak civilly to one another. Today, we are not enemies nor rivals. We are here for a common purpose. Our very existence is under attack. If all we do is argue amongst one another, then the necromancer has already won."

Kylora and Dalia gasped. Norvic didn't seem surprised however, he nearly nodded in acknowledgment.

"Wait, did you say a necromancer?" asked Dalia, wiping sweat off her brow.

I nodded. "I'm afraid so. The creatures are of her making. They're called the Hissera, and this necromancer means to destroy us all with them."

Dahrik and I told them everything Zorrel had found in the archives, as well as what Ginn had learned from her vision of Kaynah.

74

When we finish, Kylora then said, addressing everyone, "It would seem that the young Prodigy is wiser than us all. If a necromancer has arisen, then we must work together and do what needs to be done in order for any of us to survive."

"Well spoken," replied Norvic, putting his feet on the table once again. "But agreeing on the gravity of the problem isn't enough. We need to kill this necromancer before she can send more of those Hissera to finish us off."

"It sounds to me like you're proposing a quest," replied Dahrik.

Norvic chuckled. "Then you're not as thick in the head as you look, dwarf."

Dahrik tensed and tried to jump out of his chair in anger, but I grabbed him by the arm and kept him from standing. In normal circumstances, whenever Dahrik lost his temper, I would just hit him on the head as hard as I could. This was our agreement. It helped calm the irate dwarf down quickly. However, given the setting, that didn't seem like a viable option for the moment. So, he and I just locked eyes. Our gaze was intense, but despite his frustration, he knew that for the time being, he had to play nice with the warlock leader.

"Five enchanters trek across Cray to the den of a necromancer with an army of monsters," noted Dalia. "Even with the Prodigy amongst us, I don't like our chances."

None of us liked our chances. It didn't seem like there was

much hope for us. There was a long moment of silence, each of us thinking about our options. Even though it had been discussed many times, I still wasn't sure what to expect with Kaynah the necromancer. She had to be very powerful to create the Hissera because they themselves were more than formidable. Somehow, they were immune to magic, Dahrik and I had to use our scepters as ordinary staves to kill them. They actually died fairly easily when you were using raw force instead of magic. That must have been how the Culten Watch was able to fend the Hissera off until they moved to the Warlock Keep.

"We won't survive if just the five of us go," I said, breaking the silence. "We'll need help."

"Well obviously," scoffed Norvic. "Of course there needs to be more of us. The only question is, how many?"

In a low voice, Dahrik suggested, "Why not bring everyone? All of us, from every Keep. A strong, massive, force to charge in and take out Kaynah of Shale."

"Absolutely not," interjected Kylora, almost before Dahrik had finished speaking.

Dalia rolled her eyes. "Of course you would say that, coward."

Before another argument could start, I spoke again, "No, no, Kylora's right. That won't work."

Once again, all eyes were on me. I paused for a few seconds

76

before I spoke again, working out my idea in my head.

"We can't make a full-force attack, that's exactly what Kay-nah wants us to do," I said, avoiding eye contact with Dahrik. "If we're all in one place, then it will be all the easier to wipe us out. I think we need a smaller infiltrative team."

"You said it yourself, the five of us alone aren't enough," replied Norvic as he cracked his knuckles. "What then, do you suggest we do?"

I nodded. "Despite how powerful we are, the five of us are not enough, and adding more enchanters in the team won't do much good. That's why I think what we need are some warriors."

Norvic laughed. "You honestly think bringing some sword-swinging brutes is going to help?"

I nodded.

"The warlock has a point," said Dalia. "What good would ordinary warriors do?"

I leaned forward in my chair and spoke with as much authority as I could. "Like the four Keeps, Culten was attacked. Without magic, mercenaries and the Culten Watch killed more of them than any of us. The Hissera have a natural defense to magic, but not to blades or clubs or arrows. Bringing a large team of enchanters is what the necromancer wants us to do, what she expects us to do."

"Boy makes a good point," Dahrik added. "It definitely wouldn't be expected to hire some soldiers."

Dalia chuckled. "It's odd, usually we are asked to come and destroy what threatens them, now it is the other way around."

Ignoring her, Dahrik turned to me and asked, "Aren't those warriors you rescued from the desert here in Culten?"

"That's right, they are here," I replied. "Barefist and company owe me a favor. If they're here, I can get them on board."

"Then it's settled," clapped Norvic. "The five of us, plus whatever sword swingers you can bring along, will journey to the abandoned fortress and kill this necromancer. What could go wrong?"

"We should leave first thing tomorrow," Kylora added.

I nodded, "I'll go find Barefist."

Brutes Breaking Doors

The Council of the Keeps concluded shortly after. Once it had concluded, Dahrik and I made our way over to the business district of the city. Our destination was "John's Hall of Hires." There, I thought I might be able to find Barefist and his crew.

I met Barefist during my quest to destroy the Vios Almna, when I was trapped in the desert city of Suffer. Like Joel and Alexandria, Barefist helped me escape the desert. Once the Vios Almna was destroyed, I returned as I had promised and freed everyone Suffer. Barefist and his team of hunters decided that they would dwell in Culten, working as swords for hire under the moniker, the Suffer Squadron. John's Hall of Hires was where mercenaries and swords of hire could be found and pay for their services.

"I'm sorry, sir," said the squirrelly man behind the counter. "I don't need to check again. The Suffer Squadron is out on another job. It could be a while before they return."

I sighed.

"We can't go back with nothing," griped Dahrik, looking

around us suspiciously. "You made a big fuss to the other Keeps about needing warriors to help kill the Hissera. If we go back without bringing any, we'll look like fools."

"Hissera?" squeaked the squirrelly man who I assumed was John. "Is that the name for those lizard things that attacked here the other night?"

I nodded. "The very same."

"Well, if you're going after them, I may have a team with just the right stuff for the job," he said with a smile.

He then turned his attention to his book.

The dwarf's head poked up with interest. He moved over to the counter and leaned in with anticipation. John didn't pay Dahrik any attention. He scanned the book that was in front of him on the counter, moving across the page with his finger.

"Oh good, they're available," he said, tapping a spot on the page twice.

Dahrik and I looked at each other, then back at the man.

"Who's available?" snapped Dahrik, his face turning a faint shade of red.

John chuckled, "Oh, right, sorry about that. It's a bad habit of mine, not quite finishing my thoughts out loud."

The dwarf motioned with his hand for John to go on.

"What I was meaning to say, is that I have a group of clients that have some first-hand experience with those... Hissera, I think you called them," he said tapping his book again.

I put a hand on Dahrik's shoulder, hoping he would remain calm, then asked, "What kind of experience? Were they part of the city's defense?"

"Oh, more than that," John replied. "They were the ones who lead the charge until the Culten Watch and militia got there. The Lute Brutes are some of my best. Very fierce, and very efficient."

I nodded in remembrance. "The Lute Brutes, I read about them on the notice board."

"Like I said, they have experience," replied John.

Dahrik and I looked at each other again. I knew from his expression that he thought it was a good idea, or rather, the best idea he could come up with. I agreed, if Barefist was out on another job, this was probably our best option.

"Do you know how long the Suffer Squadron will be out on the other job?" I asked, certain I already knew the answer.

John shrugged.

"How much to hire the Lute Brutes?" asked Dahrik.

* * *

Kaynah of Shale stood in a chamber of the Abandoned Fortress. Years ago, she converted the chamber into a laboratory. It was a large, wide room that, in another time, was used as a dungeon. Stone bricks and tiles covered each face of the chamber, the age of the fortress showing prominently. At the far end was a large desk with papers and books stacked high.

The elven necromancer looked around forty-eight years old. She had an average build and height, with fair skin. Her long hair was pulled back in a tight braid. Her fierce green eyes twitched as her body shuddered in apparent pain. She stood in the center of the stone-bricked chamber, facing the desk, her breathing a mix of coughing and wheezing.

She slid a pair of slim, cotton gloves over the fresh wounds on her hands. Puss and blood-soaked into the fabric, but she didn't care. The pain and discomfort had been well worth it. Kaynah's use of magic came with a price, a physical price that enchanters did not pay. Each use caused her pain, injury, or mutilation, a way for the magic to reject her forceful use of it. She had been beautiful once. Her face was symmetrical and pleasant to look at. Her skin was once smooth and flawless. Now, that part of her identity was all but forgotten. Her face was wrinkled and aged beyond her years, not to mention scarred and disfigured beyond recognition. Her body was dotted with sores, warts, and gashes that would not heal no matter the remedy she applied.

Despite the costs to her body, she loved magic. Her heart

pounded with adrenalin, the thrill of using magic exciting her down to the soul. Over the past ten years, magic had become everything to her, and she would not give it up.

Moments ago, she had tried a new spell, a form of surveillance called Scrying. She had attempted it once before, but without a special gift from Jard, scrying had proven too difficult for Kaynah at the time. This had been the first successful attempt, and she had learned more than she had ever anticipated.

Scrying had allowed the necromancer to listen in on her enemies, who conveniently had, for the most part, been gathered in one room together. Leaders of the four enchanter Keeps had been there, along with the Prodigy. They proposed a quest to come and try to destroy her and everything she had built.

Anger flushed through Kaynah's body. She cried out, "How dare they think that they can just trot over her and try to dispose of me so easily. I am not the prey, I am the hunter. I am the one who's destroying them!"

She coughed. Then, realizing that she was talking to herself again, moved over to her desk in silence. She sat in the chair and considered her next move.

"Only he posses any real threat to me," she mumbled to herself, her dry throat causing her to cough between every few words. "The rest are of no consequence. Bringing warriors along with them may be a problem. My Hissera don't have the aptitude for killing swordsman."

Kaynah tapped her finger aggressively on the desk. The Prodigy had rightly discerned the Hisseras' weakness. This infuriated the necromancer more than she'd ever admit, as it put the entirety of her scheme in jeopardy.

"I need to test these warriors, find weaknesses of their own. As long as the enchanters and warriors are working together, those weaknesses will be few. Perhaps, I could send a few waves after them, separate the two groups, maybe pick them off one by one. Yes, that will work," said Kaynah, forgetting not to talk to herself.

She didn't have enough Hissera made to send another massive horde at the moment. Kaynah had the resources to make more, but what she lacked was the necessary time. There was a handful of survivors from the first raid awaiting further instruction, hiding near the gnome community of Berstad.

She would send those Hissera first. They would arrive just as the party of warriors and enchanters departed Culten. In the meantime, she would make more Hissera to send later.

Kaynah nodded, confident in the plan she had devised.

"He won't take everything I have worked for away from me. Not now, not ever!" she swore to herself, standing up from the chair.

* * *

Dahrik and I hurried down the city streets, the morning sun

illuminating the mountains in the east. The chill of the early autumn day clung to my skin bitterly.

"The Noble Griffin Tavern," griped Dahrik. "Have you ever been to that rat's nest? There's nothing noble about it."

The sound of Dahrik's heavy stomping down the street echoed off the buildings, making his step sound enormous and intimidating.

I sighed. "Dahrik, relax. These guys are supposed to be vigilant and great fighters. Both, qualities we need to take on Kaynah of Shale."

"But what does it say about their character?" he asked rhetorically, shaking his head. "The Noble Griffin is where some of Culten's worst of the worst loiter about."

"Would you stop being so judgmental," I replied, looking the dwarf in the eyes. "You know nothing about them. In fact, it was you who once told me that the best kinds of people can be found in the most unlikely of places. Not everything is so black or white."

Dahrik scoffed. "If I were a griffin, I'd be insulted by the place."

I switched my scepter to gauntleted hand, then with my newly free hand, thumped the dwarf in the back of the head.

"Hey!" he shouted in protest. "What wa-"

"If you didn't like this idea, you shouldn't have supported me on it," I interrupted, glaring down at him sternly.

Dahrik stopped walking, as did I. He avoided my gaze for several seconds, then muttered something under his breath that I couldn't understand.

"I'm sorry, what?" I asked.

"I said I think it's a good plan," he said, much louder now.

I finally met his gaze again, confusion in my eyes. "Then what's your problem? And don't say the Noble Griffin, I know you well enough to know that it's more than that."

Dahrik gave a half-smile. "That you do, because you're right, it's not really the tavern. Something just doesn't feel right."

"Of course nothing feels right," I replied, looking back at the mountains. "Our Keep was attacked and there's a necromancer trying to kill us."

The dwarf shook his head. "Well yes, but not what I mean. I get this feeling like we're doing exactly what someone wants us to do. As though we are playing right into some kind of trap."

I thought for a moment. The necromancer had taken every enchanter in Cray by surprise. The attack on the four Keeps had gotten us to react. Even I knew that people who react to a situation don't usually do what is wise. I had fallen victim to reactionary traps before. If Kaynah was at all familiar with our customs and protocols, she would know that we would call a Council of the Keeps. She would know that I, as the Prodigy, would also be here as part of the council. It was the perfect moment for another attack.

I surveyed around us, paranoid of the thought of another Hissera attack.

"They haven't come back to the city," Dahrik said, noticing my realization. "At least, I don't think they have. Not yet. This Kaynah girl, she's a smart one, I can tell."

I nodded. "She has the advantage of making the first move and knowing more about us than we know about her. If we keep reacting to her game, we'll lose."

"Couldn't have said it better myself, boy," he signed, slapping me on the back. "But that's not what's really bothering me. There's more to it than just the necromancer predicting our moves. Something else is at play that I just can't put my finger on."

"Maybe," I answered, unsure of what to do next. "But where does that leave us now? Do we go forward with the quest or not?"

The dwarf looked at me the same way that he did every time he thought I said something stupid.

"Of course we are still going on the quest," he nearly shouted.

"We can't just wait around for the necromancer to kill us."

"But it could be a trap."

"Boy, I guarantee it's a trap. That's doesn't mean we give up. We just got to be smart about it."

This time, I was the one to lower my head and avoid Dahrik's gaze. I couldn't believe I had just suggested quitting. A sorcerer was never supposed to quit, and that goes double for the Prodigy. Unlike last time, people expected greatness and leadership from me.

"Do we go forward with the quest or not? But it could be a trap," I had said. Those weren't the words of the Prodigy, they were of a man who just wanted this to be over. They were the words of a coward. I was glad that only Dahrik was around to hear me say it. He knew me better than anyone. Not to mention, who knew what kind of response someone like Norvic would make out of them.

"Hey, we all have our moments of doubt," Dahrik said, nudging my side. "These mind games can be tough to figure out, so don't worry too much about them. Together, we'll beat this necromancer, I promise."

I smiled. "Thanks, Dahrik. I think I needed to hear that."

"Now, let's go get those warriors," the dwarf said, clearly trying to change the subject. "John said they tend to drink a lot after a job, and the bigger the job, the longer the celebration.

Saving the city and getting a big reward for it probably means they're celebrating is still ongoing."

We continued down the street towards the Noble Griffin, at a much slower pace than before. Dahrik's heavy footsteps were still audible from far away. The buildings we passed were gradually decreasing in quality. Paint that was pristine a block before was now faded and chipped. The well-crafted woodwork was still there, but now splintering. These homes were made of the same materials, but looked as though they hadn't been well cared for.

Despite my efforts, my mind kept circling back to my partial admission of wanting to give up the quest before we even started it. Shame and confusion accompanied the thought.

"I'm not a coward," I told myself, trying to convince and quell my shame.

Throughout my time as an enchanter, I have fought against warlocks, imp hordes, a Sand Conqueror, and the Vios Almna. In every case, I was outnumbered, outranked, or underestimated. I faced each one with the courage required, no matter the disadvantage. Why then, did the thought of going up against Kaynah of Shale scare me so much? I dwelt on this until arriving at the tavern, coming to no solid answer.

The Noble Griffin was just like any other tavern. The ripe stench of alcohol, body odor, and urine assaulted my nose. Just outside, a sign with a handful of missing letters hung crudely above a couple of passed-out drunks.

89

"The Nob riffi Tavern," I read aloud, the l, e, and G having fallen off long ago with no evidence of them ever being there, except the large gap between the b and the r.

"It would appear so," Dahrik noted, looking up at the sign.

I laughed. "That has to make you feel better. If I were a griffin, I would be happy about it."

The dwarf smiled unconvincingly, then proceeded to knock on the tavern door. We waited for a minute or so with no response. Dahrik knocked again, this time with his black iron scepter. The door shuddered as the dwarf banged his scepter against the top left corner of the door, and as he did, the sound produced much louder than before.

We wait a moment or so more, still with no response. I took a few steps back into the street, looking up at the second story of the tavern.

"Well," I began, "John said they rent the second-floor apartment from the tavern owner. If they're asleep up there, it would make sense that they might not hear us."

He walked away from the door and stood next to me on the road, giving a light grunt in agreement.

"Maybe we should come back a little later," I suggested. "I could really go for some breakfast."

Dahrik grunted again, this one lower in pitch and longer,

suggesting he disagreed. "We don't have time to come back later. We need to get out of Culten and start our trek toward the Abandoned Fortress as soon as possible."

He was right, but aside from kicking the door down, I didn't see another option. Which is exactly why I shouldn't have been surprised when Dahrik marched back over to the door, and with a single, seemingly effortless collision with his foot, the door broke free of its hinges and fell to the ground with a loud crash. He paused for a second, as though to admire the result, then wordlessly trudged into the tavern. By the time I realized what was happening and followed after him, the dwarf was halfway up the stair to the apartment on the second floor.

The smell was the first thing I notice as I stepped inside the Noble Griffin. A palpable cloud of ale and perspiration hovered inside. The tavern was mostly dark, the only source of light coming from the entranceway. The interior revealed a larger tavern, with a long bar immediately to the left and a vast number of circular tables and stools to the right. Straight ahead at the far end, the stairs that went up three steps then turned right. The stairs continued up twelve more steps, then were blocked from view by a wall.

I reached the bottom of the stairs just as Dahrik was a step away from the door at the top. Just as he reached for the doorknob, however, a giant, hulking mass busted through the other side of the door. A pair of beefy gray arms grabbed Dahrik by the tunic, and the two of them sailed down the stairs. They were at the bottom in an instant, I barely managed to avoid getting crushed as I sidestepped away from the stairs.

Everything happened so fast, my mind had trouble keeping up. I blinked twice, now identifying the assailant creature as a troll, which snarled in Dahrik's face as it pinned him against the wall. This troll, like all trolls, was nearly nine feet tall, and several hundred pounds of pure muscle. I raised my gauntleted hand and the Gasper Emerald in the center of the forearm glowed with power. Green energy swirled and grew in my palm, I readied to release it into the troll's face.

"I wouldn't do that if I were you," came a voice from above.

I looked up and saw a dwarf pointing a drawn bow and arrow at me from the top of the stairs. Behind him stood another dwarf wielding a big war hammer, a human with a broadsword, and a sickly looking creature I couldn't identify in the dark holding a pair of hand-axes. I looked back at the troll, who was still holding Dahrik by the tunic and pinning him against the wall, then back at the four on the stairs. I lower my gauntlet and the collected energy dissolved.

"I'm afraid there has been a misunderstanding," I stated calmly.

The dwarf with the hammer snorted. "You bet there is! Who do you think you are, busting down our door and ruining our tavern?"

Before I could respond, Dahrik took advantage of the distraction and jammed one end of his scepter into the troll's side. The bare-chested colossus groaned in pain as electricity surged through his massive body. The troll's muscles stiffening, Dahrik tore himself free then shoved the troll forward. The large brute shot up the stairs like a cannonball, plowing into the four others at the top and landing on top of them with a loud crash.

Dahrik brushed some of the dust off his closed and stood next to me with a smile of satisfaction. I sighed irritably. This whole situation had become an enormous, unnecessary mess. Up at the top of the stairs, the five warriors stirred and groaned.

"Hemm, you big lug, get off of us!" came a deep, baritone voice.

The second floor creaked, then thumped, marking the troll's return to its feet.

"How in Jard's name did that happen?" asked a softer, more feminine voice. "Hemm is massive, and that guy threw him up the stairs like he was a ball of feathers."

The human that wielded the golden-hilted sword took a few cautious steps down the stairs, he and I making eye contact immediately.

"These two are enchanters," the man declared, still looking at me but clearly talking to the rest of his crew. "You can tell by the sorcerer's cloaks and their scepters."

93

The man was young, maybe only a few years older than myself, and just as tall. His skin was dark like the night and his hair was cut meticulously short. He had a coal-black goatee that gave his face a proud look. Aside from the sword in his hands, he had nothing on him except an old pair of undergarments.

"Oh great," complained the deep voice from before. "Just our luck."

I took a step forward and spoke as calmly and genuinely as I could, "We are not here to harm or rob you. John told us that we could find you here. We have paid for your services."

The man's face tensed with surprise. He looked up at his companions at the top of the stair, confusion riddled in his expression.

"Wha... What?" he stuttered. "You want our help? But you're enchanters, masters of magic! What could you possibly need us for?"

The dwarf with the bow came halfway down the stairs, stopped next to the human, and said to him, "they probably want to use us as sword fodder, I'd wager."

The archer dwarf looked at me with a frown, but his expression changed dramatically as he saw Dahrik for the first time. His eyes widened and his mouth dropped. He raised a hand and pointed a finger at Dahrik.

"You... you... you... you're Dahrik Ironhelm," he struggled.

94

Dahrik emphasized the scepter in his hand and nodded to the archer.

The archer dwarf then turned toward the top of the stairs and yelled, "Barris, it's Dahrik Ironhelm! Dahrik Ironhelm kicked down our door."

"What?" called the baritone voice. "You're kidding!"

The stairs shook as the hammer-wielding dwarf raced down the stairs, coming to an abrupt halt next to the archer. He looked at Dahrik and he gasped in amazement.

"Oh Jard," he said, his mouth hanging open. "It's really him."

The two dwarves looked at each other and then ran down the rest of the stairs and over to Dahrik, kneeling and bowing their heads at his feet.

"Please forgive us, sir," the baritone-voiced one said.

Then the archer added, "Yes, we didn't know it was you. If we had, we never would have opposed you."

"I am Barris, son of Barnard," said the deep-voiced dwarf. Then, gesturing to the other dwarf, he said, "This is my cousin, Howel, son Hammell. We are of the Bronzearm clan. It is an honor to meet you, sir."

The human, still halfway down the stairs, rubbed his eye in irritation.

"What are you two talking about?" he called to Howel and Barris. "Who is Dahrik Ironhelm? Why are you both treating this guy like he's a king?"

"Hey," shouted Howel, his face flushed red. "You show some respect. Dahrik Ironhelm is the greatest enchanter alive. He even trained the Prodigy."

The human's eyes narrowed and then fixed on me.

"Wait, so if this guy trained the Prodigy and that," he pointed to the gauntlet on my left arm, "looks like Yep's famed gauntlet. That would make this guy the Prodigy."

He now pointed at me, to which I shrugged in admission.

"Guilty," I said with a half-smile.

However, the two kneeling dwarves weren't paying attention, they were both entirely fixed on Dahrik.

"Sir, you said that you have need of our services," said Howell, his head still bowed. "But why? What need do you have that rascal adventurers such as us could provide?"

"Why don't you all ready yourselves first?" Dahrik said, motioning to the two of them who were dressed solely in their undergarments. "We have a long journey ahead of us and there will be time to explain everything."

The two dwarves looked at each other, then themselves, and

their faces turned bright red with embarrassment. Obviously, they had forgotten that we had woken them up as they were sleeping, and they, assuming we were dangerous intruders had only grabbed their weapons to defend them.

"He makes a good point," the human called to them, then changed his focus to us. "We'll ready our supplies and meet you outside."

The two dwarves nodded and ran back up the stairs without another word, probably too embarrassed to speak.

"Oh, and if you don't mind, could you fix the front door with your magic? Otherwise, we will have to charge for the damages," the human added before returning to the room on the second floor.

When the second-floor door closed, I sighed with relief. Dahrik started laughing, then slapped me on the back.

"You see, I knew coming back later wasn't the way to go," he said, placing his fists on his hips with satisfaction.

I rolled my eyes, "No, you're just lucky that there were dwarves in this group and that all dwarves adore you, otherwise this could have gone a lot worse."

He nodded, chuckling to himself. "Yeah, I know."

I rolled my eyes again and chuckled with him for a second.

We turned around, and I lifted the door up and moved it back to its place on the frame. The orange gems on Dahrik's scepter glowed faintly as he refused the wood with all of its severed pieces. Then, he connected the resolidified door to the hinges.

"There," the dwarf nodded, "not so hard, now was it?"

I made no response. The two of us waited outside the tavern in comfortable silence for several minutes. We could hear the group of warriors shuffling around on the second floor and speaking to each other, although it was difficult to make out what they were saying.

Just as Dahrik started to tap his foot impatiently, the five warriors came down the stairs and stepped out of the tavern, fully dress and each carrying a travel bag. The human came into view first, completely dressed in studded leather armor, his sword sheathed on his waist, a hunting knife strapped to around his leg, and a hunting bow and quiver slung on his back. After him, followed the remaining four, and for the first time, I got a good look at all five of them at once. A human, two dwarves, a troll, and the most unexpected creature of all, a hobgoblin. An odd assortment for sure.

"I'm sorry for our entrance, but we are pleased to be working with you," I began politely. "Allow me to introduce myself, my name is Jes Nulkin."

"Well, Jes Nulkin, next time don't knock our door down," replied the human. "But as long as you're paying, there's nothing to worry about."

"Why are you hiring us, anyway?" asked the hobgoblin, the voice surprisingly pleasant, albeit a little brittle. "You're enchanters, why can't you just take care of it?"

Dahrik answered, seemingly having the answer at the ready. "Remember those lizard creatures that attacked the city?"

The hobgoblin nodded in confirmation, "Of course, that was just the other day."

"Well, those things are called the Hissera, and they were created by a necromancer. They're impervious to magic and out to kill every enchanter in Cray," Dahrik stated.

"So, you want us to protect you from those things in case they come back," added the human.

"In a way," I replied. "We and a few more enchanters are leaving for the Abandoned Fortress in the Abic of Marsh. There, we have to put an end to the necromancer and her Hissera. You five have experience with these creatures and have shown aptitude in dealing with them. We'll need that if we are to succeed."

The five warriors nodded, looking at each other proudly.

"So do you have names or should we just call you the Lute Brutes?" asked Dahrik, his arms folded.

"I am Kernil Ravenhigh," the human replied with a hint of annoyance.

Dahrik seemed to flinch at the mention of his name but said nothing.

Kernil pointed to the others next to him. "Howel and Barris already introduce themselves. My gigantic friend here is Hemm and the hobgoblin holding the lute is Kilt."

I had seen few trolls in my lifetime and even fewer hobgoblins. Hobgoblins tend to stay secluded deep within the Nitt mountains and trolls can be very territorial, rarely leaving the swamplands of the eastern Abic of Marsh. Seeing the two of them together seemed even more unlikely.

The troll called Hemm was huge, standing at least nine feet tall and entirely made of muscle. His head was round and sat on its shoulders with no neck in between. His ears were large and round with an ebony earring clipped to the right ear. Like all trolls, his skin was a dull gray color, but his eyes were a shining green. He had steel greaves and leather pauldrons, but otherwise, he wore no armor. Curiously enough, I noticed that he didn't carry any traditional weapons. All he had was rope intricately wrapped around his hands and wrists.

Like all hobgoblins, Kilt had a leathery, greenish-yellow skin. Kilt's ears longer than its head that came to a sharp point. I didn't know a lot about hobgoblins, or Hobbs as they are sometimes called, but one thing I knew was that this meant that Kilt was a woman. Female Hobbs have long ears, while the males typically have shorter ears, about the same length as elves.

Curious enough, Kilt was holding a lute in her hand, giving context to the warriors' group name, the Lute Brutes. I hadn't known any Hobbs with any musical talent but was intrigued by the concept.

Kilt spit on the ground and brushed some dirt off of her knees. She looked tiny compared to Hemm, but in reality, she was likely a few inches taller than the dwarves. It was difficult to tell just how tall Kilt really was because she stood with a hunch.

Facing Dahrik, Howel stepped forward and placed a clenched fist against his chest. "Sir, may I again that it is an honor to be accompanying you on this quest."

Barris stepped forward also, making the same gesture with his fist. The two of them were clad in shinning chain-mail armor, over which they had dark blue tunics. Barris wore a metal helmet and greaves, with several different weapons about him. Most prominently was the large war hammer he had strapped to his back. Howel had no helmet or greaves but instead leather archery bracers, his longbow, and extensive quiver on his back.

"Oh, would you shut it already! We get it," snapped Kernil.

Both Howel and Barris scowled at the human but said nothing in return. The two dwarves took a step back and stood in line with the other warriors.

"Well, lead the way," Kernil instructed us, motioning with his hand.

Might Over Magic

The ten of us stood in front of the Howling Wolf, supplies packed and horses readied for the journey. Norvic looked disapprovingly at the Lute Brutes.

"Is this all? I must say, I expected... more," said Norvic after one look over the five Lute Brutes.

Kernil put a hand on the hilt of his sword and took a step towards Norvic. "What exactly is that supposed to mean?"

Norvic laughed. "Do I really need to say it?" He turned to me and then said, "Now when you suggested bringing a handful of magic-less warriors, I assumed we'd have a group that's a little more impressive. The troll is large, sure, but other than him..."

"The warlock has a point," added Dalia, "A troll, two dwarves, a human and an out-of-place Hobb, I was hoping there would be at least some elves. Other than that, well, I'm not sure what I was expecting, but this isn't it."

Kylora avoided eye contact with me and the warriors, it was obvious that she too was not impressed.

"See what I mean?" remarked Norvic. "They're not all that impressive."

Hemm growled, a low, guttural sound resonating from his mouth. Kilt crouched low to the ground, hiding in Hemm's shadow. Howel glared at Norvic with disdain, while Barris gripped his war hammer tightly. Kernil waved the other warriors off and they relaxed.

"My team and I are more than enough to fight off your lizards," Kernil stated firmly.

The warlock scoffed. "I certainly hope so, otherwise I don't see any reason for you to be on this quest, and I don't much care for useless people."

The two men glared at each other intensely, neither breaking eye contact.

"Like it or not, Norvic, this is who we have hired," stated Dahrik.

"They have experience with the Hissera, they're the ones who lead the Culten's defensive strike two days ago," I added.

Dahrik nodded in acknowledgment. "Exactly, they are more than impressive enough for the needs of our quest."

Norvic opened his mouth to speak, but Kylora interrupted. "It's pointless to argue about this now! I'll admit they aren't what I expected, but it doesn't matter at this point. We need to get on our way. The longer we debate this, the longer it will take us to get to her. And that will give her more time to figure out our plan. We have to get moving!"

We all looked at each other, surprised and impressed at the Mage's outburst. Kilt stepped forward and put a hand on Kylora's shoulder. She flinched at the hobgoblin's touch but made no verbal protest.

"I like this one," Kilt chuckled, nudging Kylora. "She's got some spice. I like people with spice."

Kylora's eyes widened with surprise, then narrowed with confusion. "Thank you... I think."

Norvic sighed with boredom. "Alright, the Druid has a point. We need to leave. The sooner we get going, the sooner this is all over."

Norvic marched over to the horses, the rest of us following a few steps behind. Hemm didn't have a horse, he was much too large for one, but he assured us that keeping up with us would not be a problem. The troll was so large, I didn't doubt that his stride could keep up. Kilt also didn't ride a horse, but rather climbed up on Hemm's left shoulder. The sight of it made Dahrik and I chuckle to each other.

We made our way to the northern edge of the city at a decent canter. Hemm effortlessly traveled along with our pace, and Kilt looked far more relaxed than anyone else. She grabbed her lute and then adjusted it on her shoulder, then strummed the instrument twice. It was perfectly in tune, and the Hobb nodded with satisfaction at the sound.

Kilt cleared her throat, then announced, "This first song is for everyone. I wrote it myself and its reputation is almost as renowned as our own."

What came next surprised me. The hobgoblin's voice was normally thick and gravelly, but her singing voice was very smooth and pleasing to the ears.

We're gonna sharpen our blades,
Bring out all of our spearheads and spades,
Oh, and don't forget my lute.
We will get the job done,
As long as they pay the sum,
And we'll avoid a troll-sized dispute.
Be,
'cause,
the,
Lute Brutes are he-

"Will you stop!" Norvic shouted, interrupting the song.

There was an instant of silence, as everyone registered Norvic's outburst. Kilt's eyes said it all. She was annoyed but not going to push her luck either.

"Alright then," she said to herself, using the strap to slide the lute to her back. "I guess we'll travel in silence for a while. No epic ballads necessary."

Once we exited Culten's northern gate, the wide-open fields of Aris laid before us. We followed the road north at a comfortable but fast pace. The ground boomed as the troll run beside us. Hemm's long stride put him ahead of most everyone, except for Norvic and Dahrik. The two of them were in a silent competition to lead the way. Just behind Hemm was Kylora, who seemed to not want to get too close to the massive troll. I rode in the middle of the team, next to Dalia and Kernil. Bringing up the rear was Barris and finally Howel.

The sun was shining just above the mountains, and the chill of the autumn morning had passed. There was a comfortable breeze coming from the south. We passed many of the Culten farms and ranches. Each one was peppered with gnomes and humans working and readying their fields for the harvest which was only a few weeks away. I didn't know much about farming and ranching, but the herds looked strong and the crops looked healthy. All signs pointed to a massive harvest this year. Culten's harvest was very important to all of Cray since it was the land's largest food provider. A bountiful harvest in Culten meant plenty of food and trade between the races and kingdoms, and would usually deescalate tensions throughout the land as a whole.

A shiver ran down my back.

"Who knows what this year's harvest will bring, especially

if we don't get the Hissera and necromancer problem solved soon," I thought, cautiously checking my surroundings. "I wonder what Kaynah plans to do if she succeeds in killing us all off. What comes next?"

A feeling of unease swelled in the pit of my stomach. As I dwelt on the thought, Kernil tapped me on the shoulder. When I looked at him, he gestured to the cornfield on our right.

"I heard a rumor once, that powerful enchanters blessed the fields Culten and Aris to grow enough food for all of Cray. Is it true?"

"I don't think so. Where did you hear that?" I replied.

The warrior paused for a few seconds in thought, then said, "In school, most likely. Although, it sounds like something my father would say. Myths, legends, and magic fascinated him."

I chuckled. "Then he's nothing like my father. My father was as skeptical as they come. Wouldn't believe anything unless he saw it with his own eyes."

"It must have blown him away then, when you became an enchanter," he laughed.

"Actually, no," I replied, then cleared my throat. "He and the rest of my family died before my powers developed. My village burned to the ground during the last war with the elves. I was gone, recruited for the war."

Kernil's eyes went wide, then awkwardly broke eye contact. "I'm sorry, I didn't mean to-"

"It's alright," I interrupted. "It's been ten years, and although the pain never leaves me, it gets less difficult to live with."

He frowned. "It's been five years since my family's murder, and it isn't any easier than the first day. It just all became real so quickly. One minute I was worried about returning home late, and then the next minute my home and my family were gone."

"I can understand that. I found out I was an enchanter the same day I found out my village was destroyed. Within moments of each other."

"Wow, that's quite the mixed bag of information," Kernil replied, making eye contact once again.

I nodded. "It was, but becoming an enchanter helped me focus on the important things that needed doing. And it gave me the time I needed to face my loss. I realized that if I ever wanted the pain to stop growing, I couldn't ignore it."

Kernil stroked the hilt of his sword, then snorted with frustration. "I don't think that will be enough for me. My father, my family, and my birthright were stolen from me. Only that traitor Nemul's death will satisfy me."

"Nemul?" I muttered.

The name instantly recognizable to me. For the last five years, Dahrik had been ranting about his failed mission in Tyran and Nemul the Usurper.

"Kernil Ravenhigh," I stated, pointing at him as everything started to make sense. "Kreed Ravenhigh was your father."

He nodded. "I don't usually admit that. Normally if someone comes asking for me by name, Nemul's sent them to kill me. I thought of going by another name, but then I realized, if he's still sending people after me, then he's still scared of me."

"That's one way to look at it," I said, not knowing what to say next.

Kernil looked off into the fields for several seconds, his heart and mind lost somewhere else. I had seen that look many times before. It was the same look that Dahrik made whenever he was thinking about Hilda, his dead wife.

"Thank you for answering my question, Jes. I think I'll check on Howell, make sure he's not slacking off back there."

Before I could say anything else, Kernil pulled his horse off to the side of the road and waited until all but Howell had passed him before moving again.

For a moment I sat confused. I didn't think I had crossed any lines or pressed too hard or too fast. One minute we were talking about our common losses, the next Kernil seemed disinterested. The thought occurred to me that perhaps he wasn't as ready to talk about it as I had assumed. He was clearly still angry. I knew from my experience that Kernil would never move on until he dealt with that anger. Then again, my family died by faceless elves, whereas his family was murdered by a person whom he was likely very familiar with.

I looked ahead at Dahrik, who was still fighting Norvic for the lead. Over the past five years, he had told me about the coup of Kreed Ravenhigh and everything that followed in Vain many times. Dahrik never mentioned that Kreed had a son that survived, or that he had a son at all. Which led to the question, did Dahrik even know about Kernil? Obviously, he would have pieced it together by now, but did he know before? And if he did, why did he never mention him to me?

* * *

Once Zorrel dropped Joel off outside the city limits, Joel began the long walk back home. He didn't particularly like having to walk, but Zorrel had given him the choice between walking and continuing alone on horseback. Without a second thought, Joel chose to go on foot. Zorrel protested, but Joel dismounted Amlico, waved Zorrel goodbye, and began walking. Although everything had gone without incident so far, Joel was convinced that the minute Zorrel left, that horse would turn on him.

"Better not to risk it," Joel thought as we walked toward the great outer wall of Tyran City. "I'd rather get as far away from that thing as possible."

As he approached, Joel tucked the tips of his ears underneath the navy blue headband tied around his head. He wasn't nervous about entering the city, but Zorrel's mention of Tyranians hating elves had him feeling cautious. He knew he had no reason to worry, most of the guards knew Joel by name and knew that he was a half-elf. For the past two years, he had worked as one of the King's messengers. The Job allowed Joel to get to know many types of people throughout Tyran City and it was the perfect opportunity to quell his desire to explore. Princess Rebecca had introduced the idea to her father who agreed on a trial basis. The trial was only supposed to last a week but was never spoken of again, so Joel just assumed that he had passed.

Only a few yards from the south gate, Joel could see three guards stationed. He checked his pockets for his messenger badge. His fingers traced the outline of the shield-shaped badge in his left pocket. He withdrew it and smiled as its silver surface shined in the daylight. Joel couldn't believe what this badge let him do. Whenever he wore or showed this badge, people didn't question him. They just let him come and go as he pleased. He was allowed almost anywhere in the castle. He could sit in during important meetings and planning sessions, and as long as he acted seriously, he was normally taken seriously.

"Hey kid, stop right there," called a guard at the gate.

Joel stopped, and the guard came forward, his hand resting on the scimitar at his waist. The guard looked Joel over, and it was clear that this one didn't recognize him. To be fair, Joel was pretty sure he hadn't seen this guard before either.

"State your business," said the guard, as he twirled the hairs of the bushy mustache on his face.

"Just going home," Joel replied.

The mustached guard briefly looked back at the other two guards standing by the gateway, then returned his attention to Joel.

He raised an eyebrow. "Going home, eh? You got any papers or identification?"

Joel smiled, handing the man his messenger badge, "Just this."

The guard looked at the badge and squinted, then brought it closer to his face.

"Joel Shine, messenger to the royal house of Regalock," he read aloud.

The boy nodded, stretching forth his hand for the guard to return the badge. However, the guard didn't seem to notice the gesture. He examined the badge, inspecting it as though he believed it to be a fake, all while stroking his mustache.

"You? A messenger to the king?" he asked condescendingly. "I was under the impression that Chamish had a high standard for his messengers."

Shocked by the guard's rude implication, Joel replied, "He does, unlike the standard for south gate guards. I'll be sure to mention it to King Chamish."

With that, Joel snatched his messenger badge back from the guard and returned it to his pocket. The guard scowled at him, still twirling one side of his mustache.

"May I go in, then?" Joel asked, not hiding his irritation.

"Yeah," he replied. "Get out of here and learn some manners before entering this way again."

Joel started forward, but before the guard was out of earshot, he called back to him, "Do yourself a favor and shave off that ridiculous mustache. It makes you look like a real creep."

If the guard replied, Joel didn't hear it. He walked through the gate, left the greater outer wall behind him, and casually made his way into the southern edges of Tyran City. Joel stopped and sighed. His body had returned home, but his heart and mind were still back at the Keep. Joel's greatest dream had come true, he would be a sorcerer.

When Ginn told him he had to wait a few more years, it broke Joel's heart. He could feel the magic churning inside him, he knew it was there. To his young mind, waiting to grow up just didn't make any sense. He felt ready to begin training now. Then came Zorrel. They had an instant connection. Zorrel offered him a chance to turn his waiting time from four or five years, to maybe a month or two. Sure, he'd have to start his training in the Keep's archives instead of learning magic, but it was better than waiting. All he had to do now was get his mother's permission and of course and wait for Jes to defeat Kaynah of Shale.

Joel laughed to himself. "I bet fighting a necromancer will be a lot easier."

It took Joel a long time to walk through the vast city. As he walked, he noticed something had changed, although everything looked the same.

When Joel and his mother first arrived in Tyran, it seemed enormous and amazing. This was probably because of the stark contrast Tyran City had to his birthplace of Suffer. Suffer was a small community, bonded because everyone was stranded there, kept alive by a little oasis in the center of town. Tyran City had more people living on a single street than Suffer thrice over. In Suffer, Joel had known everyone on a very personal level, but in Tyran, there were new people to meet every day.

What excited Joel about Tyran so much was the atmosphere he felt here. To him, there was a kind of spirit in the air. It held so much life, and it held a lifetime of adventures. His mother didn't feel it. Her complaints and criticisms for the city made that more than obvious. Every time Joel walked through the streets, he felt that same spirit of adventure around him. Today, however, that feeling had changed.

Joel looked around at the people in the busy markets, the

calm neighborhoods, and the army training camp. Life was all around him, nothing had changed there.

"If the city is the same," he thought, "what's different?"

He thought about this for a long time, long enough for him to reach the inner castle wall, which divided the royal estate from the rest of the city. The guards standing watch there waved to Joel with a friendly smile. These guards, Joel had seen plenty of times for each of them to recognize each other on sight.

"Hey Joel," one greeted him. "How have you been, little buddy?"

The boy stopped in front of the guard, whose name he remembered was Martin. He remembered this because everyone had nicknamed him, "Martin the Mole." This wasn't because he was a traitor leaking information, but because once he had a large mole on his right cheek. As you might expect, Martin didn't care for the name and even had a physician cut the mole off of his face. The mole was now gone, but it had left behind a scar on his cheek.

"Hey Martin, I'm doing alright. Just getting back from the Sorcerer's Keep. Jes took me," Joel replied.

Martin the Mole's eyes went wide with surprise. "Really? Wow, that's so exciting!"

Joel looked up at the inner wall. The banners of the Tyran

116

hung intermittently along from the top. The silver shield with a maroon serpent coiled around a gold star in the center, once made Joel feel so empowered and proud to be considered a Tyranian. Now, however, he just saw a flag.

Without returning eye contact to Martin, he answered monotonically, "Yeah, it's exciting. In a few months, I'll get to start my training."

"I'd say that's fantastic, but you don't seem so excited about it. What's going on?" Martin observed.

"Does the city seem... different to you?" Joel asked, gesturing to their surroundings.

Martin gave everything a quick look, then said, "Looks the same to me. Then again, I don't go out and about very much. Why? What have you noticed?"

Joel sighed. "It's not that I've noticed anything different, Tyran just seems different. I can't put my finger on why, but it's like all the excitement is gone."

The guard nodded, although Joel wasn't sure if that was because Martin understood him or if he just didn't know what else to do.

After a momentary pause, Martin said, "You came from that prison in the desert, right?"

Joel did a double-take, caught off-guard by the seemingly

random question. "Yeah, but what does that ha-"

"And you came directly here from the desert?" Martin interrupted.

"Well, we stopped in Culten for a day, but after that, yes," Joel answered, still not understanding what these questions had to do with anything.

Martin nodded again, scratching the back of his head. "I see. And when did you first feel get this feeling that something in Tyran is different?"

"Today, as I got back, I was-"

Martin interrupted again, "And have you always felt the excitement in the city? From your first day here until today?"

Joel thought for a second, then nodded.

"Just as I thought."

"What? What is it?" asked Joel, a little frustration building in his voice.

The guard knelt down, their eyes now on the same level. Joel could see the scar where Martin's infamous mole had been on his face. Whoever had removed the blemish did an excellent job. The scar blended so well into his face that if you didn't know it was there, you would likely miss it.

"Maybe Jes or another enchanter used magic to remove it," thought Joel as he unsuccessfully tried not to stare at the area of Martin's cheek.

Martin cleared his throat, bringing Joel back to the matter at hand.

"Why has everything changed all of a sudden?" Joel asked, frowning.

"Because you've changed."

Joel took half a step back in confusion. "What do you mean? I haven't changed, I'm still me."

"But your goal and aspirations have changed since you first came here," Martin replied, putting a hand on the boy's shoulder. "You came from a very small town to a large city full of exciting new things and opportunities. Now, you have the chance that only one in a few thousand people get, to train as an enchanter. With that kind of adventure on the horizon, life in Tyran City doesn't seem so exciting anymore because you want more than it could ever offer you. This place is the same, but your expectations are not. It's all a part of growing up."

Joel stared down at his feet and frowned. He knew Martin the Mole was right, being an enchanter in the near future was the most exciting thing to ever happen to him. The thought of continuing in Tyran as the King's messenger seemed so bland. A tear rolled down the boy's cheek.

119

"Hey now, it's nothing to cry about," said Martin, looking very uncomfortable with the idea of consoling a crying child.

Wiping the tear from his face, Joel sniffled and then said, "No, it's not that."

"Then what is it?"

First rubbing his nose, then looking back up at the guard, Joel replied, "What if my mother doesn't let me go? What if she says I can't be an enchanter?"

"You're right, that would be pretty crushing," Martin frowned.

"You call that cheering me up?" snapped Joel.

Martin exaggerated a shrug. "Hey, I gave it my best shot. You make a fair point. If your mother says you can't train, then there's not much you can do about it. Except maybe hope she changes her mind somehow."

Joel laughed. "Yeah, I guess there's only one way to find out what she'll say."

"There you go," the Mole rallied. "I bet, that the worst she'll say is that you should a few years until you're older. I doubt she'd keep you from being an enchanter forever, especially with Jes Nulkin always around to watch over you."

He stood up, then patted Joel on the shoulder.

"Thanks for everything," the boy said honestly.

Martin smiled and winked, then gestured for Joel to continue on into the castle. Before Joel had taken three steps, Martin called to him again.

"Hey, speaking of Jes Nulkin, I heard a rumor and since you're coming from there, you'll likely know if it's true."

"What rumor?"

Martin and the other guard looked at each other. The other guard, whose name Joel remembered was Stewart, nodded encouragingly to Martin.

"Well, you see, we heard that a pack of lizards attacked the Sorcerer Keep. Supposedly they had enormous claws and set the whole thing on fire. That can't be true, can it?"

Joel did his best to hide his shock that Martin knew about the Hissera attack. Although he wasn't sure where the fire part came from.

He gulped, trying to keep the nerves from coming out in his voice. "Where did you hear a rumor like that?"

"A bunch of guys were talking about it in the tavern," replied Stewart. "Word has it those lizard-things, or whatever they are, attacked Culten too."

Sweat moistened on Joel's forehead. He hated lying almost

as much as he hated horses. Then, he got an idea. Maybe he didn't have to lie.

Joel let out a small laugh. "Well, I don't know anything about Culten, but I promise you that the Sorcerer's Keep is not on fire."

The two guards looked at each other, puzzled.

Before they could ask him any more questions, Joel started walking again towards the castle.

"I should be going home now. My mother will be worried about me if I'm not back soon. Thanks for everything!" he called back.

* * *

We were making good time as we journeyed north, traveling at a fast but comfortable speed. In only three and a half days of riding, we had nearly reached the Crossroad of Aris. At that point the road split, leading east to Cretik, west to Panorl, or continuing north to Vain. We intended to keep north. The crossroad was our first milestone, it being considered the southern border of the new Kingdom of Aris. Until now, we had been in Culten's territory.

I looked back at Kernil, still riding in the back next to Howel. If we were entering Aris and passing by Vain, would that be an issue for him? Would he be safe? He had mentioned that Nemuel wanted him dead, so much so that the usurping king was sending assassins after him. Even if we didn't run into any trouble here on the southern border, I doubted that we'd have such luck on the northern border with Tyran.

Since Aris won their independence from Tyran, tensions had been high, and crossing from one side to the other was difficult. I realized I might be a target in Aris as well. Even though I was an enchanter, I was married to the Tyranian King's daughter. Although a foolish idea, perhaps I too might be considered an enemy. If that were to happen, what should I do? I couldn't just let myself be captured or killed, and fighting back might cause consequences for all of Tyran.

I rubbed my eyes with my non-gauntleted hand. Best to deal with these issues if and when they presented themselves. No sense in worrying about them now. Not to mention the nine-foot-tall troll that was sure to draw attention.

All-day, the sun had been stuck behind a thick stream of clouds and despite it being only midday. The sky was getting noticeably darker. Any minute now, a heavy rain would begin. I put my hood over my head in preparation.

There was a buzzing sound. Instinctively I swatted at my ear, believing the cause a bee or wasp. Quickly realizing that there were no insects nearby, pulled my hood back down and checked my surroundings. I didn't see anything unusual.

"Does anyone else hear that awful sound?" called Barris.

Kernil, Howel, and Dalia replied that they were hearing the

noise. Dahrik called the company to a stop.

"Maybe I've lost my mind, but it sounds like the swishing of large waves," Dalia commented. "But that's impossible, we're nowhere near an ocean."

I closed my eyes and concentrated. My first impression was wrong. It wasn't a buzzing noise, but I was also fairly certain that it wasn't ocean waves either.

"What could make such an irritating noise?" Dahrik asked, confusion and frustration in his voice.

"Are there insects in the area that make it? Like a cicada or something," Kilt added.

Kernil shook his head. "If there are, they've come in the last five years. I've never heard this before."

Howel stood up in his saddle, stretching himself as high as he could, and squinted southward.

"Anyone else see that?" he called, pointing to a shape on the horizon that hadn't been there before.

Arrig and I moved next to Howel. I cupped my eyes to block out the glare of the sun and studying the shape on the horizon.

"It's moving closer," I said as I noticed it.

"He's right," confirmed Kylora, who had moved next to me

without me noticing. "Whatever it is, it's headed straight for us."

"What?" shouted Norvic, actually looking a little panicked. "Are you sure?"

Nobody replied or said anything else as we all watched the horizon for several minutes. The air felt tense, as if we were waiting out a horrific storm. The dark shape grew closer and I could now see that it wasn't a single object, but rather several, maybe thirty or forty individuals packed together, heading towards us. As they did, the sound grew louder, echoing through the valley.

"That wouldn't be hissing, would it?" Kilt asked nervously.

Everyone looked at each other, fear and shock in their eyes.

"More Hissera?" gasped Dalia. "And coming from the south? How can this be?"

Norvic, who was already cantering away, cried, "We can't let them catch up to us. Ride, everyone!"

Like lightning, everyone was racing northward. I was behind Norvic, Kernil, and Barris but in front of Dahrik, Kylora, Dalia, and Howel. The increased speed put Hemm and Kilt at the very back of the company, but he seemed to keep up fine enough. As we hurried ahead, I could see the crossroad. My worst fear was confirmed. Soldiers from the Kingdom of Aris, or the Arisites, had set up a blockade. Aside the blockade, a watchtower had been constructed, on top of which was stationed a single soldier. He waved a flag, likely signaling to the soldiers on the ground that we were coming.

The hissing grew louder, I wanted to look back, but I knew from experience that this was a bad idea. We were closing in on the blockade, and it was unclear if the watchman saw the Hissera behind us. Norvic, who was still leading the flight, didn't show any sign of stopping. The Arisite guards readied their weapons, and the watchman drew a bow.

The warlock grandmaster removed his scepter from the straps at the side of his saddle and held it forth, the blood-red gems at each end glowing brightly. A surge of lightning burst from the scepter and struck the blockade. The iron gate closing off the road was destroyed, scraps of hot metal going everywhere. Guards on the ground that weren't caught in the electric blast, met their end from the shrapnel. The lightning also removed an entire chunk of the tower. After the blast, the structure wobbled violently and the watchman on the top frantically shouted for help.

It took a few seconds for what had happened to register. When we reached the former blockade, the tower began to collapse. It was folding in on itself, and looking to crash where the gate once stood, right on top of us.

My right hand went to my scepter, which was still strapped to my saddle. I used my left hand to reach out with magic and focus on the collapsing tower. I willed it to resist gravity and stay suspended in the air, allowing us to pass by unharmed.

This turned out to be much more strenuous than I first anticipated. The tower was not only broken into large pieces but into smaller pieces as well. Thankfully, my horse Arrig kept moving along with the rest of the company. Levitating the tower mid-collapse took every bit of my concentration.

Dahrik had a similar idea, although he must have known that I was focusing on the tower. He used a similar spell to stop the watchman from falling to his death. The dwarf slowed the Arisite's fall and moved him out of the way of the still charging company. Before the guard knew what had happened, he was seated comfortably on the ground, watching us pass by.

After I had passed the suspended tower and the destroyed gate, I looked back. I saw that everyone had passed through unharmed, but the Hissera were gaining on us quickly. I was about to release the tower from my spell and allow it to fall naturally to the ground, but then I got an idea. I slowed Arrig until we were at the very back of the company and I nearly crashed into Hemm and Kilt.

I released the reigns, putting my whole faith in Arrig to steer us correctly, and kept my eyes focused behind us. The small cluster of Hissera was close enough now that I could see their individual faces, although each one was just a copy of the other.

I smiled as the first of the Hissera reached the tower.

"Try this one, you fiends!" I cried as I released my hold on the tower and it collapsed.

A cloud of dust went up from the crash, but my eyes remained fixed on it. Cheers hollered from ahead of me from the party. The celebration was cut short, however, when out of the dust came over a dozen Hissera, climbing over the remains of the tower and chasing after us.

Kernil saw the Hissera and veered his horse off the road, rounding back to face the creatures.

"Stand and fight, everyone! We can't outrun them," he cried.

He drew the Sword of Vain, and the sky cracked with thunder. Kernil raised his sword high for all to see, the gold hilt shining, even in the dim light. His horse Ioc reared and then charged into Hissera. The Lute Brutes roared in support and followed after their leader. I responded quickly, Arrig and I only two strides behind the Son of Vain, my gauntlet, and scepter at the ready. Dahrik and the other enchanters were the slowest to turn around.

"For the heart of Vain!" Kernil shouted as his blade met first of the Hissera.

Just as the battle began, it started to rain. The air was thick and cold, with a soft but steady wind blowing from the east. The rain started as nothing more than a trickle, but every second the raindrops grew larger and fell faster. Within minutes, it was a complete deluge.

Before the first Hissera could slash its claws at Kernil, the Son of Vain cut its head clean off. The head bounced off of the next Hissera, causing it to stumble back. The Sword of Vain thrusted into the off-balance Hissera before it could recover. His initial luck ran out, as the next Hissera jump up and sunk its claws into Kernil's shoulder.

I wanted to help him, but two of the Hissera were nearly upon me. I fired a blast from my gauntlet, but the first of the creatures swatted it away easily. That Hissera leaped forward and landed upon Arrig's head. Before it could get with its knife-like claws, I raise my gauntlet arm in defense, blocking the attack. Acting fast, I swung my scepter at it and bashed it on the side of the head, knocking it to the ground.

As I fired my first gauntlet blast, an arrow pierced the Hissera with its claws in Kernil's right shoulder. The Son of Vain looked back to see that Howel was already drawing another arrow as he and his horse flanked to the right.

Hemm and Kilt were the next to engage. The hobgoblin drew her duel hand axes and lept off of the troll's shoulder with impressive distance. As she landed, she buried her axes in a pair of Hissera. She yanked her weapons out of the dead fiends and was faced by another Hissera. The creature hissed angrily in her face before striking. Kilt hissed back and countered each of the attacks with her axes. After a series of back and forth, the Hissera swiped with its left, but Kilt jammed an axe into its hand. The creature hissed in pain and died when the hobgoblin finished it with a strike to the chest.

When four of the Hissera saw the monstrosity before them that was Hemm the troll, they stopped in their tracks. Each one hissed in warning to the troll, moving as a group to surround him. Hemm roared louder than the thunder booming throughout the sky. The four Hissera each took a step back. Moving faster than you'd expect a body like his to be capable of, Hemm grabbed the nearest Hissera by the leg and whipped it around. He wielded the creature like a club again the other three. Within seconds, the dead remains of all four Hissera smeared across the wet ground.

Meanwhile, Barris jumped off of his horse and into a trio of Hissera that were nearly on me. Wielding his large war hammer, he crushed the skull of the first one on impact. The second Hissera got two good swipes in before the dwarf countered with an uppercut hammer-strike to the jaw. The lizard fell on its back to the ground and never got up again.

Just as Barris was turning to face the third one, it leaped on his back, sinking its claws in deep. Howel fired an arrow into the monster's shoulder but the Hissera only flinched. Angry now, Barris reached behind him and grabbed the Hissera by the neck. He attempted to yank the lizard over his shoulder, but the creature didn't budge. Seeing no other alternative, Barris slammed his back, and the Hissera along with him, into the ground. The hit knocked the creature loose and Barris immediately turned and crushed the Hissera with a two-handed blow from his hammer.

Dalia and Kylora rode side by side, cutting off one Hissera from the rest. Kylora froze the rain above her and directed it into the Hissera's face. It slashed at the ice droplets, stumbling back. Dalia formed a lasso of magical energy and looped it around the creature's neck. She sped her horse, dragging the Hissera along the ground by the neck, choking it. It squirmed and thrashed in a desperate attempt to free itself. The Hissera managed to get one of its claws hooked on the magic lasso and with a single thrust, it severed the rope.

Kylora noticed first, shooting more ice rain at the escaped lizard. The Hissera blocked it this time, putting an arm up to shield its face. The Hissera leaped high into the air towards Kylora, its claws extended and its teeth ready for a bite of druid flesh. Kylora closed her eyes, bracing herself for the attack, but it never came. To her surprise, Hemm intercepted the monster mid-jump, catching it with one of his massive hands. The lizard hissed angrily at the troll, then bit his hand with its sharp teeth. Hurt by the bite, Hemm dropped the Hissera. It tried to land on its feet, but the muddy ground was slick and the Hissera slipped and fell flat on its face. With a grunt of pain, the troll smashed his left fist into the prone Hissera. Displeased, Hemm looked at the ropes intricately wrapped around his hands. The fibers that were once white were now stained blue with the blood of many Hissera.

As I struggled with a few Hissera, Dahrik and Norvic came to my aid, each of them focusing on a Hissera. A Hissera landed a nasty cut to my leg and Dahrik assaulted it with a fireball. The fire did little damage, merely pushing the Hissera back a few steps. With a flick of his scepter, Dahrik levitated the man-sized lizard high in the air. Using the rain, which was drenching everything, Dahrik froze all of the water on and around the Hissera, turning it into a block of ice. Pushing his scepter downward, Dahrik sent the frozen block back into the ground. The Hissera shattered on impact.

Norvic was on the other side. First double-teaming one Hissera with me, then fighting his own as another attacked him for the other side. Norvic's horse took a bad cut to its leg, rearing suddenly and sending the warlock to the ground on his butt. Instantly the Hissera was on him, but Norvic called upon his magic to throw chunks of earth at the attacker. However, since the rain had thoroughly soaked the ground, he hurled mostly mud at the Hissera's face. The mud did little to harm the Hissera, but it gave Norvic enough time to get to his feet. He summoned fire, engulfing the lizard with a massive blast pouring from his scepter.

The fire mixing with the heavy rain caused nearly everything around Norvic to become enshrouded in steam. In the instant that followed the steam's creation, Norvic intended to use the momentary distraction. His vision was obscured, but Norvic could see well enough that the Hissera still standing, its claws glowing hot like metal.

"Why won't you just die?" he cried, advancing on the creature.

The Hissera nearly cut his throat with a single swipe, but Norvic stepped just in time for the hot claws to graze his chin. He yelped in pain as his flesh singed. The Hissera raised its claw to attack again, but just before it struck a killing blow, an arrow pierced through its hand and into its neck. The dying Hissera flinched and convulsed for a few seconds, then went still.

A Hissera slashed at Arrig's neck, but luckily it didn't cut very deep. Arrig reared, whinnying in pain, I nearly fell off but just managed to hang on. Levitating some of the mud Norvic had exposed, I temporarily blinded a Hissera.

"Leave me for now," I said into Arrig's ear. "Just don't go too far, I'll have to heal that cut when we're done here."

I jumped off of Arrig, leading with my gauntlet in a flying punch to the Hissera's chest. Arrig turned and retreated a safe distance away. The Hissera cleared the mud from its eyes and hissed at me defiantly. It moved towards me, claws extended but just then a thick cloud of steam obscured everything around us. I had just enough time to see the attack coming and guessed where the Hissera would likely be finishing the attack. So, I sidestepped to the right and felt the lizard's claw slash the air where I had been standing.

Using that as a point of reference, I swung my scepter wide. It collided with what I assume was the side of the Hissera's head. Twirling my scepter in my fingers, I summoned a small whirlwind to churn the air around me and disperse the steam. The Hissera stood up but was knocked down by Dahrik, who bashed its face in repeatedly with the blunt end of his iron scepter.

The rain had everyone thoroughly soaked, but it started to ease up. I looked to the sky and saw that the dark gray clouds were moving quickly to the west. In the distance near the Pyre Mountains was a sliver of blue sky that marked the end of the small, but intense storm.

The final Hissera was facing off against Kernil. He stood a safe sword-swinging distance from his horse. With the Sword of Vain raised, Kernil dueled against the necromancer's final pet. The Hissera first slashed left, then right with its claws, forcing the Son of Vain to backpedal and parry the attacks. The Hissera swiped again at Kernil, this time catching him once, then twice in the ribs. However, landing the cuts into Kernil's flesh had come at a cost. The Hissera left itself open to attack. Kernil took the advantage and chopped the Hissera's arm clean off at the shoulder.

The creature hissed and writhed in pain, its blue-colored blood squirting everywhere. Kernil raised his blade once again to end the beast, but before he could, an arrow shot into its heart. The final Hissera ceased its screeches and fell to the ground without another sound.

"Howel, that one was mine!" Kernil yelled back at the archer, his bow still aimed at the fallen Hissera.

Howel moved closer to Kernil, pulling his hood back up and wiping the rain off his face. "You know the rules. He who deals the killing blow counts the kill. Not my fault you took your time and came in last place."

"What? I didn't come in last, did I?" he replied in disbelief. "How many did everyone get?"

I looked at Dahrik, who seemed just as lost as I was.

"Three for me," called Kilt, climbing back onto Hemm's

shoulder.

The troll put up both hands, showing five of his large, beefy fingers.

"Really? Five?" remarked Kilt. "You work fast in the rain, don't yah?"

Hemm shrugged humbly, a tiny grin on his face.

"I also had three," inserted Barris, leaning against his hammer. "Although if we counted how impressive the kills were, then I'd likely be at the top, as usual."

"Except we don't," Howel replied immediately. "Especially since they were all the same size."

Kernil put his sword back in the sheath, then turned to Howel. "I suppose that means you got three as well? Making my two the lowest."

The archer nodded, smiling big.

"You stole that last one on purpose! You were set to lose," accused Kernil, pointing angrily at the dwarf still on horseback.

Howel scoffed in defense. "I did not. I might be a rascal, but I'm an honest rascal. It was screaming and flailing around. I wanted it to stop, you were taking forever, and I had a clean shot."

"What are you savages talking about?" demanded Norvic, still wiping mud off his clothes.

It was Dahrik who answered. "They kept count of how many Hissera they each killed."

"Exactly," replied Barris with a grin. "We have a little game. The lowest kills gets last pick of any loot and they have to take first watch the coming night."

"And Kernil's just upset because he lost," Howel remarked.

"Of all the childish notions," Norvic swore to himself, rubbing his forehead in frustration.

The five Lute Brutes looked at each other for a second, then back at Norvic. The warlock didn't notice immediately, as he was still concerned with getting the mud out of the crevasses of his scepter.

"As I recall," Kernil began, "it was you who doubted our abilities."

Kilt added, "What was the word he used? Unimpressive. Yeah, that was the one."

"Was it unimpressive how the five of us killed all of these lizard-things, while you enchanters couldn't kill any?" Barris taunted, gesturing to the carnage behind him.

"Actually, Dahrik Ironhelm killed two of them," Howel corrected. "Not a surprise, given *his* aptitudes."

Barris looked at Dahrik and bowed. "My apologizes, sir."

Dahrik waved the apology away, clearly enjoying Norvic's embarrassment. "No need. Please continue."

The hammer-wielding dwarf nodded, then turned back to Norvic with a scowl. "We killed nearly all of them, and all you did was cover the battlefield in smoke."

"Not to mention, I had to save your life. You would have been Hissera food if I hadn't been watching your everyone's back. Was that not impressive enough?" added Howel, his arms folded confidently.

"Enough!" shouted Norvic, turning his back on everyone. "I have had enough of this harassment."

"No Norvic, you deserve this," said Dahrik

The warlock abruptly turned back around and faced him. "And how do you figure that, Dahrik?"

The two stood inches apart, glaring at each other with fierce intensity. Barris and Howel slowly reached for their weapons, preparing to come to Dahrik's aid if a fight broke out. I waved them back and gave them a look that meant, "He can handle this himself," which they seemed to understand well enough.

"You're the one who questioned their abilities. You said they wouldn't be enough. So, here's a field test for you. They not only killed the Hissera when we couldn't but they saved all of us, including your own life."

"He's right, Norvic. We underestimated them," added Kylora.

Then Dalia spoke up, addressing the Lute Brutes. "I apologize for dismissing you as well. We Druids are not used to this kind of conflict, I was foolish and judgmental."

"We forgive you," said Kilt, leaning on Hemm's head.

Norvic turned away from the rest of the company, whistling for his horse to return to him.

"Alright, fine. I was wrong," he muttered just loud enough for us to hear.

Barris stifled a laugh. "Was that so difficult?"

Dahrik and I did nothing to conceal our amusement.

"For him, yes," Dahrik said.

Thankfully, the rain stopped shortly after. We decided it best to rest for an hour before continuing on. It was just past midday and there was still plenty of daylight left before we'd have to stop and make camp for the night. While we rested, Kylora and I focused on healing everyone's wounds. Everyone had been injured in some way, even the horses. We applied some salves that Kylora made and mixed them with the Vodro

Heal. The mystical salve and magic bandage that the Vodro Heal provided was a good pairing and very versatile.

"You'll have to teach me how to make that salve," I said, after seeing it work first hand.

She agreed, although I wondered if either of us would ever get the opportunity.

Kernil had the worst injury, with a bad gash near his ribs. I was surprised that he hadn't passed out from blood loss when we started the Lordon Heal. The Lordon Heal is powerful and effective but requires time and lots of energy from the spellcaster. Once we stopped the bleeding, we shared the energy required and place the Lordon Heal on Kernil. The heal put him into a heavy sleep. We decided that when we traveled again, we'd guide Ioc for him. That way the heal and his induced sleep would come to its natural end.

Meanwhile, Dahrik and Dalia did their best to dry out our supplies, as well as everyone's clothes. Barris was particularly pleased when Dahrik evaporated the water in his shoes. Hemm tried to wash the blue stain from his ropes himself, but Dalia eventually used magic to make them clean. Hemm blushed after the druid had done this for him.

Norvic took care of himself, not accepting help from anyone. He impatiently stood ready to continue traveling, which everyone ignored.

Once I had helped everyone with their wounds, I looked out

at the field of dead Hissera. I felt an unease in my stomach, and again my focus was caught by a dark figure in the corner of my eye. This was the figure I had seen once before, right after the Hissera attacked the Keep. I turned around to face the shadow, but it wasn't there. Once again, it had vanished.

The Last Ravenhigh

After a few more day's travel, we reached the city of Vain. It was mid-morning when the capital of Cray's newest kingdom came into view. The sky was gray, but there weren't enough clouds for it to rain. A gentle breeze kept the air chill as the sun peaked over the mountains.

As soon as the city was in view, Dahrik called everyone to stop and gather around him.

"I think it best for our situation to go into Vain and restock our supplies," he began, pointing the city behind him. "That blasted rain ruined most of our food, so it only makes sense to stop here and restock."

I instinctively put a hand on my stomach in hunger. Despite our best efforts, most of the rations we brought from Culten were spoiled by the intense rain. Norvic scolded that we should have prepared a weather protection spell on the food before the storm. This, of course, was correct, but it did little good for us now. The damage was done.

Kernil spoke first, avoiding the sight of Vain in the distance. "I'm not going any further than right here. Nemul wants me dead more than anything, and I'm not about to deliver myself to him."

Norvic chuckled. "Oh, that's right. I forgot about that. Yes, best you stay out here. We wouldn't want anything to happen to you."

I scowled at the warlock, although he paid me no attention.

"I could give a disguise," Dahrik stated, acting as though Norvic hadn't spoken. "Nobody would recognize you."

The Son of Vain shook his head. "Nope. I'm not taking any chances."

"Very well," the dwarf replied.

"I'm staying behind as well," I added, looking at Dahrik.

Norvic answered, not bothering to hide a laugh. "Ah, even better!"

"Why not?" Kilt asked, leaning in from atop Hemm's shoulder.

"I am married to the Tyranian King's daughter," I replied in a matter-of-fact tone. "That, along with being the Prodigy, gives me a high notoriety which could prove dangerous. Best we avoid that altogether."

Barris chimed in next. "But if magic disguise is an option, why would it matter?"

"I'd just rather be safe than sorry," I answered. "Besides, when splitting up, nobody should go alone."

"Fair enough," nodded Dahrik.

"What about you, Dahrik? You started a counterrevolution last time you were here. Perhaps you should stay behind." Norvic suggested the idea to the dwarf with a wide grin plastered on his face.

Kernil's eyes narrowed, bouncing between the Dahrik and me. For a second, it looked as though he wanted to say something, but he didn't.

Dahrik scoffed. "I have no problem trusting my own disguise, besides, nobody will remember me. Most humans can't tell the difference between dwarves. They think that we all look the same. Barris, Howel, tell him I'm right."

The two dwarves of the Bronzearm clan looked at each other, then nodded in agreement.

"Oh, it's very true. Happens more than you would think," said Barris.

"Norvic does bring up a good point, however," I admitted. "You should at least conceal your scepter. You *are* the only dwarf enchanter alive."

"Wise counsel, Prodigy," Dalia commented.

Dahrik waved his hand over his scepter, making it disappear before our eyes. "There, now I'm just an ordinary dwarf."

With that, Dahrik and the rest of the company rode into Vain, Kernil and I being the only ones to stay behind. I dismounted from Arrig, wanting to stretch my sore muscles. Kernil had a similar idea, dismounting Ioc and sitting on the ground a few paces away. I stared at the city in the distance, remember the last time I was in Vain.

As though he could read my thoughts, Kernil asked, "You ever been inside the city?"

I turned away from Vain and walked over to him. "Yes, but it was during the war, so didn't get to really see much of it."

"You were in the war? I thought enchanters stayed out of international conflicts."

I nodded. "Oh, we do. Dahrik and I were healers. Although before I became an enchanter, I was actually recruited for the war."

Kernil seemed genuinely surprised by this. "How does that work? You just got to leave without serving?"

"In a way, I suppose," I shrugged. "Dahrik had to petition for my release as a Tyranian citizen. After that, I was free to leave."

"And yet you ended up marrying Chamish's daughter anyway?" he said with a hint of sarcasm. "Wow, you really got the best of every scenario, didn't you?"

"Not exactly," I muttered to myself, so I was certain he didn't hear me.

Kernil looked towards Vain for the first time. He sighed, and I couldn't be sure but I thought I saw a few tears drip from his eyes.

"Have you ever gone back?" he asked suddenly after a few moments of silence.

"What?"

"To your village," he corrected. "Have you ever gone back?"

I shook my head.

"Well, why not?"

I shrugged. "I never had a reason to go back. It was burned to the ground and everyone died. I mean, I once heard a rumor that there were a handful of survivors that were rebuilding the town. But that was more than five years ago and there's still no town or further rumor of the supposed survivors."

"But what if someone you know is alive? What if it's someone in your family?" Kernil protested. "Shouldn't you go back at least and check?"

I chuckled in spite of myself. "You know, my wife has made a similar case about this."

"From what I remember about her, she's smart and witty. Sounds like I remember correctly."

I paused. It had never occurred to me that Kernil might have known Rebecca. Now that I thought about it, it made sense. She was the princess, and he had been the son of the king's governor. They were from the same social class, why wouldn't they have run into each other at some point?

"Yes, she is," I replied. "I think I will go back someday. Probably when my children are all old enough. That way, when I go, I can bring my whole family and show them where I came from."

"That actually sounds pleasant," Kernil admitted. "Although, I know I couldn't wait that long."

I sat next to Kernil and together we watched the city of Vain, illuminated beautifully by the mid-morning sun.

"This must be hard for you," I noted, my gaze still fixed on the city. "At least when everything was taken away from me, it was *everything*. You only lost part of your life. Your home still stands, but you're a fugitive from it. If I go back, there's nothing for me, no hope. You still have something left, and I think that as long as this the case, you'll still have a sliver of hope in you. That's why you still feel the pain of losing it."

The Son of Vain didn't say anything for a long time. I knew he heard me. I was right next to him and I spoke clearly. After several minutes, he began to nod.

"You are right," he said softly. "The part that hurts most of all is seeing my home and my inheritance right here in front of me."

Kernil stood up and drew his sword. "When I last saw my father, he gave me this sword. It's been in our family for nine generations. My ancestor who forged it and called it the Sword of Vain."

"It's a beautiful blade," I stated, standing up. "The hilt is very fine."

He nodded, then polished the coin-sized ruby in the pommel with the sleeve of his shirt.

"You know, it has its own battle cry."

I raised an eyebrow.

He turned the sword over, revealing the words, "*For the Heart of Vain*," engraved on the flat of the blade.

I smiled. "Didn't you shout that before the Hissera battle?"

"I did," he replied. "I used to think it silly when my father would shout it before a conflict, but now, it's almost like he's beside me when I say. Almost like it's a way for me to call

147

upon him from beyond. Foolish, I know."

"No," I stated firmly, shaking my head. "It's not foolish. I feel the same whenever I go fishing. I didn't do it for a long time but for the past few years, I've made a habit of fishing in the Neos at least once every season. Each time I do, I feel like the family I lost is with me again. You're lucky to have that sword and the battle cry, never think it's foolish."

He nodded, stroking the blade with his hand.

"You're right. It's the only thing I have to remember my family. This sword and I are all that's left of my family's legacy. I'm the last Ravenhigh and a Ravenhigh is meant to wield this blade. If Nemuel had his way, he'd kill me and take it for himself, likely to use it as a symbol of legitimacy."

I put a hand on his shoulder. "He will never have it. I promise you."

We locked eyes, and after a few seconds, he nodded confidently.

"I believe you," he said. "Or at least, I believe that you believe it. Which, I suppose, is more than I can say for myself."

I took my hand off his shoulder and faced the direction of the city once again. Where had that promise come from? I didn't know Kernil very well, but something inside me wanted to help him. Was it that we had both lost our families?

I looked down at the ground and pondered the connection. Perhaps it was because we had both been through similar tragedies, but there was something else. It was almost like a soft, nearly inaudible voice was telling me that I should help him. Like some outside force was nudging our paths together. Was I going crazy?

Kernil looked once more at the Sword of Vain before sheathing it. I removed my gauntlet and moved over to Arrig. Pulling out some extra straps from one of my bags, I began latching the silver gauntlet to the saddle.

"Isn't that your weapon?" Kernil asked, pointing to it.

"It is, but I don't think it will be of much use for a while," I said, staring at my reflection in the gasper emerald that was still set in the forearm. "In both of my fights with the Hissera, it's proved almost useless. I'm tired of carrying it around and getting little results. There's no sense to carrying it right now."

Kernil frowned. "You're right, it didn't do much, did it? Hey, but what about that necromancer? Couldn't you use the gauntlet against her?"

I shrugged. "I believe so. I mean, unlike the Hissera, she wasn't created with the ability to resist magic. She's just a normal elf, or used to be anyway."

"Used to be?"

"The dark magic she's using is dangerous and unnatural," I answered. "Every time she uses it, she has to sacrifice a piece of herself. Who knows how much of her there'll be left when we reach the Abandoned Fortress."

"Ah, that makes sense, I suppose."

Once I finished strapping the gauntlet to Arrig, I sat facing the city and the mountains. A few seconds later, Kernil did the same. A nice breeze blew past me, and I thought of my family back in Tyran. At this time of day, Rebecca would likely take the children on a walk around the castle garden. However, she was several months pregnant. So she might cut it short, or have Alexandria take Elias and Samuel around if she is tired.

The thought of my family sent a surge of homesickness through my stomach. I wanted to go back home to them immediately. I looked over to Kernil and sighed. I couldn't go home, no matter how much I wanted to. Once again, I was on a grand and important quest to save Cray. Unlike last time, Rebecca wasn't traveling beside me, which was an obvious downgrade. However, on a positive note, I didn't have a time limit in which I needed to defeat Kaynah. That had been the most stressful part of the Vios Almna quest, the fear of running out of time. Still, I had an evil to defeat and little confidence in myself to do it. I laughed a little, not much had changed at all.

After a few minutes of silence, Kernil said, "What did you mean when you said that Dahrik had started a counterrevolution?"

I froze. I had completely forgotten that I had said that to Dahrik in front of Kernil.

"Well... he's the one who organized the counterrevolution after Nemul assassinated your father," I stated, not looking at him.

I expected an immediate response, but Kernil had no audible reaction. I still didn't want to look at him, so there was a long, uncomfortable pause. After a few minutes, he spoke again.

"I heard about the counterrevolution, but didn't everyone in it die?"

I faced him. His face was flushed, his eyes were dull, and he looked back at me seeming visibly confused.

"Yes, everyone except Dahrik," I answered. "He was there leading the loyalists. However, he focused on destroying Varen, the warlock that was helping Nemul."

Kernil's mouth hung open for a few seconds, then he gritted his teeth and his eyes narrowed.

"What warlock helping Nemul?"

I gulped. I had done it again, said something he hadn't known about. I was in too deep now, and I could tell that Kernil wouldn't be satisfied with anything less than the whole truth.

"His name was Varen," I replied. "He was a master warlock

and Dahrik's personal nemesis. It was through his help that Nemul killed your father and rallied Vain and the other Aris cities to join his coup."

Kernil slammed his fist on the ground in frustration, then jumped to his feet. He began to pace, his face turning sour and more unpleasant to look at as his fury grew.

"Where is this Varen now? Why haven't I heard of him?"

I shrugged. "He's dead. Dahrik killed him. As for why you haven't heard of him, I have no idea."

He began to pace back and forth, grumbling to himself as he worked his thoughts out.

"That snake!" he yelled. "He's covered up anything to do with the warlock's help because it will make him look better to have done everything himself."

I thought about making some sort of comment but then decided against it.

Kernil then stopped pacing and looked me in the eyes. "Norvic. He's the leader of the warlocks, isn't he?"

"He is."

Drawing his sword once again, Kernil stood facing Vain, looking as though he were ready to charge.

"Then he must die too."

I got up quickly and grabbed him by the arm. He yanked himself free from my grasp but then looked at me, expecting an answer.

"I hate Norvic more than you will ever know. He's done things to my family that would leave you horrified, but trying to kill him outright isn't the answer. He's one of the most powerful enchanters in the world. I'm the Prodigy and I'm not even sure I could beat him."

With a loud huff of his nose, Kernil sheathed the Sword of Vain. We stood in silence for a moment when he started to chuckle.

"It all makes sense now. No wonder Dahrik instinctively disagrees with him on everything, even if it's the right idea."

"Well, that's Dahrik for you," I replied. "As unhappy as he and I are to have to travel with him and treat him like an ally, we have to keep our guard up. He's dangerous, very cunning, and intelligent."

Kernil looked me in the eyes and saw the sincerity expressed on my face. "You think he'll betray the company? Why? He seems to want the Hissera gone more than anyone."

I nodded. "I wouldn't put it past him, but it doesn't make sense to betray us until Kaynah the Necromancer is gone. I think we have until then."

Kernil started to speak but was interrupted by the sound of hooves clomping on the road behind us. We turned to see a squadron of Arisite soldiers on horseback coming from the southwest.

"Rats!" Kernil cursed. "It's a patrol, likely coming in to change the guard. Now we're in for it."

They began shouting at us. It was impossible to make out what they were saying, but the intent was clear. Kernil drew his sword for the third time that afternoon. I turned toward Arrig, who along with Ioc, was getting startled by the oncoming riders. I began sprinting toward the horses and Kernil was one pace behind.

The Arisites were nearly on top of us by the time I was mounted. Kernil charged immediately.

"For the heart of Vain," he cried out.

I unlatched my scepter from my saddle, and once I had it in my hand, I cued Arrig to charge forward too. Kernil and I were outnumbered, but as the green gems at the end of my scepter glowed with power, I knew it was them who was outmatched.

Kernil's blade clashed with that of the first Arisite, who I guessed was a captain by the emblems on his jacket. The other soldiers were coming up fast, but now I was ready for them. With a single thrust of my scepter, I sent a bolt of lightning in front of them. The lightning blocked them off from Kernil and the captain. They looked at me and realized with horror what I was. I kept charging, now spinning my scepter above my head. The loose earth and rock on the ground around me rose up and spun along with the scepter. I whipped the oaken rod, and the rocks whizzed toward the Arisite soldiers faster than arrows. Each piece hit, striking them in the chest with enough force to knock each of the twelve soldiers off their horses.

The captain and Kernil battled behind me. Their swords locked together and Kernil broke his sword free by raising his hilt with a jerk. Before the captain had time to react, the Son of Vain trapped the captain's blade under his arm. The captain's sword now immobilized, Kernil dropped his sword in a swift stroke. As The captain's hand fell, he shrieked in pain and clenched his bleeding wrist.

Kernil spun his head around, ready to cut down anyone nearby. Yet, to his surprise, there were no others near him. The other twelve soldiers were still on the ground. He looked just in time to see me leap off of Arrig and slam my scepter into the dirt. As the scepter's gem touched the earth, the land surrounding each of the soldiers instantly turned from solid dirt to quicksand. The soldiers, still not on their feet, sank into the ground. The soldiers panicked, reaching and thrashing out, which only caused them to sink faster. When they were halfway sunk, I tapped the ground again. This reversed the spell and turned the quicksand back into dry earth. A dozen Arisites were now trapped from the waist down in the solid ground.

With Kernil distracted, the captain had regained his senses

and stabbed a dagger into Kernil's leg with his remaining hand. Kernil yelped and bashed the captain's face with his sword's pommel. The captain was pushed back and fell off of his horse. The captain laid on the ground, unconscious upon impact.

I saw Kernil's wound, so I called upon my favorite spell, and in a single leap, I was next to him and Ioc. First, I yanked the dagger out of Kernil's leg. Blood spewed out of his thigh faster than I had expected. His face was pale and his expression went blank as he went into shock.

"Stay with me," I commanded.

I dropped the dagger on the ground and then snapped my fingers, summoning the purple flame of the Vodro Heal. I smacked it against the stab wound and Kernil's blank expression changed to one of pain. The purple fire burned into the flesh, sealing off the injury and stopping the bleeding.

"What was that?" he cried as he inspected his leg. "It's still there. How did you get it to stop bleeding so fast?"

His face was still pale, and he seemed a little slow in his speech, but otherwise, he was okay.

"I put a magic bandage on your leg," I replied. "It works faster than any other healing spell."

Cautiously, Kernil poked at the stab wound. "Wow, that's weird stuff. I don't feel pain at all anymore."

I whistled to Arrig, who responded quickly and trotted over to me. "Yup, it's good for that as well."

"How long will it take to heal?"

"A long time if I leave it as is," I admitted. "But I'll speed it up."

I brought up my scepter and jabbed it onto the wound. The green gems flashed brightly as I set the Lordon heal. I felt an immediate drain of my energy, but it was nothing I couldn't handle. Kernil flinched at the touch of my scepter but quickly relaxed.

"That's so strange," he remarked. "I can actually feel my flesh mending back together."

Just as I was about to say something back to him, a booming sound from behind me thundered.

BRRUHHHRRAAHHRRRAH!

I spun around and my jaw dropped. One of the Arisites, still stuck in the ground, was blowing on a horn, signaling others to us. I stood frozen in place. My mind was caught off-guard and confused. I thought I had sunk everyone deep enough to restrain their arms, or at the very least, stop them from grabbing any of their tools and weapons. How could I have overlooked this one?

Kernil reacted quickly. He cued Ioc forward and with the flat of his sword, whacked the horn out of the soldier's hand. Kernil then dismounted and stabbed the man through the chest.

"How could you have let this happen?" he scolded, but my mind was still slow to react.

I tried to reply but all that came out was a few mumbled syllables.

Kernil walked a few paces toward me, then asked again, "How could you let this happen?"

"Excuse me, but I didn't *let* anything happen," I said, my mind finally catching up to the situation. "It was a mistake. I took on twelve men while you nearly got killed by just the one."

"You have all the power in the world. You could have ended each of these degenerates with no less effort than it took to trap them but for whatever reason, you let them all live. That makes this your fault."

I couldn't believe what I was hearing. He was blaming me because I hadn't killed all of them.

"Clearly you don't have a problem with murdering people, and that is what it is, I can't tell you what's right and what's wrong. I don't kill people, especially when I can avoid it," I yelled back. "But you're right, I should have made sure that the horn was buried, I admit that was my fault."

He looked like he wanted to say something but then changed

his mind. He broke eye contact, which had been pretty intense, as he checked our surroundings.

"We should move, now. That horn is to signal danger," Kernil warned, wiping off his blade.

I decided to let the issue go since he had obviously decided to do the same. I mounted Arrig, then asked, "Would they have heard that all the way in the city?"

"Maybe not," he admitted, getting back onto Ioc, "but there may be other patrols nearby and I'd like to minimize the amount of Nemul's men that see me."

We decided to ride further north, eventually stopping near a stream that flowed from the Neos River.

"There likely won't be any patrols here," noted Kernil. "But keep your guard up just in case."

I nodded, but he was staring at the city, still visible in the distance. He and I kept our distance from one another, I dismounted and stood by the stream. I stared at my reflection in the clear water. I looked tired, yet I didn't feel very tired. I felt frustrated. Kernil's accusations echoed in my mind. My fault? Just because I didn't murder those soldiers? I pick up a rock and attempted to skip it across the stream, but in my frustration, it ended up just plopping into the water.

Closing my eyes, I listened to the current. I breathed through my nose, and that helped me calm down. I opened my eyes and knelt by the edge of the stream. I plunged my hand into the Neos, closed my eyes again, and thought about my family. Not my parents, or my old home of Fisher's Haven, but of my wife Rebecca and our children. I smiled. I wondered if she suspected anything yet, or if Joel had told her what had happened. I chuckled, the latter was very likely, Joel was terrible at keeping secrets. Everyone in Tyran probably knew about the Hissera attack by now.

I looked over at Kernil, who was still gazing toward Vain silently. He and I had many similar experiences, but very different philosophies. I still wanted to help him, and I had already given my word that I would do what I can, but did he expect me to do that by killing Nemul?

I took my hand out of the stream and wiped my face with the cold, clear water. Arrig came over and stood next to me. He lowered his head and nuzzled it against my shoulder. I smiled, giving his head a good rub.

Murder was not what I meant by helping Kernil. Is killing Nemul what he thought I was promising? I was thinking diplomacy, or at the most extreme, I'd help capture Nemul and the leaders of Aris to stand trial. My family was killed during the war, but his was killed, at least in his eyes, out of betrayal and greed. Kernil was still angry, and unlike me, he had a specific person to be angry at.

Although I was still a little frustrated, I thought I understood Kernil's position, so I decided to let it go and forgive him. He was still a good man and I could see us being very good friends and allies someday.

Arrig drank from the stream as I stood up and stretched. I patted the horse's side, thankful to have him with me on this quest.

* * *

Howel Bronzearm painted a mental picture of Dalia Longroot in the mid-morning light. Never before had he seen a woman of such poise and beauty. Living the life he did, Howel hadn't thought much about love. Although, after laying eyes on the elegant druid, he finally understood why so many songs had been written on the subject.

He rode next to her as the company made its way towards the market. A few times, he tried to find the courage to say something to her. He wanted to say anything that might ignite a dialog between them, but he abandoned the effort each time, too afraid of being rejected.

The company arrived at the market and everyone dismounted.

"We'll watch the horses," Kilt offered, leaning against Hemm's leg.

The troll nodded in response, his neck-less head surveying the square.

Dalia walked off towards one of the fruit stands and Howel tailed her, but careful not to make it look obvious. As it was, located near the fruit stand was a vendor selling arrows which, Howel could definitely use more of. The archer counted a dozen or so arrows with steel heads and quickly paid for them.

He looked over at his elven love and smiled as he thought to himself how beautiful she looked, even in disguise. Before entering the city, she along with Norvic and Kylora cast an illusion over their faces. The illusions hid their elf features in place of human ones. Although he preferred Dalia's normal look, Howel was very surprised at how alluring she still was as a human. Interestingly enough, she had done nothing to hide the fishhook-shaped scar on her lip.

Dalia had selected a few different fruits and moved on to smell some flowers at the next stand. The masses of people, the jostling carts, and the animals were loud, but Howel thought he could still hear the druid speak.

It sounded like she said to the vendor, "These gardenias are wonderful. I just love their fragrance."

She walked from the flower booth and joined Kylora and Barris, who were selecting some dried beef packaged specifically for travelers.

"Gardenia," Howel repeated in an attempt not to forget the word.

He moved over to the flower stand and asked the vendor, "I need a single gardenia, or whatever the flower the woman who was just here liked."

The vendor smiled. "Trying to impress her, eh? A noble effort, I must say."

Howel gave a guilty smile to the woman, who laughed a bit louder than the dwarf would have liked. He quickly checked to see if anyone, especially Dalia, had taken notice. Luckily, not a single head turned his way.

"Oh, would you relax, I bet she'll love it," she noted, handing him the flower.

After paying the vendor a few silver coins, Howel made his way toward the horses. His idea was to tie the gardenia to the horn of her saddle. All he had to do is get it there without Hemm or Kilt seeing him.

"If only I had some of that disappearing magic," he thought to himself.

Checking his surroundings again, Howel weighed his options. He considered telling Kilt and Hemm that he'd take over watching the horses but quickly realized that this would only make him the obvious culprit. The dwarf wasn't very light in his step, so he doubted he could sneak over without either the Hobb or the troll spotting him.

Then he saw something interesting. A pair of young men were staring at Hemm as they hid behind a cart packed with hay.

Howel moved closer to them and heard one of them say, "... massive. That thing could probably lift this wagon above its head with one hand."

Then, the boy who was wearing the strangest-looking blue hat replied, "It's big, for sure, but no way is it that strong."

Howel smiled. This is what he had been expecting. It was actually a common conversation to have about Hemm upon seeing him for the first time. He and Barris had a similar one when they first met their troll friend.

"Oh, trust me, he's that strong," Howel interjected, making sure he was well-hidden behind the cart.

"See! I told you," cheered the first boy.

The boy with the hat scowled. "Who are you, dwarf, and just how would you know?"

Knowing he couldn't tell the whole truth, Howel had a story ready. "I'm a traveler. I've seen few different trolls and one of that size can definitely lift a wagon of this size."

The young man scoffed, then adjusted his hat.

"Care to make it interesting?" Howel asked, reaching into his pocket and pulling out three gold coins.

The eyes of both boys nearly popped out of their heads at the sight of the gold.

Howel continued. "If I'm wrong, these are yours."

The two youths looked at each other and frowned.

"We don't have enough for that kind of wager."

The dwarf had expected as much and was ready for it. Without skipping a beat, he replied, "Tell you what, I'm so confident that I'm right you pay me nothing if the troll lifts the cart with only one hand. If I'm wrong, you still get the money."

Both boys looked at each other again, this time, a large grin on each of their faces.

"Why would you do that?" asked the first boy. "What's in it for you?"

Howel puffed out his chest, "I just like to be right. However, I am going to make the two of you go ask the troll if he can do it."

He reached in his pocket again and pulled out another gold coin.

"Offer him this to lift it."

The boy wearing the blue hat took the coin nodded. The two of them peaked around the cart, checking if Hemm was still there. After confirming that the troll was still there, the two slowly walked toward him. As soon as the youths were out of eyesight, Howel was on the move. He made a wide crescent, weaving through vendors and shoppers as he got into position.

Howell reached his spot right as the two boys approached the massive troll and the hobgoblin sitting on his shoulder. He was far enough away that he could not hear them, but he could tell by the smile on Kilt's face that she would instruct Hemm to accept the offer. Once the four of them moved back over towards the cart stacked with hay, Howell sprinted to Dalia's horse.

Moving faster than even he thought he was capable, Howel tied the Gardenia to the horn of the saddle with a cord. However, his speed has caused him to crush and even break the stem of the flower in half. The archer caught the flower as it fell, then quickly check on Hemm. To Howel's horror, the troll had lifted the cart and was displaying his victory as he held it about his head. Howel took a single, deep breath to calm himself. Like lightning, he untied the cord, then, with more care this time, tied the gardenia to the saddle horn with what remained of the stem.

Without bothering to check on Hemm and Kilt, Howel ducked down and ran back into the market as fast as he could. He hid in a secluded alley between a general store and a blacksmith's workshop. He breathed hard as he tried to stop his heart from beating so fiercely. After a few minutes, his nerves ceased and a massive smile crept over his face. The archer began to nod with satisfaction at the thought of Dalia seeing the gardenia.

He put his hands in his pockets and began to casually walk back into the market. As he did, he realized how light his funds had become. Howel had essentially given Hemm an entire gold coin just to distract himself. Even worse, the dwarf had been willing to risk three more gold coins if he was wrong.

Just as he was questioning whether or not the druid was worth all the trouble, Howel caught sight of Dalia returning to her horse, supplies in hand. Howel's heart began racing again as he watched her closely.

"What if she doesn't like it?" he thought, panic having taken over his mind.

Instantly, the panic washed away as Howel saw the smile on Dalia's face as she laid eyes on the gardenia.

She began looking around, scanning the crowd for the person who might have given her the flower. Realizing what she was doing, Howel ducked behind the stall of the meat vendor. Howel understood little about magic or enchanters, but when Dalia immediately found him, it seemed to him like the only explanation was magic. She locked eyes with him and smiled.

* * *

Joel wondered through the castle grounds gardens, inspecting the various plants that were readying for winter. He smiled from ear to ear as he saw the most colorful tree he knew of, that was planted in the deepest part of the garden. Joel smiled because he had planted the tree himself.

He walked up to the exotic tree and put his hand flat against the trunk. Joel sighed with relief. Ever since planting this tree in the garden, visiting it had brought him a sense of peace and clarity. It had been over two weeks since he had returned from the Sorcerer Keep. Since then, he had heard nothing about the Hissera or the necromancer. The situation had him on edge, especially since he desperately wanted to talk to someone about it. Joel was awful at keeping secrets, but this was an important one. Zorrel had told him so adamantly. So, Joel had said almost nothing at all about his trip to the Keep, only that Jes said he might be there a little longer than normal.

Joel leaned forward, resting his head against the trunk. He sighed once again, this time even louder and with more frustration. The result sounded like a strange mix between a bear's roar and chipmunk's chatter.

"Troubled, Joel?" came a voice from behind him, causing him to jump in surprise.

Joel spun around and saw Rebecca sitting on a nearby stone bench. He was shocked at the sight of the princess. She looked like she had grown much larger in her pregnancy since last he saw her, which was only two days ago.

She caught him staring, but smiled and waved him over to her.

Rebecca groaned with discomfort. "This baby is the most difficult one yet. Then again, three children in five years is probably hard for everyone."

Joel avoided eye contact. His mother had been very clear about him not commenting on Rebecca's pregnancy. He had done so about two years ago, while she was with her second son, Samuel. The comment was apparently so blunt that it made Rebecca cry. She forgave Joel, but Alexandria had made it clear that he was never again to comment about the state of a woman's body.

"Something wrong, Joel?"

The boy looked up and sighed. "Yeah, but I can't tell you why."

The princess nodded, then patted the spot next to her on the bench.

"Come, sit with me."

This time, Joel obeyed. The stone felt cold and damp and it wasn't very comfortable at all, but he made no outward complaint. The two of them sat in silence for several minutes. They stared at the only tree with none of its leaves shed by the season, the very same exotic tree Joel had come to see.

"You know what I like about you, Joel?" Rebecca asked, breaking the silence.

"No, what?"

"You're exactly like this tree."

Joel's face wrinkled in confusion. He had been compared to many things by many people, but never had he been told he was like a tree.

"I don't understand," he said finally, trying not to sound judgmental or rude.

The princess laughed, which made Joel a little embarrassed.

"What I mean is, you are special. You're the colorful, full-of-life tree in a garden of ordinary, withering plants. There's no one like you. You're one of a kind. You're the most honest person I've ever met."

"That part I get told a lot."

"I have no doubt," she smiled. "It's what I admire most about you, even though because of it you compared me to a cow once. I actually wish I could be more like you in that way.

Not knowing what to say, Joel looked away again. Only now, he wasn't ashamed, but rather humbled. It was the oddest compliment he had ever received. This thought made him smile, as Joel was often told that he gave the oddest compliments.

"Thanks, I think."

Rebecca laughed again, then said, "I'm very glad my husband brought you and your mother here. Both of you have been such a big help to me and my family."

"Well, it was either live here or Culten," Joel replied, "and I didn't want to live in Culten."

"Yeah, I don't like Culten very much either."

"I've actually never been there," he admitted. "Well, except when we dropped everyone off there once Jes came to get us with the griffins, but that wasn't for very long."

Now the princess looked confused. "Then why didn't you want to live there if you had never been?"

Joel pointed at the tree, then asked, "Did Jes ever tell you how I got the tree?"

"Now that you mention it," she thought aloud, "I don't think he did."

"When I found him in the desert," Joel began, "I thought he was just some guy that was dropped in our village. Then he used magic and made my walking stick sprout a living flower. It was the most amazing thing I had ever seen."

Rebecca nodded. "Ah, yes, Jes has told me this before."

"Well, that's the stick," exclaimed Joel, still pointing at the tree.

The princess looked confused and taken aback.

Joel nodded, then folded his arms. "And that's why I didn't want to live in Culten. I wanted to be here. I wanted to be near the magic. An ordinary life in Culten just seemed so boring. Luckily, my mother gave in to my pleas. She's nice that way."

The princess laughed. "And she's not easily persuaded either."

"No, she isn't," he laughed back.

"So that tree used to be your walking stick?"

"Yes, it kept growing and growing. So when Jes brought me here, he told me to plant it in the ground and see what happens. I came back the next day and it looked like this," Joel gestured to the whole tree, emphasizing just how big it had gotten.

Rebecca thought for a minute, then smiled. "Jes once said that the best magics are the unpredictable ones. I don't think I understood what he meant until just now."

The boy shook his head. "No, the best part of magic is being able to actually make some real changes in the world."

"Is that why you're out here? Because you're sad that the Keep told you that you can't start training yet?"

Joel flinched in surprise. How had she known about that? Did he somehow give that part away?

"It's okay. Jes said that it was likely to happen. It's only a few more years, I'd imagine," she said comfortingly.

"Actually, I was given an apprenticeship in the Keep's archives, so I'll be able to start a lot sooner," he replied without thinking.

The princess gasped in delight. "Oh, that's exciting. You must be so pleased."

Joel nodded. "I am. I won't start magic training until my powers start to develop, but at least I'll get to be in the Keep most of the time."

"Why haven't you told your mother about this?"

He sighed, then said, "Because I would rather her not say no."

"You think she won't let you go?" Rebecca asked.

"I don't know," he admitted. "But I would rather not find out. She gets so overprotective."

"So that's why aren't you there now, you're just afraid of being told you can't go?"

"No, I also have to wait until they rebuild the Keep or at least until the Hissera thing is over," Joel stated but immediately realized he should have.

He cursed himself under his breath as he looked at Rebecca and could see the next set of questions forming.

"Wait, what Hissera thing? And what happened to the Keep?"

she asked, looking a mix between confused and worried.

Joel crinkled his face in frustration at his own big mouth. He cursed himself for not being more careful about what he said.

"Is that what I said?" he asked, hoping Rebecca would believe it.

She seemed to grow several feet as she looked down on the half-elf, her face stern and without the joy that was present a moment ago. She nodded, then motioned with her hand for Joel to answer. Clearly, she was not going to let this go.

"While I was there," he began nervously, "the Keep sort of came under attack."

The princess's eyes went even wider than before. "Under attack! By who? Was it the Warlocks?"

"No, they actually got attacked too. All of the enchanter Keeps did."

Rebecca braced herself on the bench with one arm and rubbed her eyes with the other.

"It was by these evil creatures called the Hissera," Joel continued, embracing that the secret was out anyways. "I didn't see what they looked like because Jes hid me, but according to everyone else, they looked like big, nasty lizards that stood up like people."

The princess looked like she was going to faint, although Joel doubted that she would. After a moment's pause, she seemed to look for the words to a question, but they weren't coming together. Joel knew what she wanted to ask.

"Jes is okay, as far as I know. He and Dahrik went on a quest to find the source of the Hissera."

He considered telling Rebecca about the necromancer Kaynah but thought better of it. It would likely only make things worse and make Rebecca ask him a lot of questions that he wouldn't know the answers to. However, he wasn't a great liar, so he decided to go vague with his explanations.

"Where's the source? Rebecca asked, no longer looking as though she would faint but still very worried.

"Some abandoned fortress in the swamplands," Joel replied.

Rebecca's eyebrows twitched at the boy's answer. "The old prison?"

Joel shrugged. "I think so. Why, do you know it?"

"I've never been there before but I know about it," she said, looking more curious than worried now.

The sudden adjustment in her attitude didn't make much sense to Joel but he was more than happy to change the mood of the conversation.

He then asked, "What do you know about it?"

"It was built long ago, once Tyran's proudest structural achievements," Rebecca replied quickly, clearly already thinking about it.

Joel was going to ask another question, but the princess continued talking before he could. "The trolls allowed Tyran to cross the Abic of Marsh and put our most dangerous criminals in the fortress as long as they could do the same."

"That sounds a lot like Suffer," he noted.

Rebecca nodded. "It was. I suppose you could say it was the trial run for what Suffer would become, but with one exception."

Joel was on the edge of his seat.

"What's the most interesting part of all, was that for a short time, it held enchanters as prisoners and even tortured."

The boy nearly fell off the bench. "What? That doesn't make any sense."

"Well, you see, one of my ancestors, Queen Ariel Regalock, hated magic and prosecuted enchanters, regardless of what Keep they were from."

"How could she hate all enchanters?" Joel gasped. "The warlocks, sure, but all of them?"

The princess frowned. "I don't know, but my husband once said that it was her hatred of enchanters that helped the warlocks grow so large in number. Apparently, they still use her as an example."

Joel nodded then muttered to him, "So, Kaynah's making the Hissera from an old prison that used to torture enchanters for no reason. That can't be a coincidence."

"I'm sorry, who?" Rebecca snapped. "Joel, what are you not telling me?"

Realizing he had done it again, the young half-elf smacked his face into the palm of his open hand.

He cursed himself allow. "Why am I so bad at this?"

Joel looked up and saw Rebecca glaring at him expectantly.

Sighing in defeat, Joel decided that there was no use in trying to keep anything a secret.

"Do you know what a necromancer is?" he asked.

The Cost of Victory

It wasn't long before Dahrik and the rest of the company caught up to Kernil and me at the stream. I heard them coming before seeing them, as Kilt was strumming her lute in a tune I didn't recognize.

"This isn't where we left you," called the dwarf as he came into view.

Not wanting to yell, I waited for them to get closer before responding. Once the dwarf was in speaking distance, I shrugged then replied, "We ran into some trouble."

"Oh, did you?" inserted Norvic with a smirk. "What a shame. I hope the Arisites didn't prove too much for you."

I faked a smile, mounted Arrig, then replied, "Don't worry, they weren't."

"But if they did, it would be your fault!" snapped Kernil as he mounted Ioc.

"Oh good, you told him," the warlock chuckled. "I was afraid we'd be dancing around the subject the entire time."

Kilt, Howel, and Barris looked at each other in confusion. Hemm stared blankly, watching the clouds and not paying attention.

"So you know who I am?" Kernil asked Norvic, scowling at him.

Norvic coughed on a laugh, "Boy, we all know exactly who you are. Not that you've been hiding it."

Kernil's face turned a deep, fire red color. His eyes burned with anger as he griped Ioc's reins.

I looked at Norvic, whose eyes were fixed on Kernil, watching and waiting for the Son of Vain to make a move. Kernil's fingers twitched, slowing moving to a position where he could draw his blade.

"Okay, I'll ask," announced Barris loudly. "What's going on here?"

I answered. "One of Norvic's warlocks helped Nemul kill Kernil's father and start the human civil war."

The warriors gasped in unison.

Barris instinctively tensed as he too readied for an attack from Norvic. Hemm, sensing the tension in the air, clenched his right hand into a fist, intending to follow Barris' lead. Howel looked at Dalia and Kylora, who weren't at all surprised by the announcement.

Kilt plucked her lute in a dramatic and clamorous tune. *Buh, la, buh dahhhhh!* The last note hung in the air for several seconds.

This immediately cut the tension and diverted everyone's attention to the hobgoblin.

I grinned. This was the perfect first move to stop the fight between Kernil and Norvic before it even happened.

"What?" Kilt asked. "Don't look at me like that. I'm writing a new song about our quest. This twist is perfect for inspiring music. Keep going."

Norvic groaned, rolling his eyes. Kernil scowled at him again, this time now taking advantage of the distraction to draw his blade.

I locked eyes with the Son of Vain. I shook my head. He looked at me, motionless. To my elation, Kernil blinked twice, then put his weapon back in its scabbard before the warlock returned his attention to Kernil. He glared at me, and I understood what he was meaning. I promised Kernil justice, and I had to deliver it.

With a fight between Norvic and Kernil avoided, we rode north once again. Dahrik led the way with Norvic close behind. Hemm ran off to the side of everyone but kept up with apparent ease. Kilt rode with Barris this time and faced backward on the saddle behind the dwarf as she played her lute. She plucked and sung shamelessly as she attempted to write a new song. Kylora and I rode right behind her, and subject to the brunt of the Hobb's music. Behind us was Dalia followed closely by Howel. Kernil took up the rear of the party.

We kept along the road north for a while, crossing the bridge over the Neos River. The sound of the rushing water calmed my soul. I was tempted to linger there, but knew we had to keep moving.

"*Kaynah's reach crawls up your skin*," Kilt sung, then stopped abruptly.

The hobgoblin scratched her cheek, then asked to no one in specific, "Now, what's a word that rhymes with skin?"

"Spin," answered Barris almost immediately.

The Hobb stuck her tongue out and shook her head. "No, that wouldn't work very well."

"What about chin or begin?" suggested Kylora. "Maybe even twin or chagrin."

"Better, but not quite," Kilt replied, now staring off towards the west.

She began plucking the lute once more, only now in a completely different tune. Whether she intended this to be an alternative melody for the song, or a different song entirely, I had no idea.

"Those were great rhymes," the mage scoffed to herself.

Close enough to hear her complaint, I asked, "Do you know how to play a musical instrument?"

Kylora nodded proudly. "Four instruments. The cello, the flute, the harp and the Bells of Neah."

"The Bells of Neah? I've never heard of those."

"Not surprising," Kylora grinned. "The Bells of Neah are a ceremonial instrument used during the harvest. Only the city of Neah uses them, so many of my elven kin aren't even familiar with them."

"Kin!" shouted Kilt excitedly. "That's perfect!"

"You solved that one pretty fast," noted Barris with a laugh.

The hobgoblin immediately changed the melody and began singing anew. "*Kaynah's reach crawls up your skin, her creations drain the magic out. You can feel her drive in the air, to exterminate the enchanter kin.*"

"Absolutely charming," Kylora stated, her tone thick with sarcasm.

"I want this sung at my next birthday," I agreed, matching

her sarcasm.

As we continued north, the wind started to blow and clouds overhead covered the sun. The temperature started to drop. The clouds above didn't look like they would rain on us, but far to the west was a dark and nasty-looking storm and we were headed straight for it.

The sudden change in weather seemed to put everyone at unease, even Norvic. This storm had clouds as black as coal that surged with a purple-colored lightning. I had never seen purple lightning before, but the reasoning was obvious. The storm was a creation of Kaynah.

After we had ridden a dozen or so miles north of the Neos, Dahrik signaled us to a halt. Everyone formed a circle, then Dahrik spoke.

"Unfortunately, our destination is right into that storm," he declared, pointing to it. "To shorten our travel, we should get off the road now and cut across the valley due west. We'll meet up with the road again near the Ruins of Vahr. It won't be long to Shale from there."

"Shale? Why in Jard's name would we go to Shale?" snapped Norvic. "The necromancer's in the old fortress. The quickest road there is west of Tyran City through Bordon and Sh'rack."

"That's exactly where she wants us to go," Dahrik shouted back. "Can't you see? It's the obvious route to take. That road will likely be crawling with Hissera and who knows what

183

other nightmare creations."

I wasn't sure what the dwarf was getting at, but his conviction was clear. I looked west to the necromancer's storm. It was still far away, but oddly enough it didn't look like it was moving, just hovering directly west of us. I shivered. The wind was starting to pick up, and the air was turning bitter.

"Just because it's the clear road to take, doesn't make it unwise," interjected Kylora.

"No," the old dwarf protested. "If we go through Shale, we could take her by surprise. I'm telling you, Shale is where-"

Norvic cut him off. "There's a storm sitting right on top of Shale!"

As the warlock said this, an idea clicked in my mind. I sat upright, sure of myself.

"Exactly!" I replied. "Think about it, Kaynah is in the Abandoned Fortress, so why isn't the storm coming from that direction? If she wanted us to ride right into it, it should be cutting northeast, but instead is sitting right on top of Shale. Why is that?"

It was Barris who answered. "Because there's something there she doesn't want us to see."

"Exactly," Dahrik and I replied in unison.

"But what is it?" called Howel.

I looked west again and thought. I felt the pieces coming together like a puzzle, but couldn't quite see the whole picture yet. Luckily, Dahrik was ahead of me and had an answer to the question.

"Shale."

Kilt scoffed. "There's not much left in Shale. The whole prairie was plagued a few years ago, and now it's a ghost town."

"Kaynah of Shale," Dalia muttered. She then said it again for everyone to hear. "She from Shale, so she's probably hiding something there about her past."

"That's a good point," I replied, still gazing west.

Howel turned to Dalia, but spoke loud enough for everyone to hear his question. "Do we know *anything* about her past?"

Dalia shook her head, opening her mouth to say something, but Dahrik answered before she could.

"No, we don't, and she wants to keep it that way. I'll bet everything that Shale holds the secret to Kaynah's origin. It's likely where she met her patron that taught her to corrupt the Joining ritual and even create the Hissera."

"But we know that happened already," lashed Norvic. "It's

not worth the trouble of facing that storm."

"But we don't know what or who the patron is," I defended. "Shale could be the key to finding out, which could be the key in finding a weakness. That weakness could be the difference between victory and defeat."

The warlock groaned in frustration. "But at what cost? If you're wrong, we will have traveled through a barren prairie, through a mystic storm, and then will still have to trek through the harshest parts of the marshlands for no reason. The road through Bordon and Sh'rack holds more guarantees."

"But we won't know for sure unless we go," added Kernil, a defiant smile on his face.

Norvic glared at the Son of Vain, who glared right back at him. There was a moment of silence, no one else making eye contact with each other. I thought about what Norvic had said, and as much as hated to admit it, he was right. Going to Shale was the more difficult route, not just because of the storm.

"The Prodigy should be the one to decide," Kylora stated. "He is, after all, the one who must kill the necromancer. If he believes going west from here to Shale is worth the risk, then we should do it."

I froze, I was supposed to *kill* Kaynah? My mouth hung open for several seconds as I tried to come up with a response.

Norvic laughed. "What's the matter, Prodigy? Surprised to hear that you'll be getting your hands dirty?"

"Hold on," I said finally, ignoring Norvic. "I'm supposed to kill her? When was this decided?"

No one answered. I turned to Dahrik, expecting an answer, but he just shrugged at me.

"You're the Prodigy, boy. Who else would it be?"

Once again, I was speechless. I looked around, and everyone seemed to have thought about this except me. Dalia and Kylora looked at me with pity. Norvic was smiling, far too amused by the situation. Dahrik gave me a look that said, "I thought you knew." Even the Lute Brutes seemed to have just assumed it would be me who would take on Kaynah.

I said nothing for a few minutes. I looked again at the storm and worried that I wouldn't be enough to stop the necromancer alone. In fact, I knew I wouldn't be enough. I knew this because of the same reason Kernil thought me weak in our fight against the Arisite guards. I can't kill people. I couldn't kill Kaynah of Shale.

"Well, Prodigy," began Norvic out of impatience. "Which way do you choose?"

"West," I answered emotionlessly. "We make for Shale."

Dahrik raised his scepter high. "Well, you heard him. We ride west!"

We broke the circle and rode west into the building wind. The horizon crackled with purple lightning and booming thunder.

* * *

Kaynah reached deep inside herself as the clouds churned above her. This storm would cost her, but she feared the alternative. By scrying on the Prodigy's company, she overheard them deciding to move west towards Shale. Her plan had nearly worked, but ultimately backfired. She conjured the storm as nothing more of a deterrent, appearing stronger than it actually was. All, of course, in the hope of guiding the company to go along the obvious route. In a major oversight on her part, the presence of the storm had only encouraged the Prodigy and the dwarf enchanter.

Now, her hands were tied. She had to put some actual power into the storm. Kaynah's form stood in what used to be the center of Shale. The necromancer thrusted her hands towards the sky, purple lightning shooting out of her fingertips and into the clouds. A deafening thunder exploded as the sky surged with energy. The howling winds grew fiercer, knocking over dead trees and hurling mid-sized rocks. Had Kaynah actually been present in her old home, she would have been in danger, but luckily for her, she was merely an astral projection.

Astral projection was costly magic that allowed the user to separate the spirit from the body. Her body would remain in place, while her spirit could travel great distances at remarkable speeds. She could still cast magic while in her astral form, but the drain on the self would be doubled. The spirit couldn't be harmed, but the same could not be said for her departed body. Without a spirit, her body would be left extremely vulnerable. Astral projection is best used in short bursts, if at all, as the longer the spirit is outside the body, the weaker it becomes.

Projecting your spirit out of your body is difficult and risky magic for sure, but worth it in Kaynah's eyes. The cowardly enchanters frowned upon its use, claiming it to be too dangerous. She laughed, gazing with pride at the city of Shale enveloped in the storm she had created.

Satisfied with her creation, the spirit of Kaynah departed from Shale, soaring northward through the sky as fast as light itself. The land underneath her flashed a blinding white as the necromancer's spirit moved. Within seconds, she was back in her fortress, reunited with her body once more.

She was on the cold stone of the dungeon, tense and weak from her use of magic. Kaynah's skin felt hot as the toll of the astral projection burned and mutated her flesh. She felt it most in the legs this time, everything below her knees scorched and blistering intensely. Her muscles felt heavy and ached when she tried to move.

She cursed.

"It wasn't supposed to be this difficult," she cried, speaking to nobody.

The necromancer tried sitting up, but nearly passed out from the effort. The astral projection, along with molding the most recent batch of Hissera, had nearly killed her.

"They should be dead already," Kaynah muttered, thinking about the company. "My Hissera were supposed to have killed them all. At least they would have if those barbarians wouldn't have intervened."

She spat out some blood that was trickling into her mouth. Kaynah groaned as she fought through the pain and sat up. The room seemed to spin for several seconds, which made her so busy that she nearly vomited.

Kaynah cursed herself.

"Weak!" she shouted to herself, slapping her own face.

With the additional power Kaynah had gained from all of the enchanters her Hissera had killed, she thought it was ridiculous to feel so drained and in pain.

"You're the most powerful being in Cray, act like it," she instructed. "This is merely the cost of victory."

As it was, Kaynah was very confident in her abilities. In only a short time, she had made progress far beyond what even her patron had expected. She had transformed the Hissera of old and given them added strengths. Now the Hissera used the Joining Ritual from within and fed her their raw magical power. She outmatched the previous necromancers. Her powers grew with each successful Hissera attack. She had her growing army and became more powerful with each life stolen by her pets. She was a genius.

Yet despite all of her talent, ingenuity, and power, there was one enchanter that scared her. Who, unfortunately for her, was currently traveling straight for her. Out of all the enchanters still alive, she knew that only one mattered. The necromancer would do her best to kill *him* before *he* arrived. Deep down, she knew that the only way to ensure that all of the magic in Cray would be hers, was through a head-on confrontation.

The necromancer smiled, then started laughing uncontrollably.

"I'll be ready for you," she vowed, clutching her scepter tight. "Even if you make it here alive, I'll have the largest host of nightmares you could ever imagine waiting for you."

Bracing herself with her scepter, Kaynah stood up, ignoring the pain in her legs. Slowly, she walked out of the dungeon to where she had set up her main study and went up the stairs to the main room. It was here that her latest batch of Hissera rested in their egg sacks, ready to be hatched.

Kaynah wiped her finger along the rim of one of the earwax-colored pods. A film of yellow-brown slime stuck to her fingertip. After licking her finger clean, she nodded, pleased with the result. They were ready.

She reached into her cloak where a secret pocket held an amulet wrapped in a velvet cloth. Unwrapping the cloth, she admired the circular brass charm that fit perfectly in her hand. The amulet was old, having been buried for several hundred years when she found it. She traced the emblem of a tree that was engraved on its face. Then, Kaynah put its steel chain around her neck and felt the rush of power that it always gave her.

With a single snap of her fingers, the Hissera egg pods cracked open. They spilled a sweet-smelling goo along the floor. Each of the newly born Hissera stood from a crouched position and turned to face the necromancer. With nothing more than a thought, the Hissera obeyed her command, marching out of the fortress and to the southeast.

"That will be the last batch I send for a while," she said, walking back towards the dungeon. "I must prepare for my guests' arrival."

* * *

The further we went west, the harder the wind blew. We made little progress the rest of the day. The slowdown made us consider traveling through the night, but we ultimately decided against it. The weather made it difficult to travel, but after two days, we made it back onto the road, just south of Bordon.

"We still have a chance to go north," Norvic said, looking at the stationary storm.

Dahrik shook his head. "The decision has been made. We keep moving west."

By the end of the day, we left the Valley of the Glorious and crossed into what had recently become known as the Forsaken Prairie. Even in the low light of the stormy night sky, there was a notable difference. The Valley of the Glorious was mostly grasslands and farms, but the prairie was barren and lifeless, even at its edge. The line that separated the two regions was noticeably visible, changing almost instantly.

"This didn't occur naturally, something evil did this. Something with magic," Dalia announced as we made camp at the prairie's eastern edge, her voice barely audible over the fierce winds.

"Was it Kaynah?" asked Howel, surveying the ground cautiously.

The druid shrugged. "Possibly. It could also have been her patron."

"Will we have to fight Kaynah's patron too after Jes kills her?" he asked, addressing the whole company.

Norvic chuckled. "That likely depends on how the whole thing ends."

"Or what kind of being the patron is," Dahrik added. "Of the four previous necromancers, only two of the patrons showed any sign of aggression once the necromancer was dead."

"So it could go either way," Kernil noted.

That night, it was difficult to sleep. The wind was cold and blew ferociously throughout the night. Thunder boomed every couple of minutes, which echoed throughout the prairie. Sleep evaded me most of the night, as it did for all except Norvic and Hemm. I stared up at the heavens, which was a sea of black as the thick nimbus clouds hid the stars from view.

I tried not to think about Kaynah and everyone's expectation for me to kill her when we reached the Abandoned Fortress, but my mind kept circling back to it.

"There just has to be another way," I thought, pondering on my options.

There weren't many that I could think of, at least that I thought had a chance of success. I could trap her, but that seemed unlikely. Or I could convince her patron to take her power away from her, but I wasn't even sure that was possible.

About halfway through the night, my thoughts turned to my wife and children. If the entire trek kept taking as long it had, it would be months before I could return home. With Rebecca as far along in her pregnancy as she was, it was a horrible possibility that I could miss the birth of my third child. I shuttered at the thought.

Then there were my sons. I had never been gone for this long before, at least not in my sons' lifetimes. I wondered how Rebecca or Alexandra would explain my absence. Then again, my second born, Samuel, likely wasn't old enough to even realize I wasn't there. His older brother, Elias, however, would notice. He was very observant for his age, not quite as vocally curious as Joel had been, but observant nonetheless.

I smiled as an image of my son came into my mind. Elias was not only observant, but rebellious too. Chamish often remarked that Elias reminds him of Rebecca's rebellious nature that was present all throughout her youth. "A fitting revenge by Jard," as the king would always say.

I thought again about my unborn child. I wondered if the child would be a boy or a girl. Of course, we had already chosen a name for either option. Augustan, if it was a boy, after my father, or Isabellana, if it was a girl, after Rebecca's mother. This brought my thoughts back around to Kaynah. If I failed in killing the necromancer, if I died on this quest, then my children would grow up without really knowing me. The thought was paralyzing. I silently made a vow, that no matter what, I would not let that happen, regardless of any duty or responsibility as the Prodigy.

I got up and took over the night's watch from Barris, who was more than pleased to let me do it. I spent the rest of the night staring into the storm, the purple lightning flickering ominously, taunting me.

The following morning we moved into the Forsaken Prairie,

which is when the rain started. It came all at once, drenching us. Unlike last time, we had properly protected our food so as not to be damaged by the rain. Above us, electricity surged, which made the metal-clad warriors nervous.

The wind was blowing more fiercely than ever before. Arrig and the horses struggled to move forward, each step taking several seconds and a considerable amount of effort. After what felt like hours and little progress, Dahrik raised his hand, calling everyone to a halt.

He shouted something, but it was nearly impossible to hear him over the fury of the wind. The dwarf tried again, now shouting, but the result was the same. Dahrik's face went pink in clear frustration. He yanked his scepter from the holster on his horse's saddle and held it forth, facing into the wind. The orange gems on his iron scepter flashed, but nothing seemed to happen. The old dwarf's face flushed beat red.

He tried to dismount, but the fierce winds caused him to topple off the horse and fall onto his face. Dahrik pounded the ground with his fist, his cursing, and inaudible obscenities. He picked himself up and thrusted his scepter forward. Once again, the gems at each end flashed and it seemed for an instant that the winds seemed to slow, but quickly picked up again.

The dwarf tried a handful more times, each ending the same. Clearly, Dahrik wasn't in the right state of mind anymore to solve the problem, so I started brainstorming. If we couldn't hear because of the wind and we couldn't get the wind to slow, perhaps the best way to communicate was by writing.

I cautiously dismounted from Arrig, almost getting pushed to the ground by the winds in the process, then unlatched my scepter. I pushed through the wind towards Dahrik, each step requiring great effort. When I had reached my former master, he didn't notice me. The furious dwarf was steaming with rage as he fought against the oncoming storm.

I nodded, knowing what to do next. Raising my scepter high, I swung it down onto the top of Dahrik's skull. He instantly froze. I grabbed him by the shoulder and turned him to face me. His face was still very red, but it was clear that he was calming down.

Patting him on the shoulder, I laughed, although it too was unheard by even me. Per our agreement, I was to hit him on the head as hard as I could if he ever lost control of his temper and as always, he quickly regained control of himself quickly after.

I held up a finger, signaling him to watch me. Waving my scepter to the side of us, where all of the company could see, letters and words formed, etching deep enough into the ground so not to be blown away.

"*I don't think we can ride in this weather. What should we do?*"

Dahrik and the other three enchanters nodded, then drew their scepters.

Kylora waved her scepter. My message disappeared and a new text took its place. *"We should take shelter and wait it out."*

Norvic shook his and wave his arms in a cross formation, then, with his scepter wrote, *"this storm hasn't moved in days. There is no waiting it out. We will starve."*

He had a point. This storm was clearly meant to be stationary. I turn away from the company and looking in the west. The land before me was lifeless, muddy, and torn apart by the tempest. I raised my scepter above my head, gripping it tightly so the winds wouldn't cause me to lose it.

Dahrik had tried to quell the storm, disperse it. I was trying something a bit differently. I was studying it, reaching out with my magic to find its potential, its beginning, and its surprises. What immediately clear was that we were in the weakest part of Kaynah's storm. The eye swirled many miles away, which I guess to be over Shale.

I smiled as I found what I was looking for. The anchor. The Necromancer had tied the eye of the storm to a specific point, causing it not to move. As far as I could tell, the anchor was connected to stone about a foot long and a few inched wide. I was fairly certain it was something rectangular and was surrounded by other stones similar to it, like a brink. It felt earthy, so it wasn't exactly a brink but more likely part of a stone-paved road.

My focus shifted to the storm again. Electricity churned throughout the entirety of the clouds. It didn't feel natural, which explained the deep purple color. Most alarmingly, the hair on my arms stiffened, and the air suddenly tasted metallic. I knew what this meant. Lightning was about to strike, and it wouldn't be survivable, like an enchanter's lightning, if it struck someone.

I turned around and scanned the company. None of the enchanters carry very much metal, except Dahrik, whose scepter was almost entirely iron. Kernil and Kilt had metal weapons, but leather armor. Barris and Howel had the most metal, due to their chainmail armor, which made them likely victims. Then there was Hemm. He had steel greaves that covered his tree-trunk-like legs but otherwise had no other metal. Since coming to a stop, the already large troll had climbed up on a bolder on the side of the road, putting him several feet above the rest of the company.

I knew I didn't have much time to decide, save the dwarves or the troll. If I guessed incorrectly, someone could end up dead. There was a buzzing sound in the air and I knew my time was up. I leaped high into the air, landing next to Hemm on the bolder. I jabbed my scepter as high above me as I could, which just barely surpassed the troll's head. Just then, a huge bolt of lightning surged down from the sky and struck the scepter. The lightning impacted the green gem at the end of my staff with such force, that I nearly dropped it. There was a flash of light and wave of heat that forced me to look away, Hemm fell backward to the ground. Just as the light receded, booming thunder cracked deafeningly.

I kept my eyes closed for several seconds after it was all

over, my body tense and filled with adrenalin. When I finally decided to open them, I first notice that the entirety of my scepter was smoking, the gem at the topside end blackened. I pulled the scepter in close, then touched the gem, hoping the scorched color would just rub off. My finger was immediately singed by a blistering heat on the gem's surface. I instinctively put the burnt fingertip in my mouth to cool it down.

Next to me, the troll got to his knees. What little hair on his round head that he had was now gone, the smell of burnt hair palpable in the air. Our eyes met and I saw a combination of fear and gratitude in his gaze.

"You have saved my life," he said in a low tone.

I was taken aback by the sound of his voice. Until now, he hadn't said anything to anyone. I hadn't assumed he was mute but rather that he struggled to speak Cray's common tongue. Hemm's voice was deep and guttural but sounded aged and even wise somehow.

I nodded in response. "I did."

"I owe you a debt," Hemm said, still crouched on the ground. "I will repay it, you have my word."

I didn't know what to say. I knew enough about the troll culture to know that I shouldn't refuse. Trolls took debts and favors very seriously. Yet, I wasn't sure what his repayment would look like. Would I even want it?

I extended my hand and we shook. Hemm nodded, then stood up and brushed the dirt off his arms legs. I pulled up my sleeve and rubbed the scorched scepter gem. Luckily, the soot came off easily, leaving the scepter just as nice as it had been before.

"You two alright up there?" Dahrik called.

I turned and faced the company, all of whom were looking up at Hemm and me. I gave a thumbs up and held it high enough that everyone could see.

In another enhanced jump, I was next to Arrig a few seconds later. The noble's horse hadn't been spooked by any of it. I patted Arrig on the neck before mounting.

"That was a brave thing you did, Prodigy," said Dalia.

"It was amazing," added Howel.

It was then that I noticed I could hear each of them speak. Since the lightning, the wind had calmed just enough for us to hear one another.

"We have to get this storm moving," I announced, pointing to the sky. "Then, we'll take shelter as it passes."

"And just how do you suppose to do that?" Norvic replied, not hiding his mockery. "Dahrik tried and failed with nothing to show for it. I doubt even you could do it."

Thunder boomed above us once again, which made Hemm

flinch. I stared up at the sky and realized Norvic was right.

"That's why it won't just be me to try it," I answered finally. "The five of us must to it together."

I looked over at Dahrik, who smiled and nodded.

"That could work," Kylora added. "The necromancer's spell is meant to be stronger than each of us on our own, but not likely all of us together."

"Exactly," I replied.

Norvic rolled his eyes and groaned softly. "Very well, Prodigy. We'll try it together, but what then? Once the storm starts moving, we'll be in even greater danger than we are now."

Again, Norvic was right. I thought about our options for a moment. The best one that came to mind was creating a cave underneath the ground's surface, but with a storm of this ferocity, it would likely be very unstable.

"What about those ruins?" called Barris, pointing to the southwest as he stood on his horse's back and looked through a spyglass.

"Ruins?" asked Kernil. "Since when does Cray have ruins?"

It was Dalia who answered. "The Ruins of Vahr, yes, of course. They should be just over that way. They're the only ruins in Cray, as far as I know."

"They're as good of a shelter as we'll get out this way," Dahrik added. "Now, let's hurry. The wind is picking up again and I would like to be out of this thing before the rain gets any worse."

Barris sat back down on his saddle while the four enchanters and I formed a circle. Each of us held our scepter high, then tipped them to the point where they met. The sunset orange, blood red, forest green, sky blue, and snow-white gems on our scepters glowed brightly. I could immediately feel a rush of energy flowing through us as our magics united. As one, we released the magic into the sky, which at a distance looked like a rainbow. The colorful blast impacted against the dark clouds and was immediately lost.

For a moment, I thought our effort had failed, but then I noticed that the clouds above were inching east ever so slightly. Then the wind blew fiercer than before, nearly knocking each one of us off our horses. The rain poured from the sky, the droplets bigger than I had ever seen them.

Our spell had worked. The storm was now moving east. Without having to say a word, we charged our horses forward and made for the Ruins of Vahr. The wind and the rain made moving difficult, but we reached the ruins before any more lightning.

The Ruins of Vahr were made from a rust-colored stone that was cut into near-perfect cubes and stacked on top of each other with great precision. There were three structures, all near one another. The structures on the eastern and western sides only had a few walls and archways standing, most of their former buildings long since withered away. Curiously enough, the center building, which was the largest and the most intact, had significantly less damage. Aside from a few holes and cracks on the domed ceiling and the north-facing wall, the stone temple was nearly perfect on the outside.

We approached an archway on the northern face of the large structure. The relief from the wind was instant as a wall from the western building shielded us from it as we entered the main temple. Carved along the sides of the door-less entrance was a message in ancient elvish. As an enchanter, I had studied all the ancient languages and could read the carved words.

I spoke the words as I read them, "The point where the wall between worlds is the weakest lies here. Enter ye who seek the eternity."

"What do you think that's supposed to mean?" asked Kernil.

"Doesn't matter," Dahrik replied, walking past us and into the ruins. "We're here for shelter, not the eternity."

I looked back at Kernil and shrugged, then dismounted Arrig and followed Dahrik through the entrance.

The ruined interior was almost empty, except for a stone altar that was made from granite. It was all one large room, with withered and cracked pillars holding up the high ceiling.

"Not exactly the most sturdy piece of work, is it?" noted Barris, tapping at a fallen pillar with his boot.

"It'll be enough for what we need," said Dahrik, checking behind every pillar and corner for dangers.

Norvic laughed, his sarcasm and irritation obvious. "Well, I certainly hope so, because if not, the whole quest will have been for nothing."

I tried to ignore the warlock and inspected the ceiling. It had large cracks that were leaking into the interior, but those could easily be patched with a simple spell. Most concernedly, there was a sizable piece of ceiling missing near the northwest corner. I jogged towards it and stopped the hole just as the wind sprayed me with rainwater. The floor looked like it was made of the same red sandstone, and there was a small pool of water just underneath the opening that had formed from years of erosion. Water poured onto the ground from the outside as the rain grew heavier and faster.

"This is gonna be a problem unless we do something about it," said Dahrik, coming up behind me.

I nodded. "What do you suggest? My first thought was to patch it up with all the rubble on the ground but now that I'm really looking at this ceiling I don't think that such a good idea anymore."

"Agreed, patching it could cause the whole thing to crack further and even become unstable," said the dwarf, pointing with his scepter to the hole and large cracks that spread from it.

The two of us stared at the hole for several seconds. I considered turning the pool of water into permafrost, likely freezing any of the rain to come through the hole. I discarded the idea, however. Next, I thought about creating an invisible shield on the hole that could block the rain without irritating the cracks. It would work, but there was a catch. The shield would need a consistent supply of energy and concentration, otherwise, it would dissolve.

"Wait a minute," I thought out loud. "It's so simple. We just put a cover on it."

Dahrik looked at me, unsure of what I meant. I surveyed my surrounding once again, ignoring the dwarf's confusion and letting my mind work out the idea. I found four stones all about the same size, just smaller than the palm of my hand.

I shoved the stones into Dahrik's hands. "Hold these."

I put my scepter on the ground next to me, then untied my sorcerer's cloak. I gave the cloak a few shakes in an attempt to expel some of the rainwater on it. After I had shaken away enough of the droplets I closed my eyes and imagined what I wanted to happen next. I pictured my cloak stretching, growing larger. I then thought of the hole and its approximate size. The imagined my cloak growing larger than the hole, both lengthwise and widthwise. I felt the drain of energy that the spell had on my body and opened my eyes.

I nodded with satisfaction as I held in my hands an enormous cloak, large enough to cover the hole in the ceiling.

"Excellent thinking, boy," Dahrik stated proudly while taking a step back.

I picked up my scepter and with a flick of my wrist, the enlarged cloak levitated through the hole, then spread it out, covering it. Dahrik now understood and tapped each one of the four stones which then levitated to the ceiling. The stones spread out and stuck to the interior of the ceiling, the cloak on the anterior was now locked in place.

"That should do," I said, turning back towards the rest of the company.

We all gathered in the center of the ruin, circling around a fuel-less fire that Norvic had conjured. The horses stood nearby in a makeshift stall that Kylora had constructed from the rubble. While Dahrik and I repaired the roof, the warriors had made themselves comfortable. They lounged near the fire, completely stripped out of their weapons and heavy armor. Kilt was leaning against Hemm's leg while tuning her lute.

I took my bedroll from Arrig and laid it within the circle between Dahrik and Hemm.

"How long is this storm gonna take to pass?" Barris asked the group, the spyglass still in his hands

Dalia answered. "It felt very large, I'd suspect a few days at the speed it's moving."

The warriors looked at each other, confused.

"That long?" replied Barris.

"At least," said Norvic, looking out the doorway. "Probably a week."

There was a moment of silence as we all took in the reality of the situation. Trapped in these ruins for a week, while a deadly storm raged outside, wasn't the most comforting of thoughts.

Dahrik clapped his hands together. "We may as well get comfortable then. This temple is our home for the next while."

"Temple?" asked Kernil.

"Yes," Dahrik answered. "This used to be a temple long ago. You can tell by that altar over there."

He pointed to the narrow, stone table made of granite just a few yards away in the center of the ruin. There was a hum of recognition from the five warriors.

"So, if that's an altar," Howel began, "and this is an ancient temple, who built it and who or what did they worship?"

"No one knows," interjected Norvic. "Because it was hidden

for centuries. Until Jard found it."

Even I didn't know that last part but Dahrik didn't react, so I assumed this was true. I didn't want to seem like the least informed of the enchanters, so I kept my mouth shut. Besides, the warriors were clearly shocked by the mention of Jard, so I knew there would be a follow-up question.

It was Barris who asked it. "Jard? As in, Jard of the Grove?"

"Obviously," Norvic answered with no small amount of condescension. "Before becoming the guardian of death and destiny, he was a mortal and the first enchanter. In life, he discovered this temple which had been hidden by some ancient magic."

"Or so the legend goes," Dahrik added.

Norvic rolled his eyes. "Yes, yes, so the story goes."

After that everyone was ready for sleep, which came easily to me. Dahrik took the first watch of the night and even ended up blocking the doorway with his own enlarged cloak. The next few days the storm raged on, moving slowly to the southeast. The first day everyone spent drying their clothes, sharpening their weapons, and relaxing. On the second day, most of us passed the time by playing cards or rolling dice.

On the third day, everyone was getting restless. The warriors showed off various talents they had with their weapons. Barris could march while balancing his hammer atop his head and Kilt could juggle her axes and lute. Howell could hit a target by only using a small mirror to aim. Although, Kernil had the most impressive display. He was accurately throwing his long knife at a fair distance.

Soon after showing off, the warriors sparred one another. Kilt and Kernil were almost evenly matched, eventually being deemed a draw. Barris held his own fairly well against Hemm. He used the troll's slow movement to his advantage, which served him well enough to get a good hit in. Yet, as expected, Hemm eventually caught him and won the match easily. Howel, who was most skilled with a ranged weapon, didn't duel against the others but rather had me throw rocks at him while he would hit them in the air using a slingshot.

The sparring was so entertaining to watch that on the fourth day, the enchanters decided to duel. Dahrik and Kylora went first, but it was over quickly. Dahrik's specialty is combat magic but in the closed and structurally weak temple, the dwarf held back which caused him to lose. Norvic chose not to participate, electing to meditate away from everyone the majority of the week. I was actually relieved, knowing that if he were to duel, he'd likely demand me as his opponent. This meant that Dalia sparred each other and I must admit, I had fun. It had been a while since I had dueled anyone but I caught up quickly.

A few minutes into the duel, I overheard Howel betting the other warriors that I would lose. Barris, Kilt, and Hemm bet on my victory, but Kernil abstained from the wager, claiming that he wasn't sure who he was more confident in. I tried not to let this distract me, but the druid managed to graze me on the shoulder with a fireball as the betting was going on. To her credit, Dalia was relentless and a very skilled fighter. Our duel lasted much longer than Dahrik and Kylora's, but I managed to pull off the victory. Each of the warriors, except Howel, was pleased.

That night there was an exhausted silence from everyone in the company as we gathered around the fire. Outside, the storm raged ever onward. After our evening meal, the Hobb stood up and strummed the chords of her lute, which made a powerful, *Buuuh Daaaaah* in the ruined temple.

She cleared her throat. "I'd like to dedicate this song to all of you. You might have heard pieces of it because I've written this as we've traveled but here is the finished product. May we all survive this quest."

> *It began by the Hissera's claw,*
> *they're just around the bend.*
> *She's nothing you've ever seen before.*
> *The necromancer's draw.*
>
> *Kaynah's reach crawls up your skin,*
> *her creations drain all magic out.*
> *You can feel her drive in the air,*
> *to exterminate the enchanter kin.*
>
> *Stalking in packs by night,*
> *there's nowhere you can run or hide.*
> *Magic's bane has arrived,*

to extinguish Cray's entire light.

She's stands in her fortress, a prison of old,
The Prodigy's foil throws the gauntlet down.
Keeps unite to end Kaynah's claim,
before the hissing death leaves their bodies' cold.

For the good of Cray, the Prodigy must overawe,
as blades and scepters join the cause.
If they fail the land is doomed,
to the necromancer's draw.

"Please tell me we're not going to have to suffer your playing this whole time," pleaded Norvic, rubbing his eyes with his thumbs.

Kilt scowled at the warlock, then sat back down, strumming quietly the song's tune.

I thought the song was bittersweet. It sounded nice, and Kilt was a good singer, however, the message reminded me that everyone was depending on me to kill the necromancer. A wave of emotions hit me all at once. I stood, trying to act as though nothing was bothering me.

"I need some air," I said to nobody in particular, but casual enough that my sudden departure didn't seem odd.

I walked to the doorway that Dahrik had closed off with his enlarged cloak, ducked underneath the fabric, and out to the raging wind and rain. I was assaulted with a blast of cold air, followed by a steady spray of rainwater, which without my cloak, soaked through my clothes. The only light was the occasional purple surges of lightning off in the distance.

Cold and miserable, I looked up at the sky and silently cursed Kaynah of Shale. After a moment or two, just as I was about to go back inside, Dahrik exited the ruins and stood next to me. He and I stood silently together, soaking wet and staring off into the dark evening darkness. I felt that I should say something, sensing that the dwarf was waiting for me to speak first but couldn't find the words.

Dahrik spoke, his voice soft but concerned. "Are you all right?"

I shrugged. "I don't know what I am right now. Confused is probably the best way to put it."

"I assume this is about killing Kaynah," he stated, clearing his throat.

"Yes," I replied, still staring up at the dark clouds. "I want to do it, but I know I have to. Every enchanter in Cray is depending on me, but I don't think I have the strength to do it. Even if I could defeat Kaynah, I know I won't be able to bring myself to kill her."

Dahrik cleared his throat again. "Do you remember the night I told you that you were an enchanter?"

I looked at him and nodded.

"It was raining, just like it is now," he motioned around us. "That day, I offered you a better life, one where you would have to fight a war or take a life if you were smart enough not to."

"I remember."

My former master put his hand on my shoulder and we locked eyes. "I meant what I said then, I want you to know that. You were called for something higher than anyone could have ever imagined, being Jard's Prodigy. If I could take that responsibility from you, I would but I cannot."

I patted his hand, then took a few steps back and stared back into the darkness. "I know and I would never ask you to."

"What I mean to say is that once you became the Prodigy, that promise that I made you was null," Dahrik began. "Jard chose you to rid Cray of its worst evils. You got lucky the first time around that it was a monster and not a person."

I was aghast. "Lucky? I nearly died about six times over! I nearly had my soul ripped out me!"

"But your conscience is clear, isn't it?" the dwarf challenged.

I said nothing, but he was right, my conscience was clear.

He nodded. "That's what I thought. As I said, you were lucky last time. You didn't have to think about the morality of your responsibility, you just had a monster to destroy."

Dahrik was right. When battling the Vios Almna, I wasn't worried about whether I could or I should destroy it. I just did it, no second-guessing. Was I overthinking this?

"The cost of victory is different this time. You can do this, I know you can. Jard wouldn't have picked you as his Prodigy if you couldn't handle the challenges," Dahrik added.

I grinned. "Thanks, Dahrik. You know, when Jard had me in the Grove, I think he said something similar."

"Did he? Well, then listen to me. I know what I'm talking about."

I punched him in the arm, which he returned with much harder force.

"Come on, let's get back inside," he said, waving me towards the doorway. "I'm wet enough."

I crouched down, lifted the cloak, and stepped back into the temple. As I did so, I noticed Kernil walking away from the doorway very quickly. Dahrik followed me back inside and even he noticed Kernil walking away.

"Was he listening in on us just now?"

I shrugged. "Maybe, but why would he?"

"How should I know?" said the dwarf, walking back to the campfire.

Kernil and I hadn't spoken much since Vain. He was fixated on my hesitation with killing. To be fair, it seemed like everyone was these days. Maybe that's why he had eavesdropped on mine and Dahrik's conversation. I wondered just how much of it he had heard.

Damaged and Forsaken

Kaynah spat on the ground in anger and disgust. She slammed her fist on the floor, the stone tiles cracking under strike.

"Curse them, curse them all!" she roared in fury.

Her left arm burned and hissed from the necromancer's latest attempt at scrying. She cursed herself. Yet again, her efforts to stop the company had failed. Kaynah had hoped the storm would thin the company out, though it proved only to stop them in their tracks. Her latest batch of Hissera were also unable to continue in the storm. They now had to retreat back to the fortress because of the storm's inherent volatility. Like the company hiding away in the ruins of Vahr, her Hissera were stuck, waiting for the storm to pass.

The necromancer punched the tiled ground again, the cracks doubled and grew.

"Curse that Prodigy!" she yelled to no one but herself. "They ruined my eternal storm!"

Breathing heavily, she then started to laugh. Perhaps this was a good thing after all. Now that the storm was moving, her children were free to follow behind it. The enchanter scum had to wait for the storm to pass by them and her creations could have a head start.

Enjoying the prospect of her advantage, she considered the troll. The bolt of lightning had nearly destroyed it and the idea of the warriors dead thrilled her. Kaynah's emotions swelled but, her joy was short-lived. The Prodigy's actions had saved the giant savage from certain death. She realized now how to stop the company. She first had to kill the warriors. Without them, the enchanters and her greatest enemy would be easy prey for the Hissera.

"I must kill those warriors," she said to herself, getting off of the ground and pacing around the room.

Those warriors had enchanters to protect them, just as they protected the enchanters. She couldn't call on the Hissera to kill the enchanters without first killing the warriors, and the enchanters were protecting the warriors from everything but the Hissera. It was a puzzle that seemed to be unsolvable. The Prodigy's scheme in bringing them along turned out to be wiser a strategy than Kaynah ever expected.

Drained, the necromancer leaned against the dungeon wall. Her beautiful, perfect plan, ruined by a handful of magic-less, sword-swinging barbarians. Kaynah's dreams of taking all the magic in Cray for herself seemed out of reach, for now.

She sighed. "If only I could just kill them all at once."

An idea clicked in the necromancer's mind and her mood elevated. She pushed against the wall, launching herself across the chamber toward a stack of texts she used to inspire her Hissera creations. She found one of her early designs and snatched it off the ground. With inspired haste, Kaynah scuttled to her desk, frantically looking for something to draw with.

Her sore-covered fingers latched around a stick of charcoal, and she began making alterations to the old Hissera design. Carefully, she moved the charcoal along the parchment, all the while muttering calculations to herself as she brought her new idea to life. After several minutes, she stepped back from the page, studying again her design, this time from afar.

"This is it," the necromancer grinned to herself. "This is what I need. Bigger, stronger, and much more deadly, not just to magic."

Kaynah nodded to herself, her hands absently stroking her hair, ruining her tight braid. After a few minutes of admiring the new design, her eyes darted to the dungeon exit.

"Supplies," she gasped. "Do I have all the supplies?"

Without a second to waste the necromancer ran, up the stairs and out of the dungeon, to the creation room on the main floor. The ground was sticky from the recent hatching of the latest batch as well as the creation of a new batch, but Kaynah ignored the mess. She scrambled through her ingredients and found nearly everything she was looking for.

"Hmmm, I have to make some sacrifices, but it will be worth it," she cackled to no one in particular, eyeing the pods of her newest batch.

The necromancer started writing again on the sketch of her new creation. This time, calculating the toll this new creation would take on her supplies.

"I have plenty of venom," she muttered to herself, "but I'll have to be cautious with the Gila teeth. That will be tricky. I still need regular Hissera and this warrior killer beast will require testing."

She looked again at the pods growing the next set of Hissera. Kaynah sighed. There would have to be sacrifices one way or another, there was no getting around that.

The most unlikely sound interrupted her concentration. Kay-nah heard what sounded like the chirping of a bird. Fixated, she dropped the charcoal design and walked toward the main door. As she neared, Kaynah could hear it clearly and was certain it was a bird.

The large doors were locked but with a simple wave of her hand, they gently swung open. The necromancer stepped out into a courtyard, which was muggy and putrid from the swamp air. She looked to her right and saw it, a small brown and red-speckled sparrow sitting on a dead branch, singing loudly.

Kaynah stared at the creature, who seemed oblivious to her own presence. The featured beast confused her. She had spent years in this fortress and not once had she ever seen or even heard a bird of any kind. Paranoia crept in, causing her to look around frantically for intruders. She found nothing.

The sparrow kept singing, which put Kaynah at an even greater unease. Why was there a bird here? Had someone sent it, or had it flown here on its own? And of all things, why wouldn't it leave?

Unable to sit by any longer, she took a swing at the bird, but it fluttered out of the way of Kaynah's fist and landed a few feet over, singing and chirping all the while.

"Gah!" she shouted in frustration. "Go away!"

Flailing her arms wildly, she kept swinging at the little bird, but each time it evaded her, seemingly unbothered. After a minute, the necromancer had enough, calling upon her twisted magic. Her hands caught fire and with a windup, she hurled a ball of fire at the sparrow. The singing ceased as the flames exploded against the small creature, engulfing it in fire. The bird was no more.

Breathing heavily, Kaynah felt a stinging sensation on her elbows, the price of using her magic taking its toll on her body. She leaned against the outside of the door and stared at the stone-paved ground of the courtyard.

"What if this is an omen?" she cried out, speaking to no one in particular. "What if this is Jard trying to-"

She stopped abruptly, looking up at the sky. The clouds of her storm had passed and now had moved to the horizon in the southeast.

Kaynah smiled a vicious, dark smile. It didn't matter if the silly little bird was an omen or a message from Jard. She had already defied the guardian of destiny once, and she would happily do it again. Because now, she had a plan to dispose of those meddlesome warriors the Prodigy had brought with him.

She laughed to herself, even snorting with glee, as she walked back into the fortress. The necromancer cracked her finger joints and began to work.

* * *

Unlike most of the company, Howel enjoyed waiting out the storm. The dwarf finally had some uninterrupted personal time with Dalia, who seemed to have figured out that the gardenia was from him. She said nothing about it, but ever since he had tied it to her saddle horn for her to find, she had seemed to always be near him and had started countless conversations.

Howel desperately wanted to believe that Dalia had feelings for him just as he had feelings for her, but he also refused to let himself get his hopes up without solid proof. Talking to a member of a traveling company didn't equal love by any means.

The storm passed late in the evening of the seventh day. The noise that had been consistent throughout the last week was suddenly missing. Howel was the first to notice, shouting with excitement as he did. We all raced for the doorway, Dahrik using magic to shrink and remove his cloak from the roof as he arrived at the ruin's exterior.

The sun had set many hours before, making the sky dark, although that darkness was bright after a week of the storm. The moon was half full, shining brightly upon us. Dozens of stars gleamed between the remaining clouds.

"It's finally passed," Dalia sighed with relief.

Kernil smiled as he stared upward. "And tomorrow morning we'll see the sunshine again. It's about time."

"Finally, a chance to leave these accursed ruins behind," Norvic said, even he looking excited.

We stayed outside for several minutes, watching the storm move away to the east. The moonlight revived our mood and hope was now in the atmosphere. Howel didn't look to the sky however, his eyes were fixed on Dalia. Her brown hair, which was usually braided, hung in soft curls. The brunette's hair reflected the moonlight in a way that made it shine sliver. The archer's heart melted, unable to look away. To him, she looked like an angel.

After several seconds, Dalia turned her gaze toward him. Howel shifted his gaze, trying not to seem as if he was staring at her, even though had been. Sweat dripped from his forehead, and his heart raced. Had she noticed him? The druid didn't say anything and didn't move away, so Howel assumed Dalia hadn't noticed. He wiped his sweaty palms on his greaves.

Howel was trying to build the courage to look back in her direction when a jolt of sensation zapped through him. Dalia's fingers touched his own and time seemed to freeze. The world stopped as his mind processed the unexpected physical contact. The archer looked down and saw his left hand dangling at his side. He also saw Dalia's right hand, which was hanging next to his, the edges of her fingers brushing up against his own. A hundred questions barraged his mind all at once, leaving him in a confused haze. The only thing he knew for certain, was that he was not going to move his hand.

It was unclear to him how much time passed. Each second blurred into the next and Howel wasn't any closer to sorting out his thoughts. Another jolt went through his body as Dalia grabbed his hand and interlocked his hand with her own. Her palms were soft to the touch.

She leaned in and whispered in his ear, "You don't have to be so timid."

Howel looked into her eyes, which seemed greener than ever before in the moonlight. He smiled and nodded, causing her to smile back.

"It's a new sensation," he whispered back. "We rascal adventurer types are rather bold."

"Oh, is that what you call yourself? A rascal adventurer?" Dalia laughed.

After a moment, most everyone walked back inside the shelter. Barris and Kilt grinned widely at Howel. It looked as though Barris was going to say something, but as he leaned in Howel pleaded with his eyes. Barris seemed to get the message and leaned back out before saying anything. Without another look, he and Kilt went inside, leaving Dalia and Howel alone.

They smiled at each other, then gazed once again into the night sky.

* * *

The storm finally passed and the sun was shining once again. I gazed over the prairie landscape in front of me and was saddened. Before the storm, the land had been barren, dry, and lifeless. After more than a week of constant wind, rain, and lightning, the earth was now torn apart and laid waste.

"It looks like Vak during the war," Kernil noted as he stood next to me.

I never saw what Vak looked like during the war. I had been there shortly after to help in the reconstruction efforts, and by that comparison, Kernil was right.

"We're running low on food," I stated. "If we are lucky we might make it to Shale before we run out. I had hoped we'd be able to forage or hunt to get us by, but it doesn't seem like that will be a possibility. We must manage our stocks until we reach the swamplands."

Kernil laughed sarcastically. "Can't wait."

I sighed. "As much as I hate to admit it, Norvic was right. We probably should have gone through the troll territory. At least that way, we'd pass through towns and cities to resupply."

"Hey, no sense in doubting our decisions now," he chided. "We're on this path, so let's see it through. Besides, we have five enchanters, yourself included, in this company. We'll be fine."

What Kernil said made sense. There was nothing to be done about the past, so it was best to focus on the journey ahead. At the very least, the rain had stopped and we could continue forward once again.

I nodded. "You're right."

It seemed as though Kernil was going to say something, when Dahrik called from behind.

"Would you two quit staring off into nothing and get moving! I'm tired of these ruins."

Kernil and I joined the company and within minutes, we were

on our way. The terrain was muddy and difficult for our horses to traverse. The roadways and paths had eroded away, making the sun overhead our only guide in the barren prairie.

The Forsaken Prairie had once been known as the Bountiful Prairie. A land of plenty, full of grasslands, woods, and a thriving ecosystem. That had suddenly changed a few years ago when Shale was mysteriously destroyed and the land surrounding it was poisoned. The mages attempted to heal the land but their efforts had proven ineffectual on all fronts. Had this amount of rain fallen upon the prairie full of life, it might have fared better. Without the grasses and trees, the massive storm's waters had ravaged the land.

Travel over the next week was difficult and irritating. Even as the sun was shining during the day, the light seemed further and further away with every step. What should have taken us hours, took an entire day. Tensions were higher than ever and morale was at an all-time low. By the end of the sixth day since the storm, the ground was still saturated with water, and everyone was caked in mud.

There was no dry wood to burn for a campfire but Dahrik used his magic to fuel the flames. No one spoke as we sat in a circle, all equal in our frustration. Everyone except Howel and Dalia, who seemed moderately happy for some inexplicable reason.

"I can only imagine what things will be like when we get to the swamp," I thought to myself sarcastically. "Maybe if we're lucky, we'll be eaten by a swamp dryad or drown in bog."

As if Barris had heard me, he groaned and slammed his fists into the wet earth beside him.

"I can't stand this place anymore. I'm sick of traveling through this torn-up land of nothing and being covered in mud! I swear, we barely made any progress today!"

"Or yesterday," Kilt added.

"Or the last four days before that," Kylora finished.

Barris threw his arms up in frustration. "Are we any closer to Shale? Because for all I know, we're nowhere even close."

"Barris, calm down," Kernil commanded. "Shouting about it isn't going to make us get to Shale any faster."

"I'll shout about it if I want to," Barris snapped back. "I'm sick of this place!"

"See, this is exactly why we should have gone through Sh'rack," Norvic added.

Dahrik's face flushed red. "Oh, and be trudging through the flooded swamps. We'd be in this exact situation had we gone that way. You were outvoted."

"Enough!" I shouted, sending up a flare of fire above every-one's heads.

Everyone faced me silently, as the flames dispersed in the air.

228

I stood up straight and stared at them for a few seconds before speaking, so to seem confident, calm, and in control.

"None of us are happy to be here, so let's stop complaining and get back at it tomorrow. Bickering about it is pointless, it's not going to get us out of this place any faster. We chose this route with the best information that we had at the time, and it's too late to change that now. And unless you want to continue to quibble about it, I will take the first watch tonight."

With that, I walked away from the campfire and toward Arrig. My heart was beating fast with anger and anxiety. I took a series of deep breaths to slow my heartbeat, but it took several minutes to get it back to normal. I stroked Arrig's forehead and muzzle, which seemed to help.

"Everyone expects me to know what to do like I'm Jard's prophet or something, but I'm not and I don't know what I'm doing," I whispered to Arrig.

I kicked a small rock on the ground, but it didn't go very far in the mud. I walked away from the horses and into position for the night watch. Behind me, the fire was extinguished, meaning that everyone else had decided to get some sleep. After a few moments, everything was silent. The lifeless and torn land around me made was offsettingly quiet. Even the ordinary sounds of the night were absent. As far as I could tell, I was the only thing moving for miles.

For several hours, I kept watch over the camp while the company slept, just as I had done many times before. Alone with my thoughts, I thought about Kaynah, Rebecca, the Sorcerer's Keep, and even Joel. Stress came with most of those thoughts and I found myself staring up at the night sky, which was illuminated by the moon and bounty of stars.

My eyelids were starting to sag as the night went on, but I stayed awake until my time on watch had ended. I turned back to camp to wake Kylora for her turn, but as I did, I saw something move out of the corner of my eye. I spun toward the movement but saw nothing. Confused and convinced I was just tired, I turned back toward camp. I nearly fell on the ground with surprise when I saw a small person sprinting toward the company.

I lifted my scepter up to my shoulder, pointing it in the intruder's direction. It was running at an unnatural speed, especially for someone of its size.

"Stop right there," I shouted hoarsely, having not spoken aloud in many hours.

The intruder stopped in his tracks and turned around to face me. Despite the darkness of the night sky, I could see him fairly well. He was a small man, maybe three and a half feet tall, which made him shorter than most dwarves but taller than an imp. He had a shaved head covered by a black top hat, a blue coat and vest with gray lining, and a red scarf around his neck. At first glance, he seemed well dressed. After a few seconds of looking at him, I could see that all the clothes were tattered, stained, and dirty. Except for his shoes, which were noticeably shiny.

He winked at me, then in a blink of an eye, vanished. I blinked a few times and worried that my eyes were playing tricks on me. I looked again to where the short intruder had stopped and he wasn't there. As I stood there and considered what just happened, I felt a kick to my butt. The blow knocked me off of my feet onto the still saturated ground.

Behind me came a loud, high-pitched, rapid series of staccato, "Hee-hee-hee."

I swung back with my scepter but struck nothing. Once again, the small man vanished in an instant. I got to my feet, not bothering to brush the mud off myself, preparing for the pop-up once again. I kept moving, pivoting my stance so as not to be caught from behind again. My effort was in vain, as he struck me from behind just as I had turned directions. This time, I was able to catch myself from falling all the way over, bracing myself with my scepter.

Once again, he laughed in the same irritating, "Hee-hee-hee," as before.

I groaned, but before I could get to my feet, the little man appeared in front of me and kicked my scepter. I was using my scepter to stand and losing it caused me to fall, face-first into the mud.

"Hee-hee-hee."

"Arrrrghh!" I shouted in anger as I got to my knees.

The small creature had disappeared once more, but I knew it would be back. I waited ten seconds, turned my view south then punched the ground at my side. A ring of fire pulsed from me, flaring a crimson light in the evening darkness. The fire went out ten feet in every direction in a single second. I heard a yelp of pain right behind me, just as I had hoped.

I jumped to my feet and spun around, my scepter a the ready, to see the little man with its left hand in its mouth, sucking on it. It had a tear swelling in its eye and the end of its pant legs were smoldering.

The green gems at the end of my scepter glowed brightly as I stepped forward.

"Who are you and what do you want?" I asked calmly but firmly.

He gave no response but glared at me angrily, still sucking on his burnt hand.

I took another step, not breaking eye contact.

"Well? Why are you here? Speak!" I commanded, the gems on my scepter glowing brighter as my frustration grew.

He took his hand out of his mouth, wiped the saliva on his coat, and then winked at me, just as he had before.

Just then, a bolt of lightning struck at where the creature had been standing, although it was gone.

"Kobold!" shouted Dahrik, who was standing over his bedroll, scepter gripped tightly in his hands.

The rest of the company jumped awake, stunned and confused. I ran over to join them, hoping that the creature was either gone or would be spooked away by the increase in numbers. As if on cue, the small creature suddenly appeared next to Dahrik. It punched him in the face, laughed, and then vanished once again.

"Wha- what was that?" Kilt asked, taken aback.

Dahrik rubbed the bruise forming on his cheek. He spat on the ground, then answered. "It's a Kobold. Little tricksters that can disappear and reappear nearby. Never seen one outside of the southern Pryre. They're a constant irritant to the dwarves, always stealing our food, work tools, and treasures."

Howel and Barris simultaneously groaned at the mention of the Kobold. Both quickly grabbed and readied their weapons. Just as Howel had strung his bow, the Kobold appeared and smacked it out of the archer's hands. Howel took a swing at it but the annoying Kobold ran away at an unnaturally fast speed.

"Hee-hee-hee."

Dalia formed a whip at the end of her scepter and skillfully lassoed it around Kobold's leg. Before it could disappear and escape, she yanked the trickster off of its feet. It hit the ground with a smack, its head in the muddy earth.

"Giiiaaaahh!" it shrieked, trying to wipe the mud off of its clothes.

Norvic threw a ball of fire at its head, but the Kobold vanished just in time.

"Where did it go?" called Kernil, the Sword of Vain held at the ready.

"It still here," Barris growled. "Watch your valuables. They never leave until they've taken something important from you, nasty devils."

A few seconds later, Kilt was pushed to the ground as the Kobold reappeared behind her. Hemm roar in fury, swinging both of his fists at the little creature. It tried to run away, but the troll's massive fists crashing against the ground caused the soft earth to rumble. The slight tremor was just enough for the Kobold to lose its footing and fall on its face in the mud.

It shrieked again at the sight of more mud on its tattered coat and vest., In a frantic gesture, the kobold attempted to clear it away. Acting quickly, I swung my scepter into the ground at an angular motion. A wave of mud slid toward and covered the Kobold.

Following my lead, Norvic jammed his scepter into the ground nearby. The mud hardened into dried dirt, encasing the Kobold in a cocoon of earth.

There was a moment of silence, followed by an all too familiar, "Hee-hee-hee."

In a flash, the Kobold was gone.

"No!" cried Barris, crushing the empty dirt cocoon with his hammer. "It's over. The little devil is gone."

Everyone but the three dwarves looked around, confused.

"How do you know?" asked Kylora.

Howel answered her. "That flash of light. That's him traveling further away in escape."

"At least we can get back to sleep," noted Kernil, sheathing his sword.

"I wouldn't," replied Barris, checking his pack. "If he's left, that means he's taken something. Everybody check your personals."

It didn't take long to figure out what the Kobold had taken. Dahrik had first gone to check the food supply on his horse. When he found it missing, he checked everyone's supply, all to the same result.

"I'd bet that Kobold was the only other living thing out here," Dahrik growled, his frustration obvious. "When it saw us, it must have figured we'd have plenty of food to steal. Like fools, we weren't protecting our most valuable resource."

Norvic kicked a clod of dirt, smashing it to pieces. "Well, this is just perfect. Now we're stuck in the middle of a barren prairie with no food or water. I knew death was a possibility but I didn't imagine it would ever be for something this stupid!"

"What about magic?" Kernil asked. He faced me, but the question was to everyone. "Can't you enchanters just make food and water with magic?"

Kylora answered. "Water, yes, but food is different. Magic allows us to pull water from the humidity in the air. However, the ground is so saturated with water that we wouldn't have to do even that. Taking the water out of the ground and purifying it enough to drink is even easier. Unfortunately, food is not the same. Magic cannot create something that does not already exist."

Kernil's head sunk low as he let out a big sigh. There was a moment of silence as we all avoided eye contact with one another. I looked back up at the stars and called out to Jard for help in my mind.

* * *

Ginn looked out at the Hills of Cray as the sun was directly overhead. The week-long storm had torn the land surrounding the Sorcerer's Keep asunder. Through considerable effort over the last few days, Ginn had repaired it to its former beauty. Unfortunately, since the Hissera attack, the Keep had been acting abnormally weak. Usually, whenever the Keep was damaged, it could heal and repair itself within a matter of hours. Sometimes, if the damage was significant enough, the repair took days at most. Yet it had been over three weeks since the Hissera's attack, and still the Keep was not yet fully functional.

With a loud groan of frustration, Ginn thought about the necromancer Kaynah. The Keep's weakened state was her fault. With the Hissera stealing magical energy from the enchanters they killed, the Keep could not get the resupply of energy that it needed.

Ginn feared the Sorcerers might never recover if Kaynah continued unchallenged. Jes, Dahrik, and those who went with them in Culten were the last hope. The Keep and the Sorcerers would likely not survive another Hissera attack of that scale.

Ginn sighed. Although she had faith in the Prodigy and his former master, she feared that they may not be enough. Guilt swelled inside her, so much so that it hurt.

"Maybe I should have gone with them," she whispered.

Rethinking the idea, Ginn shook her head.

Ginn knew that her presence would have only complicated things. She hadn't seen battle in a very long time and wasn't very good at it anyway.

"Dueling a necromancer to the death needs someone like

Dahrik," she thought. "Or Jes Nulkin, for that matter. I have to believe that Jard made him the Prodigy for more than the Vios Almna."

After several minutes of admiring the beautiful landscape, the grandmaster sorceress turned away. With her back to her beloved hills, she walked back to the Keep, where duty and expectation awaited her.

"Grandmaster," called Merek, as he jogged over to meet her. "I have excellent news. Zorrel has discovered something in the library that could repair the Keep's weakness."

Ginn was surprised and very relieved but she did not show it. She wanted to shout and cry with joy but restrained herself to a simple nod. Such outside emotional passivity was often difficult for her to maintain. It was especially difficult in troubling circumstances such as these but such was the price of leadership.

"That's excellent news, Merek," stated Ginn calmly. "What has he found?"

The Keep's lead healer shook his head. "I don't know, Grandmaster. Zorrel merely told Wulfric and me that he had discovered something in the archived texts. So I came here immediately, to retrieve you."

She grinned at Merek's loyalty, not only to her but to the Keep as well. He was a kind-hearted and honorable enchanter, always seeking to do what is right. Unlike some, Merek rarely acted for personal gain. It pleased her to have him on the Council.

"Thank you, Merek. Please, lead the way."

Merek and Ginn walked back to the Keep with both purpose and anticipation. It wasn't long before they made their way through to the library archives. Zorrel and the other two remaining members of the Grand Council were waiting for them.

"Ah, Master Thea, Master Wulfric, I'm glad you both are here as well," Ginn stated warmly as she and Merek arrived. "Sorry to keep everyone waiting, I was outside meditating."

"Have you already begun?" Merek asked Zorrel.

Zorrel stood in front of the four members of the Grand Council. The book in his hand looked even older than the one the librarian had found about the Hissera.

Zorrel shook his head. "I insisted on waiting for the grand-master."

He bowed his head at Ginn as a sign of respect.

"Thank you, Zorrel. Now, please, tell us what you've found."

"Yes, very well."

He opened the leather-bound book in his hand very carefully.

The pages and spine cracked at the slightest movement. The book itself was not very large or thick, only a handful of pages between an old, leather cover.

"I've found an ancient ritual that can help heal the Keep. It's only ever been used once in our recorded history, as far as I can find. It was on a much smaller scale but it was successful, so I believe we could also use it."

Wulfric clapped his hands together in excitement. "Excellent work, Zorrel. This is fantastic."

"How does it work?" asked Ginn, her own excitement mask far better than that of the other councilmen.

Running his finger over a line of text in the book, Zorrel answered, "It's actually a rather simple in concept. We would create a beacon for the mystical energy that the Hissera stole from the dead to return to the Keep."

"That's incredible!" Merek shouted in delight.

"Zorrel, I can't even begin to explain how much this means to us," said Ginn, leaning against her scepter.

Unlike her fellow council members, Thea was less excited. There was a sour expression on her face. "This seems too good to be true. What part are you not telling us?"

Everyone looked at Thea in shock.

"Listen here, Master Thea," Wulfric began, "I'm certain Zorrel has done his research. He would not come to us unless he knew all the facts."

"That's not what I said," Thea snapped back. "What I said was, he's clearly not telling us everything. Something this good must have a caveat."

Wulfric opened his mouth to respond, but Zorrel spoke first. "Actually, she's right, I'm afraid. I hadn't gotten to that part just yet, but there is a condition crucial to the ritual's success."

Embarrassed and proven wrong, Wulfric's face went red. His head sunk low and his eyes avoid contact with everyone present, especially Thea.

"What's the condition?" Merek asked, his previous excitement replaced with worry.

"Well," began the librarian, referring back to his book. "In order for the magic that the Hissera stole to return to the beacon. The necromancer must be dead."

All four members of the Grand Council groaned.

"What?" asked Zorrel, now scratching his head in confusion. "I don't understand. Jes is going to kill Kaynah anyways, now we can take back the magic she stole."

The four masters looked at each other, all eventually settling on Ginn. Realizing what was expected of her, she cleared her throat before speaking.

"It's not that we doubt the Prodigy, because we don't. It is just that when you said that we could steal back the magic from the necromancer. I believe we all thought you meant before Jes would face her."

Then Merek added, "To give him a better chance at success."

"Yes, exactly," the grandmaster confirmed.

Zorrel frowned. "Oh, I'm sorry for the confusion. I didn't mean to mislead you all. This is still very good news, however, given the other half of the problem."

"Other half?" asked Thea, raising one of her bushy eyebrows high.

"The patron, of course," answered the librarian as though the answer was obvious. "When a necromancer dies, the stolen magic is transferred back to the patron. The beacon ritual, if done in time, interrupts that transfer and gives it back to the Keep. It hasn't been used since the very first necromancer, two thousand years ago. Though according to the record, it was a success."

"Fascinating," Ginn remarked, twisting a lock of her hair as she thought. "This whole series of events grows more and more puzzling by the day. The last few pieces are undoubtedly the most crucial."

Zorrel and the rest of the council looked at one another, then back at Ginn.

Thea was the first to break the silence. "What pieces are we missing, Master?"

The grandmaster's response was almost immediate. "Well, we still don't know who Kaynah's patron is or why they gave her the secret of the Joining Ritual. We are also missing the reason Kaynah sought out her patron to begin with."

"Very true," Zorrel nodded, "but whatever the patron is or whatever Kaynah's reasons. This beacon ritual is going to be key. Not just for us but the other Keeps as well, because-"

"The other Keeps?" Wulfric interrupted. "What do the other Keeps have to do with this?"

The librarian looked back at Wulfric in surprise. "Well, if we are the only Keep to use the ritual. Then our Keep will be the only one to receive the needed rejuvenation. A rejuvenation that is desperately needed by the other Keeps. We would be stealing the magic of their dead, and that of course is forbidden under the treaty made by the four Keep founders."

"Zorrel is right," Ginn announced. "I must alert the Druids and the Mages of the beacon, just we should."

"And of the warlocks, Master?" asked Merek.

Ginn paused in thought before speaking. "I have not decided

243

whether to tell them just yet. I have a suspicion. If I am right, not telling them of the beacon will be an amazing blessing for Cray."

"But if you're wrong?" questioned Zorrel, finally closing the book in his hand.

"Then we'll have committed treason against enchanter kind. It will destroy the delicate system of trust the Keeps have held for one another for centuries."

For several minutes nobody moved or spoke. Everyone stood still and pondered the gravity of the choice that was before them.

Merek broke the silence. "Do you think it's worth the risk, Grandmaster Ginn?"

She nodded. "I do, but before making a final decision, I think it best if I attempt to see what the future holds. Perhaps that will provide me with some of the clarity that we need."

* * *

The sun was nearly in the center of the sky as Kernil walked through the wasteland, his hunting bow nocked with an arrow. The shadowy figure ahead was coming into focus enough for him to be certain that it was moving. His arms tensed as he silently crept forward.

The company had no choice but to continue on towards Shale

after the Kobold had robbed us of our food supply. It hadn't been long enough for everyone to starve, but each of us was on edge and clearly irritant with hunger. Moments ago, Kilt had spotted several figures off in the distance, which even with the aid of magic could not be identified. So, it was decided that Howel would watch the horses and everyone else would split up and investigate one of the figures.

With every step, the figure seemed to get smaller and smaller, but as Kernil neared, he still couldn't get a good look at it because the sun shining directly in his eyes, keeping the small figure shadowed and obscured. As he stood about a hundred feet away, he started to hear what sounded like crying.

He pulled the arrow back on the bow and aimed at the figure in front of him.

"Identify yourself!" he shouted in his most authoritative voice.

The sound of crying continued. Kernil took a few more steps forward, then called out again. "Who are you?"

There was no response other than the uninterrupted wave of sobbing. Just as the warrior was about to speak again, a cloud covered the sun, allowing Kernil to see the weeping figure. Just as the crying could have suggested, the figure was a young, human girl with big, frizzy hair and skin as dark as the night. She wore a white dress with a yellow belt but had no shoes. She was missing her big toe on her left foot, but it must have occurred long ago, possibly even at birth.

Upon seeing the girl clearly, Kernil lowered his bow and returned the arrow to the quiver slung over his back. Slowly and cautiously, he walked towards her but she didn't even seem to notice him as her head was buried in her hands.

"Hey there," he said, trying to sound as calm and friendly as possible. "What are you doing out here all alone?"

She didn't answer, but her cries seemed to lessen, as though she was either calming herself or she was tiring out from sobbing so intensely.

"What's your name?" Kernil tried again, now kneeling right next to the girl, his bow placed on the ground beside him. "My name is Kernil. I'm sorry for scaring you. I just couldn't see you, the sun was in my eyes."

After another minute or so, the girl had finally stopped crying. She sniffled several times and wiped her mucus-covered nose with the sleeve of her dress.

"My name is Khii," she said in a strained and timid voice.

Kernil nodded and extended a hand. "It's nice to meet you, Khii."

The girl named Khii shook Kernil's hand, a hint of a smile on her face.

"What are you doing out here?" the warrior asked, motioning with his hands to the barren and abandoned prairie around them.

"I...I'm lost," Khii answered. "I got lost from my mother. I don't know where I am and I'm scared."

Just then, Kernil's stomach groaned with hunger. Khii smiled, even giggling a little.

"My stomach has been doing that all day too," she said, the smile fading from her young face.

"You were the first thing my friends and I have seen on this land for a long. They sent me to see if what we saw was food because we're all hungry."

Khii scrunched her face sourly. "I believe my mother has some food. If we find your she will share with you."

"That would be nice," he replied, looking again at the girl's feet. "Say, why aren't you wearing shoes?"

The girl just laughed as she stood up and brushed the dirt off of her dress. She ran without a care for her bare feet a few paces north, stopped to laugh, and waved Kernil to follow her. By the time he had picked up his bow and got back to his feet, Khii had started running ahead once again.

"Hey, wait," he called as he ran after her. "How do you know where you're going? I thought you were lost."

She once again did not answer him, still laughing as she

continued running through the wasteland. Kernil tried to keep pace with the suddenly gleeful child but the faster he ran towards her, the faster she seemed to go. It wasn't long before Kernil was sprinting at his top speed just to keep the girl in his sights. What he couldn't believe was just how easily she made it seem for Khii to outpace him, laughing and casually skipping along.

"Hey," he called out again, his breathing heavy and fast as he continually dashed forward, "Slow down. Where are... we going?"

"To see my momma and get some food, come on!" Khii replied, not looking back.

Kernil groaned in frustration at not only the child's casual attitude but also her unexpected and perfunctory speed which appeared effortless. The hot midday sun beat down on the Son of Vain as he ran, causing the sweat to drip into his eyes which stung, and yet, he did not stop running. With the sweat from his forehead stinging his eyes, Kernil was forced to squint as his vision blurred.

It was his blurred vision that caused him to nearly run face-first into the trunk of a tree, which seemed to appear from out of thin air. Kernil avoided colliding with the sudden tree by quickly sidestepping and spinning around the tree.

Curious and tired, Kernil decided to stop chasing after Khii and turned his attention to the mysterious tree. Most notice-ably was the tree's color, its bark as black as night with its leaves a popping shade of pink. The trunk was about two feet across and stood about six feet until it began to branch out. What seemed odd was that despite everything surrounding the tree being drained of life, the tree itself appeared very healthy.

Hanging from the branches were blue, oval-shaped berries that hung by a thin stem. Kernil's stomach growled with hunger at the sight of food, so he plucked one and took a bite.

"Mmmmm! Tastes just like a pit-less cherry but even sweeter," he remarked to himself, already grabbing another.

The cherries or whatever they were, seemed to become even sweeter with every bite. The intense flavor was addicting and not only filled Kernil's hunger but also seemed to make his body lighter, as though it were made of air. He set his hunting bow down by his feet and began stuffing his face with strange but delightful fruit with both of his hands.

"Addictive, aren't they?" came a voice from behind.

Kernil spun around, his mouth full of fruit and covered in blue juice. He instantly did a double-take, as his surrounding had suddenly changed. Gone was the barren wasteland Kernil had grown to despise and now he found himself surrounded by an oasis of lush, green grasses, colorful and aromatic flowers, perfectly trimmed hedges, and a sparkling pool of water. Standing in the center of the pool was a woman, who looked and was dressed nearly identical to Khii, only an adult. She was even as barefoot also.

"Welcome to my oasis, Kernil Ravenhigh," stated the woman in a calming voice.

The Son of Vain felt his body relax, although his mind became hyper alert. "How do you know me? Who are you? How did I get here?"

"My name is Loil and I know everyone that crosses my lands," she replied with a half-smile, although her eyes were filled with pain. "I know you and your entire company. Sorry for the optical illusions, I wanted to get you alone."

"Me? What? Why me?" Kernil asked, his body tensing up again with confusion and suspicion.

His hands instinctively gripped the Sword of Vain. Loil simply smiled, this time more genuine than before, as though she were amused.

"I am what's known as a Sprite, magical by nature but I will spare you my life's story, it would take too long. Immortality can seem dull to mortals. We Sprites look over portions of Cray and I am the guardian of this prairie, which as I'm sure you have noticed, my land is in a horrifying state."

Kernil had never heard of a Sprite but he had seen enough magic recently to recognize it. "Yeah, it's been destroyed. This prairie used to be full of life...kind of like this place, now that I think about it. What happened here? And what does this have to do with me?"

"It was that necromancer, that elf named Kaynah," Loil hissed, her continence becoming dark and fierce. "Everything was lovely here until her patron discovered her and gave her power. Ungrateful swine, she was born of these lands and yet she destroyed it, discarded it without a second thought. All for that stupid talisman!"

"Talisman, what talisman?" Kernil asked, now tired of asking questions.

Loil took a deep breath, then said, "An ancient artifact buried under Shale long ago. It made her creation of the Hissera much easier, but that's the least of its abilities. Kaynah must be stopped, otherwise, I fear that all of Cray will become as my beloved prairie, with no hope of rebirth. I cannot let that happen. *You* cannot let that happen."

Kernil removed his grip from the Sword of Vain and sighed. "What can we do? The enchanters are depending on me and my crew to help them defeat Kaynah, but the ten of us are struggling just to traverse this land, let alone defeat a necromancer and all of her Hissera. What are we to do?"

The Sprite's eyes glowed with ferocity, her voice rang deeper and colder, booming through the oasis. "Insure the Prodigy kills Kaynah of Shale and then bring the talisman back to me. I sense his hesitation, the conflict boiling within him. No other mortal possesses the power to kill the necromancer and break her curse, if he fails, Cray will become just as damaged and forsaken as my once beautiful prairie."

251

"H...how am I suppose to make him kill her?" Kernil cried.

"I do not know, but you must," Loil snapped back, her anger now being directed at Kernil.

His senses told him to run or to plea for forgiveness from the angry sprite, but the Son of Vain stood his ground. "But as you have said, he is the most powerful enchanter there is, and I have no magic. What use am I? Give this task to someone with magic, someone Jes will listen to. The dwarf enchanter, Dahrik, have him do it. Jes will more likely listen to him."

The prairie sprite shook her head, sparkling dust flaking from her skin as she moved. "No, Kernil Ravenhigh, it must be you."

"Why me? I don't understand."

"There is no pain quite like unjust loss," Loil began, her anger softening. "You understand that pain, I know that you do. What was rightfully yours was recently taken from you. You, like I, have lost your home. In fact, neither of us have lost our homes, but rather they were taken from us. Just as Nemul usurped your home from you, Kaynah cursed and destroyed mine. The Ironhelm dwarf might be close to the Prodigy but his losses were of his own fault, he won't understand the way that you do. He will not understand the pain of a stolen life. Jes Nulkin knows that pain. This connects the two of you in a unique manner. That is why you must do this."

Kernil didn't answer and turned away from Loil's gaze. He

looked at his own reflection in the inactive and clear water. He was just about to say something when he felt someone touching his hand. Kernil jumped in surprise as Khii was standing next to him, her face covered in the blue cherry juice.

"Khii, where did you come from?" Kernil shouted, looking back at the reflection where the girl had no image.

"Momma says you'll be rewarded if you help her," she said, ignoring his question and tugging on his arm. "She'll even give you them now if you agree to help."

Confused by the girl's sudden reappearance, as well as her promises of gifts, Kernil looked back to Loil but was again shocked to see her missing.

"Take the gifts, Kernil," pleaded Khii, tugging on his sleeve once more. "They will help you, not just now but could help you later too. You could even get your home back. Don't you want to go home?"

"Wha... what?"

An image of his Vain appeared in Kernil's mind. Everyone he loved was there, cheering and shouting in the city streets, celebrating his return. He raised the Sword of Vain, its blade shining in the sunlight, and a wave of thunderous applause came over the already excited crowd. He marched victoriously to the manor where his family had lived for generations, it looking exactly the same as the last time he had seen it.

The Lute Brutes were there too, each one knighted and made his personal guard. Nemul and the leaders of Aris were dead, his family rightfully avenged. Kernil felt the whole inside his heart begin to close. Everything was perfect, everything was as he hoped it would be.

"Well then?" came Loil's voice, bringing his consciousness back to the oasis.

Hurt and confused, the Son of Vain spun around, distraught at the sight of his paradise dissolving in front of his eyes, then sighed as he realized that his perfect scenario was only a vision, a dream of his heart's desire.

Khii was gone from beside him and once again her adult counterpart was standing atop the waters of the pond.

"Will it really be like that?" Kernil asked, his eye shut tight, his fists clenched, and his whole body tense.

"I can be," the sprite answered. "But Kaynah must die."

Kernil nodded and opened his eyes. "I'll do it. I don't know how but I'll make sure he kills her."

"Good. Cray will have a chance to heal if you succeed," he added. "Now, for your three gifts."

"We need food," he said almost before she and finished speaking.

The sprite nodded. "Then that shall be your first gift. As long as you are in my lands, you and your company shall have enough. Once you reach the marsh, I will not be able to help you."

"That is more than generous. Thank you, great sprite."

Loil frowned. "Now, what to do about the task ahead. You were right when you stated yourself powerless. Perhaps something to even the scales. Yes, something simple, but unbreakably powerful."

She reached out her hand.

"Now, give me your sword."

He started to say ask what she could want with his sword but he decided better of the question and did as he was asked. Kernil withdrew the Sword of Vain from its sheath and stepped into the pond, handing Loil the blade. The sword hovered in the sprite's hands, barely not touching her ebony skin. With a flick of her wrist, the sword plunged into the pond. The once calm waters hissed and churned as the sword shimmered with lights of every color.

Kernil thought the pond might explode like a geyser but Loil flicked her wrist once more. The Sword of Vain came out of the waters, glistening in the daylight and the pond grew calm. The reflective waters seemed as though nothing had ever disturbed them. Cautiously, the sprite returned the Kernil his weapon.

"For your second gift, I bestow an enchantment upon your family's sword," Loil declared. "From now until the end of time, the blade shall be more than just mere steel. I infused this sword with a magical charm to repel and destroy dark magic."

Kernil looked in awe at the sword, trying to discern a difference from before, but to no avail.

"I give you this great power in the hope that you might be able to bring Kaynah to her death," she added coldly.

"So, you want me to get Jes to stab her with the sword?" Kernil ask.

The sprite waved her right hand in a show of indifference. "However the events may align, it does not matter to me, as long as the necromancer dies."

He nodded in understanding, although he wasn't exactly sure what to do with the magic now residing in his sword.

"And for your last gift, a contingency," Loil said, walking further back toward the center of the pond.

"Contingency? Contingency for what?"

Once the sprite stood in the center of the circular pond, she reached into the calm waters below. She extracted a single, round stone that was a shiny black color and brought the stone to her small lips. The sprite then kissed it. Immediately, the small stone changed to a clear crystal with the slightest tint of black. Loil then marched back to the pond's edge and handed the stone to Kernil.

"What's this?"

"This is for when all else fails," she answered plainly. "Or perhaps, if you're lucky, for when everything goes perfectly."

Kernil blinked in confusion. "I... I don't understand."

Loil smiled. "This is a wishstone. Merely hold the stone in your hand, speak your desire, and it shall become a reality."

"A wishstone?" he gasped.

"But be warned," she began in the most serious of tones, "it will only work once so be certain of your wish when you use it. Also, I should warn you that this is a very fickle sort of magic, rarely does it work in the way you are expecting. So be cautious in how you use it. Be as specific as you can with your wish to avoid unnecessary consequences."

Even Kernil had heard of the legendary blessings of a wish-stone. His father often spoke of one of his ancient ancestors who had possessed such a stone. Kreed had also mentioned that wishstones rarely realized the possessor's exact wish. Which made Kernil believe stories about wishstones all the more true.

"Thank you, Loil, I am honored by your trust in me. I know

such a gift is not easily given," Kernil said with a respectful bow.

The sprite curtsied in reply. "You must not fail me, Kernil Ravenhigh. Jes Nulkin must kill Kaynah of Shale and the talisman that creates life must be returned to the prairie. I must break the necromancer's curse on my land."

The Desolate City

Fortify or attack, that was the question that Kaynah of Shale was forced to ask herself. She paced around the dungeon, limping and unbalanced.

"Everyday they get nearer," she muttered to herself. "They'll be in Shale by tomorrow and my Hissera won't reach them in time to stop them."

She cursed the difficulty her Hissera had in crossing the swampy landscape of the Abic of Marsh. Kaynah wondered that if she was just a little more powerful, she would be able to open a rift. That way she could portal her Hissera to anywhere in Cray. She chuckled in delight at the thought. As things were, the effort would likely kill her, let alone her growing number of creations.

"No," she said to herself. "I must wait for things to play out. I must not tip my hand."

She glanced over to the stairs that lead to the main floor where her most recent batch was waiting. She smiled with pleasure at the success of her new creation, a bigger, stronger Hissera.

"No, not a Hissera," she whispered to herself. "This one is in a class of its own."

Kaynah walked up the stairs to the main floor of the fortress. Waiting in the entry hall, ever so obediently, were the freshly hatched Hissera. They laid curled up on the floor, only their eyes moving as they followed her movements. Her footing was careful as she moved about the chamber. The Hissera covered almost the entire surface area of the stone-tiled floor. Kaynah avoided stepping on any of her creations and moved into the next room. She had already begun making another large batch of the monsters. They were gestating nicely so far and would add to her awaiting force.

Taking a moment to survey the progress, a wave of exhaustion came over her. The last batch had taken a lot of strength to conjure, especially the new creature. She wanted to make more and perfect this new monster. Though the time and effort would deplete her before the coming confrontation. So instead, she focused on quantity.

Satisfied with her developing batches, the necromancer moved on. She was now where the guard's dining hall likely was, where her new creation laid curled up in the corner.

"There you are, my lovely," Kaynah purred like a mother might to her child.

The creature responded to its master by standing to attention.

As the creature stood, its massive frame bumped against the corner wall. The force from the bump caused hairline fractures in the bricked corner walls.

Kaynah gripped the brass talisman that hung around her neck by a thin cord. "Very good, my big one. Now, what do we call you?"

She circled the reptilian creature, waiting for inspiration to come to her as it usually did. The large Hissera stood over ten feet tall and had thick, muscular arms and legs. It had the same pattern of scales as all of the Hissera did but the yellows were brighter and the blacks were deeper. Like the normal-sized Hissera, this one had short and stubby fingers. Its claws were more than an inch thick, over two feet long, serrated, and hooked ever so slightly at the end.

Its blood-red, snake-like eyes focused on Kaynah as she circled it.

"Hisseron," she nodded, staring back at the massive creation. "Yes, that's what I shall call you, the Hisseron. It's simple, rolls well off the tongue, and a logical variation of Hissera. My Hisseron."

The Hisseron's mouth twitched in the slightest smile before going expressionless. Unlike its Hissera brethren, the Hisseron stood tall and straight. Its broad shoulder casting a dark shadow in an already dark room.

"If only I could have an army of you," the necromancer sighed.

"But without another influx of dead enchanters, making more of you will drain me too fast."

She stared at her own reflection in the Hisseron's unblinking eyes for several seconds, when a realization came to her that made her very happy. "Of course, if I were to kill the Prodigy and the enchanters with him, I'd have enough power to make as many of you as I'd like."

In her reflection, Kaynah saw the formation of a wide grin on her face. It was wider than any sort of smile she had ever seen. It made sense, however, as the thought of killing *him* filled her with a glee she hadn't felt in a lifetime.

"Yes," she smiled, circling the Hisseron once again. "When *he* is dead there will be no obstacles in my way, then I shall make more of you, an army unseen by throughout Cray. Yet, for now, we must wait for them to get here, if they can make it here alive. If they do, you and I will be waiting for them."

However, with just one Hisseron at her disposal, she'd have to depend on her growing army of Hissera. Even then, Kaynah knew she'd still be likely to have to get her hands dirty.

"They'll send the Prodigy after me first, that much is certain. I'm not particularly worried, except for that gauntlet he carries with him."

The necromancer reflexively clutched the talisman hanging around her neck, stroking it with her thumb. She knew that if she was going to make easy work of the Prodigy, she'd have to separate him from the gauntlet, or at least its power source. Suddenly, she got an idea. Kaynah believed that all good ideas came from her destiny, as she believed this one to be.

"I think I'll visit one of my older experiments I've been keeping in the tower," Kaynah said. "With a little training, the spider monkey might just be the surprise that I need to tip the scales my way."

* * *

When everyone returned from scouting out the silhouettes in the distance, the most curious miracle happened. Our food supplies that the Kobold had stolen had returned to us. Nobody saw exactly how or when the food returned, Kernil noticed it first with his now full saddlebag. We soon discovered that everyone's food had likewise returned. The miracle first led to suspicion, so Dahrik and I made a thorough inspection. To our complete surprise, not a crumb had been eaten nor had it been tampered with in any way.

"I don't understand," said Barris. "Kobolds never return what they've stolen, even when you catch them."

Nobody had an answer or even a guess, so we thanked Jard for our good fortune, ate a deserved meal, and trekked onward. With our bellies full once again, there was an immediate relief in the tension within the company. I gave an extra thanks to Jard for that.

After another few hours of travel through the barren and

soggy landscape that had become bland and irritating to look at, Hemm suddenly threw his arms up in the air and hopped in a circle. Everyone halted, unsure of what was happening.

"Ah, hey, stop it, you big lug," said Kilt as she clung to the troll's shoulder, trying not to be thrown off by the sudden excitement.

The normally silent troll looked frustrated, then pointed ahead with both of his humongous hands and called out, "City."

Like lightning, everyone followed his signal to the land ahead. Unable to immediately see the city, I leaned forward on Arrig and tried to focus my vision. The sun had nearly set, leaving the land in the shade of twilight, which didn't provide much help to my endeavors.

"Stupid troll," scoffed Norvic after a moment. "There's nothing there!"

Kilt jumped off of Hemm's back and drew her axes. "Hey, you take that back, or else!"

"Or else what?" Norvic challenged with the slightest hint of amusement.

The hobgoblin marched forward, her face now contorted into a furious snarl. Norvic put a hand on his scepter, which was attached to the saddle of his horse on the right side next to his leg. Before either could do anything, however, Arrig and I moved between them.

"That's enough, the both of you!" I shouted with authority. "Once again, we are supposed to be a team. The minute we tear each other apart is the minute that Kaynah wins."

Kilt spit in Norvic's direction then walked back over to Hemm, sheathing her weapons.

I took a deep breath, then walked over to Norvic, who looked far too pleased with himself.

"Nicely handled, my boy," he mocked with a slow, arrogant clap. "You almost sounded like you would do something to stop us if we disobeyed. Very convincing."

"I've just about had it with you," I said with as much control over my anger and volume as I could.

The warlock smiled. "Oh, have you?"

"You've done nothing but turn us against one another and insult the warriors, who, by the way, have saved our lives."

"Ha!" he shouted. "You think I should be grateful to those heathens? Never. I am a god compared to them. They are less than insects to me and my magic."

I shook my head. "You've always thought yourself a god, Norvic-"

"True," he interrupted.

I pinched the bridge of my nose in an attempt to contain my frustration. I could not let him get me to lose control of my temper like he did with Dahrik.

"Either keep your thoughts and insults to yourself or leave. If all you are going to do is pit this company against itself, then we are better off without you," I stated.

Norvic's eyes narrowed and locked eyes. My entire body tensed as the silent battle of wills raged between us. Behind me, Dahrik clenched his scepter, in case Norvic tried something.

The warlock blinked and smiled widely. "As you wish, Prodigy. I will act like the perfect dinner host, like I did when you and I first met. I wish to see the necromancer destroyed by almost any means needed. If that means I have to put up with these brutes, then so be it."

He was trying to elicit a reaction by mentioning our first encounter, but I refused to give him the satisfaction. Instead, I returned a false smile.

"Be sure that you do that."

Our stare-off ended as he walked away. I sighed, my body relaxed. I wanted to put Norvic out of my mind, but I couldn't shake the feeling that the warlock was playing at something.

"Oh, there it is," Kernil called out, pointing to the same spot as Hemm had moments earlier. "Good work, Hemm."

Kernil turned around, facing the company, and showed a compact, brass spyglass in his hand.

"You see it?" Dalia asked."

"Well, that's obvious," Dahrik huffed. "He just said that he did. Weren't you listening?"

Dalia turned to face Dahrik, not looking very pleased. I decided to intervene before the tension grew again.

"Let's get on with it. It's getting dark and I'd rather spent my night in town."

Everyone agreed, so we began riding once more, Hemm and Kilt leading the way. As we traveled, it wasn't long before the ruins of Shale were on the horizon. I made a mental note to never doubt a troll's eyesight ever again.

It was immediately clear that something horrible had happened to this once-proud elven city. With every minute, Shale grew closer and came more into focus, as did the damage and desolation. The land immediately surrounding the city wasn't just barren, soggy, and lifeless, like the rest of the prairie, but turned a sickly brownish-black color. It was almost as though the earth itself had caught fire. The homes, farms, and buildings were torn asunder, ruined as though a thousand years of wear had been wrought upon them. The city had reminded me of the dwarven ruins of Ryone Peak, eerie, damaged, and abandoned.

The sun had set by the time we had reached the outskirts of Shale, which did not give me any great sense of comfort. Dalia, Norvic, and I provided our magical light, but it made the journey eerie as we walked into town.

"I suppose we should find a place to set up camp," Howel suggested, not sounding very pleased at the thought of it.

"Here should do fine," answered Dahrik, tapping the side of a well-sized house with his scepter.

After a quick inspection, we all determined that it was as good a place as we were likely to find. It was large enough for everyone, had comparatively little damage, and even had what was left of a stable for our horses.

Kylora was the first inside and promptly dusted off a portion of the floor and unfurled her bedroll. "I think this used to be an inn. It has that sort of feel to it."

"It was," Kilt answered. "I've stayed here before, many years ago."

"As have I," added Dahrik, unrolling his bedroll near a corner of the room with little debris.

It wasn't long before everyone had cleared a space to sleep in the derelict inn. I wasn't on watch tonight, however, Norvic was, which along with the eerie aura encompassing the city that hadn't gone away since our arrival, was enough to keep me awake. After an hour of just lying in the dark, I decided to use some breathing exercises meant to aid in relaxation. I could feel my muscles loosen up which helped. Yet even with my best effort, I couldn't find sleep.

"It's something about this place," I thought, staring up at the ceiling. "I feel... I don't know. Like we shouldn't be here, maybe. That doesn't make sense, we're here to learn more about Kaynah. We could find something that could help us understand her or her patron."

The feeling that we shouldn't be here grew the more I focused on it. What I couldn't figure out was why. There had to be a connection to this place. There was something about Kaynah or her patron and the desolation caused to the prairie. There was this sense of evil that marinated Shale. Kaynah had done something here that caused all life in this bountiful land to die, but what and why? I didn't know of any magic capable of taking so much life for such a large area for this long.

"What did she gain by doing it? Was it just to conceal any knowledge of her previous life?"

I nodded.

That thought had some promise. Would Kaynah really destroy the whole region just to stop someone from learning about her? The answer was an obvious "yes" but the more I thought about it, the more it didn't seem to fit just right.

"No," I thought. "Hiding her past might have been a perk of this destruction, but there has to be something more. Something I'm missing."

Eventually, I gave up on trying to figure it out as well as getting any amount of sleep. Thankfully, Norvic's turn watch was over by then, so I relieved Barris of his watch. Despite the sensation that evil was all around us, nothing happened for the entire night.

My watch proved to be slow. My anxiety and exhaustion caused the hours of the night to drag on. The cold, autumn air made my restless body stiff and sore. After what felt like the longest night of my life, morning came.

"So now we're here, what's the plan?" Kernil asked when everyone was awake.

Everyone looked at me, expecting an answer.

"Um... well..." I stammered, tired and unorganized in my thoughts.

"We go deeper into the city until we find the center of this poison that's be injected into the prairie," Dahrik answered for me, saving me from an assured embarrassment. "I'm sure you all can feel it, there's something off about this place, something unsettling."

There was a fair amount of nods and words of agreement.

"Like something bad happened here," Dalia suggested. "Something uncommonly evil."

"Exactly," added Howel. "It's like being on a battlefield after the fighting has stopped. You can feel the death in the air."

Howel was exactly right, that was exactly how I was feeling all night. He had just been able to put it into words.

Everyone seemed to share the same feeling. This was a relief to me, because now I wasn't the only one who felt uncomfortable last night.

"At least now, I know I'm not crazy," I thought.

"Going toward the center of town should help us get to the bottom of what has happened here," Dahrik continued. "And hopefully learn something about the necromancer while we're at it."

With little effort to conceal his sarcasm, Norvic added, "So hopefully this whole detour won't have been for nothing."

I scowled at him, angry that he would once again try to insert contention among the group so soon after our confrontation. The warlock saw my irate gaze and went on the defensive.

"Oh no, I didn't want to come this way in the beginning. I wanted to take the road through Sh'rack, but we had to come this way because you and the dwarf were certain that we'd learn something about Kaynah's past. Now that we are here, that certainty has turned into maybe we find something about her past, hopefully. It's utter nonsense!"

With that, Norvic grabbed his supplies and marched out the door, muttering furiously to himself and not waiting for anyone. I moved to follow after him but Dahrik grabbed me by the arm, stopping me. He didn't say anything, he didn't have to, I knew what he meant and he was right. The warlock master would storm off but would come back before long. Going after him now would only result in unnecessary escalation. Best to leave him be for now.

Once everyone had packed up all of their supplies, we were on the move, with no other signs of life anywhere. There was no sign of Norvic either, which made me both relieved and nervous at the same time.

After we entered the city proper, the streets of Shale got more and more unsettling the further in we traveled. Most of the homes, shops, and buildings were either caved in or fallen atop one another. Unlike the inn on the outskirts, not a single building looked recognizable to its former state. I hadn't visited Shale before now. Everything I heard about the elvish city gave me the impression it was once busy and populated. A thriving trading hub between the elven kingdom, the trolls, and even the hobgoblins to the west.

It made me sad to know that Shale used to be a great city that was now decimated beyond recognition. Desolate was the word that kept popping into my mind. The entire city of Shale was desolate, which added to the unsettling feeling.

Chunks of stone and wood, both large and small, littered the roadways. Our travel was difficult, and some pathways were impossible. More than once we had to move off the main street because of blockage. We considered taking turns levitating the rubble out of the way although, we still felt uneasy. We decided that conserving our energy was best, in case we needed it.

When we arrived at the center of the city, our jaws dropped at the bizarre sight of its destruction. Unlike the rest of Shale, the center square was different. It had no rubble and was clear of debris. In fact, there was nothing at all. There was no road, buildings, debris, or even withered plants. In place of where all those things should have been was a massive and imposing crater.

"What the..." awed Dalia, trailing off as she stared down into the concave dome.

I dismounted to get a better look, and most of the company followed suit.

The crater was perfectly circular and patted down smooth all the way around. It was almost a mile in diameter and at least fifty feet down. Near the bottom, branching out from the center, were cracks that grew into larger fissures. A sickly yellow liquid oozed from the cracks. The color made the crater's bottom seem appalling and poisonous.

"Look," pointed Howel. "Someone's down there."

Everyone looked to the crater's bottom and to our surprise, Howel was correct. There was, in fact, a person inspecting the very bottom. Kernil quickly pulled out his spyglass and groaned.

"It's Norvic."

"What?" Dahrik shouted in disbelief.

I squinted and saw a man holding a long rod in one hand. It had the red-colored gems that indicated Norvic's scepter, which deleted my last doubt.

Before I could say anything, Dahrik took a step into the crater and slid down the smooth side, gliding to the bottom with relative grace.

I rolled my eyes and followed after Dahrik. As my boots made contact with the crater side, I immediately began to slide downward. I almost lost my footing and fell on my butt but with a jerking twist, I managed to stay on my feet as I descended.

Just as I had reached halfway, I noticed something moving behind me. I turned my head without moving my body so as to keep my balance and saw that Kernil was gliding down close behind me. He looked at me with an embarrassed expression on his face as he slid down on his back.

Reaching the bottom, I was able to avoid the yellow ooze coming out of the fissures and cracks. Dahrik and Norvic were standing in the center of the crater, looking and pointing at the ground. Not wanting to slide right into them, I used my scepter to slow down and come to a stop right behind Dahrik.

Unable to stop, Kernil kept sliding so I waved my hand and magically stopped him gently as he reached the bottom.

"Thanks for that," he said, brushing the dirt off the back of his pants.

I nodded, then addressed Dahrik. "What do we have down here?"

"See for yourself, boy," he answered, stepping aside to allow Kernil and I to see what he and Norvic were standing over.

Taking care to avoid the crack seeping ooze, we stepped closer to see a small, rectangular hole. Inside the hole was a wooden box, the lid of the box sitting open. The inside of the box was cushioned with a maroon-colored velvet.

"A fancy box? How long has this been here?" asked Kernil, ignoring Norvic and directing his attention to Dahrik and me.

The dwarf shrugged. "No idea. Why?"

"Well, it rained for over a week. This thing looks dry and untouched, like it was just left here a few minutes ago," he replied.

Kernil was right. In fact, this entire crater was smooth and dry when it should be muddy and full of water.

"We should be standing in a lake," Norvic noted before I could. "Every other piece of ground for miles is completely saturated."

More questions kept forming, and I wanted some answers. After several seconds of brainstorming, I put my scepter to my neck and magnified my voice.

"Hey, Howel, get my waterskin from Arrig's saddle and throw it down here," I called to the rest of the company above.

The archer stared back at me curiously for a second but did not protest and soon disappeared from the rim of the crater. Not a moment later, Howel appeared and dropped my water container off the edge. It slid and rolled downward until it eventually came to a stop at my feet.

Not wasting any time to explain my idea, I squatted down, picked up the waterskin. I uncorked the top and poured a fair amount of water onto the dirt. As I suspected, the water disappeared when it contacted the dirt. There was no trace of it, not even a puff of air vapors or smoke. All three men stood close, watching my experiment.

"Woah," Kernil gasped. "What does that mean?"

Without answering, I moved over to the box. Standing over it, I poured the remaining water onto the velvet cushion in the open wood box. With no surprise to anyone, the water dissolved instantly.

"Well, that's at least one question answered," I stated, replacing the cork back in the waterskin. "Now all we have to figure out is why."

* * *

The rains had finally stopped, which put everyone in Tyran City in a much better mood. The autumn sun was shining bright and the sky was full of rainbows. Although it was not particularly warm, most people in Tyran City were outside. They spent the day with friends and family, finally free from the unnatural storm. It was the first time in several days there was joy and laughter all throughout the towering stone walls.

There was one man in the city, however, who was not thinking of the weather but rather stressing about the future. That man was Chamish Regalock, King of Tyran.

"Curse that Nemul!" the king shouted, slamming his fist on the long, elegant dining table.

"Father, please, calm down," Prince Nuary pleaded at his father's side.

The prince finished unrolling a map that he had received from the cartographer. It was the most current, with updated roads, locations, and national boundaries. Nuary knew that the presence of the updated map would upset his father. This was the first time anyone had dared to update it since the

Aris rebellion four years ago. The new map was an admission that Tyran had lost the war. And now, even though it was necessary, the king would not appreciate it. With a grim determination, Nuary knew his father needed it. Especially now, with the current predicaments that they were facing.

"That whelp is trying to starve us," he shouted, raising his fists above his head in fury. "He's trying to cut us off from the rest of Cray. I won't stand for it!"

Without access to the grain and livestock produced in the lands of Aris, Tyran had to depend on trade. Most of that trade came from Culten and dwarves of Underhigh and in recent months, Aris had set up blockades. The Aris army intercepted all shipments to Tyran crossing through Aris roads. Tyran was now completely cut off from most of its food supply.

"There's still the next shipment," Prince Nuary offered. "Reports say it got through most of the blockades and is nearly here."

The king groaned, slowly lowering his arms but keeping his fists clenched. "It still must pass Sentrus and I highly doubt that will happen. At this rate, we'll starve halfway through the winter unless we can miraculously come up with more food."

There was a moment of silence in the grand dining hall. The word, "miraculous" had triggered a sore subject. Countless times the king and prince had pleaded with Jes Nulkin to help them in the civil war. With the enchanter's magic, they could have saved countless lives. But after each request, the enchanter had refused. He claimed he needed to remain impartial and that it was the duty of sorcerers not to meddle in worldly affairs. The enchanter's refusal and his mystic powers frustrated both Chamish and Nuary. Even if the current situation merited differently, Jes was away. He had been gone for some weeks now on some quest westward and nobody knew when he might return. There was another wielder of magic in the city, the half-elf boy, Joel Shine. Word came from Rebecca that he was to train as an enchanter, but he was still a novice. The boy had yet to begin his magical training or show any magical talent. He was a useless option to the royal pair.

"We still have the trolls to the north," Nuary suggested, breaking the quiet. "We could try and set up some sort of trade deal with them before the winter hits. It would be a major achievement of progress for the nation that Aris couldn't touch."

King Chamish looked at his son and nodded slowly. He thought about his son's idea carefully. Tyran and the trolls had rarely been enemies, but never sincere allies either. They shared a border, and in theory, both societies had a lot to gain by forming some kind of friendship. Even if that friendship began as something simple like a trade deal.

"The trolls have an odd government. It is the structure that confuses most, myself included," the king admitted. "But Aris cutting us off from the south and the elves waiting for a reason to kill us from the west. And now with the dwarves inaccessible in the east, it makes sense to turn north."

"If only the Horthvon had come to my aid and helped me put a stop to this whole thing before it began," Chamish thought, thinking of the dwarf king's response.

The dwarves had always been Tyran's greatest ally. Almost any time throughout Tyran's history, the dwarves had come to their aid when called. Yet, this last time, King Horthvon had decided to stay out of Tyran's civil war. Or the Arisite Revolution, as the people of Aris had come to call it. Although Underhigh had refused to take sides, Chamish had seen it as a betrayal. Especially since he could no longer depend on their trade.

"I'll send our best diplomat at once," the prince replied, thrilled that his father actually approved one of his ideas.

This seemed to calm the air in the dining hall. Nuary could see his father unclench his fists and relax his shoulders a bit.

Without wasting another moment, the prince called his personal servant. A gangly-looking boy by the name of Gaius came to his side and had him send the diplomat at once. He put in a specific request for a diplomat that was familiar with troll culture. That person would likely come from Bordon. A town that bordered the trolls' swamp, but anyone well educated could potentially have just as much success.

Gaius ran out of the dining hall just as the boy Joel Shine entered. He bowed at first King Chamish, then Prince Nuary, then jogged to the feet of the king where Joel presented him with a folded note. Joel backed away just in time to avoid Chamish kicking a wood dining chair, breaking off the two back legs.

The king roared in fury as he crumpled the note and threw it across the room.

Joel got to his feet and backed away, not leaving, but keeping his distance from the angry king.

"What's happened?" Nuary cried, moving to retrieve the note at the other end of the room.

"That is it," Chamish shouted to the ceiling. "I'm going to kill him!"

The prince picked up the crumpled piece of paper, unfurled it, and began to read.

Shipment from Culten intercepted in Sentrus.

  No further shipments advised, similar results predicted.

  -Lieutenant Colonel Frenda

"Oh no," Nuary said out loud, although meant to keep quiet.

The prince turned to his father, expecting to see the king's fury growing by the second. To his astonishment, Chamish seemed calm. It was as if the last minute had never occurred. An alarm seemed to ring in Nuary's mind. His father had never recovered from a tirade or outburst so quickly before.

King Chamish normally required several minutes of kicking and throwing things in order to calm down after such news. The prince did not know what was going on or even how to proceed, as this was entirely new territory.

"Father," he said cautiously.

King Chamish smiled back at his son, which made the prince feel all the more uneasy. "I have a task for you, my son."

Nuary walked speedily back around the long table. "What kind of task?"

"They have attacked our convoys and shipments, and so declared war on us once again," the king said in absolute sincerity. "I want you to gather the generals to assemble the army, and then you are to lead the first brigade in an attack on Sentrus."

For a moment, Nuary said nothing as his mouth hung open in disbelief. Chamish didn't wavier however, he merely turned his attention to the map the prince had brought him. He studied it now as though it hid a great secret.

"Another war?" the prince asked finally. "Are you-"

"Yes, I am sure!" Chamish interrupted. "Things cannot continue as they currently are. Tyran cannot stand while divided against itself. Either we reunite or crumble. There is no other choice."

Nuary nodded, not in agreement, but out of obedience. His father had made up his mind, and when that happened, very little could be done to change it.

"What about the trolls?" asked Nuary. "Should we still try to negotiate an alliance?"

The king looked up from his map and stared into his son's eyes. "Yes, we'll need any ally we can get. That was a good idea, my boy. Now go, lots of work to be done."

With that, Nuary left his father and dining hall behind, readying for war.

* * *

"There's something that I should tell all of you," Kernil admitted, once we rejoined the company at the crater's rim. "It's something that happened back in the wasteland, right before the food reappeared."

He told everyone about his encounter with Khii and Loil. He highlighted Loil's hatred for Kaynah and her desire to help the company. He also left out any mention of the wishstone. And decided not to tell the party about the blessing on his sword, or his task of ensuring the necromancer's death. To finish his story, he recounted the sprite's casual mention of a talisman that could create life.

"She first mentioned it only in passing," he said. "It was something about Kaynah taking it from the earth and that caused prairie to die. Then, she made me promise to bring it back to the prairie, so that it could grow again, in exchange for her help."

"So, that's what was in the box. It all makes sense now," I said, happy to have another piece of the puzzle came into place.

Kylora nodded in agreement. "Taking the life-giving talisman from the ground destroyed Shale and the prairie, but why would Kaynah take it? What purpose would it serve her? It has to be more than just creating a difficult terrain for us to cross."

Everyone was silent, thinking about the necromancer's potential motives, everyone except Dahrik. "Is there anything else we should know? Any other piece of vital information that this sprite gave you?"

The Son of Vain thought for a moment, then snapped his fingers in confirmation. "Yes, there is. She said that this talisman is what made it so easy for Kaynah to make the Hissera."

That caught everyone's attention, especially those of the enchanters. I exchanged curious looks with Dahrik, Dahlia, Kylora, and even Norvic.

Dahrik nodded. "That answers that question. The talisman accelerates her ability to make Hissera. Just perfect."

"What I'd like to know is how she learned of such a talisman," stated Norvic.

"Well, that's obvious," replied Kylora. "Her patron told her what it was and where to find it. Clearly ancient magical beings, like the sprite, knew of its existence."

Norvic shrugged, then replied, "And how do we know we can trust this sprite? What if this Loil is the very patron we've been looking for? Should we promise the talisman's return to a potentially dangerous creature?"

"Hey, you weren't there, you didn't see how much she hated Kaynah," Kernil shouted back at the warlock.

Norvic shook his head. "You're young so I'll attribute your naivety to that. Hatred can be faked, the same goes for well-crafted story of betrayal and anger."

"Not like this! I saw it in her eyes. She hates Kaynah with her very soul. She took everything from Loil, everything she loves anyway. Believe me, you can't fake that kind of deep, personal emotion."

"Is that so?" Norvic scoffed.

Kernil nodded. "Yes, I know because I have the same hate for the man who took everything I love from me."

The two men glared at each other intensely for several seconds, everyone else waited in silence. The brief moment of quiet made my ears twitch, which at first didn't make sense to me. After a few more seconds, I heard it, a faint hissing noise. I turned northward, the sound was growing and definitely coming from that direction.

"Do you hear that?" asked Kilt, breaking the silence just as I opened my mouth to do the same.

Everyone waited and listened to the hissing, which was unmistakable by now. Then everyone was on high alert. Forgotten was the bitter tension between Kernil and Norvic. The company prepared for a Hissera attack, and a large one by the sound of it.

"Hemm, Barris, and Kilt, to the front," commanded Kernil, drawing his sword. "Howel, try to get somewhere with a high vantage point."

The archer looked around at heaps of rubble and destruction that surrounded us. "That will prove difficult but I'll make do somehow."

With that, Howel ran off to the southeast, his quiver thrown on his back and his bow freshly strung.

All four of the remaining warriors had their weapons at the ready and faced north. I held my scepter at the ready only a few paces behind Kernil who was on the outer left. Next to him towered Hemm, who cracked his knuckles in anticipation. Kilt then Barris stood ready on the troll's other side, their weapons gleaming in the sunlight. Next to me was Dahrik, who I doubt could see past Hemm but I wasn't worried. Norvic was next to him with Dalia and Kylora on his other side, their scepters held high.

Everyone was tense and ready for the assault. The hissing had become a deafening roar, blocking out every other sound. My foot tapped with anticipation and wavering thoughts.

"Should I grab my gauntlet? It didn't work last time, but it's a powerful weapon. Maybe it will work this time."

Then, I saw one and my thoughts were focused. It moved forward in an odd, zig-zag pattern and much faster than I had remembered. Like a yellow and black blur of death, it moved toward us, followed by several dozen of its identical kin.

"For the heart of Vain!" Kernil shouted, charging ahead to meet them.

The other three warriors followed after Kernil, Hemm catching up with the dwarf warrior in only a few strides.

I panicked. There were just too many of them. There were only ten of us, nine unless Howel found a good position. The last time we encountered Hissera, there were less than two dozen of them, but now there ate hundreds headed straight for us.

Norvic moved, clutching his scepter in both hands. He stood by and levitated the pieces of what used to a decent-sized city house or shop. With the pieces high in the air, he hurled them one by one at the oncoming wave of enemies. Chunks, both large and small, avoided the Lute Brutes. They spun past the warriors and found marks on Hissera, knocking them down or crushing them dead.

Dahrik and Dalia threw balls of fire high into the air which arched down on top of the pack of Hissera. Some creatures hissed at the approaching flames, but few seemed concerned as the balls of fire crashed into them with little effect.

Next to me came a curse.

"Why didn't that work? Is it just fire? I don't understand the difference," complained Dahrik.

"I don't know," replied Norvic. "I'm surprised the rocked worked just then. What magic affects them seems to be random, I don't understand it."

Dahrik tried again, this time levitating more chunks of debris and launching it at the pack. Just as before, at least a dozen more Hissera died.

Then something clicked in my mind, a connection of infor-mation made.

"Stone isn't magical," I blurted out excitedly, "but your fire was. They aren't unaffected by magic, just magical energy. "

The four enchanters stopped looking at the Hissera closing in and looked at me. I glanced at the pack of Hissera who had just begun their clash with the warriors. Knowing there wasn't time enough to explain, I demonstrated my point instead.

I cued Arrig a few steps forward twirling in my fingers. Just as a few Hissera broke past the Lute Brutes, I spun my scepter as fast as I could. The motion created a powerful, horizontal whirlwind. The small typhoon blasted into the Hissera driving them into the ground. Without missing a beat I leaped off of Arrig, slamming my scepter on the ground. At the scepter's contact with the earth, a fissure opened up underneath the prone Hissera, first swallowing them up and then promptly closing.

I turned back around to see the other four enchanters both shocked and impressed at my display.

"Magic energy bad," I shouted at them. "Magic plus physical objects good."

It wasn't exactly elegant, but the message was clear. I called Arrig and before I could mount him, Dahrik the others charged past me to join the battle.

Up ahead awaited a commotion like I had never seen before. Hemm was punching, grabbing, throwing, slamming, kicking, and stomping Hissera left and right. It was horrifying to watch as the massive troll hammered and pulverized the necromancer's monsters like he had been born and bred to do so. Kernil and Barris were nearby, standing back to back as they spun furiously, slashing and smashing anything that came in arm's reach. Many of the outliers were picked off by Howel, who had found a decent vantage point on the balcony of a two-floor building that was only half destroyed.

Unlike in the previous encounter with the Hissera, Kilt only had one of her axes drawn. She swung it wildly in her left hand, hacking and chopping off reptile limbs and heads with great ferocity. The hobgoblin's fierce and deadly actions were contrasted by her beautiful singing. Her song was accompanied by the skillful strumming of her lute with only her right hand. The odd mastery Kilt presented at being able to swing an axe, sing a song, and play the lute simultaneously was a sight like no other.

I recognized the song immediately. Kilt had attempted it many weeks prior but Norvic had interrupted and demanded silence. Clearly, she no longer cared if the warlock wanted her to the song or not, she was going to sing for everyone and kill Hissera while doing it.

> *We're gonna sharpen our blades,*
> *Bring out our spearheads and spades,*
> *Oh, and don't forget my lute.*
> *We will get the job done,*
> *As long as they pay the sum,*
> *And we'll avoid a troll-sized dispute.*

It was a catchy song with a good rhythm for battle. Kilt's music seemed to infuse her fellow warriors with an energizing spirit. With every strum of the lute, and every word sung, Hemm, Kernil, and Barris would strike harder and Howel would reload his arrows faster.

> *Be,*
> *'cause,*
> *the,*
> *Lute Brutes are here*
> *and we will make our foes fear.*
> *Hemm will bash their heads right in.*
> *Between Howel's true bow*
> *and Kernil's giant ego,*
> *I have no doubt that we will win.*

All of the Lute Brutes sung along during what I quickly discerned was the chorus, even Hemm, who rarely spoke. The troll and both dwarves didn't have much skill in singing. They did more shouting than anything else. All five voices together drowned out the symphony of hissing, which I realized was likely the point.

Hemm grabbed a single Hissera by the leg and whipped it around like a club. The limp creature became a weapon. And the troll seemed happy to bludgeon other Hissera with the captured one. Once the improvised weapon had proved its use, more followed. The troll began grabbing any Hissera within his reach by the leg or the arm and batted it at its brethren. After two or three swings, Hemm would toss it away in favor of a new victim weapon.

> *Now the client has paid,*
> *And we aren't a parade,*
> *We're the Lute Brutes, and my name's Kilt.*

> *Please don't sing along,*
> *It would feel very wrong,*
> *And killing you would bring me guilt.*

Kilt swung her axe upward then swiped it across, severing two arms and head. Three more Hissera were on her almost immediately but they two were hacked and chopped to death in expert fashion. One Hissera with a particularly large number of yellow scales slashed at the lute with its long, hooked claws. Kilt sidestepped the attack just in time, avoiding the lute's destruction and resulting in a minor scratch on the lute's soundboard. The hobgoblin's face shifted from horrified to furious in a single second. She flawlessly strummed the song's tune as she jumped at the Hissera, her axe embedding in its forehead. The musician was covered in blue-colored blood but it didn't seem to phase her in the slightest. She removed her axe and sang on, in search of her next target.

> *Be,*
> *'cause,*
> *the,*
> *Lute Brutes are here*
> *and we will make our foes fear.*
> *Hemm will bash their heads right in.*
> *Between Howel's true bow*
> *and Kernil's giant ego,*
> *I have no doubt that we will win.*

This time I joined in the singing during the chorus. I felt myself injected with energy, my magic flowing through me more fluidly as I sang along. I was surrounded by at least a dozen Hissera at this point but I was not afraid. I leaped high in the air, only to come crashing back down to the ground, knocking over each one of the Hissera around me. Before any of them could recover, I reached out to the water trapped in the mud at our feet and brought it to the surface. My magic moved and condensed the water at the Hisseras' heads. With a snap of my finger, the water turned to ice, killing the soulless monsters instantly.

> *The crushing hammer comes down,*
> *The chopping axe comes around,*
> *We are the best that will ever be.*
> *So just give us your coin,*
> *And your cause we will join,*
> *Oh, what a sight that we are to see.*

Dahrik had a wide smile on his face. I doubted it was from the song but I couldn't entirely rule it out either. He didn't normally take pleasure in harming people, but I suspected that he, like I, didn't see the Hissera as people. They were unnatural and mindless creatures of a deranged elf. Whatever the reason, Dahrik seemed to be enjoying himself. He leapt high into the air, just to come back down and bash several Hissera with his iron scepter. The crunch of skulls could be heard over Kilt's song, except when the five Lute Brutes and I joined in during the chorus.

> *Be,*
> *'cause,*
> *the,*
> *Lute Brutes are here*

and we will make our foes fear.
Hemm will bash their heads right in.
Between Howel's true bow
and Kernil's giant ego,
I have no doubt that we will win.

Kernil and Barris still stood back to back. Their sword and hammer both attacking as well as defending from the long Hissera claws. The Son of Vain was attacked from the right by one, then on the left by two more. Kernil did a quick feint to the one on the right, then kicked it in the chest, knocking it back. The one on his left sunk a claw into his side with the other cut his across his left arm. Pain shot through Kernil as he faltered, giving the Hissera an opening. Neither of the Hissera hesitated, going in for the kill. Kernil closed his eyes, expecting his end to come swiftly.

Instead, he heard a familiar grunt and the sound of a hammer cracking a skull. Kernil opened his eyes to see Barris now standing in front of him. He having killed one of the Hissera and fending off the other. He didn't have much time to recover, as even more Hissera were now filling the gaps. Kernil lunged at an oncoming Hissera and ignored his wounds. All his focus instead on the battle at hand.

Not far away, the enchanters and I were still surrounded by Hissera. This time, however, their numbers seemed noticeably thinner. The task of killing them all no longer impossible. The enchanters had done very well once they learned how to fight the Hissera off using physical magic. Dahrik was an obvious champion but so was Norvic. The master warlock was ferocious as he fought, going for the Hisseras' eyes, clawed fingers, and throats.

Then, something happened. Norvic made a mistake. As he smashed a Hissera's arm with a boulder and bashed another's face in with his scepter. A Hissera snuck up behind him and stabbed him in the back with its claws. Norvic's whole body went numb from the deep wound.

Norvic froze, the pain and terror filling him as he tried to connect to his magic. He began to panic as he could feel his magic draining from his body. Then, suddenly the claws retracted from his back. Most of the pain and numbness vanished as well, aside from the stinging of the fresh wounds and the blood loss that came with them. His magic was his once again as well, the familiar sensation pulsing through his body, calming the panic.

He turned around to see an arrow embedded deep with the eye socket of the Hissera that had stabbed him.

In the Mist of Deception

"How have none of us died yet?" asked Kilt as she attempted to step around the piles of dead Hissera.

"Oh, don't say that," Kernil replied. "We haven't died because these Hissera are simple and untrained monsters."

Kernil had made a good point.

"It also did wonders when the Prodigy figured out how to combat them," Kylora added.

I waved off the compliment, but inwardly I thanked Jard that I had figured it out in time. If I hadn't put it all together in time, someone, if not all of us, could have died. As I glanced around me there were at least two hundred dead Hissera in my view and the smell of death was ripe in the air. I tried my best not to breathe it in but I was still breathing heavily from the intense battle so the smell was unavoidable.

"Oh, certainly, now that you enchanters aren't helpless against them, protecting you lot will be much easier," grinned

Barris.

Howel playfully nudged his fellow dwarf in the side with his elbow. "Even then it almost wasn't enough. Norvic got himself overwhelmed and nearly earned himself an early visit from Death, until I stepped in, that is. That twice I've saved his life now."

The two dwarf warriors laughed together, but Norvic tensed at the mention of the event. A sour grimace took over his face as the color reddened. He leaned forward on his seat and I swear I could hear him growling faintly.

His angered state was offset by his vulnerable position, his cloak and tunic having been removed, exposing the bare skin above his waist to the elements. Behind Norvic, inspecting the wound on his back was Dalia.

"Stop moving," the druid snapped, "I'm trying to see if there's any poison or immediate infection. The Lordon Heal won't do you any good if we don't get this taken care of first."

The warlock twitched at the touch of her prodding hands on his wounds. "Well hurry up then!"

Dalia took several minutes to decide that there was no poison and little risk of infection. Norvic was both relieved at the news and irritated that the conclusion had taken so long. Dalia's inspection gave everyone else time to take stock of their own injuries. Which also was time to and apply the necessary healing. I offered my healing abilities to the Lute

Brutes who each accepted gladly. Out of the five, Barris had sustained the most serious of injuries, but even he was not in awful shape. Howel required no healing at all since he had been far from the actual fighting. He took the time to retrieve as many of his arrows as he could salvage.

After a brief discussion, we decided to spend another night in Shale to rest and recover from the battle. We searched for a decent structure on the north end of the city but were unsuccessful. Instead, Kylora and Dahrik had the idea of creating our own using the materials around us. It didn't take long to clear a space and move some of the larger pieces into place. Before the sun had set completely, we had a perfectly sized bunker for the night.

"I must say, I'm going to miss having enchanters and magic available when this job is over," remarked Howel, placing his bedroll next to that of Dalia. "On all of our other jobs, we've either had to go without shelter or break our backs making our own."

Norvic held back a laugh and offered to take the first watch. Unlike his last turn, I slept soundly throughout the night.

Just as the sun was rising, we left Shale behind us and headed back into the wasteland. This portion of the land seemed less tiresome to cross. The ground beneath us was no longer as muddy and saturated from the rain as before. It was by no means easy to trek through, we were after all, without a road and that did add some difficulty. The autumn sun shined overhead, there wasn't a cloud in the sky. The barren land

and the cloudless sky gave way to a heatwave. The heat dried the ground, which put everyone in decent spirits.

After two days, the treeline of the swamplands was just on the horizon.

"It's been a long while since I've been in the marsh," Dahrik said to no one in particular as was we all sat around a cooking fire. "If my memory serves, this region is among the more deadly."

Kylora nodded. "This is true, I haven't thought about it much until now. The southern region of the Abic of Marsh is infested with dryads, nixes, and swamp drakes, only to name a few."

"Doesn't sound very comfortable," Kernil noted sarcastically.

"It's not," the mage replied in absolute sincerity.

There was a few moments of silence as everyone nibbled on some food and thought about what lay ahead.

"I thought drakes and dragons were extinct," Barris said, breaking the silence.

"The swamp drake is a rare exception," I answered. "However, most of the claims of their existence don't seem all that reliable, if you ask me. If any still exist, there's only a small handful left."

To which Dalia then added, "If it's not just one that remains.

Their lifespan is rather long so the same swamp drake could be the one being spotted over and over again."

"So we won't have to worry about it then?" Barris asked.

"I'd doubt it," I said in reply.

For a few seconds, it seemed like Hemm wanted to add something but quickly chose not to. I thought about calling on the troll for his insight, since was from the Abic of Marsh but decided against it.

My explanation seemed to satisfy the dwarf warrior but only make Kernil all the more curious.

"Things never get easier with you people, do they?" Kilt interrupted, half focused on faithfully buffing out the damage to her lute. "I mean, isn't magic suppose to actually make a difference in all of this? What good is it if you're in just as much danger as everyone else?"

"I've often thought the same thing," answered Dahrik with a sigh.

I looked at him with complete shock. How long had he thought this? As long as I'd known him, he'd done nothing but convince me of the wonders of magic. Had that view changed?

"Then you're unfit for it, dwarf," scoffed Norvic. "Magic is for the superior of mind and spirit. If magic wasn't wasted on those with such weakness, Cray would be elevated to something greater than the crumbling wasteland it is now."

I tensed, ready to jump to my feet and tell Norvic he was wrong when Dahrik stopped me, putting a hand on my arm.

"Believe what you will, Norvic," Dahrik spat in defiance. "At the end of it all, I will be remembered as the third dwarf enchanter in history and the one who trained the Prodigy. Meanwhile, you'll be forgotten the minute you die and another worm takes your place as warlock grandmaster."

Norvic's eyebrow twitched as his face flushed with anger. I began to worry that he might make an attack out of anger but all tension fizzled away when suddenly he smiled.

"We shall see dwarf," he sang. "We shall see."

For the rest of the night, everyone kept to themselves. I tried not to glare at Norvic but I caught myself several times, if he noticed he gave no indication.

Tensions kept escalating within the company and Norvic was almost always the cause. Was he doing this on purpose? If he was, I couldn't imagine why. Dahrik once said Norvic was a master strategist. Was the strategy he did now getting his allies to bicker with one another?

The following day we entered the Abic of Marsh. A cold snap replaced the slight heatwave of the last few days. The humid, muggy air quickly became frigid and chilled down to the bones. My shoulders twitched and my teeth chattered continuously as we made our way through the southern end of the swamp, towards the Abandoned Fortress. After the third day, my jaw hurt enough that it was no longer numbed by the bitter cold.

Everything was wet, even more so than the rain saturated ground of the Forsaken Prairie. There seemed to be only one type of tree in this part of the swamp. Each one stood about thirty feet tall and was only a few feet in width, with no branches until the very top. Vines of various colors and thickness hung low, requiring us to often push or cut our way through them. Trees were clustered close together, blocking off most of the sky view and sunlight. We had to travel in a light no greater than you'd find during early dawn or late dusk. At night, sleep was difficult. The camp would be surrounded by the never-ceasing sounds of birds and nocturnal animal life. After a week, I became so accustomed to the noises of the Abic, that I could finally ignore them enough to fall asleep.

Our food ran out, but the company was no longer in the Forsaken Prairie. There was plenty of game to hunt in the swamps. It was an unfamiliar and odd-tasting game, but food nonetheless. Our favorites to hunt were either a black and red feathered squawking bird, Hemm claimed it was a Bog Robin. And we also hunted a brown-scaled crocodile. The crocodiles rarely bothered us, but they had the most meat out of everything in the swamp, and magic made for easy hunting. The Bog Robins were small and bony but they were the loudest and most irritating birds during the night, so hunting them became a fun sport to help make the constant travel less dull.

For several days we traveled northwest through the Abic of

Marsh. We waded through bogs, traversed through the thick cluster of swamp trees, and hunted. Spirits were high and there was no more contention or fighting among the group.

"We can't be far now," said Kernil, studying the night stars in a rare clearing of trees.

I also stared up at the night sky, the twinkling lights a welcoming sight. "Three more days and we're there, don't you think?"

"Two, if we keep up a good pace," he replied.

"Wow, two days," I said, no longer looking at the sky.

Kernil rubbed his hands together, then breathed a puff of hot air into them. "How are you feeling about facing Kaynah? I know the last time we talk about it things got a little heated, but... what's going through your mind?"

"I've actively tried to avoid having Kaynah on my mind," I admitted.

The Son of Vain nodded. "Not that I wouldn't either, but are you that worried?"

I sighed. "I don't know what to think. Despite everyone assuming that I just know what I need to do in this upcoming fight, I don't. The minutia of being the Prodigy is very unclear and my experience with last time doesn't help either. The Vios Almna was a monster, not a person. Plus, there was a predetermined way to fight it. Kaynah is an entirely different case."

"There have been necromancers before, haven't there?"

"Four," I confirmed, "but none of them ever managed to make anywhere near as many Hissera. Which, I guess we now know is because of this talisman she took from Shale."

He put his hands in his pockets and glanced back up at the stars. "Well, how were the other four defeated?"

I sighed. "I did a little research before I last left the Keep, but none went into specifics on their defeat. Well, that's not entirely true. There was a detailed record of the last time there was a necromancer. Last time, Yep, the Prodigy before me, defeated him."

"And how did he do that? Maybe you could copy his method."

I shook my head. "Doesn't apply in this case. Last time, the necromancer, a human named Crahim, had the bright idea to send his Hissera after the Prodigy first. Crahim did this, believing that taking out the Prodigy first would make the rest of Cray fear him. He also wasn't as smart as Kaynah, keeping her identity a secret. Nope, this genius wanted to watch his Hissera kill Hemm. As I'm sure you can guess, it didn't work out."

"He thought he could take down someone as legendary as Yep?" Kernil asked.

"Well, in all fairness, he wasn't quite a legend yet," I replied. "He was still quite young and hadn't yet done most of his more impressive feats."

Kernil nodded, pausing for a moment in thought. "It sounds like you are right, then, that tactic doesn't apply here at all."

"Exactly."

"Well, except for one thing," he added.

I raised an eyebrow, signaling him to go on.

"He underestimated Yep," Kernil continued. "Just as Kaynah will likely underestimate you. Use that. Someone who schemes and strategizes this far ahead might think she's outsmarted you."

"Be unpredictable," I said, liking where he was going with this idea.

He patted me on the back and smiled. "There you go, now you get it."

I felt confused after talking with Kernil. I had two, maybe three days until I'd have to face Kaynah. Would I be able to kill her like everyone expected? Did I want to? Kernil had suggested being unpredictable to give myself an advantage, but how?

The next morning, something felt off almost immediately.

The trees from then on had thinned out considerably. The air was heavier than usual and had a foul smell to it that I couldn't place. We rode on for about an hour before we came upon a curious wall of fog. It seemed to cover the Abic of Marsh going northwest, inescapable and daunting. We stopped and inspected the curtain of mist, trying to see if there was any magic to it.

Although the hair on the back of my neck stood up in warning, something evil lurked with the mist and it was waiting for us.

"We should go around it, something feels off about this fog?" I said, staring into the mysterious earthbound cloud.

Norvic groaned. "Oh, you have got to be kidding me. Not this again. You know, I'm starting to think you're inventing reasons to go the long way because you are a coward."

I flinched, insulted, but caught off-guard by the accusation. I opened my mouth to protest, but Dahrik spoke first.

"How dare you!" he spat. "Jes is the Prodigy, he's faced down the Vios Almna and destroyed it. He is no coward. Jes has looked more dangers in the eye than you ever will."

"Fine," Norvic replied with a shrug, "but we're not going around. It's just some fog. We are almost to the Abandoned Fortress, we can't take another detour."

There was a few seconds of silence, the Dalia spoke. "I agree with Norvic. I sense no danger about the mist. We need to move on, our Keeps are counting on us."

She nudged Howel, who stood next to her with her foot.

He cleared his throat, then said, "Yes, exactly. We're in a swamp, after all, fog is common. Isn't that right, Hemm?"

The troll did not respond with words but rather shrugged then nodded.

Nobody else seemed to have the same bad feeling about the mist so I credited the feeling to paranoia and we rode on.

The mist became a thick hazard. We rode blind beyond more than a few feet in front of our eyes and we assumed a slow cautious walk. The water in the air penetrated my clothes and within a few minutes, I was dripping wet. The cold that had tormented us for days had turned to blistering heat, our sweat mixed with the mist and added to the foul smell.

With every step, the fog started getting thicker, making it even more difficult to see. After what couldn't have been more than a mile, I pulled Arrig to a stop.

"Okay, dangerous or not this fog is too thick," I called to the rest of the company. "We should head back and go around."

I waited for a response, but none came. The birds and insects that for days had been flooding my ears with their constant noises had gone silent. There was a wrenching sensation in my gut.

I pulled my scepter out of the holster loops on the saddle and summoned a ball of light. The light reflected off of the white fog, making it even harder to see.

Extinguishing the light, I spun my scepter, summoning a blast of wind. I swept the scepter around me to disperse the thickening mist. A simple gale did nothing so I tried a small cyclone but it seemed to have no effect, I was just as surrounded by mist as ever.

"Can't see through it, can get rid of it, this has got to be enchanted in some way," I mumbled to myself, thinking the problem out. "I wonder..."

I grabbed my gauntlet out of the pouch in the saddle. I slid it over my left hand, the gasper emerald that was embedded in the silver forearm shimmered in recognition. Raising my hand to my eye level, I called forth the glowing ball of spinning energy. I could feel the rush of power as the magic sphere grew in my palm, the familiar sensation comforting my nerves ever so slightly.

"If the mist is magical, then this should do the trick," I said, the orb of swirling magic growing.

Once the magic had reached a large enough size, about that of my head, I pointed the ball skyward. With a twitch of my thumb the magic was released, only this time instead of the magic being focused in a singular beam, it popped like a bubble in nearly every direction.

Not only was the fog unaffected, but Arrig jumped up on his hind legs, spooked and frightened. *Wheeheeeheeheeheh!*

Before I could react and soothe him, I was thrown off his back and onto the muddy earth below, swallowed up by the fog that clustered even thicker near the ground. I laid there stunned and in pain, forced to watch my beloved steed run off into the mist.

My back had taken most of the hit but my head was spinning and I was out of breath. I was immediately sore and struggled to move for several minutes. All the while, the muddy swamp ground seeped into my already damp clothes.

"Well, that was a mistake," I groaned as I sat up, no longer able to see or hear Arrig.

With a blast of air, most of the mud was removed from my clothes, although the humidity stopped them from drying. I couldn't figure out what to do next so I just started walking. There were no trees or other landmarks so I had no idea if I was pointed in the right direction. I wandered in what I hoped was a straight line.

"Dahrik! Kernil! Kylora! Anyone?" I called, not even hearing an echo of my voice.

For several minutes I kept yelling out names and requests for a response but received none. Meanwhile, I walk forward, still unsure of where I was and was starting to panic. Eventually, my voice tired so I stopped and just decided to continue on.

For a while, the only sound I heard was that of my boots smacking against muddy ground. Then, I heard something else. It came so suddenly that I jumped in surprise. It was a rattling. The sound started out very faint but in the void of color and sound, it was unmistakable. I stopped in my tracks and looked for the source of the rattling but the mist was too thick to see anything. I leaned forward, hoping to see even the shape of something, anything that could give me a real heading. I spun in every direction but could see nothing but white fog.

Every second the sound grew louder. Before long, the rattling was louder than any of my thoughts. I pictured an army of skeletons, their raw bones cracking and shaking as they marched toward me. No such army materialized however, what did appear was far worse.

Suddenly, the air went ice cold. A figure all too familiar to me rose out of the mist. It was a large and imposing creature, cloaked in darkness with only a pair of glowing crimson eyes for a face. Its hands were long and bony while its body hovered above the ground without any legs. In one hand it carried a lantern, a fire the color of blood burning inside of it.

I dropped my scepter on the ground and fell to my knees. My entire body was in horrified shock at the sight of the Vios Almna returned once more.

"H... how? I de... destroyed you," I stammered, still unable to understand what floated in front of me.

"I cannot be destroyed," it replied, in its hollow, soulless voice which echoed in my mind. "I shall always survive."

I shook my head, hoping to wake up from an elaborate dream, but I did not. "No, that's impossible. You're not really here. You can't be."

It raised its lantern, the blood-colored fire burning bright and hot, even cutting through the thick fog. "With you, I begin again."

The familiar sensation of my soul being drained from my body was evidence enough. Instinctively, I lifted my left arm, calling upon the gauntlet's power to defend me, but through some twisted horror, it was no longer in my possession. I stared at my bare hand in fear, now completely defenseless against the Vios Almna.

* * *

Dahrik was getting angry. This was not an uncommon thing to happen, but only this time he had nothing to take his anger out on. There were no rocks to smash, no trees to fell, or any people to punch in the jaw. Only the fog surrounded him. Even his horse had left him, spooked by some unseen force, and disappeared shortly after bucking him off into the mud.

"Jes warned something like this would happen," he chided himself. "If only I had listened."

Then a thought occurred to him. "Why didn't we? Because

nobody sensed any magic coming from the mist. Only, something abnormal and mystical is clearly happening here. Jes could sense it, my horse could sense it, but I could not."

His rage was building again and his skin flushed hot. The dwarf wanted nothing more than to incinerate whatever was responsible for this mist that only ever seemed to thicken. Dahrik settled on unleashing a barrage of lightning into the sky. Electricity and anger surged through his every cell and out into the world through the orange gemstones on his iron scepter.

Once he had finished, he was breathing heavily. That had cost more energy than he had intended to put into the cathartic release. His frustration was not gone, only subdued for the time being. With nothing else to do, he continued walking.

Then Dahrik heard the rattling. His ears twitched as he tried to pinpoint the ominous sound's location, but it seemed to come from every direction.

"Who's there?" he called into the void.

When no reply came but the rattling noise's increased volume, the dwarf's face flashed red with the familiar anger.

"I said, who's there? Show yourself!" he yelled.

"Always so quick to anger, Dahrik," said a snake-like voice behind him. "It'll get you killed if you're not careful."

Dahrik jumped at the initial sound of the voice but did not turn to face the speaker. He already knew who it was.

"This is impossible. You're dead, Varen."

The elven warlock laughed, his tongue flicking like that of a snake. "And yet, here I am, back again. What a disappointment to you that must be."

"This is clearly just some trick of the mist," Dahrik said, completely calm and in control as ever. "Varen died five years ago, I know because I killed him."

"But how certain are you? Maybe I survived and have been waiting all this time to kill you at just the right moment."

The dwarf shook his head, then turned to face the image of his former nemesis. He was immediately impressed by the accuracy and detail of the illusion. Before him stood the tall elf with long, slick back dark, and crooked teeth, just as Dahrik remembered him. The mist was even able to get Varen's unsettling, snakelike voice just right, which was just uncanny.

Dahrik smiled back at the image of Varen. "If your purpose is to make me afraid by showing me the one whom I despise or fear the most, you are out of luck. I've moved on from Varen. I haven't been afraid of him since I shoved an arrow in his throat."

The warlock began to circle Dahrik, looking the dwarf up and down critically. "Is that so? I must say, I'm surprised, men like you don't usually pick up so quickly."

"Who or what are you?" he asked, ignoring the comment. "Are you the work of Kaynah?"

Varen no long spoke with his own voice but now an older, more grizzled voice that was slightly feminine. "Oh, that fussy little necromancer? No, I'm afraid I'm something much more permanent."

"What do you want?"

"Nothing, when you get right down to it," the voice laughed as the image of Varen faded into mist. "Now, if you went mad or even momentarily hysterical I'd certainly think it amusing."

Not know where to look, Dahrik looked upward. "Sorry to disappoint."

"Oh, don't be," it said with confidence, "you and your companions will be stuck here for a while, eventually you'll break. They always do, especially when they're alone. One way or another, I'll have my fun. Only then will you be allowed to leave."

Just then, another voice called to him from a distance. "Dahrik, Dahrik!"

His heart skipped a beat at the sound of the voice. He had not heard that voice in a very long time but had been longing to hear it once more ever since.

"Hilda?" Dahrik called back, his eye now fixed on a shaded figure running towards him.

The fog melted into the city streets of Vain, his beloved wife running to his side. Everything was exactly as he remembered. The smell of the festival food, the ceremonial outfits most everyone was wearing, down to the position of the sun in the sky. Of course, there was Hilda Farn, his beautiful wife. Her wavy golden hair shined in the sunlight and her smile filled Dahrik with an overwhelming sense of joy.

She ran into his arms and they embraced. The feeling of her in his arms after so long brought the dwarf to tears.

"I thought I'd never see you again," she said, her voice as perfect as ever. "I thought that warlock had killed you."

He heard himself laugh with confidence. "You have no need to worry. Even a second-rate warlock like Varen knows that he's no threat to me. I'd be surprised if he'll even show his face now that he knows I'm here."

Then it happened. Even though this was the second time in his life that he had watched this happen, it still came as a surprise. The ballista bolt zipped through the air, Dahrik seeing it just before it pierced straight through Hilda's chest. His instincts kicked in before his mind could comprehend what had happened and conjure a shield spell to block the from impaling himself. However, he did not act fast enough to save Hilda. The bolt crashed against Dahrik's magic shield, coming to a halt instantly. The momentum sent the skewered body of his wife up against the barrier, her last expression smacking the translucent magic for him to see up close.

The familiar wave of anguish filled his whole body. The dwarf fell to the ground and sobbed like he had not since the first time he had watched his beloved wife die. Her death was his fault. He had underestimated Varen and the worst of it all was that he had a chance to save her but only protected himself. The memory melted away back into the fog-covered swamp, but not before he heard the taunting words of Varen.

He leaned against a ballista and said, "We'll see who's second-rate now."

Dahrik, still on his knees wiped the eyes and tried to place his emotions back under control but the tears refused to stop. The mist deepened around him but he did not notice.

* * *

Hemm was starting to panic, which did not happen to him very often. He had heard stories growing up about a mist that separated you and then showed you images of your past in an attempt to drive you mad. However, he never considered that those stories might be true.

First, he and Kilt were cut off from the rest of the company. Then Kilt suddenly disappeared from his shoulder. He didn't even notice her missing until he realized just how quiet things had become. Now, the troll was entirely alone and that scared him.

The mass of white mist blocked out the rest of the swamp, making him lose the feeling of being back in his homeland. Hemm had enjoyed returning to the Abic. He realized it as his first foot stepped inside it once again, just how much he missed it. Several years had passed since he last returned home but the desire to see his tribe once more hadn't been more than a passing thought. Despite enjoying the familiarity of the swamp, Hemm still had no desire to go back.

The maddening mist of legend was said to draw on a person's worst fears and most traumatizing memories. Hemm had plenty of each, which caused him to sweat nervously. The Harsh Marsh is what the tribe elder had called it. Although she was never one for remembering the finer details of old stories. The only reason that Hemm remembered the myth at all was because of Yep, the former Prodigy. Yep was said to be the only person to ever escape the Harsh Marsh without going mad. Like most trolls, Hemm had grown up hearing every great dead of the mage. Yep was considered the greatest of all trolls and the pride of the tribal republic.

He tightened the knots on the ropes that were braided around his knuckles. He was smart enough to know that he couldn't punch his way out of the fog but the task gave him something to focus on. If the Harsh Marsh was going to attack him through his mind, Hemm was determined to be ready.

"Do your worst," the troll grumbled to no one.

As if replying to his request, an image formed in the fog a few feet in front of him. It was Kernil.

At first, Hemm thought that it wasn't an illusion but his friend there in the flesh. That thought was abandoned however when he saw what Kernil was doing. The image of the Son of Vain had his sword drawn, it was swinging wildly in an upward motion. Kernil sidestepped a giant fist crashing into the ground where he used to stand. Next to him now was Barris, who had a bruised eye and a cut on his shoulder. Kernil raised his sword high, and Barris did the same with his hammer. Together, they brought their weapons down upon the giant, gray-skinned fist.

The image widened to show that the owner of the fist was Hemm himself. His image roared in pain, then clobbered the two warriors with his unharmed hand. Just as the wild troll was about to deal a final blow to both Kernil and Barris, an arrow pierced his shoulder. Howel readied another arrow while Kilt moved in, both of her axes drawn.

"I'm sorry, Hemm," Kilt called while raising one of her axes, "but we just can't trust you anymore. You're too uncivilized."

Hemm's image roared unintelligibly, now attempting to bash the hobgoblin with both of his fists. Kilt sidestepped both attacks, then jumped onto Hemm's left arm, running up to his shoulder before he realized what was happening. Kilt raised both her axes, and for a single second, their eyes met. A tear rolled down the musician's cheek as she brought down her axes on the troll's neck.

Just like that, the illusion was gone. Hemm, the real Hemm, was alone in Harsh Marsh. He struggled to breathe as he fell to his knees. With both hands he clutched his throat, checking for the axe cuts. None were there. They had felt so real just seconds ago.

"How did Yep do this?" he asked himself, shaking uncontrollably.

* * *

Howel cradled his broken arm as he walked alone in the mist.

"Curse that horse," he spat, knowing that if he didn't get someone to attend to his arm, he may never be able to use a bow properly again.

Of course, he knew it wasn't likely the horse's fault. Everyone else had become separated within the intense fog, so why shouldn't a rider from his steed? As it was, the archer was used to buying a new horse after almost every job. Something or another always seemed to happen to it. Two jobs ago he stopped naming them. He didn't want to get attached to an animal that would either die or abandon him shortly after acquiring it. His bad luck with horses had become a favorite joke to the rest of the Lute Brutes. Howel failed to see how him needing to spend most of his share of the job earnings on a new horse was at all funny.

"They'd all be laughing if they could only see me now," he grumbled. "Wouldn't even care that I've gone and broke my steady arm."

Howel wasn't one to keep track of time, but even he felt that he had been walking for a long time without seeing so much as a tree. Until now, it had been next to impossible to avoid running into trees. And yet here and now he walked in the ever-thickening mist without even spotting one. Something was off, that much was clear. Had Jes been right after all? He seemed to be right about a lot of things and yet was rarely listened to by the other enchanters.

Then, he saw something off in the distance. It wasn't a tree, of that he was sure, it was much too small. Howel ran toward the figure but after a flash of blue light, he knew who it was. The dwarf smiled as Dalia's face came into view. She smiled at the sight of him, waving him forward. As the two met, they embraced, Howel very cautious of his broken arm.

"What's happened to you, my sweet?" she asked.

He shrugged at the implication of his injury. "Ran into an army of skeleton warriors. Taught most of them a swift lesson but one got a lucky hit in."

The druid laughed. "Growing up in Knaksis, I never thought I'd fall for someone like you, but I must say I'm glad that I did. These last few weeks have been difficult but well worth the struggle."

As Howel thought back on the journey northwest, he didn't have many bad things to say about it. Once he and Dalia had begun their relationship back in the Ruins of Vahr, all of the trials they had faced seemed tiny in comparison to the joy he felt in getting to spend every day with such an amazing woman. They both had insisted that they keep their relationship a secret from the rest of the company, at least until the quest was completed.

Barris had discovered them within a week but had promised not to expose them or pry into their secrecy. His cousin was normally not so observant but then again, he hadn't seen Howel act the way he did ever before.

The druid and the archer knew their relationship would have struggles, but they were ignoring them for now. They spoke in whispers or exchanged notes during the day and snuck away for a starlight walk at night. Howel had never had such happiness in his life before now and he doubted he would find such love again.

"Well, what can I say?" he began with a mischievous smile. "I'm just that charming. Rascal dwarf adventurer woos beautiful druid elf maiden, it's the stuff of legend."

She laughed again. "Oh, is that how you see it?"

They kissed.

"As a matter of fact, it is how I see it."

Dalia rolled her eyes and blushed.

She opened her mouth to reply but never got the chance, as three long, hooked claws suddenly protruded out of her neck.

The druid fell to the ground, lifeless. Her blood spewed from the neck wound, turning the wet ground an off-putting shade of red and brown.

Howel's body went stiff as he watched her die. The only part of him able to move were his eyes, able to see the culprit of his love's demise. Standing where Dalia had only seconds ago, was a Hissera. The claws on its right hand were red with blood, its pointed teeth gnashed and its tongue flicked.

The Hissera flinched when Howel reached for the dagger strapped to his belt. He brought the dagger up just in time to block a swipe of the Hissera's left hand. With a kick to the lizard's chest, the two separated, no longer standing over Dalia's limp body. The lone monster hissed, then advanced once again, both of its claws extended and ready to kill him.

The dwarf was enraged, but his years in combat had allowed his mind to focus on one thing, kill the murderer. Just as Howel took a jab at the Hissera, it leaped backward and suddenly disappeared into the mist. For several seconds, the archer stood alert and ready in case the monster returned.

Then he felt a wetness on his foot, breaking his concentration. He looked down and saw that he was standing in a growing pool of blood. He immediately sprang to the side of his fallen love, covering himself in the elf's blood. Howel cradled her in his arms, refusing to let himself weep.

"I'm so sorry, my sweet," he said almost inaudibly, "I failed to save you."

He closed her eyelids with his fingers, then shut his eyes tightly. He'd go mad if he looked at her lifeless body any longer.

In the mist only a few paces behind him, a shaded figure walked towards him. Howel neither saw nor heard the approach. A set of sharpened teeth reflected a flicker of crimson-colored light.

* * *

Kernil was really starting to get annoyed with this job.

"Last time I go on a quest with enchanters," he muttered as he stomped through the fog.

Being a sword for hire was always a risky business, but never before had so many strange and irritating things happened to him in such a short amount of time. He had come across sprites, endless storms, Kobolds, weird magic-stealing lizards, and now a horse-spooking fog. It seemed like there were new and mystical means of terror at every step, which was exhausting. The Son of Vain longed for simpler problems.

"Even with a blessed sword and Jes Nulkin's promise to help me get Vain back, there's still the necromancer to deal with and I doubt any of us will survive that."

A bitter bile coated his tongue, which he spit out in both disgust and frustration. In an attempt to calm down, Kernil closed his eyes and breathed slowly through his nose. As usual, that's all it took.

He smirked, his hand reflexively going to the wishstone in his pocket. "Then again, I have at least one ray of hope left."

Kernil stopped in his tracks as he realized he was talking to himself. After a few seconds, his anger returned. Normally, when he was alone, he would talk to Ioc but his favorite horse had been spooked and the two got separated.

Looking out into the mist, he decided to stop walking. His thought was that if he was able to escape the mist, he would have by now so may as well let whatever mystical event happen and get it over with.

He was tempted to sit but the swampy ground was muddy, so he remained upright, his eyes ever scanning his surroundings.

"Pathetic," came a voice from behind him which made him jump.

Spinning around to face the voice, Kernil's jaw dropped as far down as it would let him.

"Fa... father?" he asked, his voice weak and shaky. "How are you here? You're dead."

Kreed Ravenhigh scoffed. "And you have done nothing to avenge me. My own son, cowering in fear while his father's murderer turns Vain into a land of treason."

"No," Kernil protested, falling to his knees, "I've tried to take Vain back but-"

"-But you failed," the elder Ravenhigh interrupted. "So you're both a coward *and* a failure."

Kernil shook his head. "No, father, please don't say that. I did my best."

"You are not worthy to raise the sword of our family, you only disgrace it. Give it back to me," Kreed demanded, holding a hand out to take the sword.

Their eyes locked, Kernil's face full of tears as he silently pleaded with his father to forgive him. When his father did not back down, Kernil hung his head in shame and drew the Sword of Vain. He held it out for Lord Kreed to take, his own eyes fix on the ground, unable to look his father in the eye.

Seconds passed and still the sword remained in Kernil's hands. Had he changed his mind? Was his father waiting for him to look him in the eye? Tentatively, the Son of Vain lifted his head and saw nothing but the void of mist, his father having vanished.

"Father?" he called as he got back to his feet.

He received no answer but the endless silence of the mist. Kernil gripped the Sword of Vain tightly in his left hand while pinching his forehead with his right hand, his eyes once again shut. Things were not making sense. Was that his father's ghost? Had he imagined the whole encounter? Why did it end so abruptly?

Kernil was about to sheath his sword when he noticed something, there was a lack of mist surrounding his blade. At first, he thought he was imagining it since the difference was slight. He nearly missed it, but his hunter's eyes were trained to notice the smallest of details in the terrain around him. He swung the Sword of Vain slowly back and forth and the mist dissolved as the blade passed. He tried it again to the same effect, now standing in a pocket without any mist.

The sprite's words echoed in his mind, *from now until the end of time, the blade shall be more than just mere steel but will be infused with a magical charm to repel and destroy dark magic.* It was the sprite Loil that had said that when she dipped the Sword of Vain into the waters of her oasis.

"Dark magic," Kernil said, the words leaving his lips like ice. "So the vision of my father was dark magic. Then, this whole cloud of fog is dark magic too."

He took a step forward and swung his sword in a wide cross in front of him. The mist dissolved when it contacted the blade. Kernil's confidence grew, boldly he walked forward while waving the Sword of Vain. After several yards, he realized that still had no idea where he was going or how to reunite with the rest of the company. Yes, the mist around him was dissolving but would that mean he could find his way out?

Despite not having a plan, Kernil marched on, excavating his path out of the mist. As he moved forward, still unsure of what direction he was walking, he inwardly gave thanks to Loil for the charm upon his sword.

After walking for several minutes, he distinctly heard a sound. It was a voice, a man's voice, deep and gruff. Kernil paused to listen closely but the voice did not become more clear so he took a few more steps forward.

"Stop, please!" the voice cried out in agony. "No more, I cannot relive these moments again."

The voice sounded to Kernil like the dwarf Dahrik but the words didn't seem to fit what he had seen of Dahrik thus far. It even sounded like the taciturn enchanter was sobbing. This didn't make any sense to Kernil, so he decided that it was just another trick of the mist trying to fool him.

His blade leading the way, the Son of Vain went toward what sounded like Dahrik but couldn't possibly be him. As expected, Dahrik came into view. He was on his knees in the mud, his long iron scepter laying at his side with his back turned to Kernil.

Suddenly, the dwarf was on his feet, the scepter now back in his hands. Dahrik spun around and charged at Kernil. As he ran his scepter surged with electricity and the orange gemstones glowed. Kernil barely had time to jump back and avoid the attack.

"I said, no more visions!" the dwarf yelled as he swung.

"Woah, Dahrik, it's me," Kernil pleaded, his arms raised high. "No visions, it's actually me."

Dahrik's puffy eyes narrowed as he scanned the Son of Vain. After several seconds, his shoulders relaxed and he lowered the scepter. A moment later the staff lost its glow and no longer crackled with electricity.

"Have you seen any of the others?" he asked Kernil, wiping the brim of his nose with his sleeve.

Kernil shook his head. "You're the first one that I've found."

"Speaking of which, how did you find me? This fog, whatever it is, wants to keep us separated and drive us all mad."

With a sigh, Kernil told Dahrik the whole story about his encounter with Loil. He told him about the wishstone, the effect the enchantment on his blade had on the mist, and even about his charge to ensure Kaynah's death by the Prodigy's hand. The dwarf said nothing as Kernil explained it all. Once the Son of Vain had finished, Dahrik raised a finger and pointed to the sword.

"So that blade was blessed by a sprite to repel and destroy dark magic?"

"Yes," Kernil answered, unsure why Dahrik had seemingly ignored everything else.

Without another word, Dahrik placed his scepter on the

ground and then grabbed the Sword of Vain from Kernil's grip and examined it. After a once-over, he closed his eyes and placed his palm on the base of the blade, sliding it upward slowly. His mouth twitched in what Kernil thought might be the hint of a smile.

"I can do it," the dwarf announced, gripping the sword firmly in both hands.

After taking a step back, Kernil asked, "Wait, what can you do?"

"I can magnify the repelling magic within the sword, maybe even enough to get rid of all the mist at once."

"That's great, do it!"

Dahrik raised the sword, then abruptly lowered it, looking the confused Kernil in the eyes.

"Does anyone else know?"

Kernil blinked, confused but realizing that Dahrik meant the Loil's charge as well as her gifts.

"Nobody else knows," he answered, not breaking the eye contact.

"Good," said Dahrik. "Don't tell anyone else. Otherwise, what needs to happen might not happen. Understand?"

He nodded.

For the second time, Dahrik raised the Sword of Vain above his head, gripping the hilt with both hands. For a moment, nothing happened, the two men stood there in silence as the dwarf concentrated on the sword. Then Kernil noticed a difference in the air around him. The milky white void that surrounded him was beginning to thin and the ground was becoming visible.

Surprised, he turned around and bumped into a tree, and fell back onto a bush. After hoisting himself back up, Kernil wiped his eyes and saw that he could once again see the familiar marsh for at least ten feet in all directions. The sounds of wind rustling the branches and irritating birds squawking swelled from all directions.

Overjoyed at his escape from the mist, Kernil jumped up and down while waving his fists above his head.

"You did it Dahrik, we're out of–"

Stop," the dwarf interrupted. "It's not gone just yet, have to concentrate."

Gritting his teeth and very much embarrassed, Kernil lowered his arms and waited quietly. The mist was quickly dissolving from between the trees, and Kernil to smiled.

His smile faded as he heard a groan from behind him. It was the mage Kylora. She was bracing herself on her scepter only a few yards away. He rushed to her side, offering her a hand. Kylora took it and got to her feet. She gave him a curious look to which Kernil merely pointed at Dahrik, who was still channeling the sword's magic.

A few feet away, Hemm appeared, his eye red and puffy. At the other side of the clear stood Norvic, who looked more relieved than upset. Then, Kernil heard the strumming of Kilt's lute in a melancholy tune coming from behind him. Seconds later, the hobgoblin appeared, her lute in hand.

One by one, the company seemed to reemerge from the thinning fog. Most were on their knees and in tears. Everyone's story was the same. The fog set in and the company was separated. Soon their horse ran off, followed by a long period of wandering alone in the void. Afterward, came the visions which caused fear and despair. In a rare use of his voice, Hemm told the company the myths and legends of the Harsh Marsh. Dahrik followed up by recounting his conversation with the entity of the Harsh Marsh.

"So it wasn't conjured by Kaynah then," Kylora nodded. "Very curious."

"If only Yep himself has survived this entity, how did you manage to free all us from it, Dahrik?" asked Norvic, his eyes narrowed with suspicion.

Everyone turned toward the dwarf, all wondering the same thing.

Dahrik bit his lower lip, then opened his mouth to answer but was cut off by a cry from Dalia.

"Wait a minute, has anybody seen Howell? He's not here and I don't see him anywhere."

Dahrik's Day

Kilt found Howell's body only a few minutes later. She called us over and everyone rushed to her side. It was a gruesome scene, the back of the archer's head was bashed in, his blood mixing in the with pools of mud. Whatever killed Howell must have surprised him. His facial expression looked surprised, his eye wide and his mouth hanging open.

The death hit everyone like a knife to the back. Dalia and Barris were the most distraught. Dalia threw herself across Howell's body, sobbing intensely. Even though she and Howell had wanted to keep their relationship a secret, we all knew. And even if we hadn't, it was more than obvious now. Barris knelt next to Dalia, his head bowed and his eyes pinched together. I leaned over and closed the archer's eyelids, then shut his jaw. Once that was done, I had to look away, tears trickling down my cheek.

Kernil put a hand on Barris' shoulder as he, Hemm, and Kilt all knelt beside the friend. Each one of their eyes either full of tears or shut so tight that no water could escape them. Kilt was the most composed of the four remaining Lute Brutes.

Though her knees were shaking to the point where I thought she would tip over. She slowly reached for her lute that was strung across her back and played. I was certain that it was a song that I had never heard before, but it sounded so familiar. The tune was not upbeat and fast like all of the other songs I had heard the hobgoblin play so far. This song was slow and full of hurt and melancholy. It was clear that she was holding back tears as she sang softly into the afternoon sky.

I lost a friend today,
I didn't get to see them go.
My soul is torn apart,
The truest pain I know.

You were with me when I was lost,
Now I am alone once more.
There is no coming back,
Death has shut your door.

What will I do next?
How can I move on?
There's no answer that I can see,
Until the pain is gone.
I would give anything I have,
Down to my last scrap,
All for a moment more with you,
But that dream is just a trap.

You are like family to me,
I can still hear you laugh.
The banner of our kind now falls down,

Upon a broken staff.

I have felt loss before this day,
But this is worse than all combined.
The one thing I cannot forgive,
Is leaving me behind.

What will I do next?
How can I move on?
There's no answer that I can see,
Until the pain is gone.
I would give anything I have,
Down to my last scrap,
All for a moment more with you,
But that dream is just a trap.

Your headstone stands out,
A monument to my friend.
I will see you again,
I will join you in the end.

"That was beautiful, Kilt," Dalia sniffled, her voice hoarse.

Kilt placed the instrument at her side and nodded vacantly as she stared at the ground. "I wrote it a long time ago. It's the kind of song you only sing on the worst of occasions. Every time I sing it, I hope it will be the last... but it never is."

Nobody said anything else for a long while. The rhythm and chords of Kilt's elegy rang throughout the trees. The birds captured the tune and blended it into their own symphony.

Dahrik moved to the body and removed the quiver from off Howell's side, followed shortly by snatching the bow from the archer's grip. Everyone stared in shocked silence.

"Unless I'm mistaken, this should go to you," he said to Barris, holding out Howell's bow and quiver.

"For Jard's sake," Kernil cried in exasperation. "Can't we at least wait until he's buried before we divvy out these belongings?"

"No!" snapped Barris, taking the quiver and the bow from Dahrik. "This is the way it has to be."

Kernil didn't reply, but his facial expression was extremely confused.

Dahrik answered, "It's an old dwarf custom. Rather silly when you get right down to it, but important to our people nonetheless."

"What is it?" I asked.

"You're not supposed to be armed when you meet death," Barris answered, strapping the quiver across his back like Howell used to. "Otherwise, he might see you as a threat, an enemy. Any weapons you carry when you die need to go to your closest relative or your specified heir."

Kernil got back to his feet. "So you're his closest family, I assume?"

Barris nodded. "I'm the only blood he has left... had."

The moments that followed were difficult for a multitude of reasons. We were losing the daylight and Howell had to be buried before we could move on or set up camp. The mucky swamp made it difficult to dig a hole large enough for the dwarf, the saturated ground kept collapsing with water and mud. Even with the aid of magic, it was a considerable amount of effort. Once Howell had been laid to rest, Dalia severed a thick branch off one of the nearby trees. She burned into the shaft the words, "Here lies Howell Bronzearm, Rascal adventurer."

We waited by the grave for a while longer before moving north again. Without any of our horses, we walked. Once we decided to stop and make camp, we used magic to craft supplies and shelter. The horses had carried most of our supplies and were now gone. Nobody spoke for the rest of the day and well into the evening. Unless words were necessary, no one talked. We all kept our distance from one another as well, each one of us wanting to be alone as we mourned the loss of our friend.

Unlike when we lost all of our food in the prairie, here we did not want for food. Birds and swamp lizards were abundant and easy enough to hunt. They didn't taste very good but nobody complained. Water surrounded us and only required a simple purification spell to make it safe to drink.

What impacted us the most was our traveling speed. On horseback, we would have arrived at the Abandoned Fortress within two days, but on foot and with morale at an all-time low, it took us over a week.

Kylora was the first to spot the fortress on the horizon, just as the swamp forest was starting to clear.

"There it is, I see it!" she cried in excitement.

The sun was setting and the glare made it nearly impossible to see it for myself, but I had no doubt she was right. I felt my stomach drop and my muscles tense.

"Well then," Norvic began, "we made it. What do we do now? Shall I knock on the front door whilst the rest of you try to sneak around the back?"

His words were thick with sarcasm but I tried my best to ignore them. "Well, I guess when you get down to it, I hadn't planned out anything specific."

"Not to state the obvious, but she's waiting for us," said Kernil. "There's probably a thousand Hissera in there ready to kill us."

"Which is why no plan we make is gonna do us any good," Dahrik replied.

I stared at him in awe for several seconds before saying. "Dahrik, are you seriously suggesting that we go in without a strategy?"

He nodded. "While we have fought and struggled to get here,

Kaynah has done nothing but prepare for this moment. She's a schemer, a strategist, a woman who always has a plan. We aren't going to outthink her on this. She has every advantage here. The only way that we succeed is if she dies. So, why not just break down the front door? It might seem like the obvious thing to do, in fact, it's likely the most obvious thing to do."

"So it's exactly the last thing she will expect," Barris finished. "Her own anticipation and suspicions will expect a complex plan or trick. We come in simple and it might actually catch her by surprise."

Silence followed as everyone soaked in the idea.

"That's brilliant," said Dalia.

Followed by Norvic, who added, "Or incredibly foolish."

"Do you have a better idea?" the dwarf challenged.

"No."

Then I interjected, my own mind trying to accept that not having a plan was the best plan. "Where is she?"

Everyone looked at me with either shocked or blank expressions.

"Where is Kaynah exactly?" I expanded. "That's a big fortress and she could be anywhere inside it."

"Well," Dahrik began, "I suppose-"

Norvic cut him off with a simple declaration. "She's in the dungeon."

Eight heads turned to him, puzzled by his confidence.

The warlock sighed. "It's where I'd be."

"Sounds good enough to go on," I said. "We should wait until morning. We're tired from walking all day and I'd rather not fight off the Hissera in the dark."

Dahrik clasped my shoulder and then shouted to the rest of the group, "You heard the Prodigy, we move at dawn. Everybody rest up. I will take full watch tonight."

Nobody was bothered by the decision to wait until the morning. There was excitement in the camp. I couldn't blame them, we'd been struggling for weeks to get to this point and the end of the quest was finally here. Even I was nervous and excited. At the very least, this entire ordeal was about to be over, one way or another.

* * *

Black smoke came out of Kaynah's ears as she roared in fury. Her screams echoed throughout the old, stone fortress, which amplified the sound. Amplified her screams became roars of a wounded animal. Once she had finished, the necromancer was breathing heavy, choking on the smoke that had filled

340

the dungeon.

"*He* is outside," she spat to no one. "*He* is finally here, come to watch everything I've built slip from my grasp and take it for himself."

Kaynah started to pace nervously, her tattered shoes smacking against the stone floor. In a flash of anger, she pushed over a stack of her old research. Papers and books crashed and scattered around the room.

"No, I can't let him do this," she cried in protest. "My Hissera shall never be *his*, anyone but *his*!"

Then she abruptly ran up the stairs, leaving the dungeon behind. Her legs burned as the magic flowed through her. Her speed increased as she made her way through the fortress, counting each of the Hissera. Kaynah's breathing grew heavy as she ran in and out of every room and chamber of the old prison. She only stopped once she had gone into the lone tower, which was near the southwest end of the fortress. Once there, she went out the window and onto the roof. There, she stared east out into the blackness of the night.

"*He* is there," she coughed, the skin on both of her legs burning, bleeding, and spiting puss as the magic took its toll on her body. "I can sense him. He's brought me more enchanters to renew myself. This is good. The Prodigy will be the most useful, but he will come to me. The Prodigy will come for my life, but he has not planned the way I have. Once I have the Prodigy's power, all enchanters will soon fall to extinction!"

Kaynah laughed wildly but was disappointed that the wind, which had just begun to pick up, silenced her laughter. Frustrated, she sniffed the cold air. She smelled snow. There wasn't a lot of it but there was no mistaking the scent. Every year as a child she had looked forward to the first snow of the year. She knew what snow smelled like and this was it.

An innocent smile slid across her face, as she remembered one of the few things she enjoyed about her childhood. The smile of reminiscence was short-lived, as a heavy breeze nearly made the necromancer lose her balance on her already wobbly legs.

"Maybe I should just send my Hissera now," Kaynah said, looking down at where the Prodigy and his company were camped. "I could take them by surprise, kill them all while they slept."

After thinking on the idea for a few seconds, she shook her head in disappointment. "No, *he* wouldn't come all this way, stop on my doorstep, and be caught by a surprise attack. *He's* definitely scheming something, I just don't know what it is... "

Kaynah's thoughts scattered as the feeling that she was playing into a trap suddenly overwhelmed her. With another jolt of magic, she zoomed back into the fortress, checking every door, each window, and all the secret entrances for any sign of use other than her own.

Finding nothing but still seized by the overwhelming sensation of being trapped, she knelt on the floor of the dungeon and sobbed.

* * *

Everyone else fell asleep rather quickly after another meal of fried swamp lizard, however, I did not. No matter how hard I tried, I could not fall asleep, my mind was too anxious. After what felt like days but was only a few hours, I decided to get up in the hope of tiring myself out. I walked over to Dahrik who was faithfully watching the distant fortress and the lands in between.

"Can't sleep?" he asked, handing me a waterskin.

I grabbed it and took a large gulp. "How did you guess?"

"I can't sleep either."

"Well, you're supposed to be keeping watch, not sleeping."

The dwarf chuckled. "Then I guess it all worked out for the best."

There was a moment of silence as we both stared out into the darkness, nothing but the moon shining through the cloud cover to illuminate the world around us.

"What time do you suppose it is?" Dahrik asked, breaking the silence.

"Just after midnight. Why?"

He smiled, his usually white teeth reflecting the moonlight. "It's my birthday."

My jaw dropped. With everything going on, the quest, Howell's death, and my duel with the necromancer tomorrow, a birthday was the last thing on my mind.

"It's okay, boy, I barely remembered myself."

"Well," I began, looking at him in the eyes, "congratulations, you grouchy old man."

Dahrik laughed, much louder than I thought the situation called for, but he was never much for restraint.

"Hey, Dahrik," I started after another moment of silence, "I don't think I can do this tomorrow. I can't be what everyone expects me to be."

The old sorcerer stared back at me, as if really looking for the very first time.

Finally, he asked, "Do you remember when I first found you, all those years ago in Tyran City?"

"I do," I said with a nod. "That feels like a lifetime ago."

"It was a lifetime ago," he replied. "You have changed so much since then. It's been the greatest honor of my life to train you and watch you grow up into the wise and powerful enchanter you are today."

I snorted. "There are many things I might say about how I've turned out. 'Unfortunate' being the primary one, but wise or powerful are definitely near the bottom of the list."

"Jes," Dahrik said with a sigh, "how is it that you have this far and not learned the most important lesson about yourself? You are your own worst obstacle. You think too much. Do yourself a favor and think things through a little less. Act in the moment. Stop letting yourself be acted upon and just act. Do what needs to be done."

I sighed. Perhaps he had a point, overthinking was my specialty. When I fought the Vios Almna five years ago, I didn't overthink, I merely acted and solved the problems as they came in front of me. Then again, at the time I was under the impression that someone else was going to be there to destroy the Vios Almna, that someone else was the Prodigy.

"I wish I didn't have to be Jard's Prodigy, that he picked someone else or that there wasn't a need for a Prodigy in my lifetime. I wish it wasn't my destiny, any of it."

The old dwarf's smile was full of pity. "I'm glad it's you."

"Why? What good am I in this?"

"You have all the power in the world, yet you fear to use it. That's not something that normally happens. It's special. It's certainly not something you learned from me. I would be misusing your power left and right."

I shook my head. "I doubt that."

"Well," he began with a sigh, "I suppose we'll never find out. Whether you like it or not, you're the Prodigy, and you're the right man to be it, in my opinion. Destiny is what you choose to do with the obstacles life puts in front of you. Being the Prodigy is the same. Just do the best you can in the moments that matter. I believe in you, boy."

"Alright, stop it," I jokingly shoved him. "You're actually giving me confidence, that's not what you do. You're supposed to bark at me to stop complaining or something."

This made him laugh again. "Well, maybe I'm getting tired in my old age. Yelling anything into that thick head of yours is rough work. I thought I'd try something new."

"*The* Dahrik Ironhelm going soft, now that's a strange thought," I joked. "Here I thought that stunt you pulled with Barris the other day meant you were growing even more heartless."

He smiled but didn't laugh. His eyes flicked between me and the orange jewel on the ends of his scepter.

"That reminds me of something that I think I should have told you long ago."

346

Picking up on the serious tone that entered his voice, I asked, "And what would that be?"

"Five years ago, when I felt Ryone Peak explode, I thought you had died," he began, his fingers fidgeting with his scepter uncomfortably. "When you returned, I was overjoyed. It was around that time that I began thinking about my own inevitable death. While you returned to Tyran and married Rebecca, I snuck away back to Underhigh where I declared my heir. It's you."

My eyes narrowed in confusion. "Wait, you can do that? But I'm no dwarf, how is that possible?"

"Well, as you said, I'm *the* Dahrik Ironhelm," he grinned. "Even King Horthvon bends the rules for me."

"Huh, neat."

Dahrik stared at me for a few seconds, then said, "Anyways, what this means is that when my time comes, you will inherit my scepter. Use it how you'd like, just make sure you take it from as quickly as you can once I'm dead. I know it's ridiculous, but its custom. I have to greet death as a friend, not a foe."

He broke the eye contact as he realized he was rambling. I had never known Dahrik to believe in any of the dwarf traditions, or at least not enough to want to practice any of them.

"It sounds like you're expecting to die," I noted.

"Oh, not at all," he protested, "I'm just letting you know because it is on my mind and you should probably know for when it does happen. No, I don't expect to die for a long while. Not unless you get sick enough of me that you off me yourself."

This made me laugh. "Don't tempt me. So, why make me your heir? I know you have family in Underhigh or even Rivith. Why me?"

The dwarf looked me in the eyes again, swallowed, then said with absolute sincerity, "Because you are my son, boy."

I took a step back, but nodded, not breaking eye contact. "I know."

"And," he said more casually, trying to put the mood more at ease, "this makes you honorary but official dwarf of the Ironhelm clan. You and your descendants will be able to claim all the rights and privileges that the kingdom offers to one of its own. This includes my family's wealth."

I couldn't imagine using or needing his family's wealth. After all, I was married into the Tyranian royal family, but I suppose it was nice to know that it was there, if not for me then for one of my descendants at least.

"Thank you, Dahrik," I said. "Sometimes I don't think I deserve a father like you."

He laughed, once again too loud for what the situation

warranted. "No, you certainly don't."

"Oh, shut up."

Then, without another word, I walked back to where my cloak laid on the ground. It wasn't very comfortable but Arrig had run away with my bedroll. Despite the conditions, I fell asleep in seconds, not waking or stirring until dawn.

Kaynah of Shale

A cold droplet landed on my cheek, waking me. The sun in the east was illuminating the Pryre mountains, marking the early dawn. I opened my eyes to see hundreds of white, fluffy specks of snow descending from the sky. Most of the flakes dissolved upon impact with the ground, but a few of them clung to the fabric of my sleeves.

"First snow of the season," noted Kernil, who was also newly awake.

I nodded. "I never liked winter or the cold. This seems fitting for today."

"Alright, everybody up!" shouted Dahrik, banging his scepter on the ground with a loud boom. "Morning is here, no more stalling or wasting time. Today is the day this whole trek becomes worth it. Today Kaynah of Shale dies."

With a groan, everyone got to their feet and packed up what little supplies we had.

I fixed the gauntlet to my left arm, checking the gasper emerald. The metal glove felt cold on my arm, but a quick heating spell took care of that. After fixing my cloak and my belt, I grabbed my scepter in my right hand. It was then that I noticed everyone was looking at me.

Uncomfortable and feeling awkward, I said with as much confidence as I could gather, "Well, it's now or never. Good luck to everyone. Stay sharp, watch out for the Hisseras' claws and teeth, and remember your elemental magic. We don't know exactly how many of those monsters are in there, but it's wise to assume it will be more than we've ever faced before."

I paused, taking a breath and trying to stop my legs from shaking. "I'll break away from the rest of you and search out Kaynah once we are inside the fortress. I'll start in the dungeon, as Norvic has recommended. If she is not there, I will search the whole of the fortress until I find her. I don't expect her to want an open fight with us all, that would put her at a sincere disadvantage, even with all of her Hissera."

"Well," began Dahrik, "let's go take that fortress and be done with this."

"For Howell," added Dalia, her eyes no longer teary but fueled by righteous anger.

The Lute Brutes each nodded at the mention of their fallen friend's name. Then they looked to each other and raised their weapons in salute, "For Howell!"

"And for all those others Kaynah has taken from us," I added, raising my scepter in salute also.

Dahrik, Kylora, Norvic, and Dalia raised their scepters, the nine of us saluting together. I could feel the hurt and the anger of everyone in the company, the want for this ordeal to be over. As I looked at each one of them, I saw the confidence that they had in me, and that gave me confidence.

After a moment of silent salute, we all lowered our weapons and gazed at the fortress ahead. Without another word, I moved toward the abandoned prison. First, the movement was an intentful walk, then at a jog, and eventually a sprint. The rest of the company followed behind me, Hemm catching up and passing me in only a few strides.

With every step, the fortress did not seem to get any closer. It loomed on the horizon, taunting me as I charged forward. The cold air burned my lungs, but the soft falling snow cooled my body as ran. Then, all of a sudden, we were nearly on top of it. I blinked and the Abandoned Fortress was only a few hundred yards away. That's when the hissing started. It was like someone had kicked open a massive beehive, the thunderous collective noises seemed to come from every direction.

"Hissera!" shouted Dahrik only a few steps behind me, pointing to several dozen pouring out the front gate.

The Hissera seemed faster, meeting us within seconds of exiting the fortress door. The first one reached me and I used my scepter to vault over the Hissera. I bashed its skull in on a down-swing from behind. There was no time to celebrate, as four more were immediately upon me.

The four extended their claws, but they never got to me. I smacked my scepter on the ground, and the Hissera sank in quicksand. Once they had sunk down to their waste, I tapped the pool again and it returned to normal earth, trapping them. I smiled as I continued forward.

My ears twitched as I heard the sound of Kilt's lute, she was singing her battle song again. Like the last time, the rhythm of the ballad's tune seemed to match the pace of the battle at hand. Each pluck of the lute's acoustic strings matched a movement made, either an attack or a block of a Hissera's attack. My heart stung each time the Hobb sang the line of the chorus, "between Howel's true bow." I was sure this affected the singer more than me, but it did not show, Kilt spun and hacked with her axe to great effect without missing a beat of the song.

"Maybe she'll change the lyrics next time she gets the chance," I thought while crushing a pair of Hissera under a boulder.

Although we were all doing well against the Hissera, their numbers did not seem to be getting any smaller. With each one killed by our hands, another exited the front gate and ran out to meet us.

"This isn't working," Dahrik called over to me. "Killing them off one by one is going to wipe us out."

My former master was right, all this effort seemed futile. Maybe this was Kaynah's plan. Even if we made it through her army of Hissera, we'd be too drained to be any kind of threat to her.

A Hissera jumped at me head-on. Thinking fast, I caught and suspended it mid-air in a small cyclone of air. I channeled the magic by spinning my scepter between my fingers. The floating Hissera thrashed and kicked wildly, trying to break free but it could not escape the magic. It was completely at my mercy.

This gave me an idea.

There were more Hissera incoming, so I brought the wind-trapped Hissera down. And this sent it crashing into a few of the others. Keeping my scepter spinning in my hands, I blasted any Hissera that came near me with the cyclone of cold air. This only seemed to enrage them more, drawing them to me in greater numbers.

I smiled. It was working.

They came at me from all directions now, meaning I had to keep my eyes sharp and pivot quickly to keep them at bay. After a minute or so, I spun in a circle, the small cyclone spinning both forwards and clockwise. I focused on Dahrik during each rotation to keep from getting dizzy.

The air churned around me, the gyration of the cyclone caused the air current to change into a funnel around me. As this change occurred, I changed my position to match. I stopped pivoting and stood firm on the ground once again. In the same motion, I brought my arm, which still spun the scepter in circles, above my head. This made the funnel of air grow in size and speed, the wind all around me subject to my command. The clouds above me collected together, whirling in the same clockwise direction.

All of the Hissera flocked to the tornado I was creating, like prey to a baited trap. They seemed drawn to it, the challenge, enraged by the barrier of natural magic they were still subject to. Dahrik's eyes went wide as he stared at the tornado, backing up to a safe distance. The rest of the company stood nearby, also staring in awe.

The funnel that started on the ground connected with the clouds. The ferocity of the winds increased so much that closer Hissera got swept up by the current. Breathing was growing difficult, but I didn't let that distract me. My focus was on the motion of my scepter, spinning it in a perfect rhythm from one hand into the other. With each rotation, more magic wisped into the air of the typhoon. Magic became thicker in the winds and the air moved faster, and the wider the eye of the storm became.

All of the Hissera were now caught in the torrent, spinning and circling in the powerful gales. Each one flailed their limbs in a desperate hope to regain control.

The rest of the company moved to the other side of the fortress, yet they still struggled with the force of the blowing

355

winds. The four enchanters jammed their scepters into the ground in an attempt to keep steady. The Lute Brutes clung to Hemm who had the widest stance and the strongest legs to keep upright.

Without realizing it at first, I rose, pulled upward by the air churning around me. I was only partially aware of my ascent, my focus still on the hand motions that spun my scepter. The tornado raged faster and stronger with every passing second. Lightning from the clouds above struck repeatedly at the fast-twirling scepter. The barrage of electricity was then immediately channeled through the silver gauntlet on my hand, held captive by the Gasper Emerald. I did not feel any pain, but I could feel the energy flowing through me, building with each bolt.

Dahrik stared up at me and a realization came to him. He started to panic, knowing there was not very much time left to act. He called to the rest of the company but the words were drowned out by the roar of the storm. He tried again, calling on his magic to help amplify his voice, but it failed to the same effect.

Growing frustrated and pressed for time, the dwarf punched the ground at his feet. The earth split and compacted, forming a tunnel sloped at a steep but not unscalable angle. He peered inside, trying to not lose his balance from the push of the wind. The tunnel went only a few yards below the surface and was about fifteen feet in diameter. It was not his best work but would have to do for the moment.

Knowing that yelling would not work, Dahrik tried something new this time. With a snap of his fingers, the orange gems on his scepter flashed brightly. He snapped five times, one after another, each one accompanied by its own flash of orange light. This grabbed the attention Dahrik wanted. The four Lute Brutes and the three enchanters looked at Dahrik expectantly. The dwarf pointed to the tornado, then point to the tunnel at his side with emphasis. Although no words were shared, everyone seemed to get the message.

Norvic was the first to move, crouching low but moving fast in a straight line toward the tunnel. After a few steps, the warlock lost his balance and fell to the ground, the wind pushing him back. His misstep was short-lived, as Kylora and Dalia caught him by the arm and pulled him to his feet. The three enchanters moved together, using each other for support. Dahrik grinned at Norvic as he slid into the tunnel, the warlock glared back at him.

Hemm wrapped Kilt and Barris in one arm and Kernil in the other. The troll then slung his friends over his broad shoulders and began maneuvering toward Dahrik. Hemm's legs were long and it did not take him very long to reach the entrance to the tunnel. There was a slight shaking of the ground as the three enchanters already inside widened and deepened the cave. Hemm slid in without a word or glance to Dahrik, who followed in after them.

As I rose to where the tornado on the ground met the clouds, my scepter was moving nearly too fast for my hands to keep up. The air was thin and I was breathing heavy just to get any air into my lungs at all. I knew this had to end and end quickly, otherwise, I might lose control of the whole thing.

I took one last deep breath, then grabbed the spinning scepter tightly in the center with both hands, stopped it abruptly.

"Heeyaah!" I yelled with great effort, calling upon all of the swirling winds around me.

I plummeted to the ground, the violent gales of the tornado following my descent. The twister collapsed in on itself as we fell. Then when the violent gales hit the earth the column exploded outward in all directions. My gauntlet seized and the lightning that was no longer contained burst out. Bolts of energy struck all around in rapid succession. The gates of the Abandoned Fortress snapped off their hinges, blown away beyond my sight. Wind and lightning hit the southeast corner of the fortress and destroyed it. Walls and earth were torn off entirely, tumbling away like a pebble down a steep cliff. The ground shook and chunks of rock and dirt were ripped away. That part of the fortress was now a field of uneven trenches and craters.

I landed scepter-first and the force of my fall created a massive crater in the moistened ground. Being in the center, I felt the least of winds and escaped my own wraith. I huddled there on my knees, still clutching my scepter as hard as I could.

The chaotic winds howled in rage for several minutes before calming. Once the wind was nothing more than a light push against my body, I looked up and was horrified. The land between the Abic of Marsh and Kaynah's fortress was more torn apart than even the Forsaken Prairie had been. The fortress itself was missing a tower on one side and looked like it would collapse any minute. Parts of Hissera were in every direction and their blue blood was a grim paint on the ruined ground.

The next thing I knew, Dahrik was standing at my side. He grabbed my shoulder and pulled me to my feet. I thanked him and tried to brush off some of the dirt on my cloak.

"That was amazing!" called Kernil from behind as he gestured to the carnage around. "It was horrifying... but absolutely amazing. That has to be the most incredible display of magic I think I've ever seen."

I turned around and saw the rest of the company had left the tunnel behind and were making their way over to Dahrik and me.

"When this is over," Kilt began as she stepped over a Hissera torso, "I'm writing a song about that, something twister-like. Not sure how that'll work just yet but it will be worthy, I promise."

"Impressive display, young Prodigy," said Norvic, without his usual hint of sarcasm or passive insult.

The congratulatory remarks were cut short by a familiar sound. A loud, guttural hissing filled the air. Everyone paused, listening with the hope that it wasn't what we all knew it was, even silencing their breathing so as not to add to the noise.

After a moment or two, Barris broke the silence. "Well, I suppose not all the Hissera were outside."

"Yeah," I sighed. "It would seem so."

"It's not nearly as loud as before," Dalia noted as she gazed at the fortress.

I faced the open gates and stared into the darkness, not yet illuminated by the morning sun. She was right, the hissing from inside was not as loud as it had been before. This filled me with hope, and the adrenaline flowed through my veins once again.

"Dalia is right," I called, moving toward the entrance, "however many are in there, I believe we've seen the worst of it already. Now, let's finish this!"

Everyone cheered as they followed behind me. Kernil, who was now in front, drew his sword and held it high as he ran forward. Everyone began running close behind him, the entire company charging in as one.

"For the heart of Vain!" Kernil cried as we reached the doorless entrance.

Going through the doorway, we came into a dark room that was wider than it was deep. With a flick and a flash of my scepter, I sent a ball of yellow light up to the ceiling, giving the whole chamber perfect illumination. Now that I could see I came to an abrupt halt. A thick, puss-looking slime covered the stone floor, except for the entryway where we stood. A putrid stench seeped from the slime, assaulting our noses and causing our eyes to water.

I stood frozen next to my companions, unsure of what to do next. I looked at Dahrik for a suggestion but he looked as confused as I was. What was the most confusing was the hissing. In the stone room, the Hissera's calling cry was deafening and very close. They couldn't be very far but they were nowhere to be seen.

Finally, Hemm moved toward the edge of the clean tile, prodding the rim of the yellowish goo with his toe. He gave no reaction to touching it, which lead Kilt to do the same. After a quick, tentative experiment, she then stepped on it with her foot, testing the slime's stickiness.

The hobgoblin shivered. "It stinks and it feels gross but it won't slow us down any more than we let it."

Everyone else looked at each other, then moved forward. I found Kilt's assessment to be accurate.

The chamber had three doorways leading to other parts of the fortress, one on each wall. I trudged through the slime toward the door straight ahead when something sitting in the slime in the corner caught my eye. I walked toward it and picked it up, careful not to the slime get all over me.

361

"What is this?" I asked, holding it for all to see. "What is any of this?"

Kernil squinted at the flabby, flat object in my hand. "How are Hissera made?"

The question seemed strange. No one answered him.

"No, really, does anyone know how they're made?" he asked again.

"What are you trying to say?" asked Kylora, taking a few steps closer.

He sighed, then pointed to the squishy membrane in my hand, then to the floor of slime. "What if this is how they are made? The Hissera grow in some kind of egg or pod made out of that flabby thing, and this slime is what's leftover when they hatch."

"Gross!" Barris cried, staring down at the slime in disgust. "You mean we're stepping the Hissera's birthing fluid?"

I immediately let go of the piece of egg and shook the slime off my hand. A single shudder went up my back.

"Okay, I'm going to ask a question and maybe it's obvious to everyone else, but it's making me uneasy," said Kilt, nervously scanning the walls. "Why aren't the rest of the Hissera attacking us?"

It was Norvic who answered, pointing to the door on the right. "They're behind that door. They will strike as soon as we open it."

"So let's just go through one of the others," offered Dalia. "Who says we have to fight them now. Maybe we could all face Kaynah together, take her down as a company. This Hissera would be directionless, and possibly easier to kill."

The warlock shook his head. "I don't think that will work. This feels like a trap. We make the wrong move and all of a sudden we're facing something even worse."

"And just how would you know that? You seem to know a lot about this place and how Kaynah thing," accused Kernil.

"Because I'm good at strategy," Norvic spat back. "The necromancer has had weeks to plot this out. Did you really think it was going to be an army of Hissera sent all out at once? Use your mind for once, you mindless animal. This is a puzzle, a test of our wits."

Kernil's face reddened and his arms tensed. Dahrik took a step between them.

"Now hold on a moment," the dwarf said to both of them. "If this is a trap, how do spring it?"

Norvic shrugged. "We pick the right door."

As they were trying to rationalize which door to open, an idea came to me. I got the idea when Norvic called Kernil an animal.

his got me thinking, "How would an animal figure this out?"

I walked a few steps forward until I was at the far wall from the entrance. I held my scepter and planted it firmly on the floor while I placed my right ear on the wall and closed my eyes. The gems on my scepter shined dimly as I called forth magic to heighten my senses. I raised my gauntleted hand smacked the wall, the vibrations moving through the wall.

My eyes were shut but I could still feel what was around me, magic enhancing my other senses. I had practiced this spell before, just not in this way. It was a basic charm to help an enchanter fight off enemies when unable to see, called, "Nocturnal Mapping." It grants a heightened smell and hearing, and an ability like echolocation. This echolocation uses vibrations to give the enchanter a vague sort of sight. It isn't specific, but it can use the natural vibrations of objects to make a sort of mental map. Hence the spell's name "Nocturnal Mapping."

Just as I had hoped, I was able to use Nocturnal Mapping now to mystically sense the fortress' layout. I smacked my gauntlet against the wall twice more, the vibrations bettering my map with each hit.

"Norvic is right," I declared, backing away from the wall and pointing to the door on the right. "All of the Hissera are behind there. Kaynah is with another creature that's too small to be a Hissera in the dungeon. The door behind me leads to

364

her, eventually."

"And you know this after hitting the wall a few times with your gauntlet?" asked Kernil, his arms raised in confusion.

Kylora replied, nodding her head and smiling. "Nocturnal Mapping. Very clever, young Prodigy."

The Son of Vain looked even more confused, but let it go.

"What about through the other door, what's through there?" asked Dahrik.

"Something a lot bigger than a Hissera is three rooms over," I stated, looking at the left door. "I don't think it was moving, I think it was tied up or restrained, but it was definitely breathing so I know it wasn't just an old piece of furniture."

Dalia clapped her hands together with confidence. "Okay, so let's all head down and fight the necromancer together."

"No," I snapped, surprising myself with my own conviction, "it has to be me. I have to do this alone."

Dahrik took a few steps toward me. "Jes, maybe she's right. You don't have to do this alone."

"No," I said again. "The side with all the Hissera has another entrance to the dungeon also. I think Norvic is right about it being a trap. If you go that way and I go straight for Kaynah, things will go as we want them. No surprises."

"What about the tied-up creature through there?" asked Barris, pointing to the door on the left.

I shrugged. "If it's a friendly prisoner, we'll rescue them once this over. In case it's not, I'll seal the door to the dungeon behind me. There are only the two ways to the dungeon so it will have to come your way to get below."

Barris did not seem pleased by my answer but chose not to say more about it.

"Good luck, Prodigy. All magic be with you," said Dalia.

"And to all of you," I answered, trying my best to smile and seem more confident than I really was. "Don't worry, this will all be over soon."

Dahrik looked at me for only a second, but I knew what he meant to say.

I nodded and without another thought, I opened the door behind me and made my way toward the dungeon.

* * *

I summoned a floating ball of fire to light my way as I descended the circular stairs to the dungeon. There were torches hanging on metal racks attached to the walls. Every single one of them had been recently extinguished. I reignited each torch I passed; the firelight reflected dimly off of the gray stone of the walls and stairs. Kaynah's first attempt to intimidate me had failed, my confidence was at an indomitable high.

I soon came to the bottom of the stairs where there was a stone door closing off a wide arch. A sliver of yellow light was visible under the door's base, meaning that Kaynah was likely on the other side. Pausing for only a few seconds, I reevaluated every choice that had led me to this here and wished that Rebecca was by my side. I gave the door a gentle push and it slid open as if the stone were made of paper. Without another thought, I leaped into the chamber, ready for a fight.

"Greetings, Jes Nulkin," called a woman's voice from behind me. "This is a great honor, indeed. It's not every day that Jard's Prodigy marches into my halls and rips away my gates."

I spun around to see Kaynah of Shale, and she was just as I had imagined her. She was an elf with green eyes that were full of purpose and assurance. She had long black hair that was woven into a tight braid on her left side. Her once fair skin was cracked and covered with scabs, sores, and open wounds that looked infected. Even her face was dotted with scars and blisters. Kaynah was taller than I expected, standing just over six feet. She wore all black clothing aside from a crimson sash that wrapped around her waist. In her hands was a scepter, like one an enchanter would use, the metal was a rusty iron and the gems a calm lavender color.

The necromancer stared back at me, both of us sizing up the other. We stood only a few feet apart. I stood tall and tense, while Kaynah leaned casually against the wall next to the now open doorway.

"Did you steal that scepter?" was the first thing that came out of my mouth.

She laughed as she pushed herself from the wall and to the far end of the chamber toward a stack of loose pages. "As a matter of fact, I did. My very first victim's scepter, to be more exact. She was a mage, I think. I changed the color of the gems from this ugly lime green color. Do you like it?"

I didn't answer, instead, I scanned the large room for any sort of trap. In every other room I had seen of the fortress, there was at least some of it covered in the slimy egg residue. The dungeon was oddly without the sticky substance. There were several shattered tiles on the floor that looked like Hemm had lost his temper. Loose pages of differing sizes, materials, and ages were scattered everywhere. At one end there was a desk and a chair with even more pages and books stacked on top of it.

"Can I help you find something?" Kaynah asked, a sinister smile on her face.

I couldn't get away from the feeling that I was falling into her trap but I couldn't figure out what it was. She was trying to put me off balance with a false warm welcome.

"Enough of the lies and the games, you know why I am here," I declared, sounding an awful lot like Dahrik. "You have murdered hundreds with your Hissera and turned the Bountiful Prairie into an unrecognizable wasteland."

The necromancer snorted and began to shift through a large stack of particularly old-looking pages. "Oh, I'd say I've killed far more than you realize and as for the wasteland bit, I think the Forsaken Prairie has a much better ring to it, don't you?"

I stomped the end of my scepter on the ground, the *thud* echoing throughout the large dungeon. Kaynah stopped flipping through the pages, stood up straight, and grinned widely, her black, rotting teeth on full display.

"You're a lot feistier than *he* said you would be, I like it," her body shuddered so drastically at the mention of *he*, nobody with eyes could miss it.

I took a few steps toward the necromancer, and she sidestepped to her right. I mirrored her movements, and soon we were circling each other. The tension in the air noticeably rising. Her grip on her rusty scepter tightened, and sweat dripped steadily from my brow.

"Your patron, he knows me," I stated, putting together who she meant by *he*.

Kaynah made a clicking noise with her tongue, then smiled. "Oh, *he* knows you. *He* claims to know everything, but *he* doesn't. *He* underestimates me. I had to do it. Now *he* is angry with me, but I will kill *him* too if I must."

Her body continued to shudder at every mention of her patron. Her eyes, which only a few seconds ago seemed full of confidence and control, now flickered with anger, distress,

369

and chaos.

"I don't suppose you will tell me who your patron is," I said. "So that way I can find him when this is all over."

"No, I won't," she snorted again. "Although, *he* wouldn't like it if I did, and after all, you'll be dead in few minutes so... no, I don't think I'll say. Best to avoid... complications."

The necromancer's eyes looked me up and down once more. Something was about to happen. I readied myself mentally for Kaynah to attack, but knew there was still a few seconds left before she made her first move. I decided to try something first, something I couldn't have done with the Vios Almna.

"It doesn't have to be like this, Kaynah," I declared. "Surrender your scepter and the talisman that was buried underneath Shale, and I will spare your life. You will stand trial for your crimes, but I give you my word that it will be a fair trial."

Kaynah opened her mouth as if to laugh but abruptly closed it, resulting in an awkward facial expression. Then, she shook her head far more dramatically than necessary. Kaynah then mumbled some kind of response before stopping in front of the desk and stomping her foot thrice on the stone floor.

Wah-aaaah!

Suddenly, a small creature jumped out at me from underneath a stack of pages to my side. Before I could even see it, the creature clung to my gauntlet and kicked at my face. I tried to shake it off my arm, but whatever it was, this thing had a good grip. I then swiped at it with my scepter, but it kept kicking at my face, making it difficult to see exactly where it was. After a few tries, I finally managed to whack it off my arm.

It slid toward Kaynah, who seemed to be enjoying the display, and I finally got a good look at the small creature. It looked like a cross between a spider monkey and a lizard. It was freckled with patches of white fur and black scales. It also had a tail, stood on two legs, and had two arms not so different from that of an imp or gnome. Its head was round and hairless. Its eyes were identical to those of the Hissera, red with a diamond-shaped pupil that was completely black.

In its hands, it clutched a green gemstone that I recognized instantly. Flashing a look to my gauntlet, I felt a drop in my stomach. It had the Gasper Emerald. Screeching like when it had jumped out at me, the Hissera monkey ran out of the dungeon and began climbing up the stairs. I started to race after it but stopped at the base of the stairs. The monkey was already at the very top and making its way into the fortress proper.

"You were saying?" came a laugh from behind me.

My face muscles clenched up and my cheeks turned red and hot with anger. I had known there would be a trick and even knew something else was down here with her, and yet I had fallen for it. That creature had left me without the key to my greatest weapon.

I spun around and ducked just in time to avoid a large fireball. Still on the ground, I countered with my own fire. Kaynah smacked the flames away with her scepter, but the delay allowed me to get to my feet and jump back into the dungeon chamber. I threw another ball of fire at her, which she again deflected to her side. I expected the loose pages to catch fire and burn but they did not, likely from some kind of preemptive protective charm.

"You're already doing better than I had expected," taunted Kaynah.

"Really? Because you're doing much worse than I had expected," I smirked back, sending a gust into the necromancer.

She was pushed back only a few feet, but lost her footing and fell on her back. Taking advantage, I ripped out a chunk of the stone flooring and hurled it at her. The uneven brick crashed against her chest as she was sitting up. The impact forced her back until she slammed against the desk. Most of the books and pages stacked on top scattering onto the ground.

I brought up my gauntlet before remembering the Gasper Emerald was missing. Not wanting to waste the opportunity, I launched my gauntlet off of my hand toward Kaynah. The metal fingers open in a cupped formation. The silver glove zipped through the air hooking necromancer by the neck, pinning her against the desk. I walked toward her with speed and purpose, the gems on my scepter gleaming brightly.

I stood before her as she sat on the ground, a brick pressed against her stomach, and my gauntlet holding her by the neck. I stepped on her scepter, which she still grasped at her side, with my right foot. I pressed one end of my own scepter to Kaynah's forehead. Then, with a flick of my wrist, the gauntlet released its grip on the mutated elf and returned to my left arm.

"Where is the talisman?" I demanded through gritted teeth, breathing heavily through my nose.

The necromancer glared back at me, her eyes full of pure hatred and malice. She made no verbal response.

"Speak!" I shouted, my scepter flashing even brighter as I did so.

She still did not reply, but her eyes did tell me something quite clearly. "I'd rather die than give you the satisfaction."

Adrenaline flushed through my veins. This was it, this was the moment everything had been leading to. Kaynah, the necromancer that had caused so much death and had caused me so much struggle, was finally in my hands. It had been so much easier than I could have ever imagined. She had underestimated me out of arrogance, just as I had overestimated her out of fear.

I knew what I had to do. I called forth the magic from inside me and a pulse of electricity surged throughout my entire body. I had never struck a moral creature with lightning bluntly on the head before, but I knew it would be lethal. I

373

took my foot off her scepter, so not to electrocute myself, I stared into the necromancer's eyes and...

I suddenly saw someone different. I no longer saw the self-mutilated necromancer I had been dueling with just seconds ago. The woman before me was not a murderer and threat to all of Cray but was someone's child, another's neighbor. A living soul that had been manipulated by some malicious force along the way. She was a villain, but she was also a victim. My heart and my mind fought for control. I knew she had to be destroyed but could no longer bring myself to do it. I was frozen by indecision, and Kaynah recognized it.

Before I knew it, my back hit the ground when Kaynah swept my legs with a quick kick. A wave of terror and regret came over me and I jumped up to my feet, but it was too late. The necromancer struck me across the face with the end of her scepter. Then she took the brick that had pinned her and hurled it at my head. I stumbled back as the jewel of her scepter struck my face, which caused Kaynah to miss my head with the brick. Being struck in the face saved my life and the brick instead slammed into me on my left shoulder.

In a desperate attempt to give myself time to recenter. I swung my scepter wildly in Kaynah's direction, spraying fire and embers between us. My defense held her back, but only just enough for me to regain my footing and raise my scepter. Kaynah cut through the flames and jabbed at my side, sending a jolt of electricity through my body. The shock contracted my muscles and lowered my scepter.

With a stomp on the ground, Kaynah levitated two large chunks of stone out of the floor and hurled them at me. The first hit me in the stomach, while the second crashed into my legs below the knees. The force knocked my legs out from under me and I fell face-first onto the floor, my limbs flailing in all directions.

The necromancer cackled, the sound echoing throughout the cold dungeon. "Jard's Prodigy. You have all the power in the world, more magic bestowed to him than any other enchanter in all of Cray, and yet you weak."

I tilted my head up at her and she prodded the end of her scepter into my face. The glow of the lavender gemstone gleamed just enough that I could see her villainous grin. With her spare hand, she swiped up my scepter and dug it into my back.

"You lack the drive to do what you must, Prodigy," she taunted. "You had me defeated, all you had to do was strike. I was completely at your mercy and yet here we are, roles reversed! Pathetic, weak, unworthy of the power bestowed to you!"

Kaynah let go of her scepter but it stayed in its position, the gems glowing with power, ready to strike me dead. She stepped back, taking my scepter in both hands and holding it where she knew I could see it.

"But don't worry, I will soon put that power to good use," she spat. "Unlike you, I don't share that weakness. I am worthy of the Prodigal power."

She then took my scepter pushed it onto her right thigh, each of her hands on an opposing side. The oaken wood staff broke in half as if it were a twig. Green light flashed, blinding both of us for a few seconds. When my eyesight recovered, I saw Kaynah the Necromancer holding the shattered pieces of my scepter.

* * *

Kernil ran his sword through the chest of a Hissera. Two more were coming up behind him, but Hemm caught them first and beat them into the wall. Kernil gave a quick nod of thanks and Hemm grunted before going back to the fight. Pushing the dead Hissera off of his blade with his foot, Kernil slashed at another lizard.

There were a few dozen Hissera that had remained inside the fortress. After seeing an army of several hundred not an hour ago, didn't seem so intimidating. The eight of them were making quick work of the remaining Hissera. Most of all, Hemm had found a good rhythm, slaughtering the necromancer's minions left and right. Dahrik and Norvic were doing very well also, both very competent in using their magic in such a way that it could still affect the Hissera.

The eight of us stood in a line, backing the final nine Hissera into a corner of a large room. If they were afraid, then they did not show it, not that Kernil knew what a Hissera fearing for its life looked like. Hemm cracked his knuckles but stopped short

376

of the Hissera. At first, Kernil and the rest of the company were confused, but soon felt and then heard the rumbling of the walls and floor.

His instincts told him to get away from the wall. Kernil listened and got away just in time to avoid the wall exploding as the largest Hissera any of them could have imagined came crashing through it. Chunks of stone shot in all directions. Barris and Kylora were hit by large pieces and fell limp. Kernil watched in horror as blood flowed from their heads. As Kernil watched, stunned, Dalia ran to them and applied a purple flame to their wounds which stopped the bleeding.

Hemm stood to face the ten-foot-tall Hissera head-on, clubbing it thrice with his fists. The Hisseron was knocked back by the troll's punches but showed no signs of significant injury. Hemm ducked as the Hisseron swung its long, serrated claws in a counter-attack. Then he tried to tackle the huge lizard in a bull rush but the Hisseron kept its footing and threw the troll off.

Kilt and Kernil ran to aid their friend but were cut off by the last six Hissera. The other three had suffered a similar fate as Barris and Kylora without the application of the healing magic. The Hobb and the human warrior looked at one another and charged the Hissera, their sword and axes working as one. Kilt cut off an arm as Kernil severed its head. The Son of Vain elbowed a jaw as the musician dug her axe into a chest.

With the Vodro Heal applied to both, Dalia moved Barris and Kylora's unconscious bodies further away from the action and then examined them. The mage's head wound was much more serious than that of the dwarven warrior, so Dalia knew exactly with whom to start. Kylora had lost a lot of blood in just a short amount of time, perhaps even too much. This did not stop Dalia. She put all of her efforts into saving her friend, using her entire knowledge of healing spells.

Norvic and Dahrik joined Hemm against the Hisseron. Dahrik summoned a fiery lasso, binding one of the large beast's wrists, but the enormous Hissera broke free with a simple yank. Norvic's attempt was also in vain. He levitated a large brick and hurled it at the Hisseron's head, but as Hemm and the Hisseron wrestled tussling from side to side, the brick slammed right into the troll's side.

It was at this time that Kilt and Kernil had successfully killed the last of the normal-sized Hissera. Hemm was knocked down thanks to Norvic's brick, and the Hissera roared with triumph. Dahrik blasted the lizard with fire. It did nothing to harm the Hisseron but instead got its attention away from the disadvantaged troll. Norvic tried again, this time getting a clean hit to the Hisseron's back. It stumbled forward and then fell face-first after a low kick from a recovering Hemm. Kernil and Kilt charged forward. Kilt threw both of her axes at the fallen behemoth, embedding into its shoulder. It groaned with pain then slashed frantically with its claws, warding away any further attacks. The two warriors stopped just in time to avoid getting impaled by its long, hooked claws.

The Hisseron got to its feet and Hemm met it from behind. The troll grabbed the Hisseron by arms, wrapping his own arms around those of the Hisseron's and around the back of its head. Seizing the opportunity, Kilt jumped onto the Hisseron's leg and swiftly climbed up its side. She worked her way up until getting to her pair of axes, still stuck in its shoulder. As Kilt raised her weapons high for another downward hack, she was thrown off the creature. The Hisseron thrashed and kicked wildly, trying to free itself from Hemm's hold.

Dahrik and Norvic hurled bricks and chunks of stone at the captured monster, but this only seemed to enrage it more. Kernil ran to its feet and tried to cut off its bulky toes, stabbing and chopping and best he could. After several chops and a lot of physical effort, he cut the smallest one off. Blood sprayed Kernil, even blinding him momentarily.

The Hisseron roared in pain and anger, breaking the troll's grip and pushing him back with only his hips. With one motion, the Hissera grabbed Kernil and threw him behind its shoulder, through the hole in the wall, and across the fortress. The Son of Vain landed back into the entrance room, a large pile of slime cushioning his fall. He was not hurt but had the wind knocked out of him, leaving him motionless in the slime.

There was a flash of light off to his side. He looked toward it and saw that the doorway leading down to the dungeon had also been smashed, leaving the entry open. Kernil knew that the flash of light was from the battle below. He sat up, looked at the Hisseron fending off the company's attacks, then looked back at the open way towards the dungeon. Getting to his feet, he took one step forward then stopped.

"You must not fail me, Kernil Ravenhigh," came Loil's voice, ringing through his mind. "Jes Nulkin must kill Kaynah of Shale, and the talisman that creates life must be returned to the prairie. So that I can break the necromancer's curse on my land."

* * *

I managed to get to my feet and dodge Kaynah's first three strikes, moving out of the way just in time. She was moving a lot slower than before, I suspected that she was toying with me. Like a cat playing with a captured mouse. I hated being toyed with, my scepter was broken into two pieces on the floor and my gauntlet was powerless. I had to rely on my wits and reflexes to use whatever magic I could conjure at the right time. All without draining myself too quickly. Then again, using my energy too sparingly could have the same end result, my death, and Kaynah's victory.

The necromancer threw a wave of fire at me, the flames arching in a wide half-circle. I ducked below the fire wave and responded with an electrified punch to her side. It wasn't as powerful as a lightning bolt, but she was stunned for a few seconds all the same. As her muscles contracted, I made a grab for her scepter. Unfortunately, the shock made her grip on the iron staff even tighter. And it lasted until she regained control of herself.

Kaynah and I were locked in a back and forth, both of us clinging onto the rusty scepter, desperately trying to yank it out of the other's hands. I thought I'd have the advantage since her every use of magic had corrupted her physically, yet somehow her strength persisted. My own muscles cried out for relief, but I knew that I'd not likely get another chance. In her wild eyes I could see she was done toying with me, given another chance, she would end me.

Running out of options, I tried something dirty and kicked her in the shins. Kaynah responded by spitting in my face and then smashing her knee into my groin. I doubled over from the hit, loosening my grip on the scepter. The necromancer recognized her opportunity and took advantage of it. Taking back control, she jabbed the scepter into my side. The jolt of electricity in the attack knocked me to the ground. Kaynah then looped a fiery lasso around my ankle and spun me in a circle around her, my body dragging on the stone floor. With just a flick of her wrist, the lasso knot released, and I flew across the room until I crashed against the far wall.

I scrambled to my feet only to be caught in a circle of white fire. Kaynah laughed as she stomped closer, the circle shrinking in diameter with each of her steps. The fierce heat from the white flames cracked stones on the floor.

"Perhaps I was wrong," she coughed, puss spitting from her neck. "Maybe you do have the drive, but not enough."

The flames disappeared once she was only a few steps away. Kaynah stopped once her scepter was inches in front of my face. The glow from the lavender gem once again blocking out my vision.

"No," she hissed. "I won't burn you alive. You've actually earned my respect enough to die quickly."

The glow of the gems intensified, and the scent of lightning filled my nostrils. I knew what was going to happen next. I clenched my eyes shut and thought of my family, praying for Jard to watch over them.

Then... nothing happened.

I still had my eyes closed, but I could feel the scepter move away from my face and the light coming from it dim. I opened my eyes once I heard Kaynah cry out in pain. I was shocked to see a large knife sticking out of the necromancer's shoulder, a thick stream of blood running down her left arm. Behind her, I saw Kernil standing in the open doorway, the Sword of Vain in his off-hand.

Kaynah yanked the knife out of her arm and without tending the bleeding wound, turned to face the Son of Vain. Her pale face flushed red with pure ire.

"Nice throw, but it will cost you your life," she spat through gritted teeth.

Thrusting her stance forward, she shot forth a stream of lightning. The bright streak hit Kernil. I winced, expecting him to fall back either dead or unconscious. To my surprise, Kernil withstood the lightning, staying on his feet and holding his sword high. The blade even seemed to be glowing.

Seeing her foe alive and standing, Kaynah pressed even harder into the magic. The chamber lit up from her increasing the lightning's intensity. Kernil slowly folded, falling to his knees, his sword continually glowing with golden light. The necromancer's own legs started to shake, followed quickly by her arms.

Knowing she couldn't use up all her energy, she brought her scepter back, ending the stream of electricity. Kernil fell forward just as she did, the Sword of Vain falling in front of him. Her body trembling, the necromancer groaned in pain from the use of magic. Her back sizzled and hissed, corrupting her physical form even further. She cursed under her breath for having to use so much magic on a normal human.

Unbeknownst to Kaynah and me, Kernil was not yet unconscious. He struggled and was fighting the sensation. He inwardly thanked Jard and Loil for the blessing on his sword for taking the brunt of the necromancer's spell. His free hand moved sluggishly toward his pocket. Once he could he wrapped his finger around the small, mostly translucent stone within. His head becoming foggier with every passing second, Kernil made his wish and let the sleep overtake him.

There was a quick flutter of light by my wrist, which caught my attention. I blinked several times, certain that my eyes were playing tricks on me, yet they were not. To my complete bewilderment, the Gasper Emerald was once again set in its place on the gauntlet forearm. I could neither believe nor begin to imagine how it had somehow returned to my possession. Its magic surged through my body, making me feel full of energy and powerful. I stared and even prodded at it, just to remove any remaining doubt that it was there.

After a few seconds, I remembered the situation I was in. Just as Kaynah recovered from her extensive use of magic on Kernil, she swung back around and pointed the scepter in my face.

But I was ready.

I called forth the gauntlet's power and grabbed hold of the gem. A swirl of pure energy surged forth, compressing and ravaging the lavender jewel. The necromancer stared, wide-eyed at the legendary emerald glowing from the center of my gauntlet.

"That's impossible," she muttered, trying to pull the end of her scepter from my grasp.

I shrugged. "No, it's destiny. You'd be surprised how often this kind of thing happens."

Purple and green light flickered rapidly, and the sound of glass shattering echoed throughout the dungeon. Kaynah fell back several steps, then lost her balance. When the lights stopped, the necromancer stared in horror at the end of her scepter. The gem once at the end of her scepter was gone, crushed and scattered along the floor in front of her in tiny shards.

Her face flushed red as she thrusted her scepter at me. I didn't even flinch, instead, I called upon my gauntlet once again. A surge of electricity came out of Kaynah's scepter, but it refracted back toward her. She shocked herself with lightning until she had the presence of mind to stop the spell.

I pointed the ball of green magic that formed at the gauntlet's palm at the necromancer. My arm was steady and my mind was focused, but I felt itchy with power and excitement like I never had before. Whatever confidence I had lost just a moment ago, had now returned twofold.

"An unbalanced scepter to match its user's unbalanced mind," I stated, unable to ignore the irony.

Her face was a mixture of rage and despair, but I knew she had not given up. Kaynah scrambled back to her feet, despite the presence of my gauntlet aiming at her, and then threw her broken scepter at me like a javelin. Twitching my thumb, I shot a small portion of the magical energy that I had been building up at the useless scepter. The iron staff disintegrated within the beam of magic, leaving behind a puff of red and lavender-colored dust.

"You think I need a scepter to kill you?" she shouted, her fists clenched.

Her arms started to sizzle and streams of foul-smelling smoke came from out of the pores. With a punch, Kaynah unleashed a blast of fire at me. Without her scepter, the toll on her body was even greater, she screamed in pain from releasing the blast of fire. I ducked under flames and shot my own blast from the gauntlet. The beam of green magic energy hit the necromancer in the stomach, pushing her back to about thirty feet away from me.

White smoke that smelt like burning flesh and hair was coming out of her legs. Her face was both red and pale at the same time. Yelling with a mix of pain and rage, Kaynah stomped on the ground. The stones making up the floor jumped up from their positions like a massive wave moving toward me. Thinking quickly, I slammed my own fist onto the stone tiles at my feet, creating my own wave. The two waves collided, bouncing off of one another and scattering the tiles on the floor. Moving my arms in a circle, I suspended all of the stones in the air, then carefully moved them back into their original places.

In my mind I thanked Jard that the gauntlet was able to be used like a scepter, channeling my magic through the power in the Gasper Emerald. I had never done so before, but somehow always knew it was possible.

Kaynah's look of anger and pain was interrupted by one of curiosity. Her eyes darted to the gauntlet, as if she could hear my thoughts about it. Stretching out both of her arms, I could feel her magic trying to pull the gauntlet off of my hand. Once I noticed the pull, I brought up my right hand and grabbed the end of the gauntlet near the elbow, clenching it. Steam and smoke came out of the necromancer's body as if she herself was on fire, filling the entire dungeon. My feet started to skid toward her as her mystic pull on the gauntlet increased. I readjusted my stance and used my own magic to pull the opposite way.

Kaynah's whole body started to shudder, the smoke pouring out faster and faster, making it in harder to breathe with every second. Her teeth were clenched tight to keep her from screaming. Even from about thirty feet away, I could see the pain and desperation in her eyes. She had run out of ideas and the means to kill me.

Loose pages flew around in two of us, caught in the matched pulling forces. The walls started to shake, chunks of stone ripped out of their places, and were being tossed around in multiple directions. Even the ceiling started to bounce up and down.

"Kaynah, this has to stop!" I shouted, realizing what was about to happen. "This whole place is going to collapse if you don't stop now!"

I couldn't see her through the cloud of billowing smoke but I knew she had heard me. After a few seconds, she yelled back in a very pained voice, "Not until you're dead."

"You'll kill us both!" I pleaded. "Stop now and I'll make sure you get a fair trial!"

"No," she replied. "You die, I die, *he* dies, I don't care! Just die!"

I scanned the room and saw Kernil still laying in the doorway. I thought he was dead but then saw his eyes twitch ever so slightly. He was alive.

It was then that I knew what I had to do. I stopped the pulling force and let go of the gauntlet. Immediately, it flew off me and into the outstretched hands of the necromancer. The room calmed, and everything floating in the air fell to the ground. The walls and ceiling stopped shaking as Kaynah stared in wonderment at the sliver gauntlet in her hands.

Without a second to waste, I sprinted toward her, calling on whatever magic I had left to levitate the Sword of Vain into my hands. The grip of the golden hilt came into my palms just as I closed the gap between us. Without hesitating or missing a step, I rammed the blade into her chest. I came to an abrupt halt as the guard met her ribcage and the tip poked out the other end.

Kaynah's eyes widened, as if she hadn't noticed me until then. She dropped the gauntlet as her last breath left her body. My own breath was heavy as I stared at her corrupt and poisoned body. The smoke that had been spewing out of her every pour was now only smoldering. Puss and blood dripped onto the floor below. She was disgusting to look at, her features now unrecognizable, but I did not pity her. With a single yank of the hilt, I pulled the Sword of Vain out of the body formerly belonging to Kaynah of Shale. The corpse fell to the ground at my feet, crumpling and withering away.

Behind me, just barely visible in the corner of my eye, a figure stood. At first, I thought it was Kernil back on his feet. After only a second, I realized that it wasn't the Son of Vain.

Whatever this figure was, it had a presence that I recognized but couldn't place. My body filled with the greatest sense of discomfort and my stomach twisted into a knot.

I slowly turned to face the black figure, but it was gone. I scanned all around me, but no one else was there. The uncomfortable knot in my stomach was still there, now mixed with a mess of confusion. I had been so sure someone had been there.

I turned back and saw Kaynah's body. Suddenly, the knot was gone and I fell to my knees and a cascade of grief, guilt, and horror crashed upon for what I had done. Tears fell from my eyes, blurring and blinding my vision.

It was over, the quest had been complete, and I had lived up to what everyone had hoped for me to do. I wished with every fiber of my soul that I had not, but I couldn't take it back.

The Necromancer's Patron

I knelt there for a long time, staring down at my victim. The smoke that had at one time filled the room had now cleared. The smell of burning hair and flesh lingered, now mixing with the unmistakable scent of death.

There was a sudden shift in the stones above me after a loud *thud*. I jumped to my feet, worried that the walls and ceiling were about to cave in. A few seconds passed and nothing else happened. I breathed a sigh of relief then turned back to Kernil, who was starting to wake.

The Son of Vain lifted his head and held his upper body by his elbows. I ran to his side and offered him a hand up, which he took. Once on his feet, Kernil's knees buckled but I caught and pulled him back up without him falling.

"Careful," I said, putting one of his arms over and around my shoulders. "Your muscles are probably going to be weak for a while. You were hit with a lot of electricity. In fact, you're lucky to be alive."

Kernil chuckled. "All thanks to my sword."

"Your sword?"

"Didn't Dahrik tell you? The sprite blessed it to destroy and repel dark magic. It's how he got us out of the mist."

I looked over to Sword of Vain, still stuck in the necromancer's body. The red jewel embedded in the pommel glinted in the soft light, almost as if acknowledging Kernil's words. The Son of Vain followed my gaze and nearly lost his footing again.

"Ah, I see," he winced. "You really did it."

I sighed. "Yes, I really did it."

There was another booming *thud* from above us. This one was much louder than the last, but seemingly further away.

"Huh, I would have thought that they would have killed that thing by now," Kernil noted, staring up at the ceiling.

"Killed what *thing*?"

He looked back through the doorway leading to the stairs. "Remember that large creature you told us was on the other side of the fortress? Turns out it was a giant Hissera, even bigger than Hemm. I thought they would have killed it by now. We should get up there and help them."

Kernil didn't seem completely present when he spoke. Given

his condition, that was understandable. Part of me hoped he was just confused about the giant Hissera, but the rest of me knew that he very likely wasn't.

I leaned Kernil against the door frame as I went back for his sword. I kept my eyes on the floor, then on the sword, trying to not look at Kaynah's contorted face or shriveled body. With a firm yank of my right hand, I pulled the sword out of the necromancer. Then found my gauntlet and equipped it on my left arm.

When I returned, I held out the sword for Kernil to take, but he held up his hand to stop me. "I'm in no fighting condition and your scepter is over there broken in two, you'll need it more me when we get up there."

I nodded, then put his arm back over my shoulder. Together we climbed back up the circular staircase. There were a lot more stairs than I remembered coming down, and they were a lot steeper too. Halfway up, I was panting for breath. The adrenaline and energy boost I got from dueling Kaynah was finally gone. The bill for my use of magic had come due. I was tired, but not quite dizzy. Helping the weakened Kernil didn't help much either, but I refused to complain.

Sounds of the ongoing fight above became louder and clearer with every step up. Hemm roared so loudly it shook the torches hanging in their racking near the top of the staircase. The deepest sounding hiss I'd ever heard followed the roar. There were then three vibrating *boom*s, as if stone were clashing against stone. Just as we reached the top of the stairs, a boulder tumbled through the far wall, missing us by only a few feet.

"Leave me here," instructed Kernil, leaning against the doorway. "They need you now. I'll catch up."

I wanted to protest, but he was right and I knew it. The Sword of Vain in my right hand and my gauntlet on my left, I ran. I kept running through the rooms that separated the dungeon from where I saw the company last. I was breathing heavily as I ran, still tired, but I knew now was not the time to focus on that.

Entering the large greeting room, I felt the open air of the early winter day. Most of the walls on all sides had large holes in them or had collapsed entirely. I saw the giant Hissera first, its long claws swiping down at Kilt and Norvic at its side. Hemm was in the corner and threw a piece of stone the size of his torso at the Hisseron, striking the creature in the back. It fell on its side, and that's when everyone pounced at once.

I was about to join when in the corner of my eye I saw Dalia in the other room, huddled over two other bodies. One was Barris, the dwarf was unmistakable as he sat upright covered in blood, his eyes glossy. The other body was laying down with the druid's traveling cloak over their head.

My stomach twisted in a knot again. I studied the scene around me, taking a headcount. Dalia and Barris were in the far left corner. Kernil was back by the stairs. Hemm was smashing his fists into the recovering Hisseron. Kilt was climbing on the large beast's back while Norvic and Dahrik were using a fiery lasso to restrain the Hisseron's arms. That only left one, Kylora.

Just as the sorrow for her death swept over me, I saw the black shadow in the corner of my eye again. I spun around but found nothing there once more. I knew I had seen something, but didn't have the time to worry about it. Shaking the thought out of my head, I ran forward.

The Hisseron broke free of the bond on its wrists and roared. I stopped in my tracks as it swung its claws around in a primal rage.

It was here that Dahrik and my eyes met. He saw me without my scepter and holding a blood-covered sword and he knew what had happened. His face flashed several emotions in only a few seconds. There was relief, confusion, joy, pity, then sorrow. He knew exactly how I felt by looking at me, and I at him.

Still looking at me, Dahrik didn't have time to flinch when the Hisseron drove three of its claws right through his chest. The world went suddenly silent as darkness filled the outer edges of my vision. I felt very cold, frozen in place as I watched my mentor's mouth fill with blood. Dahrik's eyes never left me as he tried to say something, but couldn't. He exhaled a final breath, and the light left his eyes just as the Hisseron yanked its claws out of him.

The dwarf's body fell limply to the ground. His scepter

clanked against the stone, still clutched in his hand. Anger swelled and exploded from me. I leaped forward, sailing up to nearly the ceiling as I held the Sword of Vain forth with both hands. I screamed louder than I ever had before, channeling my pain and anger through it. In one swipe, I cut the Hisseron's head clean off before landing on the opposite side of the large room. The huge beast's body jolted and flinched before falling to the ground with an echoing *thump.*

Wasting no time, I ran to Dahrik's side and called forth the purple fire of the Vodro Heal. I smacked the flames against the dwarf's body, then summoned the gold light of the Lordon Heal. Tears filled my eyes as there was no reaction from Dahrik or signs that the spell was working. I tried again, first the purple fire, then the gold light. When that didn't work I did it a third and then a fourth time.

"Jes, stop," Dalia cried, trying to pull me back. "It doesn't work on the dead. He's gone."

I was sobbing by this point so uncontrollably that I didn't hear her. I pulled myself from the druid's grip and cried over Dahrik's lifeless body. What remained of the company gathered around Dahrik's body. Even Barris and Kernil in their injured states stood near.

Then, I saw it again, the shadow barely visible in the corner of my eye. I hated how it haunted me, and in my anger and sorrow, I picked up the Sword of Vain and threw at where the shadow had been. It was gone, the blade flying through the fortress, through a large hole in the damaged wall to the outside.

Everyone took a step back, unsure of what irrational thing I might do next. Kilt offered to fetch the sword for a still uneasy Kernil. The Son of Vain nodded in thanks and the Hobb brushed past Norvic as she ran for the sword.

Barris took a step forward and knelt at my side.

"Jes, his weapon," he began, tugging at the bandage wrapped around his forehead nervously. "He must be unarmed when he meets death."

I wiped my face with my sleeve and nodded. I reached for Dahrik scepter, which was still in his grip. His hands had already begun to tighten around the iron staff. Thankfully I was able to pry the rod free without breaking off any of his fingers. As I held the scepter in my hands, its orange gems flashed so brightly that everyone had to look away. After the light had dimmed, I saw a tiny comet of green light spiraling around each end of the scepter. Slowly, the tail of the comets seeped into the orange jewels, turning them into a deep forest green color. Once the transformation of color was complete, the small swirling comets vanished with another flash of light.

"Okay, what was that?" asked Barris, still shielding his eyes.

I opened my mouth to answer but stopped, unsure of what had just happened.

"Remarkable," gasped Dalia, leaning in to get a better look at the scepter in my hands.

"What's remarkable?" I asked her, turning around to face her. "Do you know what that was?"

The druid nodded her head. "I've only ever seen it once before but yes, I know what that was. Your own scepter was destroyed, correct?"

"It was, yes. Kaynah snapped it in half. Why?"

"Congratulations then, Dahrik's scepter has chosen you as its next master."

I instinctively looked down it in my grip. I couldn't believe what I was hearing. "Is that even possible?"

"Of course it's possible," Dalia replied, patting me on the shoulder. "All scepters are repurposed and given to another enchanter eventually. In this rare case, Dahrik's scepter acknowledged that both its master is dead, and you were without a scepter. So it chose you."

"No, no, I can't take it," I rejected, dropping the scepter on the ground. "It's Dahrik's, I can't take it."

Dalia took a step forward and was about to say something when Kilt arrived with the Sword of Vain. Oblivious to what had happened in her absence.

"Jes, you really threw this thing with some top-notch might!

I nearly walked right past it, it was flung into the ground all the way to the pommel."

The musician stopped short, as she realized everyone was staring at her uncomfortably. Dalia opened her mouth to speak but was cut off by Kilt again.

"I'm sorry, but where's Norvic?" she asked. "Did Jes throw something else?"

Kilt's question rung like a warning signal. I grabbed Dahrik's scepter off the ground and jumped to my feet, scanning the open room for the warlock.

"He was standing right next to me a minute ago," cried Kernil. "I didn't notice him leave."

"Why would he sneak off now?" asked Dalia. "Where would he go?"

A swift pain stabbed at my forehead as I remembered something and cursed myself for it. In my despair over killing Kaynah. And then the noises from the ongoing Hisseron battle. I had completely forgotten about the talisman. The same talisman the necromancer had used to start this whole ordeal.

"I can think of one place he'd go and why," I stated, looking toward the room with the spiral staircase.

Kernil was the first to realize what I meant, and everyone else caught on soon after. We didn't have to discuss what to do next, we all ran for the dungeon. I was in front, Dalia and Kilt close behind me. Hemm carried both Barris and Kernil because of their injuries. Halfway down the steps, I grew impatient and dropped down the center hole. I fell to the bottom in seconds only to cushion myself with a gust of air, landing softly.

I stepped into the familiar dungeon and found Norvic immediately. He was at the desk rummaging through the drawers, full of even more books and loose pages.

"Ah, Jes, you found me," Norvic said without the slightest hint of guilt.

"Where is it?" I demanded, pointing both Dahrik's scepter and my powered-up gauntlet in his direction.

Without taking his eyes off what he was doing, the warlock held up a circular pendant made of brass hanging on a chain necklace. It had several engravings, but I was too far away to see what they were.

"Give it to me!"

He smiled. "Ah, found it."

His finger rolled up a dozen pages or so, then stuff them into his back pocket. Finally he looked up at me and smile. He walked back around the desk, swinging the talisman by the chain in his hand. Then pick up his scepter and leaned against the front side of the desk.

"Relax, will you? It's over. You did your job," he offered. "Now it's time to go home and be satisfied with a victory."

I took a few steps forward, never taking my aim away from the warlock. "Give me the talisman."

"No, I'm not going to do that," he laughed. "I've worked too hard for this and planned everything out perfectly. I was afraid you would be too soft to finish her off, but hey, I don't mind being wrong from time to time."

I stared back at him, confused. This only caused his amusement to visibly grow, which made my blood boil. Then all the puzzle pieces fit together at once. Kaynah's tongue click echoed in my head.

"You're... you're *him*," I stuttered, feeling dizzy and frustrated. "You're the necromancer's patron!"

"That I am," Norvic said with a theatrical bow.

Just then, the rest of the company ran through the entrance, their weapons ready.

"And fortunately for me, this is where my part in this asinine little quest comes to an end."

He said, tapping his scepter on the ground twice.

"Don't worry, we'll meet again soon. I'm sure of it," he winked.

Gold light spun around the warlock like a small twister around his body. Acting as fast as I could, I fired my gauntlet blast. The ray of green magic shot right through where his head had been, but passed through. Norvic disappeared through his rift just in time to avoid my attack. The last thing I saw of him was his wide, irritating grin.

To be continued in, "Enchanter's Quest: The Patron of Evil"

About the Author

When he was fourteen, his friends gave him the nickname "The Esquire," and it stuck. In the same year, he discovered his love for fantasy after reading JRR Tolkien's "The Hobbit." This eventually led him to want to become a writer, with Enchanter's Quest being the first of many novels, both in and out of fantasy. Once the Enchanter's Quest tetralogy is completed, JL Esquire intends on writing series in sci-fi, mystery adventure, historical fiction, as well as continuing in the fantasy genre.

You can connect with me on:
🌐 https://privatedragon.com

Also by JL Esquire

See where the Enchanter's Quest began!

Enchanter's Quest: The Void of Souls
Discover the awe and wonder of Enchanter's Quest in this well crafted second edition.

Winner of the "Epic Epilogue Award" from reviewgoblin.com in 2019.

The kingdom drafts a young man with a destiny into military service. A princess must fight for her survival and the fate of her kingdom. A famous dwarven enchanter seeks vengeance for his wife.

In the mystical world of Cray, many dangerous things happen all the time. To offset these terrible things, an order of magic-wielding enchanters are Cray's protectors. Jes Nulkin is one of these enchanters, although he never imagined this kind of life. Journey alongside Jes as he ventures on a series of quests to save Cray.

This is a tale filled with life, culture and song. Dwarves, elves, and a fantastic world fill the imagination. The author's love of the written word is plain in every detail.

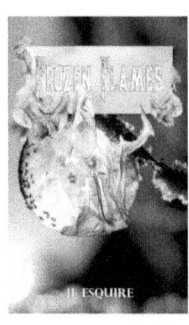

Frozen Flames

https://privatedragon.com/hub/
media/blogs/perks/quick-uploads/
frozen-flames-by-jl-esquire/frozen-
flames.pdf?mtime=1626139213

The Witchcat valley is under attack by the great dragon Ralgoz. Helpless against the monster's power, the villagers call upon Tulro, an ice mage from Boreal, for help.

This short story is free to access on the private dragon website.